"You're freezing. Come upstairs. I have a fire going in the drawing room."

Seth Weston just stood there for a moment. Doubt crossed his face. In a strange kind of elfin way, Sophy van Houten seemed timid and embarrassed, yet he knew she was playing a game. A dangerous game.

Not only was she flirting with her looks, she was dangling her money as bait. She was even breaking conventions and inviting him into her private drawing room. It was incredible what a wealthy woman would do for amusement.

He quickly weighed his chances of backing out and laughing the whole mess off as a joke, yet something stopped him. Looking down at her, he realized that Sophy interested him. Her eyes were huge with some carefully concealed emotion. As if it had taken an astonishing amount of nerve to confront him. For the first time in months, genuine delight flared in his blue eyes....

D0681178

Dear Reader,

Emily French's first book, *Capture,* was released in 1994 during our popular March Madness promotion and earned the author some wonderful reviews. Ms. French's second book, *Illusion,* is the emotional story of the growing love between a couple drawn into a marriage of convenience that is threatened by embezzlement and extortion. We hope you will enjoy this intriguing story.

In *Lion's Legacy,* the third book of Suzanne Barclay's Lion Trilogy, a Scottish warrior is hired to protect a tower from English raiders, only to discover that his benefactor has nothing to give him in return for his services but the hand of his unwilling granddaughter.

Diamond is the first in award-winning author Ruth Langan's new Western series, The Jewels of Texas, which features four sisters who think they are only children until the death of their father brings them all together at his ranch in Texas. And in our fourth book for the month, *Twice Upon Time,* Nina Beaumont's second Harlequin Historical time-travel novel, the author weaves an exciting tale of an ancient curse and a passion too strong to be denied.

Whatever your taste in reading, we hope to keep you coming back for more. Please look for Harlequin Historical novels wherever books are sold.

Sincerely,

Tracy Farrell
Senior Editor

Please address questions and book requests to:
Harlequin Reader Service
U.S.: 3010 Walden Ave., P.O. Box 1325, Buffalo, NY 14269
Canadian: P.O. Box 609, Fort Erie, Ont. L2A 5X3

EMILY FRENCH

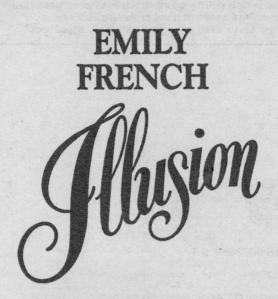

Illusion

Harlequin Books

TORONTO • NEW YORK • LONDON
AMSTERDAM • PARIS • SYDNEY • HAMBURG
STOCKHOLM • ATHENS • TOKYO • MILAN
MADRID • WARSAW • BUDAPEST • AUCKLAND

If you purchased this book without a cover you should be aware that this book is stolen property. It was reported as "unsold and destroyed" to the publisher, and neither the author nor the publisher has received any payment for this "stripped book."

ISBN 0-373-28906-5

ILLUSION

Copyright © 1996 by Germaine Kennedy

All rights reserved. Except for use in any review, the reproduction or utilization of this work in whole or in part in any form by any electronic, mechanical or other means, now known or hereafter invented, including xerography, photocopying and recording, or in any information storage or retrieval system, is forbidden without the written permission of the publisher, Harlequin Enterprises Limited, 225 Duncan Mill Road, Don Mills, Ontario, Canada M3B 3K9.

All characters in this book have no existence outside the imagination of the author and have no relation whatsoever to anyone bearing the same name or names. They are not even distantly inspired by any individual known or unknown to the author, and all incidents are pure invention.

This edition published by arrangement with Harlequin Books S.A.

® and ™ are trademarks of the publisher. Trademarks indicated with ® are registered in the United States Patent and Trademark Office, the Canadian Trade Marks Office and in other countries.

Printed in U.S.A.

Books by Emily French

Harlequin Historicals

Capture #214
Illusion #306

EMILY FRENCH

A living passion for the past, combined with the sheer joy of writing, has lured Emily French away from the cold ivory tower of factual academia to warm, heartfelt historical romance. She likes her novels to be full of adventure and humor, her heroes to be intelligent and kind, and her heroines to be witty and spirited.

Emily lives on the East Coast of Australia with her husband, John. Her interests are listed as everything that doesn't have to do with a needle and thread.

To Wayne Pierre Beattie and
Thomas Carroll Geoghegan
soldiers both
who saw service in Vietnam and World War II
and to whom freedom owes a debt

What if we fly
on ethereal highs
through cloud-soft illusions!
Our dreams are welded
to burning desires
flares in the mind's sky
…meteorites!

The author acknowledges kind permission to use
the extract from the poem, "being in love," by
Heather Farmer (*Of Dreams and Desires*, 1993)

Chapter One

Yonkers, New York—September, 1865

"Did anyone ever tell you, you're a mighty stubborn woman, Sophy van Houten?"

Taking several deep breaths to choke back the sobs that were threatening to well up in her throat, Sophy focused very hard on the street scene outside the window. She was not one of the indomitable van Houtens for nothing. She would give a good account of herself if she had to. Resist as long as she was able.

The van Houtens had always been proud. Their lineage could be traced to the settlement of Manhattan. As the only child of a wealthy industrialist, she had been given every material advantage, but she was not spoiled.

During the dreadful years of the war, she had put her talents to good use. She was not one of those women who had never faced anything more momentous in her life than a decision of accepting or refusing a proposal of marriage.

Sophy van Houten was known to be extremely fastidious. She had danced and dined her way through New York society without once having been tempted to wed. Now, circumstances beyond her control dictated that she marry, and with no further tarrying.

Her face darkened. "Why should I be forced into a marriage I do not want? They freed the slaves, but not the women!"

"Sophy!"

Shoulders stiff and squared, Sophy wrapped her arms protectively around herself. It was a posture she often adopted when she was upset. "Money! Money! It is not the 'root of all evil,' it is the cause of all distraction and worry! I hate men!"

"Nonsense!"

There was a tight feeling in the region of her heart. "It's true. They're all the same. Wanting to get their hands on me—or my money."

"Sophy!"

She scowled. "I have no wish to be a social butterfly, nor am I cut out for constant charitable works. I want to be gainfully employed, using my God-given talents, though I am sure the stuffy old-fashioned financiers in Wall Street would not give me a job," she added darkly.

Turning, she shot her companion a quick, questioning glance and then smiled crookedly. "A woman must know when to bend, or else she will surely break. I really have no alternative, do I?" Her chin rose defiantly. "I'll get married, Aunt Ella, but it will be on my terms."

"Sophy!" The other woman, perched like a nervous bird on the edge of a large wing chair, admonished her again in breathless apprehension. "Even though your father tolerated your idiosyncrasies, and understood your natural reluctance, he still wanted you to marry. The trustees are only doing their duty."

Sophy spun impatiently and strode toward a large mahogany desk on the other side of the comfortably furnished room, which was lined with books and showed every evidence of luxury and wealth.

"Their idea of duty leads to constraint, and constraint stifles compassion. Have I no duty to myself? Why should

I sacrifice my independence, be snared like a silly bird by that reptile word *duty?*"

Picking up an embossed letterhead, she marched across the Persian rug toward her aunt and ground out between set teeth, "Listen to this hogwash! 'After due care and consideration of your proposition, the trustees do not consider your request for funds to be either expedient or for a worthy cause.' What a load of drivel!"

"Now, Sophy, that is a wicked way to talk." Ella van Houten could scarcely gasp the words. "Try not to be so...so passionate, dear." Putting her hand against her chest, as if she feared she might have a heart attack, she said faintly, "You know that your uncle Schuyler and my dear brother, Heinrich, act only in your best interests."

"Aunt Ella, it's ridiculous. My uncles' living will controls Father's dead one. I am bound hand and foot by invisible threads, a conspiracy of those who profess to love me. You know I always looked after Father's investments. He trusted me to make good any cash given to 'worthy causes.'"

"I agree, Sophy, and you never once failed your dear father's trust," Ella van Houten replied wearily. Knitting her brow, the elderly woman continued, "Nicholas believed that whatsoever a man sows, that also is what he reaps, for the reaper and the plowman are one."

Sophy crouched and added a log to the fireplace. "Don't go all cryptic on me now, Aunt Ella. I know it's vulgar to talk about money, but you know none of the men who offer for me so ardently would be at all keen if I were not a wealthy heiress," she retorted, trying to keep her tone light. "I have rejected so many offers I have lost count, but not one heartbroken suitor was among them!"

Her aunt smiled pensively, feeling a tug of affection and appreciation for Sophy's prosaic attitude. Rich, beautiful, witty but stubborn to a fault, naturally she had admirers in plenty, but so far she had refused to marry any of them. She had never said so, but Ella knew that her niece had hoped to marry for love.

It was a shame that women were so bound and restricted by custom and the laws of society. With her secret core of romance and color, and a lack of convention that distressed only the unimaginative, Sophy had much to offer.

Ella's eyes softened. Sophy did seem very slender and frail in the firelight. The mass of shining hair, looped in a fashionable swirl, seemed too heavy for the finely molded head.

Yet there was something vital and vibrant in the contours of the face, the straight little nose, the arched eyebrows and generous lips. And the large eyes, dark gray with somehow a tinge of purple in them, were bright and intelligent.

"In that case, there is no reason for you not to marry one of them. Surely you will now take your trustees' advice as to the eligibility of suitors?" Ella questioned dryly.

"Oh, but I have a plan!" Sophy rose to her feet and danced across the room, merriment in her eyes. The decision made, her spirits rose like bubbles in champagne, sparkling, invigorating.

"Those chauvinistic fuddy-duddies are kindhearted and well-meaning, but they are pigheaded, and confuse logic and emotion. What I intend to do is to have *them* approve someone *I* choose!"

Her aunt's expression of patient disgust changed to one of suspicion. "What's going on inside that head of yours, Sophy? What scheme are you cooking up now?"

"I shall travel to New York City tomorrow. If I tell Mr. Tyson that I will transfer the van Houten funds to Pierpont Morgan's bank when I come of age if he doesn't cooperate, he will soon produce a desirable suitor."

Sophy spoke so violently that her aunt winced. Her niece was small and fragile, yet she was stalking the room and snarling like a tigress after its prey.

Ella realized the great mistake Sophy would make if she were allowed to pursue her fantastic scheme. A rare spirit, cursed with a strange uneasy restlessness, difficult to manage at times and unpractical to a degree, the girl needed an outlet for her pent-up passions.

She hesitated, then said in a low voice, "You have always said you had no wish to marry. A man whom you do not know, a fortune hunter, the type who would accept a bribe to marry a girl he has never seen, sounds a terrible risk."

"Oh, he will be no problem, merely a trifling drawback. I mean to be rid of him," Sophy replied airily.

"Divorce is not condoned by the church! Would you jeopardize your soul for a whim, Sophy?"

Sophy grinned wickedly, then sighed. "No, Aunt Ella, I would not." She spoke in the quiet, unhurried tone her aunt was used to hearing. "The idea of being married to a man who wants me only for my money is like living in hell. It betrays everything I believe in, all my dreams, all my ambitions, all the things that I have lived for these past five years."

She fell on her knees beside her aunt. "But, Aunt, the alternative is even more mortifying." She smiled a rather wistful smile. "Having a fortune carries a moral obligation to others, and so many people out there need help."

Ella stared at her niece. "Maybe if you suggest to Mr. Tyson that your preferences lie with someone in need, then he will be more sympathetic."

Sophy's head came up and the calculating look reentered her eyes. "Aunt Ella. How clever of you! What a brilliant idea!"

Aunt Ella groaned.

"Marry Sophy van Houten!"

The man staring blindly into the rainwashed darkness gave no indication that he had heard the banker's theatrical statement. Forehead crinkled in thought, he seemed oblivious to his surroundings.

Matt Tyson watched his client's profile for a moment, took in the tension around the eyes, the grim, set mouth with deep lines at the corners. The sort of face, young yet old, to which he had grown accustomed in the four long years since the start of the War between the States. The genuine concern he felt for his friend gave him courage. He decided to push the point.

"Marry Sophy van Houten! That's the answer! You'd get voting rights to her railroad stock, plus a wife who'd be no trouble at all. Always dutiful. Pretty manners. Good family."

The silence in the room was more thunderous than sound. Seth Weston's face was an unreadable mask; only the angry muscle flexing at the jaw admonished the banker. Minutes lengthened.

Matt tapped the desktop with his fingertips, brows creased in growing consternation. Finally, he sighed and continued. "I've known Sophy van Houten for years. Bright girl, no problem to her father. Old Nicholas used to keep her busy looking after..."

Marry Sophy van Houten! The words ringing in his ears, Seth Weston swallowed hard and tightly clenched his jaw to prevent an outflow of sarcastic words. Outwardly, his calm demeanor showed none of the disquiet he felt. The truth was he felt more than a little disgruntled. He felt off-balance. Marriage! Hell, he'd sooner roast in hell, or face a firing squad, than marry!

True, he could not remember ever having met Sophy van Houten, but the last thing on earth he wanted was a wife. If he needed a woman, he only had to take himself off to Greene Street. No need to saddle himself with a permanent fixture. A wife would demand more of him than he could give.

The war had turned him topsy-turvy. He was drained, an empty vessel. No, not empty. Filled with bitterness, like sour wine. Women were shrews anyway. He had yet to meet a woman who was loyal and loving, tolerant and resourceful, who was neither cold nor subject to fits of jealousy. There was no such creature.

Seth became aware, slowly, that the banker was still talking.

"—and Cornelius Vanderbilt would pay handsomely for that stock. Marry Sophy van Houten and you can clear the mortgage on the factory and introduce those innovations...."

Marry Sophy van Houten! Seth sucked a strangled breath through his teeth, made an impatient movement of his hand and slowly turned away from the window. With a quick, uneven step he made his way to one of the bentwood chairs flanking the banker's desk.

"Vanderbilt already has control of the New York and Harlem Railroad," he cut in curtly. "Moreover, I imagine Miss van Houten would have something to say about marriage to a broken crock of a man who plans to immediately sell off her stock. And besides—" he paused on the excuse of placing his long ebony cane on the desk and lowering himself into a chair "—I don't think she and I would suit."

Matt Tyson leaned forward, his face frowning and intent, rested his elbows on the polished mahogany surface and raised an eyebrow. "Why ever not? Told you, Sophy's a nice girl, sensible, intelligent . . . and she has lots of other attractions." He jerked his head meaningfully toward the iron door of the bank's strong room.

"I've nothing against Sophy van Houten," Seth hastened to assure the banker, a coolness in his voice. "She's probably all you say, and charming company for a social evening. I simply do not wish to be married."

Matt gave Seth a considering look. "Don't misunderstand me, Seth." He picked up a pen and rolled it round in his fingers. "You need the money Sophy can bring you. Marry her and you'll retain your empire and your dream. A man with brains could come out of this mess richer than Midas."

Seth winced, stretched out his legs and wearily leaned his head against the fanned back of his chair. "I know," he said with a sigh.

The banker moved his head in a gesture of disbelief, and the skeptical look congealed into a baffled frown. "Hell, man, use your gray matter! I've known you since school. What's happened to you?"

"Four years of a damn war that has divided this country so's I don't know how the scars'll ever mend, a factory that leaks profits like a sieve, and a leg that is useless. That's what's happened."

Matt could hear the edge to his friend's voice, hard and sudden, like fine-honed steel. He knew Seth Weston was consumed with a deep anger. He also knew Seth Weston was no fool.

"You can't turn back the clock, Seth. Count your blessings and you'll find you still have more than most. The war's over. We must repair the fabric of this nation. Even without Lincoln at the helm, I'm confident that Andrew Johnson can create a new and stronger Union."

Seth's mouth twisted faintly. "If he doesn't fall out with Congress first. If he does he'll limit his tactical choices for reconstruction."

"At least you've got a choice." Matt straightened up, his brown eyes serious. "I'm going to lay it on the line, my friend, and this is as painful for me to say as it is for you to hear. If you're mule-stubborn enough to ignore my advice to marry Sophy van Houten, then the bank will be forced to foreclose on your mortgage."

Seth stared. "What?" He had heard, but he didn't believe his ears.

"No more credit, Seth. You're overextended. Hard cash is what you need right now. There's an heiress in Yonkers ripe for the plucking. Take her, or you'll have to liquidate half your holdings. You might not be poor, but it'll be a long crawl back to where you are now."

Seth heard the finality in the banker's calm statement and repressed a shiver of rage. Without a word, he slowly uncoiled his vast length from the chair. He walked toward the door, gait slightly uneven. He was still three feet from it when he turned, leaning heavily on his cane. He could feel himself trembling as his mouth compressed with bitter fury. Danger simmered in the depths of his eyes, but his voice, when he spoke, was cool and controlled.

"I'll call on Miss van Houten in the morning."

As the door closed behind his friend and client, Matt Tyson leaned back and grinned. Seth Weston's wrath was terrifyingly splendid. Such a man, seasoned to war, to hardship—and yes, even to women—was just what Sophy needed.

Over to you, Miss Sophy van Houten. Challenge an old dog, would you? Sophy deserved what was going to happen to her. Did she really think she could get away with blackmailing him? She needed to be taught a lesson. And Seth Weston was just the man to give it to her.

The door opened slowly to reveal a short, plump, middle-aged woman dressed in a plain gray gown with a white starched apron. In the middle of the room sat Sophy, dark head bent, lips slightly parted, writing. The scratching of pen on paper was the only sound to be heard as she entered a total on her inventory sheet with a flourish.

"What is it, Tessa?" Her voice was soft and calm, but sable eyebrows rose at the interruption.

Smoothing her apron with a reproachful gesture, the older woman set a vexed mouth, before she offered dourly, "Sorry to disturb ye, Miss Sophy, but there's a gentleman downstairs says he'd like to see ye."

Sophy van Houten lowered her head again to her journal, sighed and laid her pen aside.

"I'd hoped to finish my accounts this morning. He didn't say what he wanted, I suppose?"

"No, I never asked." Tessa's voice was severe as she continued, "Ye'll ruin your eyes with all that book work."

Sophy's smile was brilliant and an imp of mischief glinted in the gray eyes. "How old must I get, Tessa, before you will realize that I am no longer a green girl?"

Tessa's round face shone with indignation as she remained standing close by the door. "None of your lip, young woman. Ye'll always be a bairn to me. Shall I tell him to come back later, Miss Sophy? No respectable person comes visiting at this hour, or in this weather! It's only ten minutes past the hour of nine! Positively indecent!"

A small smile touched Sophy's lips at the servant's impertinence. Tessa Fraser had a bad habit of thinking Sophy still needed a nursemaid. It came with twenty years of loving and caring.

"Don't fuss, Tessa. I am not about to be ravished in my own house. This is 1865, after all. Show the gentleman into the parlor, please. I'll be down in a moment."

Sophy's thoughts spun round in her head like windmills as she carefully wiped the nib of her pen, closed the journal and slipped both into a drawer. Perhaps Mr. Tyson had sent someone? He had seemed quite certain after their little talk two days ago that he would be able to find a suitable prospect.

Since then, she had discovered several flaws in her plan. She touched her lip with the tip of her tongue. Perhaps it was not too late to back out of her hastily conceived strategy?

Needing a moment to consider how she could squash her rash scheme, Sophy unlatched the French window, and stepped outside. Droplets clung to the ironwork balustrade. The view below was flat and uninspiring. A dark canyon of street, and stark black elms outlined against the dull gray sky. Sophy grimaced. Winter was early this year. A wind slanted the rain, blowing a mist into the room.

It reminded her of the gray mist in Mr. Tyson's banking chambers two days earlier. He had sat there, the smoke from his cigar veiling his eyes, and listened to her. She was sure his brown eyes had been alight with mischief when she had carefully explained what she wanted. But he had been very polite.

Of course, while she had not told any direct lies, she had not been exactly truthful either. She had just let Mr. Tyson assume she was fulfilling her father's wish that she wed a man who needed her. Where was the line between lie and truth?

It was a little late to issue warnings to herself. Fastening the window latch, Sophy straightened her back, tilted her head proudly and headed for the parlor.

Only nine-twenty! Staring into the face of an ornate ormolu clock on the mantelpiece, Seth Weston asked himself for the hundredth time why he had allowed his ungovernable temper to trap him into traveling all the way to Yonkers.

For what? Dismissal? Ridicule? He'd heard Sophy van Houten had rejected so many suitors her father had laughingly declared she would die an old maid. .

Within weeks of Lincoln's assassination, her father, returning home on the *Sultana* after arranging the return of Union soldiers from Southern prisons, had been killed when the steamer exploded on the Mississippi. Now she was left quite alone, the old maid her father had predicted, before she was twenty. Also a very wealthy one.

Seth shivered, bent and poked the ashes in the grate with the silver tip of his walking stick. No warmth there. Cold. Cold as last year's love. Probably as cold and frigid as the van Houten woman. Another shiver ran through him. Hell, it was chilly even for October. He should leave now, before he made a fool of himself.

Instead, he removed his hat and gloves, drew the collar of his jacket higher about his neck, straightened his shoulders and faced the door to await his nemesis.

Small sounds indicated her arrival, light footsteps crossing the hall, a soft musical voice requesting coffee, the rustle of fabric. Dark against the open doorway appeared the shape of a woman dressed in black. She was small. He doubted she reached five feet.

She stood there, perfectly still, a dark shape around whose head the lamplight fashioned a halo of flashing daggers that pierced him with unease. Seth heard her soft exclamation. For a moment she stood there, hand gripping the door-knob as though it were a lifeline. Then, with another excla-mation, she swept toward him.

Entering the parlor, Sophy gave an involuntary gasp of surprise and stopped in confusion. Here was a new type, someone she had never seen before. Her heart was in her throat, pounding.

The lean, darkly powerful man who stood aggressively across the room from her was handsome, but there was an uncompromising severity about his dark eyebrows and the hard, controlled line of his mouth. A long, straight nose and firm chin added strength to his features.

Some interesting lines marked his finely chiseled face, giving it an elegant maturity. It was the face of a man who had stood at the doors of hell. Sophy looked at the tall length of him, the splendid breadth of his shoulders, the stiff-legged stance and ebony walking stick.

Stunned, her hand tightened on the doorknob to prevent it from going out to him. Eyes of brilliant blue met hers with some indefinable expression in their depths. Hard. Calcu-lating.

A ruthless man, Sophy decided, and a relentless one. He would go where he wished to go, do what he wanted to do, with implacable will and drive. Her stomach lurched, and for a moment a strange, unfamiliar sense of dizziness al-most overwhelmed her.

Sophy was looking for something in life; she did not know what. All the men she had met she could rule. None of her would-be husbands had made her feel as this one did!

She tore her eyes from his assessing gaze with a distinct effort, directing them toward the empty grate. For a mo-ment, she battled with an odd uncertainty. Then she began to breathe again and coherent thought replaced the drum-beat in her head.

Sophy strode forward, hand outstretched. Her slender body moved quickly, and she walked with a purposefulness that few women possessed.

"Good morning. I'm Sophy van Houten. What can I do for you?"

The words were no more than a whisper, and seemed to come out in an exasperated rush. Her heart was pounding so hard, she could scarcely breathe. She looked up at him, but not as far as his eyes. She avoided his eyes. Instead she looked at the slant of his jaw, the wide, uncompromisingly masculine mouth, the curve of his upper lip.

Hell, she couldn't even look him in the face! All he could see was a swirl of black hair, shiny as a raven's wing, concealing most of her face. Seth wondered why he felt a vague sense of disappointment. His mouth tightened. Surely she had been aware of his disability when she put forward her audacious proposal to Matt Tyson? Or was this some trick?

His suspicion was a weakness, momentary and unwelcome. But he could not stop the thoughts that buzzed round in his head as he accepted the hand waving vaguely in his direction.

The instant pressure, warm and firm, was like a bolt of electricity to his system. Her head jerked up. Around its edge glowed a shimmering halo. Seth jerked, released himself and fumbled with the collar of his jacket, which, for some reason, suddenly seemed too tight. Even his voice sounded hoarse, as though he had a sore throat.

"Seth Weston. I called to... that is, I was at the bank yesterday going over my affairs with..."

Sophy's eyes widened at the deep, well-modulated voice, which clipped the words with the precision of an executioner. It was a voice that carried the authority and menace of a master. It would seldom need to be raised.

She rubbed her hand against her skirt to rid it of the nerve-tingling sensation his cold flesh had generated. The tingle grew, radiating out to encompass her entire body.

Illusion

Face aflame, Sophy feared she looked ridiculous. Breathing raggedly, a strange knot deep in her throat, she blurted, "You're freezing! Come upstairs. I have a fire going in my drawing room. We can talk there."

Seth Weston just stood there for a moment, as though he didn't understand the language she spoke. Sophy knew she was gabbling, but she had to do something to dispel the tension. She shrugged, trying to appear calm and disdainfully unconcerned.

Doubt crossed Seth's face, but only for a moment. In a strange kind of elfin way, she seemed timid and embarrassed, yet he knew she was playing a game. A dangerous game.

Not only was she flirting with her looks, she was dangling her money as bait. She was even breaking conventions and inviting him to her private drawing room. He thought he saw her game. It was incredible what a wealthy woman would do for amusement.

He quickly weighed his chances of backing out and laughing the whole mess off as a joke, yet something stopped him. Looking down at her, he realized Sophy van Houten interested him. His probing gaze burned into her tense features.

She had a little pointed face and her eyes were huge with some carefully concealed emotion, as if it took an astonishing amount of nerve to confront him. For the first time in months, genuine amusement flared in his blue eyes.

Sophy took a step forward, about to take his hat and gloves, just as Seth shifted his weight to one hip. In her haste, she accidentally pressed against him. For some reason, this seemed to knock him off-balance, and he grabbed her shoulder to right himself. Sophy's eyes flew to meet his. Both went rigid with shock.

The clock ticked in the silent room.

Eyes more violet than gray, as fathomless as the sea, fringed by dark, long lashes, widened to an impossible extent. Seth did not think he had ever seen such a look of gentle allure in a human being before. He was suddenly taken with a longing to see those eyes darken with passion.

For a long moment he stood as though paralyzed before he swallowed a faint sense of chagrin. For an instant, he had glimpsed the promise of a wife, and children he could love and cherish.

An illusion. A dream. Dreams were for children...and fools. The thought brought a strangled sound from his throat.

Sophy came out of her state of stunned immobility. As though she had been scalded, she stepped back abruptly, and the color deepened in her cheeks. Her eyes flashed between the soft lashes.

Seth watched her. His sharp eyes saw through people. He knew she was nervous, and not stupid, and he wondered what caused this state of mind.

His eyelids drooped a fraction as his eyes shifted to the curving lips of a full, shapely mouth. The underlip, edged with a trace of moisture, was drawn over the upper, as though she were thinking deeply.

Sophy was. She didn't know what was happening to her, but something liquid seemed to be collecting deep inside her. A new experience to meet someone who could make her feel so strange! If her stomach kept turning somersaults, she would have Aunt Ella prepare one of her potions!

"First door on your left. You go on up. I'll just tell Tessa to bring the refreshments there."

Sophy's light, musical voice sounded distracted to her own ears, but she did not want to humiliate Mr. Weston by making reference to his affliction. While issuing instructions to the maid, she watched him surreptitiously as he made his way up the stairs.

He limped, barely able to move his right leg, and there was a way he held his shoulders that made her think every step he took was painful.

Every instinct urged her to offer assistance to her visitor to mount the stairs, but she knew pride would result in an angry refusal. So she allowed him five minutes before she ran lightly up the steps. He was standing composedly by the fire in her drawing room.

"Warmer in here, isn't it? I'll leave the door open so all will be correct."

Sensing his instinctive withdrawal at the comment, she waved toward an antique silk-upholstered sofa. They did not speak again until coffee had been served, each busy with private, uncomfortable thoughts.

How neatly he had been backed into a corner by Matt Tyson, Seth reflected bitterly. A yoke of matrimony hanging about his neck to weigh him down, or the loss of all he had labored for over the past ten years. He couldn't let that happen, whatever the cost.

Sophy absently stirred her coffee. The war was over. Had been for nigh on six months. Yet still the legacy of misery lingered. She did not know how much excruciating agony Mr. Weston must have undergone, but he still seemed in pain.

Sometimes the test of courage was not to die but to live. It would be good to ease this man's hurt. Deliberately she took a grip on her thoughts and looked up at him through her lashes.

"Did you want to tell me the reason for your visit, Mr. Weston?"

Seth watched her face for a long moment. His blue eyes seemed to see right through her gleaming head. Then he appeared to reach a decision. Leaning forward, he set down his cup on the low cherrywood table, an air of sudden determination in his eyes.

"I wanted to talk to you, Miss van Houten, on a very personal matter. With the war and all—" indicating his leg "—I've been out of commission for two years, and become a social hermit, I'm afraid."

"Yes, I suppose you have," Sophy replied slowly. A fleeting smile touched her lips, and she looked him straight in the eyes. "I promise to do whatever I can to help you."

"I know it's asking a great deal, but . . ."

Hell, this was more difficult than he'd thought. Damn, but Matt Tyson had put him in one hell of a spot, Seth fumed. Another six months and he could have traded out of his financial quagmire.

"Go on, Mr. Weston."

Seth ran his fingers through his hair. He didn't have another six months and Sophy van Houten was looking at him so intently, with such unblinking fervor, he felt as though she were reading his mind.

She sat, hands folded in her lap as she waited politely. He was aware she had rejected dozens of offers of marriage. His would be another. It seemed a calculating look had entered her cool gray eyes.

She was probably enjoying herself immensely! Fresh as the violets tucked into her belt, she appeared a product of the present day's spoiled, overindulged young womanhood. Such a creature could be of no interest to any thinking man, except for one aspect, and he was much too busy to bother with such things at the moment.

"In order to be honest, I shall tell you I have numerous assets, including several factories, but no ready cash for working capital. The trouble is that even with hard work and a lot of luck, it will be years before modern manufacturing methods can be introduced."

Seth looked at her just a trifle savagely as he leaned forward in his seat, absently kneading his right thigh. His resolve was diminishing with each passing second.

Fresh autumn air, gray eyes and pink velvet cheeks, to say nothing of a Cupid's bow cherry mouth that owed nothing to artifice, were upsetting factors. The most insane desire flooded him to kiss those dusky eyelashes and crush the little fragile body in his arms.

As he pulled himself together with a jerk, a scowl settled upon his stern face. If he wanted her fortune, he would have to marry her. He looked at his hands and took a deep breath.

"It goes against the grain to appear mercenary, but it's been borne in upon me lately that the only real solution for me is to acquire access to a reliable source of funds. To be blunt, to marry an heiress."

Sophy's eyes widened in shock. His honesty touched her. All her previous offers had been accompanied with vows of undying love. This man offered no such commitment.

Here was the first man who was plainly not dazzled by her. She had been hoping for this, but she had not expected it. A faint blush started over her cheeks and she began to speak, but he silenced her with a wave of his hand.

"I do not want to marry except for the reason I've given, but I'm not in love with anyone." His lips curved wryly, revealing even white teeth. "Don't believe I could be. All the romance was knocked out of me long ago. So, well, what I'm leading up to, Miss van Houten, is this. Would *you* consider marrying me?"

Chapter Two

The question hung in the air. Sophy sat as still as death while she felt her face grow scarlet and then drain of color. Pricked by a sudden doubt, she waited to recover herself before she answered.

"I, too, would like to be honest with you, Mr. Weston. While my father was alive I became accustomed to organizing my own finances. However, my trustees feel that these same funds would be better utilized under the firm control of a husband. I don't relish the idea of giving up my freedom."

Sophy's voice was deceptively calm. Her cheeks were wild roses once more. The thought of being made to play the role she despised so completely infuriated her. Her vexation gave a new charm to her glowing face.

Seth could not fault that sentiment, even if it was a radical one for a woman. "I, too, would want the advantages of being married, without giving up anything of myself," he assured her.

Sophy's eyes snapped toward him. For a moment she studied his face. The marks of the past four years were on it, a disturbing intensity in the strong features. While she did not want to appear reluctant to become his wife, she could not help but worry at the bitter edge of cynicism in his voice, the contained tension of his body and the despair reflected in his countenance.

To her surprise, Seth Weston became distinctly uneasy under her assessing scrutiny, and moved restlessly.

For a few seconds they sat looking at each other and then, almost roughly, he said, "Miss van Houten, I had thought this over, of course, but I didn't realize how it would all sound until I spoke those last words. I think the proposition I just made you is actually insulting, and I hope you'll excuse me. It was an impulsive thing to do and I'm ashamed of it. So forget it. I'll see myself out."

He had the silver knob of his cane in his hand when Sophy found her voice. "Mr. Weston, I would like to accept your offer."

Seth's head came up. "You mean you'll marry me?"

He leaned toward Sophy, his eyes narrowed, as if taking her measure, a measure that somehow puzzled him.

It did. The woman was rich and exceedingly attractive. Why connive an arranged marriage with a man she didn't know from Adam? He found himself watching her mouth. On lips firm and full, a soft, mysterious, somehow inviting smile bloomed. Behind their protective lashes, a secret, pleased look flared in her eyes. It was an echo of her sensual smile. Seth felt his features lock into an unrevealing mask.

Sophy smiled faintly, finding it difficult to conceal a strong sense of elation. She had succeeded in her plan to break the trust. Now she would have only a single male to contend with ... her husband.

Husband. The word made her insides squeeze all sick and scared. Husbands usually meant knowing each other in an intimate way! Sophy felt her stomach leap to her throat.

Husbands meant babies! Her stomach flipped again. Her whole body stiffened, and she felt her panic growing. Maybe he wouldn't want her in that way? Maybe he would be content with her money? Her words were sober, but her eyes betrayed her.

"You've made your points very clearly, Mr. Weston. One thing, though, you didn't mention. Since this would be a marriage of convenience, did you mean it would also be what I believe is called a 'marriage in name only'?''

Seth paled. A frown creased his broad forehead into a network of lines, and something undefinable flickered in his eyes. He looked off over her head. There was a long pause. Sophy began to suspect she had offended him.

"Well, no," he said slowly, his voice soft, deep as summer midnight, richly textured as plush velvet. "I didn't mean that, I guess." He stretched out his weak leg, absently rubbing his thigh through the fabric of his trousers.

Sophy nervously touched the round silver disk suspended from a delicate chain at the base of her throat and stifled a pang of fear. How had she expected him to react? The truth was, she hadn't thought it all through that far. Just as she hadn't considered she was being totally unreasonable in expecting him to forgo the expectation of a normal marriage and children.

She needed to think logically and calmly about the situation. Perhaps if she told him the truth, he would understand. She drew in a quavery breath, searching for cushioning words.

"I want only honesty between us. You seem to understand my situation, and I had hoped to come to some arrangement with you." Sophy managed the words with a steadiness that surprised herself. Inside she was a bundle of agitation and chaotic thoughts.

Seth looked at her curiously for a moment, his interest heightened by her sudden diffidence. Sophy's eyes were on his face, but he felt as though she did not actually see him.

There was a darkness in her eyes, a fear in her face that he had seen before only in the eyes of men going out to battle. Then she held out her hand. He looked surprised at the gesture but took the slim fingers in his own large ones. They were icy cold.

"What is it?"

There was a deep note in Seth's voice that reached out and touched Sophy, bringing her back to reality. Suddenly her eyes were focused on his, and for a moment both of them were very still. His strongly magnetic eyes seemed to enter her very being and cause some strange fluttering near her heart.

She waited, aware of a breathless feeling. Her fingers trembled in Seth's large hand, and she knew he must have felt it. The lines around his mouth deepened, and a muscle flickered in his jaw. His voice was steady, without emotion. "I cannot help you, if I don't know what is wrong."

His fingers tightened on hers, and he smiled, but his eyes gleamed with an unreadable emotion. Sophy's senses reacted to the subtle force of his personality. There was a cool perception and an underlying intelligence in Seth Weston that she would do well to acknowledge. Deception or lies would not sit well with such a man.

She licked suddenly dry lips. "If it would not...inconvenience you too much, Mr. Weston, would you consider a marriage in name only?"

There was a distinct pause, then Seth asked cautiously, "Are you afraid of me, Sophy?" The question hung in the air between them.

"No." Abruptly, she felt a searing need to share her secrets. She swallowed and gathered her courage. If they were to start off their married life right, she was going to have to be honest.

"As a charity worker in the army hospital, I helped tend hundreds of wounded soldiers, both Union and Confederate prisoners. The agony and misery I witnessed affected me deeply. I have sworn that I will never bear a child and so perpetuate the terrible things that brother can do to brother."

The harsh contours of Seth's face seemed to harden at the depth of despair in her voice, but he did not release the grip on her fingers. "The idea still distresses you?"

She frowned uncertainly. "No. But I made a solemn vow. One which I intend to keep." Her fingers flexed against his palm. "Now that you know I will never give you a child, do you want to withdraw your offer of marriage?"

Seth's eyes narrowed to blue slits as he examined her face carefully. Her eyes were wide, reflecting an appeal of which she wasn't aware as she waited for his reaction.

He found his gaze drifting to her mouth, observing the way the lower lip slid beneath small white teeth. Was the action to prevent its trembling? Or a contrived expression of mystery, sensuality and allure? Whichever it was, Sophy van Houten was not what he had anticipated.

He had expected a weak, easily led woman, helplessly adrift without the support of her father, and instead here was a creature who, though she looked fragile, possessed a devastating candor, an integrity, that set all his preconceived notions of women in a spin.

Humor flickered briefly in the set features of his face. "Is that all? You don't want children? That is your terrible confession?"

Sophy's chin rose at the trace of amusement in his voice. "I am constantly told I am too unconventional, too reckless, that I must curb my foolish thoughts." A little ghost of a smile touched her lips. "I am also aware that, even in a city that prides itself in being on the cutting edge of the new morality, to go against custom is to invite ostracism."

"Money will open most doors, and we've just finished four years of bloodshed to confirm all men are born equal." He slanted her an odd glance. "In any event, one man's rose is another man's cabbage. It seems we have things in common, after all. Children are not high on my list of priorities from this marriage."

Recognizing in the simple statement both the truth and the utter insufficiency of the words, Sophy closed her eyes for a moment, relief surging through her. He had no intention of withdrawing his offer, she thought, with a trace of wonder. It was comforting and slightly scary, but it also gave her an oddly warm feeling right behind her breastbone.

Silence fell around them. Sophy stole another look at him, wishing she could sit here and savor this warm, comfortable feeling for the rest of time. Her fingers quivered a little in the warmth and strength of his clasp, and she smiled brilliantly up at him.

"We can call it settled, then?"

Seth went still. The unnatural quietness in him was unnerving. Deep down, it sent prickles of a very primitive, very feminine alarm through her.

"Not quite." His voice was gentle. "There is one detail I would like to clarify. It might not be fair to either of us to commit ourselves to the arrangement you propose on a permanent basis."

Sophy marveled at the perfectly neutral tone of his words. Whatever happened, marriage or no marriage, would not be a neutral event to her. She leaned forward earnestly, breathing tremulously, searching his face for hidden meanings.

He was watching her with a startling intensity. "I know that you consider this marriage to be founded on necessity, so I am prepared to wait until you feel comfortable enough to fulfill the . . . er, shall we call it, duties of a wife."

His thumb stroked the back of her hand, tracing the lines of the bones there. "I've tried to make it plain that I can't give you romance. That part of me does not exist anymore." His jaw tightened. "But I promise to be a faithful husband, Sophy, and I will not act the cuckold. Do you understand?"

Sophy could feel the tension emanate from his body, a tangible thing, matching her own. A deep wariness and a grim determination lit his eyes, as if he were silently setting down the rules of war. The challenge was there, in his eyes, waiting for her.

With a feeling of sliding from a great height, she responded, her fingers tight on his. The suggestion of warmth and laughter that was reflected in the curve of her mouth became a full-blown smile.

"Yes."

It was all that she could manage, that one syllable, but nothing could halt the rush of red into her cheeks. She had won a glorious victory! The matter of marital intimacy had been satisfactorily resolved. She had control of herself and the situation.

Realizing suddenly what he'd agreed to, Seth pulled his hand from hers as if her fingers were a sheaf of snakes. Damn her to hell! Had he consented to a marriage he did not want simply to save a factory? Sold his soul to the devil for thirty pieces of silver?

No. Not quite true. Most men would kill for a smile like the one she had just given him. The smile that was on her face was like the rising of the sun. A sweet, feminine gift, which dazzled the senses.

For a second, he'd stepped into an illusion, allowing it to enclose him so completely that he'd felt her delight as if it were his own. And, in reality, the kind of marriage she was offering was precisely the type to which he was most suited.

They each had something the other wanted, or needed.

Sophy moved restlessly in her seat, hurt at his abrupt withdrawal. She wanted to leave her hand in his, warm and safe. The pain seemed to grow round her heart, but there was self-deprecation too. She should not have dared to show such foolish emotion before him. She glared at Seth as he poured fresh coffee from the porcelain pot on the cherry-wood table.

An odd smile edged Seth's mouth as he looked into those well-spaced gray eyes. He raised an eyebrow at her and held up the pot in salute.

"Well, Miss van Houten, it would seem that you and I have ourselves a marriage contract. I hope you consider the bargain worthwhile." He shut his eyes in brief irritation when his leg protested angrily at the movement. He shifted position gingerly. "Would Sunday week suit you?"

"Whenever you wish. I won't change my mind," she said gravely, accepting the cup he passed to her.

Seth gave her a sharp look as though to detect levity, a slight frown hardening the lines around his mouth. When Sophy's eyes solemnly met his fierce blue ones, her whole body went tense.

There was something about the way he looked at her that confused her. Something shrewd. Something dangerous. The taut strain in him was etched around his eyes, making her want to lift her fingers to soothe away the lines. A nervous tremor skittered along her nerves, and she tore her eyes from his, breaking the spell.

"I'll wait on your uncles tomorrow to make the necessary arrangements."

Relieved, Seth realized his voice was even, as though he were in full command. For a moment those soft gray eyes had stirred feelings that were strange and unwelcome, yet pleasurably compelling. It was a long time since a woman had so disturbed his equilibrium.

Sophy lowered her eyes demurely to the contents of her coffee cup. Thinking she shouldn't even be considering the suggestion and knowing it was already starting to tantalize her, she glanced up at him through lowered lashes.

Setting down her cup with great care, she put her small hand to her mouth, shocked by the heady notion. It would be a bold move to try to squeeze further concessions from him, but why not enter into marriage on terms favorable to the wife?

Her mouth tilted slightly at the corners. *Fortune sides with him who dares.* She tried to make her voice bland. "I would like to continue with some projects I've been working on, maybe even undertake some new ones."

Seth's eyes met hers over the rim of his cup. Sensing his annoyance, Sophy sat up a little straighter, and blinked owlishly. Her voice was a shadowy breathless sound. "No questions, no reproaches, no *comments* even from a husband."

Seth set down his cup, the firm line of his mouth hardening slightly. From the displeased expression on his face, Sophy could tell he found her demands excessive.

Sophy blinked, uncertain of his sudden change of mood. Maybe she should compromise, just a little? She wet her suddenly parched lips with the tip of her tongue and hurried on before she lost her courage. "And I promise no tears. I've heard wives cry a lot to gain their points."

Seth's features were forbidding as he studied her. Sophy's jaw muscles went tight. His gaze seemed to penetrate into the very heart of her, as if he were trying to discover her deepest secrets.

He stared at her for a moment, then he laughed. A short, sharp expulsion of air. But definitely a laugh. To his ears the tone sounded surprisingly rusty, but then it had been literally years since he had laughed out loud so spontaneously.

"I couldn't stand that! Anything more?" His question was more curious than anything.

Sophy shook her head slowly. "No."

He eased his leg back against the sofa, watching her, a cool, flicking assessment in his bright blue eyes. Sophy could feel the probing inspection as if he had reached out and touched her.

Something feminine and disturbing flowed down her spine. She shifted uncomfortably, unable to look away from his suddenly hooded gaze.

"I take it that this is the end of our negotiations? That you will not come up with new demands and stipulations every other day?" His voice was steady and calm, though she could feel the coiled energy in him.

Sophy felt herself blush at the gibe, but she felt a sense of relief that he was willing to ignore the tension flowing between them. She had to establish firm terms and conditions in her relationship with this man, or she would be lost. She lifted one shoulder and shrugged dismissively.

"Of course not." She moved her head once in denial. "I simply wanted to have things cut-and-dried before you committed yourself. There is one more thing, though." She was annoyed to recognize the hint of uncertainty in her voice.

"Let's hear it." There was resignation in his tone, but wry humor flickered behind the dark lashes and tugged at the corners of his mouth.

Sophy drew in a deep breath and let him have it. "As I mentioned earlier, I was actively involved in many of my father's financial dealings. I would like to learn all I can about textile manufacturing as well, assist where I can."

There was a charged silence while Seth digested her proposal. He sat there, looking as if he were reflecting on his response as he idly ran a finger around the rim of his coffee cup.

Sophy eyed his lowered lashes, a queer feeling in her stomach. It was like a great bubble that threatened to expand and explode the fantasy she had begun to weave about the nature of this man.

It was this element of uncertainty that caused the powerful effect on her. Her heart beat a slow thud, pressing the bubble up behind her breastbone, pounding a thought into her brain.

Had she made a terrible miscalculation?

The silence was becoming more than a little frightening when he looked up suddenly, his decision made.

"Fair enough. I have no objection. If you accept that I reserve the right to try to influence your decisions, you have a deal," he agreed easily.

The small victory banished Sophy's apprehension. Once again she felt in charge of the situation. The notion was strangely satisfying. Sufficient for her to proceed recklessly.

"As my wedding gift, Mr. Weston, I intend handing over my father's entire estate to you. It is not insubstantial and will make the payment of your debts infinitely easier and any plans for expansion less troublesome. Unless you have any objections, I shall retain only those assets and funds I have acquired through my own endeavors.''

Seth gritted his teeth, reached for the cane and started to get to his feet. And he had thought she was vulnerable, a target for fortune hunters like himself!

An uneasy shiver feathered his spine and he shook his head. He had a gut feeling she was not going to be the biddable, obedient wife Matt Tyson had promised.

''The idea of a wife who drives a hard bargain intrigues me, Sophy van Houten.'' He slanted her a deliberate glance. ''It's going to be interesting being married to you.''

He had never envisaged that married life was going to be a pleasant experience, not by any stretch of the imagination. The point to recognize was that Sophy van Houten was only a woman, and an unseasoned little squab at that.

He had merely to show her who was in charge, and all would be well. Seth Weston was a man used to giving orders, and to seeing them obeyed.

Time enough after they were married to bring her to heel. He had other things to do today. He was going to visit Wall Street and give a certain banker a small but hopefully salutary piece of his mind.

Sophy's eyes were bright and steady with exhilaration as the door closed behind him. Every hope she had ever held was blossoming afresh.

Her prayers were answered. All she had ever wanted was within her grasp. A small voice within her whispered, *Be careful not to ask for what you want. You just might get it.*

It spun through her mind that, if she were wise, she would leap up and run from this marriage as if the yawning pits of hell gaped at her feet. But Sophy knew how often the gamble was worth the risk.

The game was never lost till won.

The day of the wedding was one of October's smiling ones, still and unseasonable, almost warm. There was the feel of a gentle determination in the air, of tenacious life, a

movement, a subtle tremor of restless nature, beneath a
shining sun. The curtains were pulled back from the bow-
shaped windows, letting the light spill into the dressing
room.

Standing in front of the long mirror, Sophy gave her hair
a final pat, and her delicately arched brows pulled together
in a frown. Would she be a disappointment as a wife to Seth
Weston? He had made it perfectly clear it was only her coin
he wanted. It wouldn't have mattered if she were a hunch-
back with four eyes, her wealth was attractive.

There was no reason for her to feel as strangely unhappy
and uneasy as she did. After all, she had agreed to the wedding bargain. Her only doubts lay with the unknown quantity of Seth Weston and her growing awareness of him as a
man. Sophy touched the tip of her tongue to her lower lip,
suddenly nervous.

Her maid gave a knowing grin. "Now, don't ye be fret-
ting over something that hasn't happened yet. Things have
a way of working out." Giving Sophy a caress on the cheek,
Tessa adjusted Sophy's cap.

Sophy had finally settled upon black silk and lace for her
wedding attire and a small cap, black, embroidered, with
just enough veil to suggest the bride.

"I guess you're right, Tessa," she conceded. She wished
she had asked Aunt Ella about the intimacies of marriage,
but she had not wanted to embarrass her straitlaced aunt.

"Have you never wished to marry, Tessa?"

"Nay, lass. My clan were poor. From the day I arrived in
America, I belonged to Nicholas van Houten and his bonny
lassie. They were all the kin I ever needed, just as yon man
will be your life."

Sophy stood helplessly. A thousand thoughts possessed
her, none of them rational enough to voice.

Seth Weston ...

She had not seen her fiancé at all during the two weeks
preceding the wedding. Only a brief message with Matt Tyson to say the marriage contract had been drawn up, and, if

it fulfilled all her conditions, would she please sign as necessary.

There had been other callers, including her two uncles and her cousin. Uncle Schuyler had seemed relieved that he would soon be able to discharge his final task as trustee. Her mother's brother had never wanted such a responsibility in the first place. Sophy, with her independent ways, made him uncomfortable, but he was determined to do the right thing by his niece.

He had pompously declared Seth Weston to be a man of excellent character, who would safely see to Sophy's welfare. He had also sadly reflected that it would have been more seemly if dear Sophy had respected the customary period of mourning before committing herself to marriage, and left.

Sophy had a sneaking suspicion that Uncle Schuyler was secretly impressed that Seth had survived the bloody battle of Gettysburg and still remained a respected textile manufacturer.

While Uncle Heinrich wished her well, he also considered the haste unseemly. Did she not feel the weight of remorse? he asked trenchantly. Did her conscience not trouble her?

A pained expression on his face, he closed his eyes, muttered a prayer for forgiveness, then made the caustic observation that Seth Weston would regret tying himself to such a willful baggage.

But Uncle Heinrich also felt under obligation to see that his brother's daughter was married well, and pronounced Seth to be a man of honor who had fought bravely for the Union. Any man who could control a regiment of soldiers should be able to control one small woman.

It was left to Cousin Pieter to ask her bluntly if she loved Seth. Sophy flushed, unable to reply. Pieter believed in the cause of freedom, not only for black slaves, but for women. What could she say now?

That love was an illusion, cut to the measure of one's own desire? That her desire was for independence, not love? That she was desperate for freedom? That Seth Weston was willing to give that freedom to her?

Pieter's eyes had narrowed with suspicion. Sophy gulped, gnawed at her bottom lip, trying to figure out how she could distract Pieter's thoughtful attention.

"If there's one thing I've learned since Father's death, Pieter, it's that I don't want my life the way it was. I want more," she ground out, her throat tight with tension. "I'll make Seth a good wife if it kills me," she vowed, "or if he doesn't kill me first!"

The sound of church bells, ringing as clear and crisp as the autumn sky overhead, accompanied Sophy as she entered the sacristy of the old church at Sleepy Hollow.

Sophy had difficulty in concentrating on the service. She thought it might have something to do with the potion Aunt Ella had given her earlier to quell the butterflies in her stomach.

As she entered the church on her uncle's arm, her whole being was concentrated on the man waiting at the altar.

Seth Weston...

It was quite remarkable; she knew without looking up the very moment he turned his head to look at her, and felt his start of surprise. At the last moment, she had impulsively plucked some late-blooming roses and pinned them to her cap. A novel touch. Incongruous. Defiant.

The wreath of vivid red roses lent a sweet, pungent scent to the air as she stood before the pastor and prayed for God's blessing on the marriage. The minister opened his book and began to address the congregation.

"We are gathered here today to join this man and this woman in the bonds of holy matrimony...."

Seth was conscious of the slight figure standing at his side. Whoever heard of a bride wearing mourning black—and red roses? Not exactly proper. In fact, downright unconventional! Like a reflection on water, his first impressions of Sophy were beginning to waver.

That sort of picture did tend to ignore the small irregularities. A dangerous mistake. Although it was only a tiny error in the mental image of her that he had fashioned, it bothered Seth.

A seasoned campaigner, he knew little mistakes, small pieces missing in the puzzle, could lead to much bigger and more dangerous miscalculations. There were still too many unknowns in the mystery that was Sophy van Houten.

No. Sophy Weston. He made a quick adjustment in his mental construct of his bride. His bride. Hell, what on earth was he doing here? It was too late now to get out of it, but he had a feeling that someone had set a trap for him and he had fallen into it.

"Wilt thou take this man to be thy wedded husband... for better, for worse, for richer, for poorer... in sickness and in health... to love, honor and obey...?"

Confusion and a strange kind of fear thudded with Sophy's heart, which was pumping in quite an uncertain manner. As Seth's fingers closed over hers, her insides churned and she felt a deep throbbing wave of excitement. It was startling and disturbing to react as strongly as this to his touch.

I shouldn't be here, she thought, staring blindly at the preacher. She knew nothing of love, so it wasn't so bad that they didn't love each other. Seth was marrying for security and she was making a respectable bargain, the kind many women in her position struck. It was just that she felt uneasy. Besides, it was too late now to change her mind.

Sophy felt a moment of panic, and her throat was so tight that the "I will" demanded of her would hardly come out.

There! It was done! She was married to Seth Weston.

Seth Weston...

He stood beside her, in stiff military style, a soldier girded for battle. She heard his responses, firm, strong and, in some way, completely impersonal.

Somehow, that bothered her. An unaccountable tension gripped her. She felt as though she were standing on the brink of a very wide, very deep chasm.

"—what God hath joined together, let no man put asunder."

Lost in thought, Sophy scarcely realized the ceremony had concluded. Seth, too, stood as if made of stone, not moving, staring into space. The silence was awkward.

Finally, Cousin Pieter, who had acted as groomsman, gestured toward Sophy. "Go ahead and kiss the bride, Seth."

Sophy was overwhelmingly conscious of the tall, powerful figure at her side. Face aflame, she forced herself to meet her husband's eyes. A quickening shivered through her middle. She attempted a smile, but her mouth felt soft, tremulous.

The deep glow in his eyes was suddenly so intense that she was forced to look away or be scorched by the heat. Why was he looking at her that way? It was vaguely unnerving, and it took a great deal of courage not to step back. Instead, her small, pointed chin rose in challenge.

Seth paled considerably. He drew in his breath sharply, and his eyes blazed with the sizzling heat of a lightning bolt. Then he appeared to reach a decision. Sophy had the feeling that he always made decisions that way, quickly and surely.

What would it be like to be kissed by him? Sophy's eyes widened. She knew he was going to kiss her, and she knew she wanted him to.

Yet, at the same time, she felt trapped, unnerved by the strange feelings coursing through her. The quickening rippled outward from her belly, into her limbs.

I can't, she thought in panic. She sucked in a quick breath, and turned her head sideways. Seth's breath was soft and warm in her ear and she felt chills on her arms as his moist lips landed just above her earlobe.

Sophy could see the sudden flush on his cheekbones, and his blue eyes seemed to see right through her head. Crystal eyes, frost eyes. And they were filled with a brilliance that subtly invaded her being, causing her to shiver, to remember that her first impression of him had told her that he could be a dangerous man.

She watched Seth's mouth draw downward, his weight shift to one hip, heard his intake of breath, which mocked her.

"I beg your forgiveness, Mrs. Weston. My aim is not what it was." There was something slightly contemptuous, or was it scorn, in his tone? She looked up at him and saw in his eyes an almost blazing anger that was quite unmistakable.

Startled by the extent of his reaction, Sophy's throat tightened on a sudden urge to cry out. She had not intended any offense. It was merely a spur-of-the-moment act of self-defense. So why did she suddenly remember one of Aunt Ella's maxims? *Who digs a pit shall fall therein.*

Chapter Three

"Teatime, Sophy."

Intent on her work, Sophy was busy cleaning out the numerous drawers of her tall Empire secretary. She gave the maid a quick smile.

"Put it on the table, thanks, Tessa. I'll join you in a minute, Aunt Ella. I'm just about finished here."

Boxes of books and papers, all precisely wrapped and labeled Mrs. Seth Weston, were neatly stacked, awaiting the removers.

Mrs. Seth Weston.

She frowned. What a mess, a frightening, overwhelming mess her life had become. Nothing was going as planned. Even her wedding day had not gone as anticipated. It seemed as though she had taken a wrong turn and, without warning, found herself on the lip of a great abyss.

From that moment in the church when Seth had faced her, his eyes twin blue flames, the marriage had been a debacle. For a shattering second she had been torn between running into her new husband's arms and running as far away from him as she could.

True, he had been a perfect gentleman. She could not fault his manners. A small smile curving his mouth, he had bowed, brought her hand upward and kissed the delicate flesh on the inside of her wrist, before placing it on his extended arm.

There had been something in that smile that wrung an instant response from her, something intimate that she was too inexperienced to define. Blood-pulsing. Nerve-tingling. As though he knew of, and understood, her dilemma perfectly.

She had groped for something to say before they turned to greet their guests, but it was too late. Whirling in upon itself, her mind paralyzed her tongue, and the moment passed.

Color flowed under her skin, staining her cheeks a dull pink at the memory. She'd been scared by that kiss! Terrified by the churning inside her. In vain she tossed the memory aside, but perfunctory though the gesture might have been, the spot he kissed still tingled and throbbed.

Tossing a sheaf of notes into the wastepaper basket, Sophy had the uncomfortable feeling that she had been outmaneuvered. It was difficult to recall, even now.

Dredging it up was like opening the edges of a slowly healing wound and probing for the nerve. Although he held her arm, she had not dared to look at him. She was conscious of his nearness, conscious, too, that he was tense.

The relief was there in her eyes when a servant had handed Seth a telegraph. She knew it, but couldn't disguise the emotion when he paused in the act of reading the message, and met her eyes very directly. His blue eyes narrowed, he explained he had to leave for Chicago immediately.

That had been two weeks ago. The days had passed for Sophy in a flurry of activity as heavy trunks were filled to overflowing. Seth had decreed that Richard Carlton, his New York agent, would give any assistance she might need.

"Drink your tea, Sophy. You're looking quite pale."

Aunt Ella sat on the edge of the settee, ramrod stiff. Sophy's ceaseless activity was disturbing to say the least.

"If I stop now, I'll never get everything organized."

Sophy locked the center drawer of the walnut writing desk and dropped the key into her capacious apron pocket. The closer the hour of Seth's return, the more apprehensive she was becoming.

She was not quite certain what she had expected from this marriage, but she knew she was feeling a decided sensation of pique and neglect. Whoever heard of a husband going off the very day of the marriage?

"What's the matter?" Despite her rigid back, Ella's tea-cup rattled in its saucer, belying her calm. "Are you regretting your reckless decision to marry in haste, my dear?"

Sophy laughed lightly. "No, of course not! I simply want to have all my personal bits and pieces unpacked before Seth returns."

By keeping herself frantically busy, she was able to keep her uneasiness, her doubts, at bay. But despite her attempts, one question throbbed in her brain. Had she made a dreadful mistake? After all, she hadn't made a very good start. She knew so little about the man. Still, it was said that all things in life balance themselves out. She hoped so.

Timidly, Ella expressed her own reservations, "Perhaps it would have been better if you had considered the consequences of marriage, Sophy. A woman is only a secondary consideration to a man beside his work, or where his interests are concerned."

"It's too late to fret, Aunt Ella. We must deal with reality. The deed is done. *Until death us do part.*"

Sophy dismissed her aunt's qualms with a facetious shrug, and picked up her cup. Her nose crinkled at the dark, syrupy brew. Sometimes, Aunt Ella's concoctions tasted quite poisonous. There was a brief silence between the two women as Ella drank her tea and Sophy contemplated how she was going to greet Seth.

Would it be permissible to kiss him? In her fertile imagination, she could see Seth holding her gently, stroking her hair, murmuring soft endearments. Beyond this point, there was no form or substance, only an ill-defined longing which made her weak. Mostly because she was a bit vague about the next bit. She had only a dim knowledge of sexual matters, and was not at all sure what "doing your duty" entailed.

Unable to sit still, Sophy wandered over to the one set of bookshelves that had not been denuded. Idly she plucked a thick, red, Moroccan leather-bound volume off the bottom shelf.

A small package fell from between the pages, to land with a thud on the carpet. She instantly picked up the packet, and warily turned it over in her hands.

Ella sat her saucer on the table in front of her. The cup rattled again, and her back straightened even more. "What is it, dear?"

Sophy carefully undid the knotted red tape and unrolled the folio. Pressing it flat against the desk, she stood studying it for a long moment. Eventually she looked at her aunt, dark brows raised in curious question.

"Did you know Father owned property in Greene Street, Aunt?"

To her surprise, Ella blushed and looked away quickly, as if she was anxious not to let Sophy see her expression. It was almost as if she knew something.

"Nicholas never discussed business with me."

Sophy frowned over the faded ink record of ownership. It was hard to believe that her father kept secrets from her, or that Ella might have been privy to that information. So it was with deliberation that she faced her aunt.

"I remember he often mentioned appointments he had in Greene Street. Once when I wanted him to put a proposal to John Rockefeller regarding an investment in the Cleveland oil refinery, Father said it was 'a convenience and a delight' to transact business there. Do you know what he could have meant?"

Just as deliberately, Sophy studied the older woman's reaction. Ella's expression was closed and she looked uncomfortable, even as she shook her head.

Relentlessly, Sophy continued, "This seems most mysterious. I think I will visit Greene Street. Don't you think that will be amusing?"

"No," Ella replied with the gloom of one who knew that, like Pandora, Sophy might do best not to pry.

The night was almost silent, except for the tick of the tall clock set in the angle of the stairs, and the muffled hiss of the gas fire, which burned softly in the grate. Sophy came awake suddenly. Something had disturbed her.

Was there a noise? The question remained unanswered. She wasn't sure whether it was a sound, or whether it was the beating of her own heart.

In any case, she was awake. Better to investigate than to lie in bed worrying. Her mouth a little dry, her heart beating a little faster than usual, Sophy searched for a weapon. Picking up a silver candlestick, she crept down the stairs and along the corridor, toward the soft, muted sounds she now identified as coming from the kitchen.

She heard her own footsteps echo on the marble hallway. They seemed to echo very loudly. At the kitchen door, Sophy paused, straining to pick out any movement. A slender, uncertain little figure, she stared wide-eyed into the gloom. Relief flowed through her as she recognized the tall figure and gleaming head of her husband.

A wide smile lit her face. She was too delighted to do anything but exclaim breathlessly, "Seth! I didn't know you were back!"

In the dim light, Seth's elegant broadcloth suit glimmered richly like polished obsidian, and his crisp white linen shirt created an illusory pedestal on which rested the chiseled form of his handsome head.

"Didn't you?" A trace of amusement flitted over his face at the obvious pleasure she did not know she had betrayed. "You must have missed me, to greet me so enthusiastically," he added softly, indicating the silver weapon still clutched in Sophy's hand.

Self-consciously, Sophy thrust the candlestick onto one of the kitchen benches. "I thought it was a nocturnal intruder." The words came out in an unsteady rush.

"You look...mussed. Did I waken you?" As he moved toward her, his halting stride unhurried, his face was shadowed.

Sophy cared little for his words, only his presence. She smoothed her hair, feeling such a flood of warmth and pleasure that she felt weak. "It doesn't matter. Welcome back." Her voice was shy as she gave him her hand.

Seth's jaw muscles went tight. In dishabille, her feet bare and with her hair flowing like a length of ebony silk about her shoulders, his wife looked very young and very fragile. Like a drop of morning dew waiting for the sun. The illusion of sweet, trembling innocence was heightened by her demure, white cotton negligee, trimmed with broderie anglaise.

Mildly irritated, he realized something about his pixie-faced wife had gotten to him. The determined lift of her chin, the mouth wide and ready to smile, the sweet clarity of her eyes drew him.

Curse her. Curse her. Curse her. She had already stripped him of his pride, his self-respect. Never in his life had he envisaged marrying a woman for her money, or having a wife who was richer than himself.

He had to be strong, or he was in danger of losing his honor, as well. The answer was simple. He must overcome this weakness induced by a pair of guileless dawn gray eyes and three years' abstinence. Resist the temptation to press himself against her, beg her to let him make love to her.

He took a slow, steadying breath. Hell, where had that idea come from? It put him off-balance. He smiled in self-derision, taking her hand to his lips in a practiced, masculine gesture.

"It is nice to be back, Mrs. Weston." His voice was low and thick.

Sophy's brain was awhirl with delicious confusion. She had forgotten the sound of his voice, the low but distinct quality that seemed to intimate much more than the simple words he spoke.

It shook her to her core. She trembled involuntarily, and she could not think why. "I daresay you are tired after the rail journey from Chicago," she heard herself say, still somewhat unsure of herself.

He let go of her hand and bowed slightly, as if he were a mechanical doll. "I am, a trifle."

His voice was dry, but before Sophy had time to dwell on it, he had adroitly changed the subject by asking about the possibility of getting a hot drink.

Sophy studied Seth in silence for a moment, noting the tautness of weariness around his mouth and the shadowed hollows over tired eyes. A rush of compassion made her forget his neglect, whether it was real or fancied, and want to assuage that utter exhaustion glimpsed in his face.

She struck a match and lit the gaslight, adjusting the jet on the wall sconce, an air of sudden determination in her eyes. "Sit down and make yourself comfy. I'll make some coffee."

His brows went up. "Here?"

"It'll only take me a minute to make some. Would you like something to eat? Some cold meat? An omelet?"

"You can cook?"

He made a faint curl of his mouth, not quite a smile, but not quite an insult. Sophy's answering grin was both taunting and triumphant.

"I'm not just a wealthy heiress. Not only can I cook, but I've a talent for organizing business affairs. I am a master when it comes to keeping accounts and I have a gift for solving riddles and puzzles. That's how I know you're hungry now."

She pertly tilted her head to one side, studying him, her eyes wide with a quaint mixture of concern and eagerness in their depths. Their message all but shattered his reserve, and her gamine smile touched a place within him that no one had touched for a long time.

Seth felt as though he had received a blow. He felt the impact deep in his body, and winced. It was as if something vital had disintegrated inside him, collapsed in on itself, solidified and condensed in his loins, taking what he had of himself with it, leaving an empty shell that stood there like an idiot, unable to function.

He released a soft rush of breath, and smiled whimsically. "I hadn't realized the extent of your accomplishments. You've whetted my appetite. I'd love an omelet."

The quiet words broke the spell they had been bound in, and Sophy set to work briskly. As she calmly broke eggs into a bowl, she was pleased the kitchen was a modern one, with a new gas cooker and icebox, even if, somehow, the room seemed smaller when Seth was in it. Certainly there was a sense of unreality in having him sit there, watching her prepare a midnight snack.

Seth seemed disinclined to small talk, content to sit in silence, regarding her with an enigmatic expression.

That steady, silent regard began to wield a strange effect on Sophy, making her feel awkward and unsure of herself. Her heart began an erratic thumping, and she felt hot one minute, chilly the next. A long breath escaped her lips, and she felt light-headed. When their gazes collided, she found she could not tear her eyes away from his.

Seth leaned his elbows on the table. If he didn't know better he would say his wife's fascination was oddly innocent and totally genuine. His white teeth glinted, and his eyes crinkled in sardonic amusement.

"A watched pot may never boil, my dear, but an unwatched omelet will always burn!"

Cheeks scarlet, Sophy lowered her lashes quickly. She found her husband had an unsettling effect. Disturbing. Making her a stranger to herself. Restless in a way that she didn't like.

What she did like was the way Seth tucked into the fluffy omelet, oozing cheese. His Adam's apple slid up and down as if he savored every mouthful.

In truth, Seth did. For several years he had been accustomed to camp fare, which, more often than not, consisted of basic army rations subsidized, on occasion, with a scraggy chicken or jackrabbit stew. The cook he employed had neither the expertise nor the desire to embark on any recipe more exciting than boiled meat and potatoes.

"I must commend you on your cooking, Sophy. That was delicious." He scraped the last morsel off his plate.

"You ought to taste my *coq au vin* and my *boeuf à la mode*."

"When did you learn to cook like that?"

"One of the many indulgences my father gave me was cooking lessons from a French chef." Sophy knew she was gabbling, her tongue working faster than her brain. "Father paid Marcel's passage from Paris on condition he stay with us for six months. Marcel stayed for a year, found himself an American bride and now owns a restaurant downtown."

Seth arched one dark eyebrow. "You look like a bride yourself, all decked out in white, waiting for her husband."

Instant warmth flooded Sophy's cheeks. Suddenly she was painfully conscious of him, of his maleness, of all that this night could mean. She stood uncertainly. She did not speak, but simply looked at him, her eyes very wide and pleading in her small face. Her lips trembled.

It seemed an eternity passed before he moved. Slowly, gently, he put his hands on her shoulders, and drew her toward him. The warm masculine smell of wool and leather, and something indefinable, flooded her senses. Sophy's hands came up and clutched the white pleated folds of his shirt. She saw the brown skin of his throat, and felt the vibrations of his heartbeat through her fingertips.

Instinctively, Sophy stood still within Seth's arms. The caressing hands slid across her back, warm through the frail barrier of cotton, his touch as delicate as a butterfly's, as light as down.

Her fears and hesitation fled, and she snuggled closer. His arms tightened. Slowly she let her hands, still shy in their response, slide up to his shoulders. Touching him meant merging reality with dreams.

Seth withdrew from her slightly to stare into her eyes, his own fiercely blue. She quivered in his arms like a fragile, windswept flower. His palms tested the contours of her waist before his hands came back to her shoulders, moving lightly back and forth, over her collarbone, circling lower and lower with each stroke.

The buttons of her negligee gave way beneath his fingers, and he brushed the fine material aside. Sophy's thoughts became scattered and unfocused. The tips of his fingers trailed across the tops of her breasts, curved down, round, to softly cup the underside of the soft mounds.

It was shocking, and somehow shameful, but very low down, below the pit of her stomach, her organs began to twist and coil, to converge throbbingly in a tightly laced ball. A deep shuddering sigh convulsed her body, which was soft and yielding in a way it had never been before.

Seth whispered something incoherent, and then his mouth came down hard on hers. Sophy clung to him, her mind reeling, her insides quivering. She arched against him, her mouth finding his with answering passion.

She murmured in protest when his lips left hers, but Seth only slipped lower, kissing the hollow of her throat. He made a groaning sound, and his thumbs stroked the rounded flesh.

Sophy pushed in denial of the hand at her breast, but then came a tremulous joy, so strong it was almost painful. A rising, thickening pleasure that drew her muscles taut. The universe shrank to the size of a hand and only his fingers were real. They probed the hardened peak before he drew it into his mouth.

The warm wetness of his mouth, the roughness of his tongue, made Sophy squeeze her eyes shut. She gasped as a bolt of fire pierced her loins, rippled down her thighs, up her belly, leaving her quivering, muscles trembling in a deep, hurting need.

She was going to die! She whimpered and dissolved into his body, raking her fingers through his hair, wanting, needing something only he could give.

The solid strength of his body touching hers made Sophy feel weak. Full-length against him, she was aware of his labored breathing, of every muscle in his long legs, the fiercely masculine outline of his body. His responses became slow and hesitant, as if he feared hurting her, though he made no attempt to camouflage his desire, as he pressed her to him.

Seth was straining her to him so intensely, pressing her curves into the hard planes of his body with kneading, wanting hands, that it came as a shock to Sophy when he suddenly thrust her back from him and held her inches away in a hurting grip that told her how hard it was for him to break contact with her. She glanced up at him in bewilderment, and saw the faint uncertainty in his features before his face hardened into its familiar unemotional mask.

Feeling much like a man caught in a tidal wave, Seth made a desperate attempt to battle against an irresistible force. He had promised to give her time! His body surged with desire. He felt ready to erupt!

There was chaos in him. He couldn't give in to lust. How could he not? He couldn't. It was destruction. He was a man of honor. He must resist, give her the time she had asked for. His voice was low and rough.

"Go to bed, Sophy. I'll tidy up here."

"Will you be joining me?" Her voice was an airless whisper. Her breath had been taken by an explosion of ecstasy and confusion.

"No. I am travel-weary and tired, Sophy. Let's leave it at that."

Silence filled the kitchen. Sophy waited for a heartbeat. For an instant, she felt as though everything inside were collapsing. Her knees were shaking and she felt weak and cold all over, as if the blood were draining from her body. Seizing her composure with a stubborn will, she stiffened her spine. Pride alone kept her chin up.

At last she spoke in a voice that seemed to echo the thundering of Seth's pounding pulse. "As you wish."

He watched her go, quietly shutting the door behind her. He had an overwhelming desire to call her back. Still, he kept himself in check. For a long time, he stood there, looking at the closed door, listening for the sound of her footsteps. A very long time. But he couldn't hear them, for the beating of his heart.

"For heaven's sake, lass. Whatever's the matter with ye?"

A face-crinkling frown replaced the morning smile of greeting that had spread over Tessa Fraser's face as she drew the bedroom curtains.

Sophy shrugged. "Seth came home last night." The words were flat, without expression, like black stones dropped into a stagnant pool.

"Oh, my precious lamb! Do ye want to tell me about it?" Tessa's voice was all concern.

"I should never have married him, Tessa. Never."

Sophy pulled up short. She could have bitten off her tongue for letting that out. Where on earth was her mind wandering? Conscious of her own dissatisfaction, she had been so occupied with her chaotic reflections that she had not given a thought to her words.

"There, there, now." Tessa shook her head in her inability to refute the vehement declaration. "What's done is done." She gently wrapped her arm around Sophy's shoulders.

Sophy whirled. Thrust off Tessa's comforting hand. Shook her head in denial. This attraction she felt for Seth made her feel out of control, and it wasn't a feeling she was at all comfortable with.

"No, it's not done. Seth Weston has a lot to learn about marriage. He made a bargain. Signed a contract. I am not a weak and pliable creature to be pushed to one side."

There followed a long moment of silence in which Tessa watched Sophy jump off the bed and insert her feet into the mules beside the bed.

"Merciful heavens! Has he been unfaithful, then? When ye've only been married a few weeks!" Tessa's words were faint, filled with disbelief, matching the surprise in her face.

Sophy flushed to the roots of her hair as a most unlady-like certainty goaded her sharp reply, "Of course not! His mother was ill, but that does not mean I am to be left behind like some ornament on a shelf."

Tessa's robust face paled considerably, and her lips twitched briefly in a bleak smile. "Aye. 'Tis right sorry I am, my wee bairn, to find ye so provoked. 'Tis thinking I am that wanting and marrying are two different things to a man."

Sophy shrugged testily. She managed to curb her tongue and did not answer. There was no need, no reason to make that assumption seem trivial. After all, Seth had what he wanted from the marriage... her money.

What she had never anticipated was that her own emotions would betray her, challenge long-held convictions. But one thing was certain. She had not married to be subjected to the sweet kind of indulgence usually reserved for children or to be treated like some kind of parcel!

Tessa dared no further comments, for she sensed by the brusqueness of Sophy's reactions that she wished to speak no more of the matter. Instead, she deliberately engaged in an inconsequential one-sided conversation about some phantom creatures invading the kitchen in the night.

As Tessa brushed and styled her hair, Sophy resolutely kept her eyes shut. That way, she could envisage Seth lying across her bed, lazy and content, relaxed in a magnificent sprawl, like a huge jungle cat, satiated with love. Somehow the vision shifted, changed. He was now a medieval knight, ready to defend her honor, her very life.

It was an illusion she could cling to, one she could hold dear. How one converted the image into reality was another matter, especially when love was not a factor in the equation that was her future.

Her father had always advised when in a situation requiring instant answers to trust her inner voices and good common sense. What would he have said to her present situation?

Sophy could almost hear his voice. *Well, my girl, pride and arrogance have gotten you into a fine mess! You're the one who set the limits to the relationship. You're the one who'll have to renegotiate.* How she missed him!

Resolutely, she turned her mind to more prosaic matters. Like her new project. Her face brightened. Like finding a house in Greene Street.

Sophy drew her brows together in mild exasperation. The warm day had darkened rapidly as fleeting wisps of cloud gathered to form masses of gray slate across the sky, casting a pall over the sun. The wind moaned as it drove clouds into a tumbling, threatening horde above the comb of chimney tops.

The carriage turned into a narrow street where stately brownstone mansions nestled behind grilled-iron doorways. Midway along the thoroughfare, the carriage stopped. Bidding the cabriolet driver to wait, Sophy hurried up the semicircular shallow marble steps, peered at the nameplate and rang the doorbell.

A servant opened the door, took her card and disappeared.

She took a deep, spine-stiffening breath as the door opened again and the servant gestured to Sophy to enter. Though the house was strangely silent, Sophy thought she heard the muffled tones of voices raised, and even the peculiar sound of suppressed laughter.

Entering the drawing room, Sophy stared in awe at the brightly patterned pink wallpaper, the large diamond-paned windows, the lavish mahogany paneling glowing with a rich luster. An exquisite rose-and-gray Aubusson carpet covered the floor, while against one wall a small iron stove glowed, exuding warmth. Hanging over all in the center of the ceiling was a tremendous crystal chandelier.

Sitting among a plethora of pink velvet cushions was a golden-haired woman. Voluptuous. Elegant. Dressed in a low-cut gown of watered silk, a ruffled shawl of bobbin lace over her shoulders. Her legs were covered with a gray woolen rug patterned with pink hearts. She looked up as the door opened, making no attempt to rise.

"What can I do for you, Mrs. Weston?" Her voice like warm black velvet, thick with a French accent.

Sophy put down her muff. "I am looking for Madame Bertine. I wish to speak with her privately."

The woman inclined her perfectly shaped head. "Speak, *ma fille.*"

Sophy stared directly into a pair of intense dark eyes. She took a deep breath. "I have come, Madame, because I have discovered my late father bought a certain piece of real estate." She pulled the ribbon-bound deeds from her reticule. "He then gifted a certain Marie-Simone Bertine a life-interest lease on the property. I want to know why."

There was a long pause. A half smile glimmered at the corner of the woman's lips. Perfect lips, sculpted in ruby, curved round flawless ivory teeth.

Finally, she spoke. "It would seem Nicholas van 'Outen was a trifle old-fashioned. 'E kept some secrets from 'is daughter."

Sophy could hear the amusement in the woman's voice. She felt her mouth open, then shut with a snap. "That is preposterous nonsense. I handled all my father's business affairs. He kept no secrets!"

"*Mais non.* You knew nothing of this arrangement." Madame Bertine shrugged off Sophy's vehemence dismissively, then changed the subject altogether. "You should wear red, *ma chérie.* It would suit you. You have such lovely skin."

Sophy glanced at the woman suspiciously for any signs of mockery. Seeing none, she sighed. "I am in mourning, Madame Bertine." She touched her black silk gown lightly. "Black is a cold, dignified color. One to gain respect in a man, not love. It's not a color to entice or excite."

"What an extraordinary girl you are. With your dramatic coloring, and dressed accordingly, you could entice *les hommes* like bees to a flower."

Sophy fought the urge to throw back her head and laugh hysterically at this absurd conversation. "I already have a husband."

A husband whose heart belonged to his business. *If only...*

Madame Bertine nodded slowly, as if her thoughts were not really on Sophy's reply. She was silent for a long while. "Red is a very bold color. It stands for something. It makes a statement." She lost the thoughtful look. "I associate it with the strong emotions, passion, anger, desire, *l'amour.*"

Sophy felt a lump form at the back of her throat. She swallowed. Fixed her eyes on her wedding ring as a focus.

"I do not know that a marriage of convenience, a business arrangement, requires strong emotions. Though I do like heads to turn when I enter a room."

No, only one. Seth's head. If I were in a daring low-cut red satin dress, then he might take me in his arms, press his lips to mine, stir again those strange, fluttering sensations. If only...

"If you want a man to long for you, find yourself a motif. One he will associate only with you. When he sees it, even if you are far away, he will think of you."

Madame suddenly became interested in the fringe of her shawl. She gave a small sound that might have been a sob.

"I surround myself with 'earts. The 'eart 'as always con-
noted affection."

Sophy's eyes widened as a sudden realization struck her,
igniting a flame of suspicion in her mind. She gave Madame Bertine an astute look.

Father's lacquered cigar box had an arched floral crest
pierced with hearts! How could she have been so blind? She
tried to suppress her inner excitement, but her high color
belied her outward calm.

"Were you my father's lover?"

Madame Bertine gave another Gallic shrug, and straightened the rug over her knees. "I 'ave been the lover of many
men, my child. Nicholas van 'Outen was but one of them."

"But he must have meant more than the others. He
bought this house. You live in it!"

"Ah, *mais oui*. Marie-Simone catered for 'is needs." Her
eyes met Sophy's with a suddenly troubled expression.
"Nicholas van 'Outen was an honorable man. He would not
jeopardize his social standing and risk gossip by taking a
mistress while 'e 'ad a daughter at 'ome. So 'e compromised 'is principles and set me up in a business 'ere in
Greene Street."

She laughed gaily as Sophy looked puzzled.

"I see you do not know what I am talking about. It does
not matter, *ma fillette*. Follow the dictates of your 'eart,
rather than the logic of the mind, and you will win the
prize."

Sophy closed her eyes, expelling a long breath. She
clasped her hands together and defied the logic of her mind.
"Madame, could you help me? Could you teach me how to
win my husband's affection?"

Chapter Four

"In spite of Lincoln's death, there seem to have been..."

Seth let Richard Carlton's voice wash over him as he idly surveyed the scene below. Suddenly, his idleness vanished. His fingers dug into the polished sill. Surely that was Sophy!

A smile tugged at the corners of his mouth. He would recognize that distinctive walk anywhere. A skip, then a hop. There was nothing sedate about his wife. She bounced. Like an excited pixie.

"—the meaning of freedom remains unresolved...."

Seth craned his neck, searching the crowded street for another glimpse of the woman. A tantalizing swirl of skirts and then she was gone.

Frowning, Seth stared up at the piling masses of clouds, then down at the slowly moving line of carriages. He was sure it had been Sophy. What the hell was she doing in Greene Street?

"—nothing but a ceaseless round of parties these past seven months celebrating the end of the war. Do you agree, Seth?"

"Definitely. Richard, I'm sorry, but I must go. Just remembered something important I must do. I'll have a look at the inventory lists another time."

Seth did not wait for Richard to call a servant. He had collected his walking stick and bowler hat and was clattering down the stairs before the agent had a chance to reply. At street level, he realized how importunate he must have appeared. He glanced again at the ominous clouds, and his mouth thinned.

Greene Street was definitely not a place for an innocent young woman. Even Bishop Simpson proclaimed there were as many whores in the vicinity as there were Methodists!

Could Sophy have seemed so untouched, so innocent, if she was indulging in an illicit affair? He couldn't—didn't want to—believe it. Headstrong and spoiled, perhaps, but he knew his wife was fiercely loyal. So what was she doing in the area?

Sophy ran downstairs light-footed and flung open the door of the dining parlor. All round the room the gaslights were blazing, and the table was set with an astounding array of crystal and silver. In the center of a simple floral decoration burned one scarlet candle.

Her mouth curled. Seth would soon be home. She felt excited and no longer afraid. It was as if she had shed the last shrinking of anxiety about the future like a discarded skin and was now emerging with wings. A conqueror about to discover a new and unknown land.

There was a wild elation at the knowledge of the marriage act as explained by Madame Bertine. Exhilarated, Sophy spun in a pirouette. As though released by a spring, her wide-skirted gown of stiff corded black silk followed her body's movement.

The mere contemplation of such delight was too much for her to face just now. She had to push it away from her, hold it off like some dazzling dream that she must not think of yet. Now there was dinner to consider. Now she must join the company in the drawing room.

The cold drizzle had started during the ride back to the house on Fifth Avenue and, an hour later, with the rising of the wind, it was battering at the window of the large drawing room. A maid had just drawn the heavy brocade drapes when Seth came into the room.

A faint chill washed over Sophy at the grim expression on his face. His brows were straight dark slashes in a face so pallid that it might have been hewn from marble. The glance he swept her felt like iced water as the magnificent blue eyes glimmered with strong emotion.

Concentrating almost fiercely upon his wife, he seemed unmindful of anyone else in the room. The silence stretched, broken only by the tap of his cane as he came to her, dragging one leg and leaning heavily on his stick.

The clear shining of the wall sconces seemed to gather about his shapely head in a nimbus of light. The brilliance of it was entangled in the piratical darkness of his hair and there seemed sparks in his jewel-bright eyes.

Forehead furrowed, Sophy stood staring at him through her mothwing lashes. There is nothing wrong, she repeated over and over to herself. Why then was her heart beating so madly that it constricted her breathing?

Their eyes locked.

Seth studied her face with the innate fierceness with which he had applied himself to the preservation of the Union. Abruptly, he felt idiotic, like a madman trapped in the nightmares of his own mind.

He drew a breath, torn between reason and instinct. His wife's misty gray eyes were wide and shy, her soft lips quivering, ready to broaden in a smile at the slightest provocation. He found himself staring at those lips, waiting.

Sophy clasped her hands together, as they went up instinctively to quell the tumult in her breast. Something flickered in the pools of his eyes, and she felt some of her apprehension dissipate. She smiled, and once more that magical transformation took place, giving her face light and warmth. It was as if the sun had come out.

"Isn't it splendid? Uncle Heinrich, Cousin Pieter and Cousin Bernard called, in this weather, too, to see how we have settled in. They are to stay for dinner."

Seth started, his eyes slanting to the van Houten brothers. He shifted a cramped knee, and the preoccupied expression left his face.

"Hello, sir." He held out his hand, with a brief flash of the smile that Sophy so longed to see. "Pieter."

His grip appeared strong and confident, but tonight the poor man looked worn-out. He moved with a queer jerking motion as if he were manipulated by strings. Sophy longed to ease his suffering.

The warmth was still in his countenance when he greeted the younger sibling. "How are your designs for a steam engine that runs on roads coming along, Bernard?"

Despite his harsh appearance, Seth had the gift of inspiring confidence. The boy's ruddy complexion deepened a shade. At fourteen, Bernard van Houten retained the snub nose and the chubbiness of youth, but his mouth and chin were determined to the point of obstinacy, and he had the same direct gaze that characterized his cousin.

"I am working on a prototype using compressed air, piston rods and valve gears." A thought occurred to him. "Have you seen the hydraulic elevator that Mr. Otis has constructed at Haughwout's Department Store?"

"No, but if you would care to come down to the plant room at Weston's Textiles, you can inspect our new rotary engine; which is driven by gears." Seth's eyes, alight with unholy amusement, met Sophy's. "If she has nothing better to do, I am sure Sophy would love to accompany you."

He was speaking lightly, but there was something in the look of his eyes that made Sophy uncomfortable, and she felt a sudden sense of relief when dinner was announced.

A few minutes later, a large uncovered dish was placed in front of Seth. He blinked at the huge crusty pie filled with chunks of beef and redolent of fresh vegetables and herbs.

Sophy's spirits soared, and her eyes danced as his gaze followed the dish of potatoes mashed with butter, cream, sautéed cabbage and a sprinkle of chopped young onions, which the maid placed in front of her.

"One of the reasons I called so late, Sophy, was because I knew you would invite me to a meal," Pieter confessed, accepting a good-size portion of pie on his plate.

"Good management of a household leads to domestic happiness." Heinrich's voice carried its own conviction. "Sophy was never interested in sensible things like crewelwork and watercolor painting or the pianoforte, so we were relieved when she made friends with Marcel and learned to cook."

"Much better than stuffing her head with all that mathematics, politics and financial knowledge, which is neither attractive nor necessary in a woman," Pieter teased, with considerable glee.

Bernard simply enjoyed the food. It was, after all, no use trying to slip the least word into the conversation with Sophy and Pieter becoming immersed in one of their endless arguments on women's rights.

Sophy glanced at Seth, who had a mouthful of pie and was chewing with enjoyment. He was satisfyingly engrossed in the meal. There was no reason to dissemble, so she took up her cousin's taunt, a fire of righteous indignation heating her words.

"Don't be so idiotic, Pieter. The winds of change are already blowing. It won't be long before women take their rightful place in society."

The suppressed fierceness in her voice caught at Seth. He looked up, met her misty gaze. She stared at him as if they shared an immediate, unspoken secret. It was a spark, like the new electricity he had seen demonstrated once, a spark that jumped the space from wire tip to wire tip.

For a moment something very soft and vulnerable flickered across his face before a ghost of a smile creased his cheek. Tonight, sentiment betrayed him. Sophy. Her laughter compelled him to share it. Her glance compelled his to meet it.

Pieter grinned at his cousin, his eyes challenging. "Women are all fools, even the smart ones. No, especially the smart ones. They are so determined on outmaneuvering their men that they cause themselves, and everyone else, endless trouble.''

The spell broken, Seth returned his attention to his laden plate.

"How can you say that?" Sophy demanded. "Women react as they do because men give women indulgence as a substitute for justice. I tell you it is not good enough!''

Seth found himself at once irritated and bemused by his wife's philosophy. Because she used her tongue as a weapon? Because there was an element of truth in her assertion? Perhaps because of the deeper truth, that no man can entirely relinquish all remnants of his own masculinity.

Catching Bernard's eye, Seth gave him a conspiratorial smile and put a forefinger to his lips. "Why not?" His tone was one of innocent inquiry.

Surprise flashed across Heinrich's face, and he practically choked on a piece of asparagus.

"Why not?" Sophy tried to restrain her sudden surge of annoyance, failed and launched into her argument. "A woman's entire future depends on her husband!''

Seth's eyes, which had been communicating with Pieter's over the top of her head, came back to her. What a little firebrand she was, so easily touched to the quick, changeable, lashing out. *Never lose your advantage.* Of course, the colonel had been talking of the battlefield, but the advice was apt here.

"Just as it should be. How else are we to keep our wives in their place? If this idea of universal suffrage gets out of hand, we'll find women dictating terms to us, and what will happen then?"

"Anarchy and revolution!" Pieter contributed.

"Can you imagine it?" Seth murmured, with an air of masculine amazement that set Sophy's teeth on edge.

Pieter drained his wine and announced in sepulchral tones, "This movement must be nipped in the bud."

"Just think what would happen if women were entitled to vote? The infection would spread. Next they'd be wanting to become doctors and lawyers!" added Bernard with enthusiasm.

Sophy, seeing him seething with barely suppressed delight at the gathering dispute, felt decidedly annoyed. Bernard was too young to have any opinions on the matter. And, if he did, he was young enough to change. It would be one of her projects.

"But that is iniquitous! It leaves women with no choice, no pride, no..." She trailed off, realizing she was being baited.

A serene smile touched her lips. "Odious creatures. Do not tempt me into an argument. You promised, Cousins, if I fed you, not to mention universal suffrage or discuss the role of women."

Seth caught the tranquil smile, and his heart leaped. Perhaps he had been mistaken. Perhaps seeing her in Greene Street had been a figment of his imagination. The mask of politeness that had been clamped down upon his face suddenly split into fragments, and he laughed.

"Promises and piecrusts are made to be broken."

This time, everybody laughed.

"Isn't Sophy an angel to put steamed fruit dumpling on the menu?" Bernard appealed to Seth a little later, licking the last dollop of cream from his spoon.

"A veritable angel indeed," Seth agreed, turning to Sophy, watching the mobile curve of her mouth.

All his doubts came rushing forth, sucked back by memory. The inconceivable happened. The words that had plagued him for hours in his mind sprang from his lips.

It came as quite a surprise to Sophy when he leaned forward and asked, his voice rich and warm, "How did you get on in Greene Street?"

His question had been quite casual, but it had an instant effect.

Utterly shocked, Heinrich van Houten nearly choked on the portion of dessert that he had just placed in his mouth. He managed to splutter just one word, "Sophy!" as if the sky had fallen in.

Bernard made a peculiar sound. Seth thought it was a quickly stifled chuckle. Pieter preserved a tactful silence.

Sophy felt the heat flow into her cheeks as she recalled the scene with Madame Bertine. Swiftly averting her eyes, she played for time. She looked down at her spoon, rubbing her thumb against the embossed silver handle. Her lashes rose.

"Greene Street? What do you mean?"

Seth's expression hardened. Her hair framed her face in a mass of dark ringlets that cast strange shadows on her elfin face. Candid, clever, guileless face. A strange conflict rose in his breast. Propriety bade him prod her no further, but he felt his anger returning.

With a menace that would have made any soldier tremble, he probed. "Did you, or did you not, go there this afternoon?"

Sophy swallowed. Her heart pounded unbearably at the bitterness in his voice. She thought she recognized what was wrong. In her ignorance, she had blithely visited an area where, she now knew, no decent woman would dare to go.

Seth's sense of honor was offended. Which was very stupid. She had never doubted the usefulness of knowledge, and Madame Bertine had proved most informative. Of course, she had never paused to see with what coin such information could be bought.

She nodded. "Er... yes, I did."

He curled his palms around the neck of the glass in front of him. Smiled at her, the merest slant of his mouth. The smile of a beast hot on the scent of its prey. "Well, how did the visit go?"

Sophy recalled Madame Bertine's sage advice on love, sex and marriage. Her eyes lit up. "It was... interesting."

Uncle Heinrich gave a deep sigh, which seemed to come from the very depths of his being. Twin blue flames glittered in Seth's eyes. Pieter ran his eye swiftly over Seth's face, and raised his eyebrows. Bernard rolled his eyes as he pursued with his tongue an errant drop of cream that was rolling down his chin.

"I see. Do you intend going there again?" His words were level, but his eyes spoke a different message. They were accusing, questioning, as if in some way she had hurt him.

Sophy's ringlets vibrated. She looked enormously pleased as the affirmation issued from her lips. "Oh, yes. I have another appointment for the day after tomorrow."

"Perhaps you would like me to accompany you?" There was a lazy, taunting quality in Seth's voice. He took a sip of his wine. "As your husband, it is proper that I share your...interests. Will you take me along on your next visit?"

Without hesitation, Sophy shook her head, her voice warm and earnest. "Oh, no. No. I couldn't do that. I don't think you would be interested in what I have planned."

The moment she had spoken she realized that she had made a foolish admission that might lead him to suppose that something less innocent than concocting a new wardrobe was on the agenda.

But he only shrugged and remarked, "Of course. No interference in your projects, no *comments* even, isn't that what we agreed?" Seth spoke smoothly, covering his anger. His hands clung to the wineglass as to a lifeline. Not where he'd like them to be—around his wife's neck.

"It's not that!" Sophy's heart was pounding, but her face showed nothing of her inward agitation as she quickly retrieved her error. "This is simply a private arrangement between ... friends."

Pieter suddenly threw back his head and laughed. "It is good to know marriage has not changed you, Cousin." Turning to Seth, he declared, "Sophy is incorrigible. I see you have your hands full already, Cousin Seth."

Any other time Sophy would have been furious with Pieter. Now, she took a firm hold on her temper. She knew her cousin was being deliberately provocative. He could never resist an opportunity to stir up a promising dispute. Her little chin went up and her eyes flashed.

"Pieter, you will mind your business. As for you, Seth, there is no need to storm and bluster at the dinner table. It is neither the time nor the place to discuss my private affairs."

"You are right, Sophy. It is discourteous to our guests. We will discuss your 'private affairs' later."

Uncle Heinrich pounced on this break in the conversation with alacrity. "An infusion of funds from war bonds to industry will get profits leaping again, Seth. Don't you agree?"

"I hope there will not be too many points on which we do not agree, sir. Would you like some more dessert, Bernard?"

"Capital. I don't mind if I do."

Sophy allowed herself to breathe a great sigh of relief.

"Your coffee, sir."

The valet entered the room bearing a small silver tray on which rested a white china cup and saucer.

Seth gratefully accepted the proffered cup and sipped the steaming, deep brown liquid. After all the wine he had drunk at dinner, he was inordinately thirsty.

He lounged in a tufted leather wing chair, the cup loosely held in one hand. With the other he absently rubbed his injured leg. A glass of fine Madeira stood on the table beside him.

"Anything more, sir?"

"That will be all. Thank you, Ned."

As Seth dismissed his valet, his mind raced over the day's events, the frustration and the dilemma of Sophy, his wife. His emotions were compounded equally by amazement at Sophy's personality, puzzlement at how he was to deal with her and anger at himself for being so reluctant to claim the privileges due as her husband.

His little wife had brazenly admitted to visiting Greene Street, which even the superintendent of the New York police acknowledged was a den of prostitutes. And she had audaciously revealed further planned assignations.

Yet the air of innocent bravado that clung to her intrigued him. He wanted to keep her safe and warm, protect her from harm. It was all very honorable and very genteel and, to his mind, very unnecessary.

Sophy challenged. Sophy dared. Sophy was trouble.

Unbidden, the memory of her soft form rose in his mind. He could see those morning-dew eyes, framed by sooty lashes, that lured and enticed him to her.

Feel again the warmth of her body, shoulders bare, breast exposed, the supple feminine sway of her hips as they melted against him. Smell again that elusive feminine scent drifting from her raven-dark hair. Hear the little gasp of pleasure she gave as his fingers slid over her breast. Taste those dusky peaks, the salty sweetness of her flesh.

Desire ripped through him, hot and potent. There had been no one like this since . . . He could not remember.

His heart leaped. Fate had answered, and he should follow the inclination. It was time to see how much she dared. Meet her challenge. He drained his glass, and struggled to his feet.

"Your chocolate, Sophy. Will ye be wanting anything else?"

"No, thank you, Tessa."

Sophy waited until the door was firmly shut before she sat down. She had to sit down. She could feel the trembling begin in her legs and travel up her body until she was forced to wrap her arms around herself. She was working herself up into a fine case of nervousness tinged with anger, the anger because she had no reason to be nervous.

Had not Seth been avoiding her since their marriage? Had he not been inordinately angry about her visit to Greene

Street today? One would think she had broken some law, or committed a felony.

When all she had done was to confirm a long-held suspicion that her father kept a woman for his "convenience and delight." A woman who had explained that she, Sophy, had it in her power to give Seth pleasure or to make him miserable. And, moreover, she had revealed *how*.

The difficulty was for Sophy to find a way out of the stupid impasse she had thoughtlessly created. It had taken some fast-talking to convince Matt Tyson to agree, but Sophy knew there was no real alternative.

Work absorbed all Seth's spare energy. He needed the money to restore his battered pride. Only then might he change his outlook. Allow his leg time to heal. Find time to live, to love.

Thoughtfully, Sophy eyed the carved wooden jewel box that hid the telegraph message. The problem appeared in sharp outline again. She had been thorough. There was no way Seth would discovered her deceit. She had a mind for detail.

What concerned her was that there had been no information available from the insurance company, not even a compilation of contracts covered. A sure sign that someone was systematically draining funds from Seth's business empire by fraud. She would find the evidence.

It would take time. Later, there could be a thorough examination. Now, she had more urgent work to do. Seduce her husband.

Sophy was still planning how to get Seth to join her when the door opened. He stood there, still dressed in his evening attire. His gaze was unreadable, but the fighting stance of his body was not.

Legs braced slightly apart, he looked prepared for battle from any quarter. He gave her a strange smile, as if he knew what she was thinking.

Immediately all the compelling emotions she'd felt when she first met him came back to her. Her heart leaped.

Gathering her shattered composure together, she managed a faint smile. "Good evening, Seth. Would you like some chocolate? I was just about to have a cup."

She poured as she spoke, as if she fully expected him to join her in this small domestic activity. Her hands moved quickly, slim, exciting.

Before he could reply, Seth found he had accepted the cup and saucer. So he leaned against the barley-twist brass bedpost and swallowed a mouthful. He grimaced at the sickly sweetness of the thick brew.

"Chocolate is good for you. It is a natural source of energy."

Sophy smiled at him, a shy and pleased expression, then went back to the marble-topped dressing table and began brushing her hair. The gesture, so deliberate and full of meaning, hovered in front of Seth's eyes as he silently drank the warm chocolate.

Minute by minute the storm within him mounted. With her dark hair streaming down her back, she looked as meek as an angel on the chapel ceiling. He realized with a sinking, helpless feeling that it was going to take every ounce of willpower he had to keep his emotional and physical distance from Sophy.

"Leave that! I want to talk to you," he commanded, unable to keep the heaviness out of his voice. He so much wanted to put his hands on her hair that his fingers tingled.

Sophy looked up, blinking. He was standing beside the dressing table with the cup and saucer in his hands, watching her with his intense eyes. She stared at him mutely, then put her brush down.

Seth considered her, and hesitated for a moment. When he spoke the words came out with quiet ferocity. "I would be obliged if you would refrain from such activities as you indulged in today."

There was a flash of indignation. This was not what was supposed to happen. Sophy drew in her breath. Her chin tilted up.

"You expect me to be kept here like a parrot on a perch with a chain around my leg?" Her voice was high, ten decibels above her normal speaking voice.

He picked up his cup, drained it, then set it down with a grimace before he spoke. "You signed a marriage contract. You are my wife, sworn to obey me."

Sophy jumped to her feet. "In the eyes of the law, infants, lunatics, felons and married women have limited contractual ability. Accordingly, the contract I signed is worthless," she flung back, mimicking his tone of voice with biting accuracy.

"The contract stands *until death us do part.* You will *honor and obey me,* Sophy. Do you understand? That means accepting my decisions in all areas, including your little projects!" His voice rose, and his eyes were blazing with fury.

Sophy could sense the suppressed violence in him, and it took a great deal of courage not to step back. If anyone else in the world had said such a thing in the tone of command Seth used, she would have resented it strongly, and would have gone in the opposite direction.

As it was, her small, indomitable chin took on a defiant curve and her lips folded in a willful, stubborn line. Unable to speak for a minute, she emitted an aggravated little sound.

It hadn't even occurred to her that he wouldn't be easily fooled. Her foot tapped the carpet. When at last she found her voice, it was charged with indignation. "I must insist on the terms of our wedding bargain."

Completely unaware as she stood silhouetted in front of the fire that her body was clearly outlined in the flickering light, she stood legs apart, like a diminutive, obstinate mule.

A tightening began in Seth's loins, and he shifted to relieve his discomfort. The action didn't help. She raised her eyes and they were like the soft mist of dawn over a clear spring sky. While he gazed at Sophy, the excitement grew stronger, a potent reminder of his self-imposed abstinence.

It was like warfare when the hardest part was in the waiting. It fed the tension. Chewed at the nerves. Eroded self-discipline. He reminded himself he had promised to abide by her rules. To wait until she felt ready to assume her wifely duties. The reminder served to escalate his already flaming emotions. Clutching at the one thin thread of sanity left in him, he drew in a harsh breath.

"You will do as I say! I will not have you associating with a woman set up as a professional courtesan. *Is that clear?*"

Sophy's tone matched his. "Only if I am so inclined!"

Damn and blast men. They were always wanting to interfere. Always wanting to impose their will. When all she had wanted... Seth's sharp, angry tone of authority cut off Sophy's thoughts.

"Or perhaps it is your trade? The way you earn money *by your own endeavors?*" He gazed down at her with frost blue eyes. "What will you be charging me for sampling your wares, Sophy?"

"What?"

He paused as if expecting her to say something, then leaned toward her, frowning, his shoulder against the mirror frame. "Your fee, Sophy. You paid me a handsome sum to wed you. How much do I pay to bed you?"

Shock washed over Sophy. He couldn't comprehend what he was saying! She wet her lips and stared at the base of his throat.

"I don't understand. What game are you playing?"

"Do the young men you save your favors for enjoy your games?" His voice sounded crude, even to his own ears.

"The young men I..."

Sophy stood very still. The contempt in his voice could not be feigned. Puzzled, outraged and frightened by the shock of his allegations, she felt the color drain from her face. She took a deep breath.

"Who told you these lies?"

Her question seemed to fall between them like a stone dropped into deep water. He stood there silently, just look-

ing at her, not saying a word. Stillness surrounded them and
time seemed to cease its coursing as they faced each other.
The whisper of the fire in the grate was now the only sound
in the room.

Sophy stood there, her two hands fisted tight and bound
together, pressed against her chest. Her throat felt as if it
were in a vise. This was awful. Her lips fell open as her tor-
tured lungs labored for air. It seemed to her that it was
rather like a mad jigsaw puzzle. None of the pieces seemed
to fit and yet she felt that somewhere there was a clue to it
all.

Seth's lip curled. For a long moment, he looked deeply
and searchingly into her eyes. He was reading mixed signals in everything she said. It isn't possible, he told himself.

There was a message there, he knew, but because he had
buried it so deep it had been slow to work its way to his
conscious self. He frowned at that, closing his eyes, en-
deavoring to concentrate. His nostrils flared.

Well, why not? How could he view her unexpected visit
to Greene Street without suspicion? And yet he had been in
the vicinity himself, meeting with his agent. His lashes
flickered.

Why did Sophy's reasons need to be sinister? Could her
purpose in visiting the area have been equally as innocu-
ous? His fists clenched impotently as a curious, lost sort of
tremor ran over him.

"Seth?"

The name seemed to hang in the air, vibrating with emotion. His eyes jerked open. Sophy was staring at him oddly,
all enormous eyes. He could feel her indecision, could almost hear her mind working.

Though she might tell herself she did not want him in her
bed, he didn't think it would take much to persuade her to
welcome him there. Why should he try to run away from
her?

His eyes traveled over her open lips, the flaring tip of her nose, to the misty violet slightly out-of-focus depths of her wide, uncertain eyes. Her vulnerability was perversely endearing.

Had she no idea what she was doing to him, standing there holding herself, limned in firelight and fear? How sweet and soft she looked. Nymphlike. Ethereal. Incredibly delicate. Sophy was fulfilling his sweetest dreams.

Inside, he grew a little cold, wondering what awful power his wife wielded. His body seemed to lose every nerve, everything that held it together.

It terrified him.

The silence grew. Flame flickered, sending waves of faint light across her face. Seth wished he knew what images went through her mind. She was staring at him so strangely. Was she judging him? Wanting him? Was she caught in a trap of her own making? His heart leaped at the thought.

Unexpectedly, he found his anger ebbing away. Her appeal was now almost irresistible. *She was his wife!*

It was that simple . . . and that dangerous.

Chapter Five

Swept off-balance by surging emotions, Seth regarded her through narrowed lids as his long fingers closed on her upper arm. It would seem offended male pride and physical frustration made an explosive combination.

He realized he was beginning to harbor lustful thoughts toward his new wife. It was a disturbing realization. Sophy was displaying a talent for being able to push him to the edge.

If he were wise, he'd stop this charade here and now. Yet even as the thought raged through his mind, he knew he would not.

Would not, or *could* not . . . ?

Sophy's eyes widened in surprise. She stared up at him mutely, aware of his punishing grip on her arm and the utter determination in his face. He seemed to be in a fine welter of emotion. Pain sometimes did that to a person, she decided philosophically. Made them fractious. For a moment, she simply stood quite still, not knowing what to do next.

Holding her arm, Seth felt the heat from her body, the subtle shift of her flesh beneath the thin cotton sleeve. He swallowed convulsively, and the sound seemed loud in the silence. "Besides, we both made a vow. And a vow by definition demands fulfillment."

He lifted one of the heavy ringlets and put it aside, touching his lips to the warm column of her throat, breathing in the fragrance of her skin. She smelled of flowers. It seemed that the very air was perfumed.

He had meant to tell her she was mistaken if she even thought she could make him look a fool and get away with it. But when he felt the shudder that trembled through her at his touch, and saw the way her lip quivered, his jaw snapped shut.

Suddenly he didn't want to snarl at her. He wanted to press himself against her, lose himself inside her, let passion soothe away the ache of his body and allow sweet physical satisfaction to bring peace to his tormented mind.

Without uttering another word, knowing he should not do this, but unable to deny himself any longer, he reached forward, and pulled her swiftly into his arms. With an air of sudden determination in his eyes, he smiled. A crooked, purposeful smile that echoed the intent in his eyes.

Sophy watched as Seth's mouth came closer and closer to her own. Her heart raced and she felt a little quiver go through her. She blinked, and swallowed with an effort. His hand slid down past her waist, and his lips seized hers in a hungry assault.

His mouth was hot and hard and tasted of chocolate. Trembling, she absorbed the shape, the texture of it. He sucked gently, sending shafts of heat darting through her body. Her heart somersaulted as her whole body tightened in reaction. She could feel herself softening, and a warm glow begin deep inside as his mouth moved over hers.

Sanity fled. Her lips responded, and her body surrendered almost joyfully to his greater strength. Her long lashes fluttered as she slumped against his chest, clutching the folds of his shirt. Her hands clenched into fists, relaxed, curled and uncurled. His lips left hers and pressed feverishly against her throat.

Sophy closed her eyes and drew in her breath. She could feel the heavy pressure of his loins against her, and she felt

her breasts tighten as if he had actually touched her. Slowly
she let her hands steal up his shoulders, to his thick dark
hair, ruffling it, mussing it. Instantly his embrace tightened.

"Sophy." Seth's voice was a strained whisper, an ago-
nized thread of sound, hoarse with passion. A powerful
surge of emotion swelled in his chest, purely male, purely
majestic. He could tell from the way she was responding that
this ensnaring desire was claiming them both.

Her eyes flew open.

Raw desire was there, in his face, in the twin blue flames
of his fierce eyes. Sophy could feel it. It seemed to pour itself into her, swamping her senses, wiping out rational
thought. She trembled in his grasp, aware of the heat of his
body, and the musky male smell of him, which set her tingling in her most private places.

Seth gazed down at her passion-softened face with eyes
that held the heat of burning coals. He was totally unprepared for this overwhelming temptation. She looked like a
tiny doll, a porcelain miniature to be put in a glass case,
protected from the elements.

Disquiet stabbed his mind. Where was his control? Deep
inside, he tried to command his sense of righteous self-
discipline, but couldn't. The driving sensual force within
him was too potent. He hesitated a fraction before, curious, his inner self stepped back and let it happen.

A still, small voice inside him was mockingly calling him
a fool, even as his hands found the ties of her wrapper. His
nimble fingers flicked the buttons of her nightgown open,
and deftly slid both garments off her shoulders until they fell
in a pale, shimmering pool at their feet.

When Sophy felt the first feathery-light sensation of his
lips on her breast, she shuddered and gave in to the heady
excitement. She had never imagined her body was capable
of such shameful sensations. His hands slid down to cup her
buttocks, skimming them like warm wind and creating
wanton goose bumps upon her skin.

Lost in the magic of his touch, she held her breath. Something strange was happening in her stomach, a slow, delicious thickening, which sent a wondrous recoil clear to her toes.

A sound escaped her, a sound of need, a faint moan. Feeling as though all of her bones had suddenly turned to water, and were seeping between her legs, she let her cheek rest on his warm, hard body.

Seth stopped moving instantly, but he did not let Sophy go. Scarcely daring to breathe, he bent and kissed her on the ear, taking the lobe gently between his lips. She thought she might faint under the intensity of the sensations he provoked. Excitement flooded her. She knew she had to get closer or go mad.

She wrapped her arms around him, pulling her body closer, nestling into him, inhaling the scent of his body, kissing him softly on his parted lips. There was a strange pounding of her blood, a thickening in her throat.

With a sense of curiosity and mild trepidation, she brought her hands up to undo a shirt button. It was an astoundingly intimate gesture, but somehow she wanted to touch his flesh, and hold him very near to her heart.

A sensation of intoxication was stealing over her, the curious thrill of passion, when it is holding the senses. Seth hung above her, breathing deeply, unevenly. Her soft mouth smiled tenderly, her eyes became dewy.

Sophy felt the trembling in him as her fingers fumbled with his shirt fastenings. Suddenly, his hands took over the task. With a deft shift and lift, his vest and shirt were swept away.

Then his pants, too, were gone. It seemed he understood everything that she was feeling and delighted in it. He held her fiercely for a long sweet moment before he stepped back.

Shivers tingled up Sophy's spine, and down her arms. The feeling seemed to originate in her belly, expanding and filling her. Her breath became ragged, and her eyes shone.

Heavens! Seth looked nothing like the illustrations of Michelangelo's sculpture, *David,* even less like Caravaggio's impudent painting, *Amor Victorious.* He was heavy, satiny, perfectly balanced. His whole body throbbed!

She blinked, fascinated by the play of muscles across his broad shoulders, the rippling sinews along his ribs, and the taut, flat belly, with its tracing of hair down to the erect evidence of his desire, jutting aggressively from its nest of dark curls, the long straight legs.

Her heart hit the roof of her mouth, and she fought for breath at the sight of the large scar that marked one thigh. The enemy soldier's aim had been poor. Another handbreadth higher and her husband would not be so swollen with conceit!

Sophy placed her soft, open palms on his chest and felt a subtle warmth that grew rapidly into a fine, encompassing heat. His magnetism reached out across the closing expanse to embrace her in a kind of self-generated fire.

The burning heat of his skin beneath her hands was an experience so pleasurable she simply closed her eyes and let them roam at will. She wanted to feel as much of him as possible. The muscles rippling below his smooth skin were sleek. Sleek and powerful, like velvet over steel.

The sight of Sophy's parted mouth and the glaze of passion filming her dazed violet-gray eyes fed Seth's appetite until it was rapacious. Well, he would hold himself as well as he could without spoiling pleasure.

His thoughts collided and merged, and finally the dialogue ceased. The small warning bells going off in his mind were ignored. His heart was pounding, a dense clamor in his head that shut off any rational objection.

Fingers trembling, he took her chin, turned her face toward him. Though Seth allowed her little room for response, what Sophy did manage to give was received with shatteringly eloquent evidence of the effect she had on him. She heard the rasp of his voice, indistinct and unintelligible, yet with an urgency that revealed his need and his desire.

He moved one leg so his thigh was between hers. She was conscious of the strong grip of his hands, the male scent of his body close to hers, the rising, thickening pressure against her belly. It excited her.

She was suddenly the huntress full of guile. Boldly, she put her arms around his neck, stood on tiptoe and kissed him full on the lips. Tentatively, shyly, she touched her tongue to his, and was stunned at his shuddering reaction, the tensing of his entire body.

Her fingers gently caressed his nape, feeling the toughness and the resiliency as they moved slowly down the rigid contours of his back. Seth drew back, gazed at Sophy's flushed face, her closed eyes.

Something deep within him responded to her unspoken plea. The little alarm bells of doubt were almost muffled now. In a haze of mounting sensation, he could barely think, only feel. Excited beyond the point of return, he thrust her toward the bed, and surged up against her body.

Sophy lay on the bed trembling, her breath coming in ragged little gasps. She became aware that her consciousness was shifting, centering within her abdomen, until she relaxed, arching her back and closing her eyes.

Seth spread himself atop her and entered her in one swift, powerful motion. As he did, she had the sudden, utterly shattering sensation of being transported from a warm, intensely exciting heaven to a cold, alien planet. It hurt!

Sophy knew there was to be pain, but never had she imagined it would hurt like that! He moved minutely against her. She gave a guttural moan, started to struggle, pushing against his chest, then became aware of that other, dizzying sensation beyond the pain, as though there were eagles swooping down from the mountain at the world's end.

Rushing at her from out of nowhere, they lifted her to great heights, toward some unknown destination, some high place she had not yet been. It did not matter. She only knew that she wanted to go there more than she had ever wanted anything.

For a second, Seth froze at that peculiarly female sound. Sweat was pouring off him and his heart was banging against his ribs. His breath was tight, clogged. She pushed him away, then seconds later, pulled him back against her.

The feel of her stiffened nipples grazing his chest was a sweet counterpoint to the aching, raging need between his thighs. His mouth was so dry that he could scarcely swallow and his knees seemed to be folding up beneath him, as though they were no longer part of his body.

His body was white-hot and throbbing for release. He was on fire. The shaky feeling increased, and he moaned, a long, male sound of anguish. Then he stopped thinking.

Sophy knew she would never forget this night. Never want to lose the memory of what he was giving and taking with every concentrated cell of his body and mind. The sound, the smell, the impact of him.

She clasped him tightly, clung to him, urging him to do as he willed, glorying in his strength, his power seeping into her. The firelight flickered, sending whorls of light, scarlet, yellow and an eerie green over the ceiling, before it broke into fragments, scattered in tunnels of time, a blur.

Ecstasy without end . . .

In the soft gray light of morning, Sophy awoke to find her cheek resting on Seth's shoulder. She felt his breathing. It seemed to encompass her universe.

Soft, light fingertips traced the outline of his mouth, traveled upward over his cheeks and gently caressed his forehead. Finally, almost reluctantly, Seth's eyes opened.

The blue eyes regarded her lazily, and she fancied there was the faintest trace of a smile on his mouth. He kissed her on the top of her head.

"Sleep well?"

"Well enough." She raised herself on one elbow and smiled down at him. "I must get up. It seems to be . . . quite late."

He shifted, rolled to one side. His hand reached out, brushed the smoothness of her cheek and slid to her breast. "Must you?"

Seth smiled openly now, and she was annoyed for suddenly feeling so nervous. Was there some hidden meaning in his voice? The identical chains that bound her to him existed for Seth. Or did they? The thought had the same impact as the opening of a great pit beneath her feet. Her eyes slid away from his amused ones.

"I really must. There is much to be done."

"Have you nothing to say to me?"

His voice, low and husky, made her heart jump, alarming her, thrilling her and spinning her into turmoil all over again. What did he want her to say?

"There's nothing I can think of."

There were things she would never forget, but the matter of putting them into words was beyond her.

"I thought . . . perhaps . . . well, it doesn't matter."

Something in his expression told her it did matter. She studied his face. His eyes were their usual stunning blue, but it seemed that a cloud covered them, reminding her of a tempest gathering at sea, of the latent passion in him.

Sophy's mind was a tumult. She could feel the blood rise, coloring her cheeks. Her face burned. Was her approbation important? Or was he concerned that she would now make demands on him? That must be it.

Or was it because she was something new in his experience? A virgin versed in lovers' tricks, who somehow knew how to please a man? She wished she had confided in him before he came to her bed.

A terrible thought struck her. He might beat her if he ever discovered the truth. Sophy caught her breath. His mouth was set in a line that made her wary, but Seth Weston was no wife beater.

How she knew, she did not know. She just knew.

The knowledge eased her, making her feel that she was beginning to right the wrong she had done, and that all might yet be well despite it. Time enough to confess when he had eaten a hearty breakfast. It would be easier for him to accept such information then.

Seth's confusion deepened. Women's motivations were so opaque. He drew up his legs under the bedclothes and winced with the pain that accompanied the movement.

"Sophy, we must talk." His low, husky voice seemed to vibrate through her. "There are plenty of servants to stir jam and mend sheets. There are other accomplishments I seek in a woman."

Deliberately she misunderstood the note of intimacy he had introduced. "I would prefer not to talk about it, Seth." It was not what she had meant to say, she thought, confused.

There was a peculiar, tense silence. Only their eyes moved minutely. Sophy sucked in her breath, and color swept over her face. She hadn't realized she had been looking at his bare chest, thinking about touching the soft curling hair on his smooth skin with her index finger.

He had not moved, but the quality of silence had changed, become charged with a curious tension. What must he think of her? She had no answer. There was an awkward silence.

"Disconcertingly truthful as ever, Sophy. Still, I'd not have you different." He gave a mirthless laugh and rose from the bed. There was a rustle as he pulled his shirt over his head.

Sophy was silent. What was she going to say now? What would he think of her when he discovered she had lied not once, but twice? She was aware of unhappiness, knowing she was something she had sworn never to be. A cheat.

She slid off the bed and picked up her discarded clothes. Her eyes were luminous. He was watching her, his face impassive. She tried to unscramble her thoughts.

"Will you...?" Her voice, for all her willpower, faltered.

There it was, the inevitable question. Seth felt a chill current curdling through his veins. There was a lump in his throat that made swallowing painful. He tried to control his features, clamping his jaw tight over hot words that could only hurt them both.

"Cancel our wedding bargain? No. I'll give you a straight answer. I will not."

Sophy waited a moment. The seed of anxiety grew. She turned her head. "Because... because you think I want to profit from what's happened?"

"Would it be that?"

His face had changed, all the proud coldness transmuted to something warmer, gentler, yet tinged now with amusement. Of course, he would look so if his intention had been to quell her rebellion. He'd think she'd capitulated.

Sophy stared uncomfortably at him. She had no answer to this question. The tip of her tongue came out and traced her lips. "Not altogether. It's just that I want to know where I stand."

Seth gave an exclamation that was almost like a pistol shot and bit out curtly, "I see." Seconds passed. "So it didn't matter too much?"

Was there a dryness in his tone? She could not be sure. It was her doing if there was. Her own feeling was that she was losing a battle she had never really stood a chance of winning.

Sophy moved away from the bed across to the fire, bending to adjust the gas injector. She made a sharp gesture with one hand. She dared not tell him the truth. The knowledge that she must choose her words with care was apparent, especially now with that delightful interlude between them.

"It was nothing," she said when she had mastered her voice. She kept her eyes on the fire. "It is forgotten already."

That was a lie. They both knew it. A horrible stillness seemed to thicken in the room. There was another long pause and then Seth slowly nodded his head as if having arrived at a difficult decision.

"You needn't fret about last night, Sophy. I'm not blaming you."

Her head was bent, exposing her exquisitely slender neck. To his horror, Seth realized that the sight of her was rousing desire in him so strongly that it was almost painful. His impulse was to fling himself across the room and reach for her. With an effort that was near physical pain, he suppressed it.

Instead, he pulled on his pants, then walked slowly to the window. He stared out through the high panes of glass, rubbing his jaw. The previous night's storm had brought a heavy fog to the city, bleaching out all the color from the land, reducing visibility to a few feet. The air was gray, cold and heavy with dampness.

He shivered.

Sophy came to stand beside him, so close her skirt brushed his trousers. It was the sound of dry leaves rustling, hollow. Empty. Distant. Like the loss of her dreams. Dreams were illusions. Doubtful. Reality was certain. Reality was that she was deliberately deceiving her husband. Reality was that Seth would regain his pride.

The world seemed much brighter with that conclusion. Sophy's natural ebullience revived. Every woman made a few mistakes in her life when it came to dealing with the male of the species. She would try compliance.

She looked up at him. The ghost of a dimple showed in her delicate cheek. An unspoken apology. Her voice was very small.

"I forgot to give you this telegraph, which was delivered yesterday."

Seth accepted the proffered slip of paper. It was from Matt Tyson. The words danced in front of his eyes. Mocking. Taunting.

Lloyd's of London has agreed to underwrite the insurance on signed contracts canceled because of the war.

Sophy eyed his blank face. "Is it good news?" she asked doubtfully, watching him frown.

"Yes." Seth's voice was heavy. His capital was secure. A few hours earlier, and the marriage could have been annulled. Now it was too late. Sophy had neglected to give him the telegraph in time.

Anger bubbled inside him, turning without his knowing on Sophy. He wished she had given it to him the day before, although what he would have done differently he did not know.

They still had that stupid wedding bargain. No questions, no reproaches, no comments on his part; but Sophy permitted to poke her pretty nose into his business to make matters worse. And he had the gut feeling he was going to fall in love with this beautiful spoiled heiress. Damn it, damn it, damn it!

Lightning forked the sky outside and raindrops formed a million tiny eyes against the glass windows. Sophy touched his arm and he glanced at her.

"I wanted to tell you of it right away, Seth. It's important that you believe that." Her voice was haunting and quite gentle, her eyes oddly lonely.

"I do." It was remarkable how she could defuse his rage so utterly. She had only to touch him, to turn those eyes on him, to whisper softly, and all the blackness curled like ash inside him.

Seth made to leave the room but Sophy stepped forward and blocked his exit. Her fingers dug into his arm.

"Not just say it."

"I don't say anything idly, Sophy." He put her away from him, gently but with the utmost decision.

Sophy squeezed her eyes shut on hot tears. Determinedly she blinked them back.

"I was lucky to find such a bargain, Seth Weston. A knight in shining armor."

It was a joke but he did not take it that way. "It is too late. We are bound together and had better find a way to live together."

There was no bitterness in his voice, no emotion of any sort. His voice was flat, and very calm.

In another moment, he let himself out of her bedchamber. The door closed without sound behind him.

For three days, Sophy saw little of her husband. He departed the house immediately after breakfast, and did not return until dinnertime. At the meal table, he was unfailingly courteous, considerate and civilized.

He discussed any number of things, from the imminence of a thirteenth amendment to the constitution, which would formalize the abolition of slavery, to Walt Whitman's poetry collection, *Drum-Taps*, which epitomized the war in verse.

What he did not discuss was anything personal. He neither asked how she filled her days, nor told her what he did during his absence from the house. Nor did he inquire whether she had kept her appointment with Madame Bertine.

It was as if he had resolved not to interfere in any way in Sophy's life.

This should have pleased Sophy. He had withdrawn his control over her actions. She was free to do as she wished. Yet a faint sense of disappointment went through her. This was not the way things were supposed to be.

She tried to tell herself that his present indifference was only a temporary aberration. Like a ship in a good wind, he would come about and all would be well. Now it was simply a matter of waiting.

But self-effacement and patience were not Sophy's strengths. She was restless. By day her face was calm, her daytime self resumed. But as she lay fitful and uneasy in her bed at night, her thoughts went round and round in an end-less, useless circle.

She spent endless hours wondering how anyone could embezzle money from a company as well run as Seth's business was. That it was soundly organized, she had no doubts. But the discrepancy with the insurance did not correlate with sound management.

Still, the suspicion had been there, knocking on the windows of her mind, trying to get her attention ever since the wedding reception. After her visit to the bank, she couldn't keep ignoring it. Drifts of a cryptic conversation overheard came back to her.

Discounts and rebates. An eye-for-an-eye-type thing.

Cut the crap, Charles. Lay them out by dates and dead-lines. Crack the Code of Hammurabi.

Babylonia. Right. Thought it was the Walls of Jericho.

You have until Thanksgiving. Then, it's Alas Babylon.

Although she could not see the men, hidden as they were behind a screen, Charles must have been Seth's trusted confidant. It seemed Charles Lethbridge was not what he seemed. Whoever it was, the guilty one was nefarious and devious, so questions like "how," "when" and "who" needed to be answered.

A part of her insisted on feeling that something elemental had changed in her life and she wasn't going to escape the consequences. She wanted Seth to care. But caring and romantic love were not the same thing, a little voice whispered in her head.

She'd known that when she'd made the wedding bargain. That was why the cautious part of her had insisted on a platonic relationship. She had said she didn't want a child, but that had been another fabrication, another lie.

The truth was that she would like a child, one with cobalt blue eyes, to remind her of her love. The truth was that she could not forget her misdeeds.

There was something to be learned from this experience. In bowing to her trustees' wishes, she had also managed to achieve her goal. She had gained what she thought she wanted in her wedding bargain, but now, too late, she discovered it wasn't what she craved at all.

She did not feel free and untrammeled. And although she was convinced of the justice of her actions, she was not at all certain Seth would agree. Whatever had happened, she was in the wrong.

But what in the world was wrong with her? She'd only acted in his best interests, even if she had compromised her ethics. Before going into this partnership she'd instructed herself to keep the relationship strictly professional, and now she wanted Seth to love her.

If Sophy suffered heartburning and second thoughts, so, too, did Seth. The truth of the matter was, Seth had not felt like himself since the day he had married Sophy. In fact, he felt he had been seeking his identity since almost the moment he met her.

Before Sophy he had known who he was and what he was. An entrepreneur dedicated to his pursuit of success. A man who had once savored the cream of life, who had lost it in the misery and brutality of war, and who had then come to terms with the future. Long gray days. Of emptiness. Of loneliness.

But Sophy had changed that. She was the last thing he had expected in a bride. She had stirred long-forgotten emotions, turned his staid upright world upside down. From her audacious wedding bargain to her outrageous visit to a bordello, she filled him with a vague expectancy, an uncertain anticipation, and not knowing quite how to cope with it.

He had the uncomfortable feeling that if he insisted that she do as he ordered, she would defy him. Perhaps for the moment, at any rate, it was best to let her have her own way, although, God and His angels knew, he would have to put his foot down sooner or later. This decision made, he went about his business and left Sophy to her own devices.

Time hung heavy upon Sophy's hands. In desperation, she looked for something to take her mind off her troubles. She busied herself planning a new wardrobe, selecting fabric, poring over *Harper's Weekly* and *The Season* for hours and choosing the latest fashion styles. She conducted interviews and appointed several additional domestic staff, including a new cook. But she did not visit Madame Bertine.

On the morning of the fourth day, Sophy was already seated at the breakfast table when Seth entered the room.

How long this charade could continue she dared not guess, but she was determined to break this impasse. As he passed her, she held out a detaining hand. His muscle flexed under her palm.

"Good morning, Seth." She raised her face.

He did not move toward her, or away. A grim smile hovered about his mouth, then he bent and touched her forehead with his lips.

"You're down early." His voice was noncommittal as he moved around to his place at the breakfast table, but his eyes burned like twin blue flames.

Seth opened the morning paper, a barrier as palpable as a steel wall. When Sophy had greeted him at the breakfast table, turning toward him with her wide eyes, a primitive need rose up in him.

He could actually feel the blood coursing through his veins, and his heart beating against his ribs. Behind the protection of the newspaper, he drew a deep breath and made an attempt to control his emotions.

Sophy, gnawing at her underlip, poured out his coffee in silence. Her hand was unsteady, and some of the steaming liquid slopped onto the saucer. She set down the pot with a bang.

This was not as she had imagined it would be. She had a feeling that it would not be in her husband's nature to take her confession with complacence.

Sophy swallowed hard, and found her voice.

"I wanted to have a word with you in private." She spoke with a restraint that made the words sound cold. Her accursed tongue again!

Seth lowered his paper a fraction at the crisp demand in her voice. He tilted his head sideways to study her face, his eyes lazy looking, almost hooded.

"This farce has continued long enough and I..." Her voice trailed off at the sudden blaze in his eyes. She drew in a quick breath and continued before he could speak.

"I...I think I ought to tell you...."

Chapter Six

Sophy was saved from having to confess her deception by a frantic hammering on the front door. Then the morning room door burst open with a bang, heralding the tempestuous entrance of Bernard van Houten, breathless and hatless.

"Bernard! What brings you here at this hour?" Sophy gasped, and half rose from her seat. Her voice took on the sharp edge of anxiety. "Is something wrong with Aunt Ella? Aunt Ilsa? Uncle Heinrich? Pieter?"

"No, of course not! Why on earth would you think that!" Impatiently, Bernard turned to Seth, who had risen to a standing position. "Pieter says the *Orion* berthed last night, sir. Can I come down to the docks with you and watch them unload her?"

"Sure." Seth eased himself back into his own chair. He was relieved to have the subject changed. He didn't want to hear what Sophy had to tell him in case it upset the rigid control he had over his emotions.

The thought brought back all the turbulent desires of a few minutes ago. Her intrusion into his life, his mind, had become dangerous, almost made him forget the gentleman he'd been raised to be.

How long could he hold out? This attraction he felt to her was not part of his plans. It was foreign to his nature to bow to the whims of a woman, even if she did send the blood coursing to his head. He could not let her defeat him too easily.

If he allowed her to gain the upper hand now, she would laugh and dance across his heart like a dragonfly over a stream, when all the time her feet would be as heavy as lead. He would not allow Sophy to govern him the way Abigail Lethbridge ruled poor Charles.

Marriage should be a partnership, not a battleground. There had to be a winning situation for both of them. He was being foolish, of course, but still . . .

He slanted Sophy a speculative glance. It was an instant caught in crystal. She gave him a tentative smile. His face softened. What a fascinating blend of intelligence, sweetness and coquetry! It was impossible to be mistaken about the appeal he saw in those unusual violet-gray eyes. He capitulated.

"Would you like to join us, Sophy?"

"Oh, what a splendid idea!" Sophy's eyes lit up, and her mouth tilted upward in her first real smile in four days. She felt absolutely buoyant, as though she might float up to the ceiling. "I'll just go and get a bonnet."

The prospect of an outing was like a draft of heady wine. For two days a steady downpour had pelted from leaden skies, accompanied by a chill wind that dashed the last of the leaves from the trees and sent them swirling into mushy little piles.

The world today was brighter and much more pleasant. Though even this morning conditions were less than ideal for unloading a vessel, with a good westerly wind and fitful sunshine.

As they moved along, Sophy pressed her face to the carriage window, looking at the fine brownstone buildings that drenched Manhattan like coffee. When the carriage swept into South Street, she could scarcely contain her excitement. Her gray eyes sparkled.

Seth descended from the carriage, and turned to assist his wife to alight. She was too quick for him and jumped eagerly to the ground. With a merry smile in Seth's direction, she sped after her impatient cousin. Her full skirts rustled vigorously as her tiny feet danced along the timber wharf. Seth's arms dropped stiffly to his sides.

In another woman, he might have suspected coyness, but in Sophy it was again that elusive quality, as if at the very moment of discovering her, she had gone. He found himself walking almost blindly, enmeshed in his own turmoil, toward the river. As he stalked toward the vessel, his limp was more pronounced than ever.

The *Orion* was easily identified, a tall, aloof, self-conscious presence among the trim sloops and cutters, the lemon-sailed craft of the fishermen, the long schooners and the heavy working barges. The gray-green water, a little agitated by the wind, slapped lazily against the clipper's hull.

Bernard scrambled nimbly across the narrow gangway. The lift and surge of the craft terrified Sophy, but she gamely followed him, slipping and sliding, across the wet planking.

She was wearing her new woven extension skirt, which she was learning to use in place of hoops. An ingenious cage affair of graduated steel springs and taped weavings, it was lighter and cooler than the bulky crinolines, but at the moment she missed the added stability of the old style.

Suddenly, strong hands gripped her waist and the wind rushed through her lungs. Exhilaration did a sharp rigadoon inside her. As she spun, the green waters of the bay were beneath her, the timbers vibrating, the whole platform shaking, the world blurring out of shape. Her eyes closed as her legs flew freely in space like a rag doll's.

Seth swung her onto the deck as if she weighed no more than a kitten. She was aware of his breath upon her ear, light and airy as blown sea spray. Of the way his hands, warm and hard, fit around her waist so perfectly, his body only inches away from hers. Her breath came faster. He released her with a soft laugh.

It sounded like bells to Sophy. Mellifluous. Sweet. She could hear the creaking of cordage, the slap of the water, and the mewing of the great gulls that were circling all about them. A paean of joy. Of exultation. For a moment she was caught up in the sound. She wanted to run, jump and shout with the joy of it.

"You can open your eyes now, Sophy."

Seth's voice was just a whisper. His breath rustled her hair. Sophy could feel his heat, his strength, the tension in his body. Her hands clung to his shoulders until the earth stopped spinning. Slowly, she opened her eyes, letting reality settle around her.

Boots planted wide, Seth gripped the rail as though he had need of its support. Or was he bracing himself against pain? There was an odd expression on his face, and for the life of her, she couldn't begin to interpret it.

Sophy's heart missed a beat as she realized he was without his cane. "Oh, my God," she breathed, appalled. "You've hurt yourself!" She looked around for her cousin, but he was nowhere in sight. Her expression softened. "Will you be all right while I fetch Bernard?"

Seth straightened. Aware that he was leaning too heavily on his injured leg, he shifted his weight to the opposite foot. A groan, quickly choked off, escaped him. Tentatively he released the rail. The vessel moved and he stumbled. Grasping for support again, he cursed softly, fluently and with great depth of feeling.

Sophy shot him a doubting glance, and stepped forward. To his surprise, she slipped her arm about his waist and moved his arm about her shoulders. "Here, let me help you."

The feminine scent of her was all around him. He inhaled, long and slow. Heat began to spiral through him, centering in his groin. The soft promise of her body, so tantalizingly close to his, was an open invitation to cast aside the facade of indifference he had sheltered behind.

He was torn between caution and desire. Caution won. He grinned down at the feathered confection of a bonnet, which barely came to his shoulder.

"Perhaps if you handed me my walking stick I could manage. It is over there, by the bulwark."

Sophy caught the gentle mockery in his voice. Mortified, she drew her teeth over her lower lip, and handed him the cane. He didn't say anything. He just stood there, gripping the knob of his walking stick, and staring at her mouth.

Her heart tripping fast in confusion, she swallowed convulsively. She knew he wanted to kiss her, and she smiled so he would understand that it was all right. Without a word, he turned away and limped along the deck toward the bridge. Pink and flushed, Sophy silently followed him.

An hour later, she was back on the wharf following a whirlwind inspection of the clipper, her mind still sorting her glimpses of a jam-packed hold, furled canvas, gleaming brass instruments and the narrow bunks of cramped living quarters.

From the shelter of the shipping office, she stood entranced, listening and watching, as barrels and bales of merchandise were hoisted from the ship under the supervision of the boatswain. As the goods came ashore, these were checked off against a ledger Seth held open on his knees.

Richard Carlton was there also. A heavily built man who seemed huge, his shoulders broad and powerful looking. He wore a dark jacket and plaid trousers. He had a wide face and big but pleasant features, with dark hair cut short and standing upright. There was no pomade on it, and it gave him a kind of unfinished look.

He smiled and put out a hand. "Nice to see you again, Mrs. Weston. Settled in okay?" His eyes were velvety brown in color, and very clear.

"Yes. Thank you for your assistance." Sophy put her gloved hand on top of his.

"You're welcome." He looked past her. "Hello, Charles. You've met Mrs. Weston?"

The two men made a sharp contrast. Charles Lethbridge was a head shorter than Richard Carlton, and thinner. He had a shortish nose sprinkled with freckles, finely chiseled lips and hazel eyes. His hat was pushed to the back of his head, showing wavy, sandy-colored hair.

Sophy damped down the sudden sense of distrust. There was nothing about the man to suggest skulduggery.

"Yes." Charles nodded. He bowed stiffly, but did not accept Sophy's outstretched hand.

He was staring at her so strangely that she was afraid he could guess what she was thinking. She felt as if she were being weighed on a mental balance. Just for a moment she was discomposed. Then she gathered her wits.

"You don't sound as if you approve."

"Not at all. Glad to see Seth married so advantageously, even if the news came as a surprise." The words sounded innocent enough, but somehow the smile that played across his lips seemed false.

Sophy tucked her hand back into her muff. "Life is full of surprises. That's what makes it so interesting."

The papers Richard Carlton had been studying were lists of the various manifests that had been unloaded in the past month. She gave a high-pitched little giggle.

"Don't you find it difficult to concentrate on all those silly figures?" That deceptive cloak of cherubic innocence fooled a lot of people.

It did not fool Charles. He looked stunned, as though he knew she concealed a motive behind every word and action, and was setting up a mark. He opened his mouth to speak but then seemed to think better of it.

Richard Carlton's smile didn't change. He folded the papers and put them into a flat metal box he held under one arm. "You've reminded me of work, Mrs. Weston. Please excuse me. On my desk at the moment there are manifests for seven different clients, all awaiting my attention."

"I'm going onto the *Orion* to do a couple of quick sketches. I've got an idea for a design with a nautical motif. See you around."

The chill in his voice sent shivers up her spine. She was letting her imagination run riot. The thought made her angry with herself. She had to stop being so suspicious of Seth's friend.

A clock struck somewhere far down in the town. Shortly afterward, when Seth picked up his books and went off to speak with Richard Carlton, Sophy roused herself. Holding up her bombazine skirts on each side and picking her way cautiously around a stock of cotton bales, she wandered among the piers that bristled along the waterfront.

As she passed the shelter of the shipping offices, the keen cold air hit her like a blow in the face. It stung her cheeks, making them glow, and sent the ribbons of her bonnet fluttering, and her black cloak flapping. Wisps of hair, coming loose from her long, coiled braid, framed her cheeks.

It was filthy, noisy, smelly and exciting, especially the odors, from the distinctive boat smell of tar, paint, shellfish, to damp hemp and bilge water. The sun was strong and the glare intense. It was nearly low water, and there was little traffic on the river.

Sophy was studying a collier brig with consuming interest, when Bernard materialized beside her. He took advantage of the opportunity to air his knowledge.

"That one unloading over there is the timber barge *Belle Rosa*. She brings logs across from New Jersey."

Alight with excitement and too full of energy to need any encouragement, Bernard began to explain the process, pointing out the huge grappling hook that caught the logs and unloaded them from the barge.

A dimple appeared on each side of Sophy's mouth. Her young cousin's enthusiasms were always all-absorbing and passionate. She listened with half an ear and smiled as Bernard talked, but she scarcely heard him.

Her attention began to drift, so engrossed was she with her own thoughts, and the problem that was nagging her: Seth's pride and her own sense of honor.

Having zealously delivered his wisdom on timber barges, Bernard had just begun to expound on the advantages of steam over sail when one of the men standing by the barge semaphored with his arms. "Hey!"

Bernard whistled to indicate he had understood the signal. Arms akimbo, he stood and watched the engineer as he stood to his levers. The main line holding the logs in place began to spool slowly in on the drum. The line tautened like a fiddle string, and the ponderous machine vibrated with the strain of its effort.

Holding her ballooning skirts down with one hand and her bonnet on with the other, Sophy kept walking slowly. She was not surprised to find her reverie drifting to Seth, nor did she wonder why she was thinking of him now. He seemed to fill all her thoughts.

The sound, the touch, the impact, the smell of him had stayed with her for hours. It seemed to flood through every corner of her mind, just as the keen air was pushing through her clothes to every part of her body. He felt so close! It was like a dream. It was because it was like a dream that she took no notice when she heard a sharp peal, as of a struck bell.

Suddenly, all hell seemed to break loose.

As Seth limped past the haul-back cable toward the barge, he saw the line come slack. His response was instinctive. Flinging himself across the dock, he hit her in a tackle that brought them both crashing to the timber boardwalk just as the cable whipped sideways, the sibilant hiss only inches above their heads. Another flicker of an instant, perhaps a tenth of a second, and he would have been too late.

Sophy lay immobilized, her breath crushed from her lungs. As she heard the sudden commotion of voices, she became acutely aware of the vibrantly male presence pressing her down...broad shoulders, strong forearms and thigh muscles like steel.

Groggily, she attempted to sit up as the body rolled off her, but fell back, trying to catch her breath. Her lungs worked like bellows, in an effort to get enough air inside her. She was aware of her whole body gasping.

"What the bloody hell do you think you were doing bringing her down here while they're unloading timber!" Seth exploded. His voice was harsh, filled with fury.

As though through a mist, Sophy heard the raised, angry voices. She opened her eyes. Seth and Charles were there, and Bernard. Her cousin stood with legs braced as though to spring into counterattack as Seth gave him a thorough tongue-lashing.

Seth was taut, incensed, his blue eyes blazing, his finely cut face set, as if on some old Roman coin. His tone of voice had turned savage, and the veins stood out on the sides of his temples.

Sophy felt her stomach contract in sudden panic. The sight of her husband and cousin standing on the very brink of violence stunned her. She struggled to rise, to speak, but her limbs and throat would just not obey.

Only sounds amplified in her head. The jagged beat of her pulse. The inner rush of her own fear.

She tried to raise her arms but they felt as if they belonged to another person. There was no strength left within her.

She tried again, "Seth..." before her voice faded and the swirling mists thickened into the darkness of oblivion.

As though attuned to Sophy's mental airwaves, Seth broke off in mid-sentence and ran to her side before she fell to the ground. He swallowed hard at the broken sound of her voice, the harsh tension leaving his body as he gathered her close.

Holding her as though he would never let her go, he stumbled grim faced toward the shipping office.

Sophy slowly opened her eyes, and groaned softly. She felt as if she'd been knocked over by a steam engine! Every part of her ached, but moved without difficulty. As she lifted her arm to push a strand of hair off her face, her eyes were caught by several bruises marring the creamy skin.

She lay puzzled for a moment, then sat up abruptly as the memories came crowding back. It was the sound of raised angry voices that had brought her back to awareness at the docks. Seth, Bernard and, confusingly, Richard Carlton were shouting at one another, the words cutting back and forth like knives. She could not understand the words, but she knew they were there.

Seth's arms had been clamped around her body like imprisoning bands of steel. As she struggled to free herself, he had stopped in the middle of a sentence, to look down, eyes blazing blue sparks.

"Are you all right?" he whispered, setting her on her feet.

Sophy nodded, not daring to speak, and allowed him to lead her to a chair. She sat there trying to control the tremors that continued to shake her.

Cursing under his breath, Seth began issuing harsh instructions to Richard Carlton and Bernard. Charles seemed to have disappeared. In what seemed like moments to Sophy, she had been transported back to Fifth Avenue, into the charge of Tessa, who had promptly insisted she rest.

Feeling somewhat restored, she now slid off the bed. It was time to face Seth with the truth. There was obligation. There was duty. As her father often said: *To see what is right and not do it is cowardice.* Too impatient to call Tessa for assistance, she gave her hair a cursory brushing to remove any tangles, and went in search of Seth.

Reluctant to face him, she hesitated in the partly open doorway. It had to be done. Deliberately she made herself relax, fortifying herself with a deep breath. One hand on the doorknob, she swept a quick glance across the living room, past the fluted columns with their gilded trim and the low table decorated with mother-of-pearl, to Seth seated in a deep cushioned chair in front of the carved fireplace.

Only the low-burning fire illuminated the room. He was so magnificently masculine and wonderfully handsome in the soft glowing light that Sophy's breath caught in her throat. Insides jumping with foreboding, she tightened her grip on the door so much that her knuckles showed white.

As if suddenly alerted by her interest, Seth swiveled in his chair and turned his head in her direction. The vision of Sophy with her dark hair cascading around her shoulders set his heart pounding.

His blue eyes, dark with sudden intensity, devoured her face with unblinking scrutiny. He studied her for a moment, absorbing the wide gray eyes riveted to his, the crisp, straight nose, the unsmiling lips.

Sophy's heart swelled, and she felt a wave of deep shyness go through her. Words failed her. The silence beat about their ears. To her overactive imagination, the large chair creaked ominously when Seth rose slowly, awkwardly, to his feet and went across to the table, returning with a glass in his hand.

"Drink this," he said quietly.

Sophy flicked him an uncertain glance. "What is it?"

"Brandy," he replied succinctly. "You look as though you need it," he added, running his fingers through his thick dark hair.

"I'm fine, thanks," Sophy informed him, her nose wrinkling in distaste.

Seth placed the glass on the mantel. "Fair enough." His lips tightened, but his response was made in an expressionless tone of voice.

"I'm sorry for causing any drama." Sophy attempted a peace offering.

She should really tell him about the forged telegraph. There had been no insurance with Lloyd's of London. No telegraph. Only her wicked scheming. Perhaps he would understand. Her heart hammering with expectation and trepidation, she began a muddled explanation.

"I...did want to...apologize...I hadn't intended any real harm...." She wanted to convince him of her genuine concern, but it was so complicated. All of her reasons for the deception were not clear to her, and she was riddled with guilt for deceiving him in the first place. She was full of mixed feelings.

Seth's firm mouth twitched. The stubborn feminine tilt of Sophy's firm little chin contrasted sharply with the haunting, trembling promise of her lips. Warm, honey-sweet, sensual lips that dazzled the senses, and sent logic spinning.

He was a man of discipline. Of rectitude, of courage, he had always thought. Yet he had almost been too late to save her from annihilation. His instincts told him that the incident today had been too close to have been an accident, too near disaster to have been coincidental. The thought sent a shaft of disquiet from his heart clear down to his boots.

"I'm touched by your contrition, but no real harm was done, so let's skip the inquest." He rallied, although any frivolity attached to the words was devalued by the darkening of his blue eyes.

A wave of unease swept through Sophy as she moved closer, into the circle of light. This was getting worse and worse. She had to tell him. She had to!

"I hope you are right, but I still owe you an explanation. I think it was overreaction to..."

Seth put his fingers on her lips to stop her from speaking. "Forget it. I should never have let you wander off. It was all my fault. I take full responsibility."

As though he could not help himself, he caught a strand of her silky straight hair between his fingers, rubbing gently. It smelled of lavender and fresh air, and that underlying heat of her body, tantalizing, innocently provocative.

"I like your hair this way," he declared in a voice of thickest satin. Fascinated by it, captivated by the scent, he breathed deeply, filling his lungs with it.

Sophy stood immobile. Her heart pounded at this declaration. She found herself staring at him in bemused wonder. He filled up all of her vision. The firelight behind him crowned his head with a glowing nimbus, casting his face into a dim silhouette.

A rush of satisfaction sizzled through her as she studied him. He was her husband!

Seth's fingers continued to play with her mane. Watching his long fingers caress the loose weight of her hair, Sophy shocked herself remembering how they felt moving over her body that way.

She hesitated. The moment was so ideal, yet she didn't want to ruin what promised to be so wonderful. There would be plenty of time later to confess, maybe after they'd eaten.

Sophy bit her bottom lip to stop its sudden quiver. Perhaps it would be best to take one step at a time and follow her instincts? But how far could a woman trust her instincts when she was hovering on the brink of love?

The realization of where her thoughts were leading her brought a small chill of uncertainty. Eyes wide, she looked up at Seth.

Seth looked down into her luminous eyes, and went still. For what seemed endless moments, he held her gaze before he dipped his head and brushed his lips softly across her mouth.

It was the merest contact, but it laid siege to rational thought. His lips were persuasive, irresistible. Some emotion more powerful than any she'd ever known before stormed her senses. She leaned into his body, and her hands rose involuntarily to clutch at his shirtfront as she instinctively closed her eyes to shield her emotions.

"Seth?" Sophy's voice was small and uncertain. She shook her head to clear it. Her wits felt scrambled, and she was not at all sure what she was wanting.

A faint smile flickered briefly on Seth's face. Like potent wine, hot excitement flooded through him, but he didn't try to deepen the embrace. Instead, his hands came up to gently clasp her shoulders, and his breath touched warmly at her temple.

"I also like the way you overreact." His voice was a soft murmur as he lifted her hair to nuzzle his face in her neck. When he bent to taste the sweet hollow of her throat, his tongue seeking out that sensitive pulse point, a muffled sound escaped her.

His tenderness was unnerving, intoxicating, and caused a response within Sophy she had not expected. Blindly, she turned her face toward his, seeking the comfort and warmth he offered.

The frill of his shirt softly tickled her chin. As she burrowed against the hard wall of his chest, her lips opened and moved involuntarily against his thumb.

Seth felt their soft brush on his flesh. Desire raged through him with the force of a stormy torrent, and he felt his skin tighten, as if the roiling blood inside were pressing against it, trying to burst out.

Sophy's arms wound themselves around his neck, her fingers twining themselves into his lustrous hair, ruffling it, mussing it. Her sudden passion surprised Seth, and he gathered her closely to him, even as a tiny voice warned against the fire that was now threatening to burn up his control.

He could not believe the intense need that threatened to overpower him as if he were a green, callow youth. He tried to deny it, but his body ignored his mind's orders. His hand pressed Sophy even closer against the whole pulsing length of his body.

Molded to his hard frame, Sophy was physically aware of his needs and desires. She felt herself yield to the hard pressure of his hand. The guilt she'd been experiencing over keeping her secret from him faded as she, too, was filled with desire.

More than anything in the world at the moment she was wanting his touch, his kiss, and unwillingly let him go when he gently eased her to arm's length suddenly.

Seth's face was tight and the blue eyes glittering and unfathomable. He sucked in a deep, steadying breath, then he smiled slowly, his eyes crinkling at their corners.

"I'm sorry, Sophy. I didn't intend for this to happen," he said thickly, stepping back. "Especially after your ordeal today. Forgive me for my lack of tact and sensibility."

Without his arms around her, without his warmth enclosing her, Sophy felt chilled. She shuddered. Her lips were still parted slightly, bereft.

She could not believe her response.

It was the middle of the day! It was madness. A wild, wanton madness to allow herself to be distracted in this way.

A brief wave of shame swept over her, and, unbidden, a swift flood of color tinged her cheeks, lending a rosy hue that was mortifying. To cover her embarrassment, she picked up the glass she had rejected, nervously swirling the contents.

Daring to lift her chin a notch, she swallowed convulsively. "I came to tell you something."

Seth's body still throbbed with need, but he ignored it. He looked down at the fireplace, pushing aside the shocking thoughts that had crept into his mind.

"What did you come to tell me?" There was no expression in his tone. No emotion at all, but she saw a dark hollow form at the edge of his mouth, and his eyes narrowed.

Sophy tried a sip of the brandy. "I think that someone is stealing from you." Seth's lashes came up quickly and she found herself staring into his jewel-bright eyes. "I think the villain should be flushed out."

He stood there, not saying anything, as she sought for the right words. Why, oh why, was this so difficult?

Gathering her courage, she drew a deep breath and plunged on. "Which is why I had Matt Tyson arrange for a transfer of funds to cover a non-existent insurance claim."

Clear as a bell, her voice echoed in the sudden silence.

Seth didn't move. He looked completely dumbfounded. Then, Sophy saw the truth of it hit him. His face went rigid, his mouth hardened, and she could see the pulse beat in his throat.

The silence lengthened, grew deafening.

Seth's tongue was frozen in astonishment. He stood and stared down at her, a curious expression flickering over his handsome face. For an instant his eyes were twin blue flames, flaring the way a predator's gaze flickers before the final leap.

Sophy's eyes were huge and wary in the shadows, but they met his bravely. For a full twenty seconds they stood gazing at each other, before he rallied and broke the silence.

"Why have you done this?" he ventured, feeling his way so cautiously he might have been trying to walk on hot coals. Under the circumstances, his voice was dreadful in its calm.

Sophy abruptly turned her head away from his blazing eyes, her hair fanning over her face as she searched for words. How could she confess the truth? That the wife whom he had married entirely for her money had fallen in love with him? That she felt his pain as if it were her own?

Sophy groped for something to say. All coherence seemed to have fled from her thoughts, so she shrugged her shoulders with assumed nonchalance, and replaced the brandy glass on the mantel. She hoped her voice wouldn't shake when she finally spoke the words she was desperately trying to frame in her mind.

She swung around to confront him. "I wish only to be your wife and make you happy. Seth . . ."

Sophy was suddenly crushed in Seth's arms, as if he would envelop her slender frame in his. "Sophy! Sophy! You give me so much, and now this . . . without asking anything in return."

His voice was thick. He, too, seemed to be having difficulty breathing. She stood on tiptoe to place a quick kiss on the pulse hammering in his throat.

"I am not so sure I will always be amenable. Father always said I was far too independent and cocky to be kept in line."

She heard the breath hiss between his teeth, then his face was buried in her hair. "Sophy, I have no wish to completely rule your life, and if I try, resist me, fight me, do anything but give in to me."

"I do not understand. I love you, Seth. You are my life, why should I..."

"I desire you more than any woman I have ever known, but, as I told you before, romance was knocked out of me in the war. If I could give you love, I would. I'd even write it into your damned contract."

This was no claim but an offering.

"I think we will have go through our wedding bargain, and rewrite it, clause by clause."

He answered the unspoken question. "Agreed."

She felt his response to her closeness and pressed herself more firmly against him. She would accept what he offered. "Change number one. The nights are yours, but the days belong to me."

Chapter Seven

Sophy ran her eye over the superb selection of fabrics in the draper's establishment. Fine silk, velvet, crepe, muslin, faille, poplin and moiré, tangled with braid, ribbons, tassels and lace.

The gleaming rainbow choice of colors was bemusing. Dazzling blues, greens, pinks and yellows contrasted sharply with gentle grays and lavender. The striking patterns, too, were overwhelming, with spots, stripes and exotic flower sprays all vying for attention.

She examined materials, shook out samples and looked carefully at the quality of a piece of black gauze. Her gaze lingered on a coral velvet, but went reluctantly on. *Red would suit you.* No, that was going too far. But not a drab, demure half mourning either.

She spied a flame red silk. It would be perfect made up in one of the elegant designs the French couturier, Mr. Worth, had sent to Madame Bertine. No, those modish styles revealed more than they concealed. It would drive Seth mad to see his wife in so daring a gown!

Sophy slowly put down the gauze. If she was going to leave off her black, she was going to do it properly. Seth Weston needed a bit of color and excitement in his life, and she, Sophy Weston, was going to provide it. Such a daring gown could be an effective secret weapon.

Hurriedly, before she could change her mind, Sophy pointed out the brilliant silk to the draper, who sent a junior employee rushing to fetch it down.

"A shrewd choice, madam," he conceded, unrolling the bolt of fabric with a flourish, cascading the river of flagrant flame over the counter. "The very finest Weston's silk, excellent quality, and just the shade to complement your complexion..."

His flow of sales talk was not needed. Sophy had already decided. She fingered the silk, her cheeks dimpling with elation. Unspoken, unspeakable thoughts raced through her mind.

Aunt Ella looked scandalized. "Sophy! You wouldn't be wearing such a heathen color! And your father not dead above seven months! It's unseemly!"

"Don't fret, Aunt. It will make a lovely lining for a black silk crepe evening cape." Sophy looked Aunt Ella straight in the eyes, but her lips curved in a conspiratorial smile.

Gathering up their parcels, the women made their way to the horse-drawn "railroad," which carried passengers all the way from City Hall to a depot on Forty-Second Street. At several places along the length of the busy road were pickup points.

Here, the ticket collectors were busy, and newspaper boys stood screaming the headlines. A drop of moisture hit her cheek. It was going to rain again. Zinc-colored clouds, streaked with dark, clotted undersides, stretched across the sky. The tram was overdue.

Sophy saw a heavily built man stop to buy a paper. He had his back to her, but he looked familiar. Before she could identify him, someone bumped into him, and he moved off.

The boarding platform was crowded with men, women and children, pushing and shoving. Several times Sophy was edged toward the rails. She didn't mind.

At all costs she wanted to catch the tram. She wanted to deliver her purchases to the seamstress, but, more important, she wanted to check whether there were any replies to some special letters Seth had dictated the night before. She was pleased Seth's house was on Fifth Avenue. It was much more convenient than her father's house in Yonkers.

Her head swam with the sights and smells of the morning's excursion, and with her memories of the previous evening. They had sat in the library after dinner, Seth with a sheath of papers before him at the table, Sophy on the chair opposite with her notebook and pencil.

She had taken down his swift, clipped sentences until page after page was filled with her neat script. It seemed Seth was taking her seriously.

He was involving her in the business, making her feel useful. At times she suspected he was testing her, teasing her, with a jumble of information and unfamiliar terms, but she always understood.

Occasionally she stopped him with a question.

"After the stock was ruined that time, Seth, what percentage was salvaged?"

"Eighty."

"Only eighty? Then there was a substantial loss on cotton consignments even before the cessation of trade with the South?"

His mouth curved ruefully. "Often happens. It's practically impossible not to suffer some commodity damage in transit. The trick is to make it up in profits on the finished product."

"Does anyone else besides Richard Carlton have access to the ledgers, like...well, Charles Lethbridge, for instance?"

"Yes. George Dunwoody." Sophy put her head on one side and looked at him, wholly beautiful. "He manages the Paterson plant." His mouth softened and the corners lifted slightly. "Well, let's finish up. The nights are mine, remember?"

In the hustle and bustle of the Ladies' Mile, Sophy remembered, and once again repeated to herself, *Half a loaf! Half a loaf. That I do have. Maybe I should be content.*

Her lip crept between her teeth. She was damned if she would give up. She knew he was a man who could be taught how to love. He just needed a little practice.

Sophy heard the iron wheels of the tram rattle on the cobblestones. She craned to see how near it was. The horses were actually in her line of vision, when a man fell against her heavily.

The lead horse reared, nostrils flaring. She staggered wildly, and a woman screamed. There was the chink and rattle of brass and leather harness. Then someone grabbed at her and pulled her back, as the steel-clad hooves flashed past.

Weston's Textiles inhabited an iron-fronted warehouse on Forty-First Street. The building was located a short distance beyond the main garment-manufacturing district, near where Broadway began to angle its way into Longacre Square.

Seth liked to be at the factory before eight o'clock when the new shift started. There was the material to be examined that had been dyed the previous day, as a final check for shade, before sending it on for further processing.

The path to the rear of the workshop nestled between two tall limestone structures. After the rain it was slippery, but he negotiated it with the minimum of effort, letting himself into the drafty complex.

The workroom was empty, except for Charles Lethbridge. White shirtsleeves rolled up to his elbows exposing his freckled forearms, the designer was already busy sketching a pattern.

Bolts of cloth lined the walls like rows of orderly soldiers, while sample books, newspapers and magazines were spread haphazardly about the drafting table. Seth picked up some pencils, and dropped them into a glass jar.

His mouth quirked at the corners. "Your clutter reminds me of planning on a battlefield. All we need is the colonel to start our own campaign."

"I could do with some inspiration," Charles grunted, his sandy eyebrows crinkled in thought. "Stewart's are flooding the market with French silks. Even with the services of a textile designer who studied at the Ecole des Beaux-Arts in Lyons, how can Weston's compete?"

Seth eased himself onto a stiff-backed wooden chair. He reached out and picked up a sample book.

"Diversification. Extend our market. Mix and match our designs. Expand into the furnishing fabric trade, woven wallpapers, brocaded damask for curtains, matching brocatelle for furniture, et cetera. With the use of aniline dyes we can produce unusual color combinations."

"How's Sophy?" Charles added a pencil mark to a design.

"Fine."

Charles thought about that for a moment, then added another couple of squiggles. "Got over her fright at the shipping yards, then?"

Seth put the sample book down on the cluttered bench. He leaned back in his chair, his face set in a dissatisfied frown. That niggle of worry returned. He wished he could confide in Sophy, but he didn't want to frighten her.

The thought of her warmed him instantly. Sophy's effervescence was contagious. His new wife was no meek and mild creature, obedient to his every wish. She was possessed of a passionate nature.

It shone in her eyes, in the unselfconscious way she moved her body, in her wide, delicious smile. In the way she welcomed him into her bed.

In some obscure way, he was pleased she was taking an interest in the business. Feisty, insolent, disobedient, she had bounced back with a vengeance! The realization brought an unexpected rush of pleasure. He pushed away his doubts.

"When I last saw her, she had an army of servants prepared for combat with buckets and mops. I judged it prudent to engage in a strategic retreat."

"Sophy worrying about housework? With all of your money?" Charles looked up in amazement, and bit the end of his pencil.

"I think she felt provoked, and when women are provoked, they do strange things." Seth gave an eloquent shrug. "Sophy does housework."

Charles wasn't sure, but he thought he was beginning to understand. "You haven't been accused of neglecting your bride already, have you?" He surveyed his friend with dry amusement.

Seth paused for several minutes before speaking, rubbing his temple with his fingers. The barest hint of a smile touched the fullness of his lips.

"Sophy has an absurd notion that she wants to be seen as more than just a person who came with a dowry."

Charles chuckled, unruffled. "It was ever so with the female of the species, contrary creatures at best, and wives can be the very devil," he said, his pencil moving, his head down.

Seth refused to be drawn. He knew Abigail Lethbridge to be a veritable waterworks if she failed to get her own way. He'd make damn sure Sophy didn't follow suit. He watched the pencil stop on a line, and shrugged his shoulders.

"She also has it in her head that there is skulduggery afoot in the plant, and that, if I let her investigate the matter, she can expose the culprit."

Charles looked up from his papers. For a moment the two men regarded each other.

"She's smart." Charles returned to his drawing. There was no hint of crisis there. "What are you going to do?"

"I'm inclined to let her have her way. There are trade-offs involved." Seth had found a fascinating pattern of shadows on the floor. Sophy was a generous lover, and it would be a shame to crush so rare and delightful a creature. She might vex and irritate with her quaint ideas of independence, but she filled his mind at the oddest moments.

"There always are with women." Seth said nothing and Charles continued. "How are you getting on with your own investigation?"

Seth rubbed his thigh, cursing the pain that flooded through his leg. "Uphill all the bloody way. I'm still no nearer finding where the money went. Why?"

Clear blue eyes bored into hazel.

Charles met the look without flinching. "Didn't you say Sophy was interested in the stock market?"

"What are you suggesting?"

"Play by the familiar rules of war. Devise an initial strategy to stun the fellow's responses. Defeat him in one decisive assault. He won't be expecting a female. Use Sophy's knowledge of Wall Street. Maybe that's where your man has been putting his ill-gotten gains."

"That'd be a bit flagrant, wouldn't it? If it'd been me, I'd salt it away in a bank account somewhere."

"Yes. Well, not everyone is as careful with their money as you, are they? Others might put it on the roll of the dice, hoping to make more."

"The idea has merit. It's worth a try."

"Are you going to put in an appearance at Horace Greeley's soiree this evening, then?" Charles asked conversationally.

Seth was instantly alert. "I have a great respect for Horace as editor of the *Tribune*. Some contentious issues have been triggered lately. This could be an opportunity for genuine debate on the issue of Reconstruction."

"It could also be an opportunity for Sophy to check out the investment bankers. Catch the enemy sleeping and undefended, so to speak. I'll check out the tables." Charles permitted himself the smallest of smiles. "Be ready for Abigail."

Seth let out an audible breath, and felt the tension leave his shoulder blades. "So what have you been doing?"

Charles recognized the signs. He put down his pencil, and turned his latest creation toward Seth.

"Like it?"

"Mmm. Nice light style. It could work on silk taffeta, if the pattern was created from a woven rib, and then over-printed after the cloth has been taken from the loom."

Seth pulled a notebook from his pocket, immersed once more in business. "Get the artists to color-test a sample to-morrow."

The big grandfather clock in the hall chimed six as Seth came down the staircase. He noticed the smell of fresh beeswax. There were flowers, too, in the brass urn at the foot of a bearded icon, which filled the alcove near the window.

Feeling inexplicably lighthearted, he crossed the small entresol, meaning to go into the drawing room, and had reached for the knob when the door opened and Sophy walked straight into him.

A jolt went through him, from his belly to his fingertips, when he caught her arm, establishing balance. In the sub-dued light of the hall, she seemed ethereal, more lovely than he could have imagined.

He gazed assessingly down at her, his fingers releasing her arm. Her hair was drawn back from her forehead and coiled low in the nape of her neck. The charming hairstyle added a mature elegance to her small, erect figure. It made her neck seem much longer, a flawless column of rich ivory ris-ing from the high-buttoned black evening cape, giving an immaculate, almost Madonna-like serenity to her face. But nothing could extinguish or subdue the luminous shimmer of her eyes, or the enchanting expressiveness of her mouth.

Sophy stood still for an instant, her hand on the knob of the half-open door. Then she smiled radiantly. He was practically eating her with his eyes. She felt her knees loosen under the sensual assault.

Under the all-concealing voluminous cloak, her new fashionable satin gown rustled most becomingly over its hooped petticoats. She took a few steps toward him, de-lighting in the effect she had created.

"Hello, Seth, are you ready, then?"

Seth could hear the smile in her voice. Her eyes were bright and shining with expectation. His expression sharpened with suspicion.

"Sophy, you are up to something."

"Not at all. I'm merely eager to show off my new dress at Mr. Greeley's gathering."

There was a smile at the corners of her mouth as Sophy straightened an imaginary wrinkle in her glove. In the words of the great General Grant: *Never let your opponent think for a minute that you will waver in your course.* She felt him gather himself to say something and intuitively she forestalled him.

"I'll be no trouble. I will not even provoke you by informing you that I thought it was time that all women took an interest in politics!"

For an instant, Seth looked totally nonplussed, then he laughed. It was a low, infectious laugh of genuine amusement.

"No trouble, hmm? I cannot tell you how much that comforts me!"

New York was in a gala mood. Optimism prevailed. Sophy was interested in the momentous political changes taking place, but personal concerns loomed larger. She had more than a few distinct qualms as she and Seth entered the spacious foyer of the Greeley mansion.

Now that the moment of denouement was imminent, her courage was evaporating rapidly. Her conscience gave a hard knock, and she swallowed nervously. It was too late to change tactics now.

Clutching the folds of her cloak tightly together, she stared across the room, and willed herself to stand still. The tip of her tongue ran along the fullness of her lower lip.

"I did not imagine there would be so many people."

There was amusement in the depths of Seth's eyes as he watched her take in the scene. The throng of guests dressed in the height of fashion, the babble of voices, the glittering crystal chandelier, the stairs that curved gracefully upward.

The broad marble steps rose in a single sweep to the center of a wide, cantilevered gallery above. There was a large silver bowl on a mahogany plinth standing at the head of the stairs, displaying an arrangement of autumn foliage.

"I know what you mean." He hesitated, then continued with uncharacteristic diffidence. "There's nothing wrong, is there, Sophy?"

Sophy raised wary eyes to his. At the gentle concern revealed there, she felt a guilty warmth rise in her cheeks. She swallowed uneasily, shaking her head, and looked away from him to see their host bearing down upon them in a peculiar rocking gait.

Horace Greeley was a portly man in his fifties, with light auburn hair that was just beginning to turn gray at the temples. He wore an exquisitely cut evening coat of gray silk, and his round moon face was smiling broadly within its frame of flowing red whiskers.

"Good to see you out and about in company again, Seth." The two men shook hands, and their host inclined his head toward Sophy. "Nice to see you, too, Sophy. I miss your father's fellowship."

Blushing even more deeply, Sophy held out her gloved hand to her host. He clasped it briefly, then waved an expansive arm and stepped behind her.

"Here, let me take your cloak."

Every sane and sensible instinct warned her to abandon the field and beat a hasty retreat while she could. Instead, she inclined her head graciously and said, "Thank you, Mr. Greeley."

A faint, wry smile curved her mouth as Sophy allowed the evening cape to slide off her shoulders. She'd never set out to deliberately seduce a man before, and the likelihood of success was limited, especially when her first sally was fired in public!

Moisture beading his upper lip, Horace stared down at Sophy, eyes blinking through his spectacles. "Ah...call me Horace. Why don't you and your husband join me later on for supper? Or have you something planned, Seth?"

Seth had been admiring the editor's dark red sideburns, and so was quick to catch the sudden appreciative look, and to hear the note of surprise in Horace Greeley's voice. A sudden sense of unease seized him, and his features tightened almost imperceptibly as he dropped his glance to Sophy.

Flattened at the front, spreading and widening at the back, with a narrow border of scarlet, her black satin gown was embroidered all over with sprigs of butterflies, no two alike. Made high in the neck, the clinging material revealed the gentle swell of small, high-tipped breasts. She looked bizarre, but at the same time the whole ensemble was outstandingly chic and arresting.

It was not until she turned toward the editor that Seth caught sight of the rear of her gown. Rage swept over him as he saw what she was wearing.

The back bodice, if it could be called that, plunged in a triangle of transparent gauze from the center of her neck out to the points of her waist. Sophy certainly was not wearing a corset since her smooth pearly skin gleamed through the filmy thin fabric.

Seth stood transfixed, as his inner being heaved about a heart that seemed to explode. It made him light-headed. He slanted her a savage glance. Deliberately, she shrugged as he continued to stare silently at her.

"I thought you'd be pleased if your wife chose to wear Weston's fabrics."

Horace Greeley looked at her as if totally fascinated. His normally florid complexion was even redder, and his shrewd blue eyes twinkled, as he pulled on his scarflike tie.

"What an exquisite little creature! She makes the other females look dowdy and unfashionable. Maybe you should let her handle the advertising for Weston's, Seth. Your wife will do more to boost the economy without a word than a hundred politicians with all their talk.''

From beneath her lashes, Sophy watched the effect of her striking outfit on her husband. He shifted a little, and moved his head in a gesture of disbelief. A dangerous fire burned in his eyes, and his strong, well-formed features assumed the inflexibility of a death mask.

It was obvious she was going to have to goad him further. If she could find a crack in the seemingly impenetrable wall that surrounded his heart, perhaps she would have a chance of gaining his love. She looked past him at a face she recognized on the other side of the room.

"Oh, there's James Pike, a reporter at the *Tribune*. I must go and have a word with him. Will you excuse me?"

Dimly through the confusion that claimed his brain, Seth heard her. He swallowed with effort. His mouth twisted wryly, and when he spoke, there was an edge to his voice.

"Beat a strategic retreat while you can, Sophy," Seth said. "Your hour of reckoning will come."

Sophy managed a very brilliant smile in his direction before she sped toward the chattering, superficial throng. As she crossed the room, she was aware that he followed her with his eyes, eyes that were barbed and frosty and full of lethal intent.

Lethal? Surely not! Lethal meant fatal, terminal, deadly. Seth was out to discipline her, not to kill her! A man of excessive passions, he would succumb easily to anger, but there was nothing about him to suggest that he would resort to murder to settle his problems.

James Pike grinned boyishly at the sight of Sophy. Slender, not above average height, with tightly curling black hair and merry brown eyes, he had features almost too delicately carved for a man.

"Hello, Sophy. Any good tips tonight?" There was a hint of laughter in his voice.

Sophy gave a breathless little chuckle. "What an avaricious fellow you are, James!" She looked back to see if Seth was still watching her. He was. She turned her back to him. "If you have a spare dollar, I'd recommend Andrew Carnegie's Pittsburgh stock. Iron and steel shares should be a good investment."

One black brow arched inquiringly, as if he could hardly believe his ears. Sophy had spoken in an artless tone of voice, but from past experience, James Pike knew that she knew exactly what she was saying.

"Have you met Samuel Clemens?" James indicated his companion. The grin that curved the young reporter's mouth widened. "Keep an eye out for 'The Celebrated Jumping Frog of Calaveras County' by Mark Twain. It is due to go to print with the New York *Saturday Press.*"

Tall and broad with a loose-limbed, athletic body, Sam Clemens looked to be about thirty. With a wide, well-shaped mouth and high, intelligent brow, his pleasant features offered a normalcy that was somehow inspiring. He gave Sophy an open, friendly smile.

"Take no notice, ma'am. James loves to hear himself talk."

Sophy flashed him a smile. "People will talk whatever you do, so you may as well give them something to talk about!" Smoothly she changed the subject. "Have you heard Macy's intends holding a special parade on Thanksgiving?"

Seth stood leaning against one of the gilded Corinthian pillars, which created an imposing entryway to the immense reception room, exchanging small talk with Matt Tyson. He also kept one eye on Sophy. His brows twitched as his eyes followed her every movement.

It was more than infuriating to be so easily outmaneuvered by the little minx. It was absolutely humiliating. He was feeling disturbingly light-headed, not because of her outfit.

Sophy's physical attraction had become meaningless for the moment, transposed into something far more precious.

She had struck with unerring accuracy, aiming at his most vulnerable point with a skill that elicited his respect even as it made him furious.

When Seth nodded absently for the third time, Matt Tyson followed the direction of the younger man's gaze to the circle of men pressing around Sophy. He surveyed the group thoughtfully. So that was the way the wind blew. There was a mischievous gleam in his brown eyes as he raised his glass in a brief salute.

"Always thought Sophy a beauty, but she's positively glowing tonight. Marriage obviously agrees with her. Seems to have developed an enchanting panache, wouldn't you allow?"

"If that's what you call trying to get a rise out of me!"

Matt compressed his lips firmly to prevent a grin, but could not prevent a gentle prod. "She seems to be enjoying herself."

Seth's hands tightened briefly on his glass, irritated afresh at the memory of Sophy's provocative dress. She had definitely grown on him. It was impossible not to appreciate her determination and impudence even as he recognized his own angry reaction.

"Sophy has a . . . a sort of elfin gaiety that is contagious."

A dark elfin creature, with a smile like sun after rain. A defiant, mischievous sprite who bewitched him until he lost his senses. He was watching her now, under his lashes, idly turning the stem of his glass.

The two men had been too engrossed in their conversation to notice the woman wending her way toward them. It was not until Seth felt a hand clutch the sleeve of his coat that he became aware of another's presence.

"Seth?"

Abigail Lethbridge! Clad in a beautifully designed gown of soft green silk, Abigail appeared to have come direct from one of her husband's drawings. Two golden corkscrew curls framed her angel-sweet oval face and her hazel eyes shone with tears. Magnificent emeralds glittered in her ears and around her neck, enhancing her fair coloring, and accentuating the glitter in her eyes.

Matt Tyson glanced from her worried countenance to his longtime business associate. There was no doubt that, at times like this, discretion was the better part of valor. He held his empty glass to the light.

"See you later, my friend. I'm off to get a refill."

Neither Seth nor Abigail noticed the banker go, or the petal that floated down, detached from the arrangement directly above their heads.

Abigail did not remove her hand from Seth's arm. Two big teardrops trembled on her brown eyelashes, and her mouth quivered.

There was a long pause, during which Seth's features settled into a stony mask. Abigail's sniveling had somehow been overlaid with Sophy's wide-eyed sincerity, her genuine smile, her frank speech.

Sophy would not have sat by and watched her husband fritter away her marriage portion. Her sense of honor would not allow it. His little wife would have boxed his ears and set him about his business!

The silence around them was broken only by the sound of Abigail's quick breathing. A single teardrop slid slowly down her cheek. Then, as if the words were being jerked out of her, she spoke. "Charles is at the gambling tables, Seth."

Seth's shoulders rose in a shrug and he handed his glass to a passing waiter. When he answered, there was a suspicious lack of inflection to his voice. "I suppose he's losing, as well."

The shimmer in the green eyes became a small waterfall. A flush brightened Abigail's dewy skin, and her chin wobbled dangerously. This time several petals fell, as if in empathy.

Seth rolled his eyes heavenward in a long-suffering manner and turned toward the staircase. Abigail moved to follow him, her tears cleared away, as if by magic.

* * *

Sophy was enjoying herself thoroughly. She could scarcely have been more pleased that two personable men such as James Pike and Samuel Clemens had taken her under their wing, introducing her to other guests. She had made several valuable future contacts.

Seth had rapidly been besieged by old friends, struggling through the crowd to shake hands and congratulate him upon his return to social functions, so she felt no guilt at deserting him.

Shortly before midnight, people began to drift toward the refreshment room where supper was being served. Sophy declined several offers of an escort, as she searched for Seth. He had been given enough time to think.

Complacency left her abruptly, as she snapped back to reality. He was standing clasping the hand of a beautiful fair-haired woman, the lamplight waking a rich golden sheen on the woman's head.

There was the strongest impression that the urn above their heads moved. The flowers seemed to sway. Something clicked in the back of her brain, and a tiny part of her screamed danger.

For a moment, Sophy stood rooted to the spot, her breath stifled. Then, almost convulsively, she sprang across the room, pushing her way through the milling guests. But the bulking crowd moved in and stymied her. Her mind whirled and the room tilted as she hit the wall of solid flesh.

She staggered, then regained her balance. A shiver rippled down her spine as with a sense of inevitability she ran toward the couple. She struggled across the packed room toward Seth and Abigail Lethbridge. They seemed miles away, much too far for her to make in time.

Her breath caught in her chest. Could no one else sense the danger? Her rapid heartbeat matched the insistent pulse of the bass drum being played in the ballroom.

"Seth!" Was that her voice, so shrill and tight, filled with the agony of fear?

Seth lifted his head and looked her straight in the eye. His conditioned reflexes had him frozen in a crouch before he'd even identified the danger. An instant later he was flattened against the pillar, Abigail thrust protectively behind him.

The urn wavered and fell. There was a tremendous crash that seemed to splinter the very foundations of the Greeley house. The urn lay shattered on the floor, in the exact spot where, only seconds before, Seth had stood.

Its contents lay scattered on the white marbles, the red autumn leaves resembling great drops of blood on an altar stone.

Chapter Eight

Sophy stirred and felt the warmth of the male body beside her. She could hear him breathing quietly. As she turned to look at Seth's sleeping figure, the night's memories came back, bringing a light flush to her cheeks. It was an unbelievable relief simply to lie there and know he was unharmed.

It was so quiet. She cocked her head, listening. Nothing but her own heartbeat and the quiet, even sound of the man's breathing. The peacefulness was unreal, even uncanny.

The excitement was over, the questions answered, and they were home safely, but Sophy couldn't dismiss the faint feeling of unease. Various incidents replayed themselves in her mind and began to fit together like the pieces of a puzzle.

She stirred restlessly upon the bed. Something was not quite right about last night's events. She was teased by an uneasy thought that she had forgotten something significant. Something she'd heard that could be a key to the puzzle.

As far as she could judge, four people had access to Seth's affairs. She made a mental note of them.

Charles Lethbridge.

Richard Carlton.

George Dunwoody.

Matt Tyson.

All of them had been at the previous night's function. Richard Carlton and George Dunwoody had left early, before supper, but had that particular timing been really coincidental? Or a deliberate decoy?

Something felt wrong. Things were not as they seemed. Somehow, she had missed a vital clue.

She was sure of it.

Careful not to touch the warm body next to hers, Sophy drew her knees up to her breast and hugged herself. Was she justified in wanting to believe Charles was the villain, and assuming therefore that all the others were innocent? But it was only guesswork. It didn't amount to more than a theory.

Impressions weren't evidence. Impressions could get her off to a good start in her investigations, that was all. And Charles had been gambling last night. Badly dipped, too, according to a hysterical Abigail.

She absently dragged her fingers through her hair. The night air was damp and clammy. She got out of bed and padded to the window, where she stood with one hand on the soft damask drape, gazing idly down into the square.

It was completely empty and completely gray, as though the November night had drained all color from the world. Gray avenue, gray sidewalk, gray tree trunks, blank gray sky.

She shivered. Torn, tattered fragments of smoke streamed from chimney tops, shredding in the wind, like the gray phantoms of terrible things come to seek revenge for the wicked wrongs that had been practiced.

Sophy pulled herself up sharply. She was being ridiculously fanciful. It was an illusory terror. No shapes of doom, no torture, no punishment, came from the darkness.

The darkness. It was her nemesis. A child's fear. Like the fear of a devil or hobgoblin. Her father thought her fear was something to do with a fertile mind, her mother dying and the war happening, both at a time when she was at an impressionable stage. Whatever it was, she had to overcome it, rout these stupid fears from her mind.

Seth came fully awake within the space of a heartbeat. In the faint yellow glow of the fire, he could make out the quiet, almost regal little figure standing by the window.

All the incipient doubts about allowing Sophy to become involved in the investigation came racing to the foreground. He already had two incidents on his mind that might have been fatal. He could not countenance another.

Ice water spread through his belly. He would have to renege on his promise to Sophy. It was getting harder all the time to thwart her. Come to think of it, having Sophy angry at him might keep her busy scrubbing and polishing, or whatever else she did when she was mad.

What he had to do was keep her busy, out of harm's way. Keep her safe. Give him time to put the puzzle together.

"Sophy?"

She came back to the bed, shivering a little. Seth put his arms around her, drawing her close. His arm brushed against her breast. He forgot what he had intended to say. He couldn't think of the words.

Her cold little toes curled against his calves as she tucked herself against him. A warm feeling rushed over him. Before he could analyze it, she gave a delicious wriggle and all coherent thought left him.

He only wanted to hold her, touch her, kiss her, become drenched in her beauty, lose himself in her softness and scent.

The next time he awoke, it was morning, and he was alone.

Sophy came into the dressing room with less than her usual bounce. She had awoken in a somewhat subdued mood, and the sight of Seth did nothing to elevate her spirits.

It was as if she had gone to bed with one man and woken up with another. He was frowning a little, in obvious agitation.

"Why so serious?" she asked gently.

Seth hesitated. He seemed suddenly even taller, his chest expanding as he drew a deep breath.

"Do you believe in premonitions, Sophy? I do, and I think it would be best if you keep close to the house for a time."

Seth watched her through the corner of his eye. She was wearing a pale lavender silk dress, a delicate thing that didn't hide the willowy shape of her body.

"I believe in what I feel and what happens. I believe in right now, not yesterday. Right now you have windmills in your mind, distorting your thinking. Don't let these stupid suspicions jeopardize both your business and our happiness!" Sophy couldn't keep the shock, and the passionate appeal, from her voice.

What could he say? He wished things could be different. He wished he could give her what she wanted. He whirled to face her, his fist tight on his waistband.

"I've got mysteries and you want miracles!"

"You're going to renege on our bargain, because of a couple of unrelated incidents?" she protested, angered now.

"Sophy, this is a security issue, not a deliberate attempt to back out of our bargain."

A tense, strained silence fell. Seth clenched his right fist, squeezing his fingers tight into his palm. A blue vein was visible in his temple.

"Rubbish!" Sophy snapped. "I will not be fobbed off with fairy tales."

If Sophy continued with her protests, he'd soon resort to lies, and more lies. That, or else be abrupt with her. He shifted a little, and shrugged into a gray gabardine coat.

"I thought I was being practical." She made a wordless noise of disgust, and he went on. "It's hard enough to tackle facts without flying away after theories and fancies. The facts are that there have been two unexplained *incidents* since you became involved in the investigation.''

Seth's words sent a chill down Sophy's back. "You're letting your imagination go too far.''

"Under the circumstances, it's a natural reaction. The less you know, the safer you are.''

There was a pause. "Last night was a misfortunate mishap, that's all. I wasn't even nearby.'' Somehow the words did not seem convincing even to her own ears.

"You don't know a damned thing about men, and how they react when cornered. A hunted man doesn't go to ground like a fox. He lashes out in self-defense. Sometimes uses scare tactics.''

"I know a lot about money. How to make it. How to keep it. How to lose it. I know men who own big companies who can't keep a straight set of books. I can pick an error in the records like a hound picks up the scent of the fox!''

"I'd rather not have to worry about you.''

"And so, out of a misguided sense of protectiveness, you want me confined to the house?''

Her arms were folded, which was not a hopeful sign. His leg hurt. He eased his weight against the dresser. Her eyes shifted around in agitation.

"What would you do if faced with a similar situation?''

"I don't know. It doesn't make any difference. . . .'' She stopped, put off by the echo in her own mind. A Sunday-morning preacher warning about the wicked paths, the evil in the world and the redeeming power of love.

A great love cannot come into fulfillment and peace before it has passed through the heights and the depths of proof, and indeed endured the acid test. It is the little loves which go by merrily, and smoothly.

At the time, the words did not make sense. Now they did. What *was* the best way to help Seth?

"Don't you want to hear what I want, Seth?'' His name was a whispered plea.

"I want to hear, but I don't want to pay the price for it...my peace of mind." He took his weight off the dresser, sighing. "I'm not going to let you goad me into changing my mind, Sophy. Not even negotiate a compromise!"

"Well..." She paused, wondering where to begin. Unspoken, unutterable thoughts raced through her mind.

I know you mean it for the best, and I would gladly obey your orders, if you...

If you love me. Her lips silently formed the words. No. She could never, ever ask him outright. Her back straightened. "You promised me the days." Her voice had lost none of its strength, but there was a hollow inside it, a vulnerability.

He closed the distance between them in a single step, touching her arm gently. "So I did. Tell you what. I'll wait around until the mail arrives. We can check if any fish took the bait from the missives we sent. That way you're still involved."

A soft chuckle issued from her throat. "That's a real relief."

Her voice cracked the shell of his fear. Seth forced a smile, holding the door open, catching the scent of lavender as she stepped into the hallway.

Panache. The single word thrust like a picture plane into his mind. The last place in the world he wanted Sophy snooping on her own was at the factory, where accidents were commonplace at the best of times. He wanted to know where she was. Home. Safe.

An hour or so later, Sophy paced the floor of the library, devising and rejecting options that might crack the armor around Seth's heart. She was going to need a lot of incitement to banish the memory of one or two unfortunate mishaps, to make him laugh again.

Having been up against Seth's implacability before, she decided not to let him provoke her without some return fire.

This would vex him, but sometimes a woman had to put her back to the wall and stand up for what she believed.

This wasn't one of those times, though. She was sure he was mistaken. Seth was becoming obsessed with her safety. He had connected two unrelated events and given each a sinister motive.

Accidents don't mean death....

But they do if they were intended.

Sophy blanched, and a bubble of apprehension lodged in her throat. What about the half-forgotten incident at the tram stop? Had that been a near miss, or a deliberate attempt to push her into the path of the moving vehicle?

This was no charade they were playing. It was reality, and one that could prove to be frightening, and even dangerous at that.

Seth needed her help. She had to get him to change his mind, no matter what subterfuge she used. That forgotten factor still teased her.

Sophy stopped pacing, and cast a speculative look around the room. Planned by William Strickland, the architect who had designed the Merchants' Exchange in Philadelphia, the library was a clever example of Greek Revival style.

Lofty stacks of books, crowned with busts of classic literary figures, rose from the floor to the ceiling, which was arched and painted with a magnificent panorama of biblical figures. A carved, almost life-size likeness of Daniel nestled in one corner, while a desk and globe held court in the center of the room.

Long windows were set with patterns of stained glass, which let in the sunshine and threw a kaleidoscope of color upon the floor. A gallery running around half the room was served by a small, curving staircase, and everywhere there were books.

Books exquisitely bound in tooled leather in soft, warm colors that, blending one into another, seemed to make a pattern for the walls more beautiful than anything that could have been devised by a painter.

Sophy went quickly to one of the tiny alcoves tucked between the rows of books, and dragged out a small wooden ladder. There was not much time.

At the edge of her mind nibbled the sly demons of unease. Undaunted, she ignored them. She was not about to abort her plans because of some idiotic concern about Seth's male outrage at being bested by a woman. He needed a caretaker and she was elected!

Shutting out the vague disquiet, she wrinkled her nose in dismay. She was not very tall, and the top of the ladder looked a long way up.

She heard a quick, uneven tread in the hall and closed her eyes, drawing a deep steadying breath. He was coming! The matter of timing her moves now loomed all-important.

Common sense warned her that even the best-laid plans seldom went exactly right. She pushed aside that unsettling thought and, clenching her teeth, climbed up the small wooden ladder. Even at the top of the ladder she couldn't quite reach the top shelf, so she put one foot up on the spooled railing beside her and stepped onto it.

The door was flung open.

"Where in the devil have you been, Sophy? I've been..."

Sophy let out a discreetly quiet scream, closed her eyes and swayed convincingly.

"Sophy!"

Quick footsteps. Silence. She opened her eyes.

Arms braced on either side of her legs, her husband looked up, a strange smile coming easily to the hard mouth. A smile reminiscent of glittering, secret amusement. It was as if he could read her mind! He tilted his head curiously. His voice was level, baiting.

"What is it that is so important my little wife must risk life and limb to read?" One hand reached up to pluck the leather-bound volume from her nerveless fingers. Gravely, he studied the engraved leather binding.

"Hmm. Mr. Deslandes. *Manhood: the Causes of Its Premature Decline with Directions for Perfect Restora-*

tion.'' He grinned suddenly in open challenge. ''Your taste in literature is execrable, Sophy. I should have thought you would at least be studying some learned text on mathematics, or even John Stuart Mill's *Essays on Marriage and Divorce.*''

His smile sent Sophy's senses spinning. Her toes curled. Warm, sensual, candid, it banished the cynical, hard, tense lines that had made him seem so frightening. He looked, for the first time since she had known him, young and carefree.

Sophy took a deep breath and pulled her scattered wits back into order. She smiled down into his upraised face.

''Such reading is too domesticated. I prefer the tales of Poe. *The Murders in the Rue Morgue* or *The Mystery of Marie Roget!*''

Seth carelessly dropped the book he was holding. ''Such stories of mystery and imagination are dangerous to an inventive mind.'' He eyed the tiny silk-covered foot nearest him. It was under his nose. It was a thousand miles away.

He leaned forward and grasped one slender ankle firmly. His eyes danced in the morning light. ''Are you flirting with me, Sophy?'' His fingers began a slow massage of the sole of her foot.

There was a smothered sound from Sophy. Immediately, she knew he was trying to rile her again. She clung to the rail, and tried to draw her foot out of his grasp.

The firm grip did not loosen. The massage did not falter. She closed her eyes briefly and clenched her teeth to keep from saying what she wanted to say.

The pressure deepened. A wave of pure physical pleasure that had its origins in her toes moved through her. Excitement rippled all along her body in a massive shudder, making her hot, making her weak. Her universe condensed down to a thin corridor where physical sensation was all that mattered.

Seth watched her with unconcealed interest, tenderness in his eyes, in his touch. ''I have a feeling in my bones that, if you ask me nicely, you could let go of that railing and come into my arms!'' Though his insides were jumping, his smile never wavered.

Conscious now of the angle from which he studied her, the way her leg was thrust out in front of him, thinly veiled and plainly visible to the calf, Sophy skewered him with her eyes.

''What do you mean by that?''

Seth stiffened, but the smile stayed at the corners of his lips. The impish, speculative expression in her eyes told Seth that, though she was watching, waiting, poised for attack, she hadn't quite calculated how to outwit him. It was like watching an intelligent, organized butterfly unfolding her wings and getting ready to fly off into the unknown with no thought of potential disaster.

He cocked his head to one side, and his eyes narrowed. Mixed with the air of innocent invitation and soft womanliness was an impudent spirit of mischief. She had deliberately challenged him, and his instincts prompted him to accept. He was under no illusions about her determination to change his edict.

Unless he disarmed her first. Directed all that hidden fire and seething passion where it should be. In a bed. His bed. It would be most effective for him to take the offense.

Seth released his hold on her and stood back, the barrier of his arms removed, his voice taunting. ''All you have to do is ask.''

The words were soft but Sophy heard the ghost of an indulgent smile. Alert to the new and perhaps dangerous element in the atmosphere, she glanced down at him in quick assessment. He made her wary. Just his touch made her body sizzle, and her mind vaporize.

''Don't be daft.'' She emitted an aggravated little sound, and put one foot on the ladder.

It tilted precariously. Seth swore softly, something harsh and violent. Off-balance, Sophy clutched blindly at the rail for support. One little foot flew sideways. Time hung suspended for a moment before she tumbled into his arms.

Together they crashed to the floor. She landed on top of him, her head on his breast, one leg sprawled across his thighs. She blinked, dazed. It was as if she had struck a wall.

She could smell the fragrance of him. A faint essence of shaving soap, a hint of a clean, manly scent. Her pulses leaped when she heard a quick intake of breath, then felt his arms tighten convulsively around her.

His mouth was very close, his breath moving the little tendrils of her hair that had escaped their pins. He was warm and hard, and strangely compelling. She felt the taut strength in his arms and knew a sense of satisfaction. Soundless tremors racked the tensile muscles of his body. She gave an experimental wriggle. More tremors, stronger this time.

Slowly, with the most indescribably wanton sensation, Sophy brought her hands up between them, then let one hand slide down the inside of his leg. Hands of iron crushed her against his muscular body, and he buried his face in her tousled hair. His maleness rose between them, hot, hard, insistent. A suppressed sound caught in his throat.

Involuntarily Sophy's toes curled into the material of the carpet as a warm, twisting sensation began to invade her limbs. She had never felt so helpless, so lacking in control.

The wild clamor of her body was indecent. Tremulous with her own desire, she pressed herself to him, all of her, molding her young body to his hard frame in wild, impassioned invitation, a soft battering ram against his hips.

She heard him groan deep in his chest when her movements brought the juncture of her thighs in contact with the rock-hard pulsing power of his manhood. His breath beat fast and warm upon her face, and she found herself longing to touch him with an eagerness that shocked her.

Sophy's heart was fluttering, her fingers faintly unsteady as her hand crept up to explore the throbbing source of his potency. He shuddered convulsively at her touch.

She was horrified at her wanton behavior, the overpowering need to touch him, the pleasurable sensations running through her fingers. It was daytime. They were in the library! Her heart skipped a beat, and her eyelids trembled as she kept them shut.

Suddenly, Seth rolled over, pinning her to the floor, his knee between hers, her skirt bunching between them. He straddled her, grabbing both wrists in one hand and pulling them over her head to keep her from tormenting his fiercely burning crotch.

The fingers of his other hand flipped buttons, loops and drawstrings, laying her open to his avid eyes. He sucked in his breath, his common sense and his desire in conflict.

"Sophy."

All the agony of his thrumming senses was projected in that single word. Seth's free hand moved round the soft underswell of her breasts, slid over her ribs, caressed her hip, drifted down the little angle between her belly and the curve of her hip.

His touch, as delicate as a butterfly's, as light as down, trailed in sweet vengeance over her inner thigh to the warm, wet cay of her femininity.

Sophy heard an uneven whimper, and realized it came from herself. He released her hands, allowing her to wrap her fingers in his hair, instinctively pulling him to her, unable to resist.

Seth covered her open mouth with his, aware of an explosive need rising in him. When he pushed her clothes aside and lowered his face to her breasts, a rasping sigh escaped her.

His lips touched one dusky tip gently, and his tongue swirled about it caressingly. Her entire being quivered in response as his teeth nibbled gently. There was no way he could prevent his hand finding the damp, secret core of her, pressing gently with his palm.

Totally unprepared for the flood of emotions that washed over her, Sophy stiffened, vaguely aware of some new, vital want. His palm rocked back to the heel of his hand. Her mind was reeling, her insides quivering. The sensation of fire lapping along her flesh washed over her. A fire that promised to build and build.

Her hips arched into his touch with an urgency all of their own. He kept up the motion. The knot of tension within her was growing to an intolerable degree of intensity. Her breath caught. There was a roaring in her ears, an ache deep inside her, and she felt a sweet, sweet dizziness as she hovered on the brink of a deep, all-consuming void.

Unable to bear the engulfing excitement, she jerked away from his touch, with a slight moan. "Seth!" There was a plea in her voice.

His hand stopped, but his voice was ragged, laced with desire.

"Say it, Sophy. Say it!"

She didn't know what he wanted her to say. All she knew was that she wanted him, all of him, so badly that she was almost in tears.

"Seth!" Her voice was a ragged whisper.

He gave no quarter. The pressure of his hand began again, became more insistent. His mouth tugged and sucked at the hard little berries crowning her breasts. The soft, moist and warm feminine scent of her filled his mind. He felt ready to erupt.

Sexual climax burst upon Sophy, like shimmering light, in strong, rhythmic spasms, totally shocking and magnificent, and she quaked again and again in the aftermath, stunned by the shattering sensation.

Seth watched her, face tightly drawn, raw masculine hunger etched on his features. He knew that he had never in his life wanted a woman as badly as he wanted this one. The smoldering fire in him flamed. He pressed into her, closing his eyes and shuddering fiercely as his hands reached for his trousers to free himself.

There was the sound of the door being opened, followed by the harsh inhalation of breath as three women demonstrated their intense horror.

Seth's eyes came open.

Sophy's long dark hair cascaded freely in wild disarray over the carpet. Her hand lay limp, the fingers curled into themselves.

Beyond her tumbled hair, he saw the door. A jolt went through him. Aunt Ella, Tessa Fraser and *his mother* stood transfixed at the scene of total decadence being enacted on the library floor. There was a charged silence. Seth sucked in his breath.

"Mother! What are you doing here?"

At sixty-two, sparrow-thin Agnes Weston still stood straight as a spruce. Her figure, clad in strident magenta velvet and a heavy plaid shawl, remained amazingly supple. Her piercing blue eyes shone as bright and clear as the sky on a summer's day, and only a few gray strands were visible amid the dark hair piled fashionably on top of her head. She looked down with sharp interest.

"I decided it was time to inspect my new daughter-in-law. To see what sort of woman managed to get my ever so responsible son's thoughts out of his head into his pants." Her voice was harsh, metallic. "I haven't superhuman patience, even if you have. I want grandchildren."

The edge of Seth's mouth hardened ominously as he slowly sat up. The ignominy of his position, a position due to his own carelessness, bit deeply into him. Both as a man and a lover he had failed Sophy utterly.

There was a flash of sympathetic amusement in his mother's extraordinary eyes when she turned her attention to the woman still sprawled on the carpet.

"I'm pleased you married someone with enough sass not to bore you out of your brain, and bright enough to know how to give me a grandchild. I expected one of those silly young virgins who's scared of her own shadow."

Although the words were pungent, her tone was matter-of-fact. She might have been discussing the weather.

Partially shielded by Seth's big body, Sophy willed herself to stop shaking. The wickedness of it! Making love in the daytime, *and* on the library floor! She hadn't meant for this to happen. She'd only meant to tease him, keep him home, where he'd be safe!

The scandal of it! Yet the wild and delicious delight still enveloped her. She gave a tiny, strangled sound.

Seth could feel the ragged tremble of her breath vibrating against the hollow of his throat, smell the hot woman-scent of her. She was quivering in his hold. A tiny wave of compassion washed over him, to be immediately swamped by a more powerful surge of emotion, one of pure male satisfaction. She was his!

Over to you, Sophy Weston. Challenge a war veteran, would you? See if you can wriggle your way out of this one.

Still bound in the iron chains of desire, he rose to his feet, went to his mother, squeezed her shoulder affectionately and kissed her cheek. He did not need to stoop. She was as tall as he. Their eyes cleaved together for a long moment. There was an indigo glitter in his eyes, and his features were very, very taut.

"There's no hurry." Seth's voice had an edge of passion that he did not attempt to conceal.

Agnes Weston's eyes twinkled with distinct humor. She held up a warning finger. "You're thirty. You've waited too long already."

Ella's face was turning a mottled color. Torn between shocked indignation at her niece's improper behavior, and relief that Seth's mother seemed to approve of her son's marriage, hands fluttering helplessly, she stiffened herself abruptly, and her voice came sharply.

"Do get up, Sophy!"

Tessa closed her eyes against the indignity of it all.

Embarrassed at her undignified condition, furious with herself for having instigated it, Sophy scrambled to her feet, a tumble of hair and elfin wantonness. Pride alone kept her head up. Everything, to her dazed eyes, was a blur, a sea of faces lost in a wavering haze of mortification.

Shaken to the core of her being, she clutched the edges of her bodice together, and returned her mother-in-law's gaze haughtily. She had to preserve her composure, and some semblance of dignity. The moment seemed to stretch into eternity.

Agnes Weston seemed to be measuring her as an opponent. The old woman's eyelids fell and rose again as she raked Sophy from head to foot, with a slow movement like a parrot's.

"You are a strange young woman. I think we will have no illusions about this. I will not say I like you particularly, but you seem to be honest in your approach to my son, so I'm sure we shall deal very well together."

Sophy inhaled with shaky relief as she heard Seth's voice, telling her to turn around. She turned to him, defenseless, like a caught hare. For the first time, her poise wavered.

Seth touched her crimson cheek gently. "Code number one. Lock the door!" His fingers rapidly adjusted her clothing as he spoke.

Sophy backed away from him, her slim figure unyielding. She could feel the anger brewing in her, like the wind gathering force and building to a hurricane. Her voice had no volume, but it was full of violence.

"You're quite abominable!"

Seth smiled sardonically, enjoying again the fury and elemental excitement that gleamed from the enormous storm gray pools of her eyes, recognizing the rich promise of hidden passion in the taut hostile body.

Life with Sophy was nothing if not unpredictable. Her momentary appearance of defenselessness had been an illusion. His elfin wife would never be defenseless.

With her chin angled defiantly, her shoulders straight, small hands fisted at her sides, face flushed and vivid, she was a creature of mystery and fire, ever reckless, ever certain of herself, ever extraordinary. He could not contemplate life without her. He made a movement toward her, but she backed away, avoiding his outstretched hand.

"Pax, Sophy?" Seth invited with a small secret smile, holding the new awareness to himself.

Sophy stared at him a moment, her lips pressed tightly together. A wave of heat swept over her as indignation flared. The world condensed. All else became blurred, everything except Seth's dark face. She drew a long breath.

"You're making a lot of assumptions, Seth Weston." Her lips hardly moved as she spoke. "Didn't the army ever teach you the ground rules of war? Honor is never satisfied until there is unconditional surrender by one of the combatants."

She picked up the flounced train of her skirt, flung it over her arm and strode out of the room.

Chapter Nine

Hours later Sophy sat, straight backed, staring at herself in the long panel mirror. The sweet face of the woman reflected there looked troubled. The ivory-and-silver comb, brush and hand mirror set her father had given her for her fifteenth birthday glinted in the gaslight.

Thoughts swirled around in her head, as the leaves did in an autumn wind. Her withdrawal from the library had been ignominious, to say the least. She had shot to her bedroom like a rabbit into a burrow, in what was a full-scale retreat in the face of a superior enemy force.

Knuckles white, she savagely anchored her braids with two bone hairpins. Hooker could scarcely have felt more frustrated when he failed to capture Fredericksburg!

Sophy shook her head, trying to harness her mind, to think coherently. Really, there was nothing to get embarrassed about. After all, she and Seth were husband and wife. They had every right to distract themselves in their own library.

In truth, marriage was an adventure, one way or another!

Through a mouthful of pins she managed to enunciate clearly, "Make sure that Mrs. Weston has a pot of hot chocolate when she retires. Even though she rested this afternoon, we will have an early night. At her age, and having so recently been ill, the rail journey from Chicago must have been totally exhausting."

"How long is she to stay?" Tessa Fraser moved around the room, picking up Sophy's discarded clothing.

Sophy dug into a small French box of fragrant, inlaid wood, which held her hair ribbons, curled into obedient circles.

"I don't know. She couldn't come to the wedding because of a fever. That's why Seth left immediately after the ceremony. The doctor feared it might be typhus." She knotted a thin scarlet ribbon to her coiffure.

Tessa folded a jacket and placed it in an old Dutch chest, inside which lay other garments, lavender sprinkled among their folds.

"Cook mentioned that there's been an outbreak of typhus in Water Street."

"It doesn't surprise me. The housing conditions in the tenement buildings are appalling. Seth has been appointed to a committee to address the lack of even basic facilities, such as fire escapes."

"Yon man has a conscience. Happy, my pet?"

Sophy nodded her satisfaction. "Oh, yes, Tessa. Marriage is most agreeable."

"Dinna get all starry-eyed, now. Just because a man is willing to dally with a woman when they're first wed, doesn't mean he'll love ye forever. Men have important things to do."

"Oh, Tessa! You Scots are so romantic! Seth doesn't even love me yet, but he will."

"I wouldna want ye to be hurt or disappointed, lass. Love is not always necessary in a marriage. There are other things . . . duty, devotion, children. . . ."

There was a squawk like an angry parrot. The shadows on the face in the mirror changed position.

Sophy swiveled her head around. Her old nursemaid held up a short, lightly boned corset.

"Mercy! Ye'll never be going downstairs without wearing your stays, lass!"

"Truthfully, Tessa, what difference do they make? How could anyone know I wasn't wearing that uncomfortable monstrosity?"

Sophy straightened up, standing arms akimbo, the folds of her gown falling gracefully about her. Her eyes danced, and her voice quivered with amusement.

The high-buttoned, long-sleeved dress of black silk with its double skirt, pleating and rosettes of the same material, narrow scarlet satin banding and belt, was a model of decorum. Her scant figure did not by any stretch of the imagination require either restraint or support.

Lips pursed, Tessa ignored the provocative words, and avoided a direct answer, but her disapproval could not be contained. "There's things that are right and things that are wrong." Mouth set, she folded the offending garment and thrust it into a drawer.

Two dimples appeared in Sophy's cheeks. She'd known Tessa too long not to know that a fit of the sullens invariably lasted but a short time. The drawer slammed shut. Her grin widened.

"How very reassuring to know that wearing stays is one of them!" Without waiting for a reply, she left the room.

Dinner was served promptly at six.

Seth and his mother were standing by the fireplace when Sophy made her appearance. From the dining room ceiling, elaborate gas fixtures spouted like inverted fountains. Their handsomely etched, amber-hued glass shades created a subdued radiance, and cast fleeting miniature rainbows upon the shining array of silver adorning the table.

Sophy's heart gave a queer little jump at the sight of Seth. How handsome and vital he was in the formal evening dress, which set off his smooth skin, neatly trimmed sideburns and brilliant eyes. As she advanced toward him, he gave a little bow.

"You look very fetching, my dear. Do I recognize another Weston's fabric? Yes? I like it." His comprehensive glance was at once a caressing appraisal and a challenge.

Sophy had the uncomfortable feeling that he was flirting with her. There was a note in his voice that sent a slow tremor through her. In front of his mother, too! For the sake of convention, she realized she should speak, but she knew that any words she uttered would be inane and meaningless.

For a split second their eyes locked, and it was as if sparks flew from the magnetic contact. She felt her heart beating hard. Just looking at him produced the same sensations as when he had touched her in the library. He knew it, too!

Ignoring the glint in his eyes, she merely nodded in agreement. Acknowledging her mother-in-law with the same smiling inclination of the head, she tugged the bellpull.

Mrs. Weston said nothing, merely stood waiting, but the soft sibilant sound of her breath exhaling was like a shudder. Seth gave her a thoughtful glance, and put his hand to her face.

"An early night for you, Mother. I might even get Dr. Bailey to call in tomorrow. That chest infection is far from cured. Shall we be seated?"

The new cook had outdone himself. Oyster soup, luscious beyond description, was followed by an exquisite bisque of crayfish and a *casserole de poussin,* chicken prepared with green olives, almonds, peppers and saffron. Apple cobbler and a fascinating dessert of fruit sorbet and whipped ice cream completed the meal.

Distracted partly by the domestic chatter of the women assembled at the dining table, and partly by his inner tension, Seth ate the meal with less than his usual enjoyment. His leg ached. It had just begun to be manageable. He must have hurt it today with his tomfoolery.

He sat there, allowing a little wave of fatigue to claim him for a moment, and tried to rub his leg so neither woman would notice. The pain was making it difficult for him to concentrate.

It was a relief to relax, letting the women's inconsequential conversation drift over him, the appalling price of French lace, the virtues of Mrs. Beeton's *Household Management,* the best way to make mulled wine, losing himself in the sounds of their voices.

Lulled by the hypnotic pull of Sophy's seductively sweet voice, he was idly making a swirl in his ice cream with a spoon when the import of what she was saying penetrated the soothing trance.

His spoon stopped its aimless circle.

"You think what?" There was thunder in his voice. He sat perfectly still, but a pulse beat rapidly in the side of his neck.

A charged silence invaded the dining room. The fierce look in his eyes filled Sophy with apprehension. She blinked at him. All signs of tolerant amusement had fled. What could have upset him?

Color invaded her smooth features and crept along her cheekbones. "I think Charles Lethbridge is being blackmailed."

"Is this your idea of a joke, Sophy? If so, I do not find it amusing."

Seth almost audibly ground his teeth, the authoritative thrust of his jaw and clean, strong bones of his face emphasized by the stiffly starched, upright collar of his white shirt.

"You are serious, aren't you?" Sophy's slight breast heaved, and she nodded. She was in earnest, and not, as he had suspected, merely bent on goading him. "Who would blackmail Charles? And for what?"

The glinting glance that accompanied this question made Sophy's insides clench. "I don't know."

Seth muttered in annoyance. "Damn it, your imagination runs wild. Charles is as straight as a die. What makes you think otherwise?"

Sophy's head moved defensively. Unwilling to get into an argument, she avoided a direct answer.

Instead, she said as calmly as she could, "I do know he's always around when something happens. And he gambles..." Her voice faltered, and her words trailed off.

"Just because a man has a flutter on the cards does not mean he is either an embezzler or a potential murderer! Don't run around with your idle accusations."

"Why? If they *are* idle, what do we have to fear?" A muscle clenched in his jaw, but his expression was impossible to read. Sophy clasped her fingers in her lap to keep them from shaking. "Anyway, I wasn't accusing Charles of anything. I'm simply looking for clues. Abigail is a chatterbox."

For a split second Sophy caught his look of agreement, before white teeth clamped over the corner of his lower lip. Encouraged, she leaned forward, her lovely violet-gray eyes shining, the words spilling out of her lips.

"She's also a lamb when it comes to being fleeced by anyone from the butcher to the baker, and anyone in between. I'm going to take her under my wing and teach her a thing or two about handling household finance."

Seth was taken aback. The suggestion was a good one. Sophy drove a shrewd bargain. Then he remembered Abigail's seemingly constant tears, which vexed him like the humming of an insect. His jaw gripped tightly.

"Hell, Sophy. You can only cause trouble between Charles and Abigail if you poke your nose into their private affairs!"

Mrs. Weston wiped her face with a napkin. "Sophy's idea that she become friends with Abigail Lethbridge is sound. It is amazing how much information can be gleaned in social chitchat without asking questions!"

A cool wind blew through his brain. How the devil had Sophy won his mother over in such a short time? Agnes Weston was protecting Sophy like a mother hen with only one chick. Maybe it went with the species. Wives, witches, pixies, elves and assorted mischief makers. He forced himself to relax his clenched jaw.

"Thank you for your advice, Mother." The spoon went back to its slow swirl.

Sophy gave Agnes Weston a grateful smile, then cast a pleading glance at him. "Last night I realized we have somehow missed something elementary in our investigation. There's a piece missing that I'm convinced is the key to it all. I had meant to consult with you this morning. As you are aware, I was distracted."

This was a much more successful shaft. The disarming confession was an unwitting, very feminine sort of seduction. Seth began to realize that in his diminutive wife, he had found an opponent to be reckoned with.

"I daresay you could be forgiven for failing to mention the matter in the heat of the moment!"

He gave her a long, brooding stare. It was hard to resist the appeal in her expressive eyes, or the temptation in her soft parted lips. His body had already gone thick and excited.

The ice cream was reduced to a mass of melted pulp. A servant removed the mutilated dessert, and replaced it with a half bottle of bourbon and a plate of curious little sugar-frosted cakes. The look of a boy eyeing an unexpected treat crossed Seth's face.

Sophy put her small hand to her mouth to stifle her laughter. She felt an almost overwhelming urge to reach out and touch him. A bubble of mirth rose to her throat, as her sense of humor betrayed her. She lowered her hand.

"They're called *gemaakt van suiker*, angels' food. The adage goes something like this—*Man did eat angels' food....*"

Inwardly relieved at her sudden change of mood, Seth gladly entered her game and sought the answer to her riddle. He arched one brow, took a cake and bit into it with his strong white teeth.

Sophy flashed him a mischievous grin. His eyes blinked. He paused in midbite, and grinned around the cake. Swallowing the delicious morsel, he completed the quotation. His voice held pure satisfaction. "—*So did they eat, and were well filled: for He gave them their own desire.*"

Sophy did not even realize she had been holding her breath until he spoke. The sudden exhalation of suppressed air surprised her.

A footman was removing the remains of the meal, while the butler directed another to draw the yellow velvet draperies against the window. Mrs. Weston caught her breath, and coughed. Suddenly exhausted, she stifled a yawn.

"If you pair of lovebirds don't mind, I am going off to bed. It's been a long day."

Seth released Sophy's hand and walked his mother to the door. The greenish gaslight from the wall sconces accented the strong bones of her thin face, and the fatigue that pinched her face and shadowed her eyes. He kissed her on the cheek.

"Have a care, Mother. Else you will not get to see those grandchildren you keep commanding me to provide." His voice was a whisper.

Agnes Weston let her hand drift across her son's dark hair, her face soft. "Make them sons, with their father's courage and their mother's winsome ways."

Sophy waited until he was reseated, his injured leg resting on a fringed stool by the fireplace, before she asked, "Did you remember to bring home the designs?"

Amusement lit his eyes. She was like a small terrier, not about to release the bone. They had been married only a month, but already she had left an indelible mark on him.

Sophy had breezily entered his life and turned his staid existence upside down. Wonderfully organized, efficient and bright, within days she had the household running like clockwork.

He was pleased and interested that she took an interest in his work. She had a flair for business, and he had begun to involve her in a couple of special projects.

A man learned a lot about a woman given a month. She was warm, charming and blessed with an inner passion that brought fire to their marriage bed. A tiny smile played around his lips. He also knew she was scared of the dark, that she loved ice cream, and was as stubborn as a mule.

True, he argued with her frequently, occasionally growled impatiently when he was in pain, and sometimes he snapped when she overstepped even the wide bounds he had indulgently allowed her. But he never really got angry with her.

Not even now.

She moved her head as if in protest at his probing scrutiny, and her face went from light to shadow. He was left with an image, a wisp of spirit, not in the mockery of a coquette, but in the enigma of a mystery he could not fathom.

He nodded in assent. "I have been gathering documents like a bee gathers pollen."

Surrendering to the peculiar craving inside her, Sophy impulsively laid a hand on his wrist where it rested on his thigh. A strange thrill ran through her, and she could see him bite his underlip.

He did not move his hand, but his eyes sought hers. She smiled slowly, a little shyly. A silent message passed between them. *A man's needs are sometimes bigger than his common sense.*

Sophy's touch had a tightening effect on Seth's already simmering desire. The deep, thrumming need inside him was painfully strong, and he didn't seem able to suppress it.

Even the pain in his thigh intensified. Tension. Pure, unadulterated tension. His hand turned, and his long strong-boned fingers lightly closed over hers.

Sophy tilted her head to one side. Her fingers felt crushed in the warm pressure of his touch. She made a slight effort to withdraw her hand, but it was held too firmly. She left it there.

"St. Nicholas Hotel will be ideal for a launch of the new fabrics. I asked Richard to book the ballroom for the event," Sophy said matter-of-factly.

As Seth had already broached the idea of a large-scale launch of the latest range of Indian-style patterns with his merchants, this revelation failed to pierce his armor. He watched his wife a moment in silence, his blue eyes narrowed.

"The Astoria."

"I beg your pardon?"

"We'll have the ball at the Astoria. If you're going to take over Weston's Textiles, we may as well do it in style."

"I'm not trying to take over your company, Seth. Only help out where I can."

He was beginning to circle his thumb in the hollow of her palm, a subtly erotic caress that sent tremors flying along her nerves. She was horrified by the pleasurable sensations running through her. Could he feel her quickened pulse?

"Then check with me from time to time, will you, Sophy? It might save you making foolish assumptions, and will create the illusion that I'm still in charge."

The shock of his feelings on her attempts to help startled Sophy. Her fingers curled protectively into themselves as she snatched her hand away. She gave him a straight look.

"I don't play games, or make foolish assumptions, Seth. I have a good head for business. I also have a maxim. There is no comparison between that which is lost by not succeeding and that which is lost by not trying."

Seth detected the iron determination beneath the gentleness of her voice. Yet, because he had dined so well and didn't really have the will to argue, her presumption only amused him.

He smiled indulgently, and made no further comment.

By the time she entered her room, Sophy was decidedly out of charity with herself. Tension and tumult both still coursed through her, having been released in enormous quantities by the stress of the day.

Husbands did that to one. Just living with a man bred uncertainty. And uncertainty led to ill temper. She paced the bedroom, her arms folded under her breasts.

I love you.... In what foolish daydream had she ever imagined Seth Weston would say words like that to her? Love was not a little cake to be cut up to suit their appetites.

Neither of them had any illusions about this marriage. It was simply an arrangement. They had made a bargain. Before her marriage, Sophy had not aspired to love. Just a measure of freedom. To live her life as *she* willed, and not beneath the domineering rule of some man.

Now she was caught in a net, and did not even wish to escape.

Sophy bit her lip, experiencing a surge of nervous tension that almost broke her resolve. It was impossible to relax. Something inside her was bubbling with unnatural energy.

She was his wife, after all, and she had not been forced into marrying him. Most women had little say in the choice of husband. She must not let emotion blind her to what must be done. As her father had often pointed out to her, nothing ventured, nothing gained.

Seth was kind and that gave her a kernel of hope. He was in pain and that gave her a chance of helping him. She had a job to do, and she had to do it without letting petty emotion get in her way. After all, affections could not be stolen, they must be given freely.

Right now, the only thing that mattered was to ease his pain. She really had no choice, and it was this that brought her here to his door. Pressing her hands together, she straightened her shoulders and stepped into his bedroom.

He lay there, his long frame stretched naked on the bed. Strain and pain had sharpened the angles of his face and pulled the skin tightly over them.

The light from the wall sconce spilled over his rippling muscles, outlining his body so he resembled a jungle cat, lithe and masculine. And infinitely more dangerous. Yet his face was all angles and shadows. He was palpably disconcerted to see her there, inspecting him.

She took a step toward him.

Through her lowered eyelashes, Sophy could see the fine dusky hair that powdered his chest tapering to disappear under the cloth he had draped over that shocking, strong, vital, pulsating part of himself. His hips, solid and trim, supported by a mound of pillows, were thrust upward in a long-limbed sprawl. He was rubbing his wounded thigh.

Seth's eyes flickered over Sophy. The screen of her lashes hid her eyes. One of the frilled edges of her peignoir had slipped off the curve of her shoulder. A shining silver pendant gleamed between her breasts. Her skin had a more subtle sheen than the lace-edged satin shaped to the curves of her breasts.

Her hair, her eyelids, the tip of her tongue just peeking from between her lips all invited his touch. His loins ignited. He wanted her. But his pain was stronger than the impulse that compelled him.

Swiftly masking his instinctive reaction, he instilled a harsh note of impatience in his voice. "I'm sorry, but I don't feel like hand-to-hand combat tonight, Sophy."

Sensing the unusual fatigue in him, Sophy regarded him intently. A frown pleated her brows as she noticed the pinched lines at the corners of his eyes, the tired droop of his mouth. She supposed even experienced assault commanders got tired occasionally.

Deliberately, she summoned up a determined casualness.

"Don't be such a grumpy old curmudgeon, Seth. You won't get rid of me by being ungracious."

Seth gave her a blazing blue glare. Sophy ignored him. She walked right up to the edge of the bed, and gave him back glare for glare.

"I know a lot of men get vile-tempered and sharp-tongued when in pain, but being disagreeable does not help." Her voice was husky, despite her resolutions, and her fingers were digging into her palms.

Silence stretched tautly between them. Had she gone too far? Wasn't he going to say anything?

"You surprise me." He swung his legs to the ground, leaning with one hand against the carved bedstead for balance. Pent-up pain was inside him, burning away, shortening the fuse of his temper. He shook his head from side to side.

There was passion there, too. He wanted to crush his mouth on hers, feel her body close to his. She ought to be in his arms, arching and writhing with the uninhibited sensuality underlying the calm self-possession of her manner in public.

A jolt of pain shook his hard frame, nearly shattering his carefully honed self-control. His hands shaped the edge of the bed as the pain in his leg intensified. His face contorted with agony.

Sophy noted the hard thrust of his jaw, the way his knuckles showed white as he gripped the bedstead. She almost reached out to touch his hair, perhaps to rub his neck. Nettled, she thrust her hands behind her back. She stood there blinking at him, suddenly aware of the sleek and bulging biceps that paralleled her head, the pulse beat of his throat. The recognition sent a tiny jolt through her.

He growled something low and impatient, then ground out in a deep, dark voice, "Next thing you'll be telling me you know just the panacea. Save yourself the effort, Sophy. Pain takes precedence over everything, even sexual attraction."

He knew all about it. Pain was scarlet and jagged and edged with fire. Pain was something one watched from a very great distance, and even admired for its perfect hideousness. But one did not mock it. Not after so long in its company.

Sophy swallowed her growing compassion, and forced her eyes up. He was staring at her, his face hostile. His piercing stare seemed to reach out and touch her. She had hit a core of some deep emotion. His eyes flashed blue fire as his jaw tightened.

She studied the curve of muscle on his chest and ribs, the dark coins of his nipples, the jagged purple streak staining the gilded gleam of his thigh, trembling now in spasmodic cramps, the muscles jumping out of control under the sheath of his skin. Her mind slowly probed the problem till an idea crystallized and took shape.

Without a word, she swung on the balls of her feet and walked out. Seth struggled to his feet, falling back onto the bed as his leg crumpled.

A flash of agony sent spasms through his frame, and the veins stood out on the sides of his temples. He made a quick violent motion with his head. To hell with it! To hell with everything!

Before he had finished cursing, Sophy had returned, carrying a laden enamel tray. She set it down with a sudden air of determination.

"I'm not precisely experienced in the act of kneading muscles to stimulate circulation and relieve strain and tension, but I have heard that it is most beneficial for withered limbs. I would imagine that it would be quite comforting for wounds such as yours." Sophy sat on the edge of the bed, offering him a cup of steaming liquid. "Drink this."

The last words came out in a suspiciously neutral tone, and Seth looked at the cup warily. He took a long breath, and raised a speculative eyebrow at her.

"Not trying to do me in, Sophy?" The words were deliberate, but whispered so softly that his voice was scarcely audible.

There was an uncomfortable sensation at the back of Sophy's throat as she met his cool, assessing glance. It seemed as if the flesh of his face were carved out of granite. Her cheeks glowed pink. She wet her lips, and shook her head curtly.

"No, it is only a simple tisane. A paregoric to soothe the nerves. A mix of dandelion leaves and poppy seeds. It's quite harmless."

Seth's gaze rested on her in musing silence for a long moment, as if trying to make up his mind about something. Then he lifted one shoulder indifferently, and held out his hand. Propped on one elbow, he obediently drank the cup of bitter liquid, feeling it warm his throat and chest.

When Sophy removed the cup from his fingers, he rolled over on his back. Her heart was fluttering, her fingers faintly unsteady as she placed the empty glass on the table. Her whole being was concentrated on Seth.

He lay perfectly still, watching the silver pendant swing back and forth, and allowed her to do as she willed. His face glistened now with a thin film of moisture.

Sophy opened the stopper and poured a small amount of the aromatic liquid in little streaks along his injured thigh. His firm muscles rippled beneath her touch. He lay with one arm flung behind him, his wrist resting on his forehead. Like a beautiful pagan effigy stretched on the bed, all sinful temptation.

Impassively, she began to smooth the oil lightly over the hard knotted muscle and scar tissue. His face never changed, but yet she felt his intensity, his active acceptance of the agony this must cause. She bent, moving her fingers up and down his thigh. It was like trying to catch an eel with your fingers, she decided, feeling the heavy muscles stretch and retract under her ministrations. They were their own universe.

Beneath Sophy's probing fingers, the tight muscles of Seth's leg began to relax and the pain eased from his body. She continued to stroke outward, exerting slow pressure, gently rubbing and patting the injured tissue. His whole being seemed to focus and fuse into her touch. The silver pendant swung like a pendulum, spinning in time to the movement of her magical fingers.

Seth shuddered as if with the ague. His chest heaved. Pain was all-pervading. It rode his thigh like an expectant predator. With a muffled groan, he acknowledged the victory. A sane, sensible part of him told him to stop her. But when he tried to move, nothing happened. It was as if his body were no longer obeying his brain.

Bereft of coherent thought and reason, he could not think, just feel. He focused on the gently swinging pendant. It was right in front of him. A blur of silver. It made him feel apart, independent, free.

His body was invaded with a sweet lethargy that was shot through with red threads of anticipation. His mind had suddenly become an immense vacuum that seemed to be filling with flood after flood of hot blood, which raced from his head down to his thighs.

Sophy's fingers continued their stroking, softly but insistently. A muscle high up in Seth's thigh jumped and she gasped. The subtle scent of the sandalwood oil mixed with the hot, masculine smell of his hair-roughened skin invaded her nostrils.

Breath caught in her throat. Her lips parted a little, but she worked on and on with agonizing slowness. The tips of her fingers were numb when, at last, he shuddered convulsively and gave a fierce, startled cry that seemed to rip through his entire body.

She looked at her husband, and all the love she felt for him rose in her in a single wave. His features were somehow different from what they had been earlier, calm and serene. His eyes glittered like glass, quite opaque, from another world entirely.

Within moments, he was in a sound sleep. She was pleased that somehow she had helped to dissipate the demon of pain that had been planted in him. To undo was far more difficult than to do.

The silver pendant was the key. Shimmering, glittering, vibrating, it lured Seth's pulsating senses into uncharted realms. Of reality and illusion. Of dreams and fantasies. Seth felt as if he were sinking into a visceral microcosm, where nothing but carnality mattered.

With each shiny swing of the pendant, new energy seemed to pulse through him. He was rushing toward some unknown destination. His heart pounded. The pumping blood sounded in his ears. He started to feel dizzy. He could only watch the pendant, and let his mind flow like a river to its source.

In his mind's eye he rearranged Sophy's ministrations. He felt the palms of Sophy's hands, her fingers sliding over his flesh. He saw the fierceness in her face, the determination. Lightly, with just one oil-slick finger, she traced a line from his throat, over the soft dusky hair of his chest to his tapering midsection, down over his belly, until she reached the top of the cloth. His body strained up, rigid.

The fabric moved restlessly. It seemed to have a life of its own. His desire was a tangible entity, which was both disturbing and exciting. In his illusion, her fingers trailed the line of his scar, slid with satin softness under the cloth. Her fingers closed around him intimately, warm and caressing. His body trembled.

Of their own volition, his hips pressed forward, and his head arched back. Each breath was an effort. He heard himself gasp for air, the sound raw, shaky. He convulsed upward like a rearing stallion, bucking into the heat of her firm rhythmic strokes. Unbearable pleasure washed over him, as, with a harsh rush of air, his senses claimed victory, and his body exploded in spasms of white-hot flame.

Chapter Ten

As Seth passed the big grandfather clock on the staircase, it chimed nine o'clock. Sophy's influence was unmistakable, he noted with amusement. A bevy of bright-cheeked maidservants in print dresses, neat little caps and frilly white aprons were busy with domestic chores, polishing, scrubbing and dusting.

The girls were all too well trained to stare, but Seth knew they peeped at him as he passed through the hall to his study. He acknowledged their surprise with a whimsical smile.

It was not often that they were rewarded with a view of the master of the house descending the stairs at this late hour of the morning. Punctilious to a fault, Seth Weston kept to the Spartan discipline acquired in the army.

An early riser, he would normally have departed on business several hours ago. This morning he had woken late, illogically disappointed to find himself alone.

Fleeting recollections of the previous night unsettled him. The movement of Sophy's pendant had set the lights flickering madly. Her face above him had swung crazily, her eyes clear and so deep that they seemed to go on forever.

Last night, Sophy had offered comfort and practical assistance. Her touch had been gentle and soothing. His agony had merged into desire the minute she touched him.

Never had his body reacted with such instinctive passion, such overwhelming release.

Today, he walked stiff legged, and somewhat awkwardly, true, but strangely sure of his balance. The immediate sensation was one of enormous freedom. He felt healed and renewed. Energy tingled his flesh. Today, he was uneasily conscious of an obligation.

Through the welter of sensations that he had experienced since his first meeting with Sophy, both physical and mental, he suddenly realized that everything about his relationship with her took on overtones of chance.

Looking back, it was chance that they should marry. Having married, it was inevitably chance that his bride was a loving and generous woman who threw herself into every project she undertook with unbounded optimism and enthusiasm.

Sophy could be downright single-minded when she decided what she wanted. It seemed he had become top priority on her project list. She was just waiting for a chance to ambush him.

The dangerous part was that he was enjoying the anticipation, and had every intention of letting her succeed. Her talents could only be an asset to Weston's Textiles.

In the short time he'd known Sophy, he'd seen just how skillfully she managed her finances. Her shrewdness overlaid a sweet honesty that appealed to his own basic integrity.

Seth looked down at the tiled floor as if it held some undeniable truth. Something curled inside of him, a subtle tightening of his body, something that had nothing to do with passion, when he thought of Sophy.

It was like a seed buried deep in the earth, being coaxed out into the warmth of the beloved sun. Inexplicably, then, it seemed chance was not finished with him. It lay in anticipation, lurking, waiting to entangle his soul, draw him out of the darkness and engulf him in a loving embrace.

As if spurred by random chance, Seth crossed the hallway and turned toward the study.

Curled up on the long recessed window seat, legs tucked under her, Sophy was engrossed in some intricate calculations when she heard the study door open. She did not turn her head, hoping that whoever it was would not see her and would go away.

"So this where you hide."

At the husky sound of her husband's voice, Sophy laid aside her book, held out her hand and smiled brilliantly.

"Good morning, Seth!"

Blood rushed in his ears like a battle cry. He was thrown out of his stride by the genuine delight in her greeting, and stared at her.

Cheeks bright, eyes sparkling, Sophy seemed full of life and vitality. She wore a deep violet silk gown embroidered with self-colored piping and fringe trimming. Her gleaming black hair was drawn tightly back from her face, exposing her slender neck.

Seth stood ramrod straight, concentrating on controlling his breathing. It was an effort to ignore the sound of the hammering of his heart, which felt as if it had lodged in his windpipe.

He paused, searching for some emotion deep inside himself as a guide. Until the previous night, he had begun to think he was immune to the wiles of a woman. There had been no question of love being involved in his marriage. No illusions of it on either side.

Last night, Sophy had changed the ground rules. She had relegated their war to another battlefield. Here he would either survive or perish emotionally.

The experience reminded him of the hallucinatory ecstasy engendered during the ritualistic chewing of cacao leaves he had witnessed in primitive tribes. During the war, when drugs were unavailable, several doctors had used hypnotic trances to anesthetize patients for surgery.

Could Sophy have hypnotized him? He slid her a prob-ing glance, a smile edging his firm mouth, as he realized how foolish he was. No. Never in his life had he experienced the phenomenon, but he was aware hypnotism required the willing cooperation of the subject.

He took the hand that unfolded like a flower reaching for the sun's warmth. Around Sophy, he seemed prepared to let chance have its way, to take a few risks. A smile playing along his lips, he gently kissed the delicate fingertips before returning it to her lap. Something intense glittered in the vi-olet-gray eyes.

"Working on a secret weapon, Sophy?"

There was a faint humor beneath the words, as Seth nod-ded at the book resting on the braided edge of her silk skirt. Sophy's smile faded slightly. Her heart skipped a beat, and she felt something inside her trembling like a leaf before a rising wind.

"In sort of a way." She ran her palm lightly over the cover of the ledger, unsure of where this was going. When she spoke, her voice was so soft it could have been the night wind. "I was calculating what percent of the market Wes-ton's Textiles needed to capture before they posed a threat to importers of French fabrics."

She tilted her head to one side, studying him. Eyes wide and reflecting an appeal of which she wasn't aware, she waited for his reaction.

Seth was leaning his arm along the mantelpiece, and had been looking down into the fire, but at that he raised his head sharply and shot a penetrating glance at Sophy. What was she up to now? What new game was this?

Innate caution restrained him, prompted him to fence. "Why should that be of such importance at this hour of the morning?"

Sophy's hands flexed around the ledger. Lord above! How handsome and vital he was in the navy velour jacket with its brass buttons, which set off his smooth skin, dark sideburns and vivid blue eyes. Her chest had tightened uncomfortably, as if she had forgotten how to get air into her lungs. She took a deep breath.

"W. H. Carryl's Philadelphia store has just been taken over by Walraven's. As you know, they were this country's main importing house for French fabrics."

A curious tension hovered between them. His eyes were bright chips as he acknowledged this fact. Sophy clasped her hands in front of her, the fingers tightly interlaced.

For just an instant, she felt her heart contract in her chest at the thought of Seth's possible reactions to her plan. She tightened her mental stays. She would need all her ingenuity to win this skirmish.

She forced herself to continue. "What you may not know is that I am the major shareholder of Walraven's."

Seth made a harsh, discomforting sound. He stood there, a dark frown pulling his brows together, his eyes hooded and unreadable. He seemed to be debating the issue in his mind. The only thing Sophy could be certain of was that his earlier good humor had evaporated.

Seth lowered his voice. "As the transaction seems to be a *fait accompli*, there is no point in discussing the ethics involved. Congratulations, Sophy, on such an astute business deal." The repressed ferocity in him was unsettling.

"Oh, Seth. I could *shake* you at times!"

Sophy sprang to her feet in exasperation, her hoopskirt billowing. A strange desire to save this man's pride was insidiously eroding her resolve.

She closed the distance between them, moving like a wraith across the room. Heart thundering within her rib cage, she prodded the top button of his stylishly cut waistcoat with the tip of one finger.

"Get it through your thick skull, I am not trying to undermine Weston's! My father always told me never to allow one's private life to interfere with one's business judgment. He was right."

Bright blue eyes became as penetrating as gimlets. It would be a considerable challenge to discover what lay behind this captivating creature's motives in going into direct competition with her husband's firm.

A desire to ruin him? The notion was ridiculous. Still, he must be cautious. But a part of him didn't want to be cautious. A part of him longed to trust her.

Mouth suddenly dry, he attempted a smile. It went wrong. His lips curled like those of a friendly wolf.

"That's always reassuring to hear, of course."

It was Sophy's turn to become wary. She felt her insides tremble involuntarily, pierced by that basilisk gaze. There was tension in the way he rested an elbow on the carved marble mantelpiece. A tension that signaled marginal success for her campaign.

She bent over and took a deep, deep breath, on the pretense of jotting a note in her ledger. "When Carryl's import contract was signed, it included a proviso that the Alsatian manufacturers must provide the fabric within one hundred days."

A slight pause followed, while Seth absorbed the significance of Sophy's curious statement, mulling it over in his mind. He looked down with an odd expression on his lean features, as if this were a new concept to him.

"Are you suggesting Weston's go into the import business? Gather our heavy artillery and breach the opposition's defenses?" His voice was arctic. "That's quite impossible!"

Sophy shook her head once in a sharp negative. Eyes glinting, she smoothed full, wide skirts.

"War makes impossibilities plausible, doesn't it? Fortunes of war sometimes turn out for the better. The War between the States has turned society upside down. Many old rules and standards are being forgotten."

Her voice changed, sounding blunt and businesslike. She tapped her chin with the end of her pencil. "I'm suggesting it seems a propitious moment for Weston's to take stock of the situation and use it to the best advantage. Snap up the slack in the import market."

Again she came under that hard scrutiny. Seth leaned his face close to hers, jawline jutting and firm as carved marble. She had cut him to the quick without realizing it.

"Calculate and rationalize as you will, Sophy, I doubt whether the Archangel Gabriel and the Twelve Apostles, plus all the labor they cared to summon, could accomplish such a miracle in so brief a time."

His terse manner somehow gave Sophy confidence. She sought to press her advantage. She allowed a full smile. "What about using tactics of war?"

She stood bolt upright, clasping her hands tightly together against her chest, and hesitated, just a beat. She had yet to learn the secret of patience.

"Think, Seth! What battles were successful? Why? Which ones were unsuccessful? Why not? Was there some point when the losers could have won? What significant moment did they miss? You're an old campaigner. Use the same harsh logic in business."

Sophy tried to drawl lightly to counteract the latent resentment and skepticism in Seth's expression with something approaching amused affability. The words came out all wrong. They sounded provocative, eager. She was doing it again. Rushing in where angels feared to tread!

Seth was so much taken aback that for a moment he did not say a word. He looked at her doubtfully, scanning her face with care. From the first moment he'd seen her, it had been as if she had some secret hold over him.

The pale morning light fell full on the wide planes of her face, bleaching it to a colorless effigy. Yet the lips, mobile and full, were those of eternal Eve, and the eyes, soft and liquid, like the moon on a wild and cloudy night, were those of the temptress, Delilah.

How curious that this appealing elfin woman should maintain such an unerring sense of aloof self-possession in business, but was also able to retain a genuine gaiety and radiant warmth that could plunge him into complicated throes of passion. It was as if some mysterious force bloomed inside her, something he could not name.

Suddenly such a wave of desire for her flooded his veins that he felt light-headed. It was as though all his essential rational props had been pulled away.

It was hard to resist the sweet appeal in her eyes, or the temptation of those soft parted lips. But he had to face the hard fact. Someone was out to bleed him dry. Someone who didn't mind using scare tactics to slow down the hunt.

Getting Sophy involved held a lot of potential risk. She could be in danger if he allowed himself to indulge her in this. Something convulsed sharply inside him. He had to find the culprit, fast. Then, and only then, could he allow Sophy to have her way.

At his hesitation, Sophy felt a measure of reassurance. She was becoming accustomed to his habit of coolly, calmly thinking things through. At least he was debating the issue in his mind. He was deep in his thoughts now. While she looked at him, she found herself fighting a strange emotion. She could feel it beating at her.

Those blue, intense, seen-everything, done-everything eyes were searching her soul, penetrating like light through deep water. She could only guess what was going on in his brain.

Was he thinking of some clever excuse to veto her suggestion before demanding that she surrender the shares? Or plotting devious ways to strike back? No. That was not like Seth.

There was so much that they did not know about each other, but from the start, instinct had told her that Seth was an honorable man. He might be something of an unknown quantity, but no one could ever accuse him of being underhanded.

The blue eyes held steady, no shift in intent, just a fraction too level. She could practically see him turning over her responses in his mind.

Suddenly her body broke out in gooseflesh. He suspected her motives, but chose to play the game she had started! She was certain of it. Abruptly and utterly certain. The thought was strangely alarming, and at the same time exciting.

Seth broke the concentrated stare, and leaned back against the rose-colored marble mantelpiece again, pushing one hand into his hair. He had come back to earth, his feet were firmly planted in reality, his mind cool and detached. It seemed so obvious to him now.

"The Battle of Bull Run." He straightened and snapped his fingers. "Maintaining supply lines has always been a problem in war. The Confederates' use of the railroad to bring up troops from Piedmont Station was crucial to their success at Manassas, for the reinforcements arrived fresh as well as fast!"

Sophy felt as if an immense weight had lifted from her chest. She had made the suggestion of applying the analogy of war to business jokingly, although with an element of seriousness.

She looked at Seth, her lovely violet eyes wide and sincere. "There are odds, and odds. Opportunities, and lost opportunities. The moment in an engagement when the least maneuver is decisive and gives victory. The one drop of water which makes the cup run over."

He nodded once, not looking at her. Memories, habits, disciplines, all carefully nurtured in the field of war, flooded his mind.

Stubbornly, she demanded, "What gave the Confederates the advantage at Bull Run?"

Several different emotions chased themselves quickly across his face. Sophy waited with interest. She loved to watch his face. To her infinite satisfaction and relief, Seth enthusiastically cottoned on to the idea.

"Procrastination. McDowell intended to capture Richmond, but finding the Confederates under Beauregard well entrenched, waited for three days before attacking."

He lowered his voice and leaned forward, making a disparaging gesture with the palm of his hand. "Those three days enabled Confederate reinforcements to be brought up, and the result was a Union failure to capture the position, followed by demoralization and retreat back to Washington."

"Procrastination is the thief of time, and an opportunity lost is one never regained. Take advantage from McDowell's mistakes, and be wise today!" Sophy chose her words with care. "Weston's could offer contract bids for special designs to Walraven's." Her lips curved slowly into a cajoling grin.

Seth drew a breath deep enough to lift his jacket's brass buttons. "We could develop pattern services. I've been tossing around an idea for some time of supplying designs in several forms, including drawings, engraved plates and fabrics, and grouping them into themes by design type or material."

Almost before the words had escaped him, Seth was making rapid mental calculations. Every possibility had to be explored. It could be the way out of the dilemma that faced the textile industry as a result of the cotton shortage caused by the war. The scheme just *might* come off.

"It's tempting, but better still, we could substitute local American textiles that mix cotton or linen with silk to achieve the same effect as the costliest imported fabrics. Create our own taste and style." His teeth gleamed briefly. "What do you think of that idea, Sophy?"

This was exactly what Sophy had in mind, but she thought it better not to say so. She was too pleased to see that shuttered, protected look in his eyes disappear.

In the few weeks of her marriage, she had discovered Seth liked the challenge of winning in a difficult situation. He liked the sense of power it gave him to be in control.

It was amazing what you could discover about human nature by studying war games, like a weakness in her own line of defense! Sophy shivered. To overestimate the capabilities of one's own forces was just as dangerous as to underestimate the strength of the enemy. She would ignore Seth's masculine force at her own peril.

Like the little wooden sticks used in a game of jackstraws, all her strengths and weaknesses were tumbled in an abandoned heap. Pride, anger, envy, hate and jealousy tangled with compassion, hope, tolerance, charity and love. The knack was to extract the right one out of the pile without disturbing the heap.

Sophy put her hands together, interlacing the fingers. She needed time to fix on a strategy. She didn't want to remind Seth of her ambitions. Running roughshod over his masculine convictions, or splashing her wealth around, was not the way to win his heart. Nor was using her feminine wiles as a weapon.

Sophy stifled the momentary qualm, and managed a little smile. A very bright, very feminine smile that completely hid her inner turmoil.

"I think it's a great idea. I don't want to harp on it, Seth, but—" She broke off, biting her lip, then leaned forward. She simply couldn't restrain herself. "I am very good with figures. The first thing my father taught me was how to look for profit leaks. As I told you before, if I could have access to Weston's accounting records, I might be able to pinpoint any deficiency in the acquisition or disbursement system."

"I've been able to buy time with that very convenient injection of working capital." Seth gave her a quick smile to let her know he did not hold any grudges because of her duplicity. "I don't like the idea that Lloyd's contribution was part of a compromise."

Sophy stiffened, her brows drawing together in a quelling frown. She wasn't certain she liked the implication of a compromise. It suggested that Seth perceived a balance of power in the relationship that she'd never intended. That disturbed her.

Her concern rose another notch. She was caught in a trap from which she was unsure how to extricate herself. Instinctively she stepped back a pace as if preparing to meet a physical assault. Indeed she felt very much like a boxer who had met a punch head-on. Her hooped skirt swayed.

"That was a low shot, Seth, and unworthy of you. In your heart you know that is untrue." Her breasts heaved up and down with her breathing. "I want only what is best for you. Just because I have tried to convince you that it is best to use my talents, does not mean I am trying to make you less than a man."

The smile was wiped from Seth's lips in an instant, to be replaced by rueful comprehension. She started to speak again, but he beat her to it.

"Hell, I'm not handling this very well, am I?" He shot her an assessing glance. Awkwardly he offered, "Blame it on the inexperience of a bruised masculine ego."

Her smile was tremulous, her eyes wide and glittery. "I'm sorry, Seth. I didn't mean to flash my money around. It was just that..."

He moved, and for a moment sunlight filtered in from the window and highlighted his handsome face, with its striking cheekbones. He was smiling now, his face lit with a sudden warmth. Mysterious lights played far back in his eyes, like summer lightning in the mountains.

Staring at up into those glinting blue eyes, Sophy forgot to speak, think, breathe....

"Don't apologize, Sophy. I like your style. You're a strong woman, and I find that a challenge. But you're also soft. I think you've been looking for someone to make you yield, whether consciously or not."

And so do I, Sophy admitted to herself. The worst part is that I like the way you take over, every bit as much as I resent it. Her chagrin stumbled. She swallowed hard and clenched her fists, forcing herself to speak calmly.

"I suppose it was a stupid idea. I guess I'll go back to my alternative plan. Check out the women. Sewing circles, dinner parties, shopping expeditions, a word here, a suggestion there, that sort of thing."

Seth regarded her with a strange look in his eyes. "You could do both."

His shift in tactics was disconcerting. Sophy's pulse fluttered.

"Both?"

"You have a point. We could use tactical planning. Mobilize all our forces. Advance and retreat. Confuse the enemy."

A sharp pain in her palms made her realize she was digging her nails into them. She deliberately loosened her hands and took a deep, steadying breath.

"You have changed your mind? I can be part of the investigation?"

Seth considered the matter carefully before he answered. He was acutely conscious of her presence beside him, the feminine smell of her and the way she seemed to lean toward him. He tried to collect his wits. Something told him that if he blocked her now, he would live to regret it, but, before he revealed Weston's secrets, he had to find an answer to the question that was gnawing at the edges of his mind.

"Sophy, about last night . . ." The faint twinge of uncertainty that made him pause was irritating but not unexpected.

"Forget it, Seth." Anxious to erase the small chill that had coursed down her spine, Sophy silenced him by placing her fingers firmly against his lips. "The ledger's balanced. We need to start again."

"We need to start over," Seth repeated with a patience that sounded extremely tenuous, "but that doesn't mean we can forget last night."

Sophy decided not to pursue that avenue of discussion. How could she win Seth's love? How could she prize open the compartment in his mind where he had buried his capacity to love?

She wished with all her might that she had the answer, but, of course, that was a useless wish. In fact, any wish, her father had told her more than once, was useless. *If you want something badly enough,* he had said, *then you must do it. Those who sit and wish for things accomplish nothing.*

Her father's words ringing in her ears, Sophy tried to deflect the debate. "What about my assignment? Will you make the arrangements for me to investigate Weston's?"

Seth hesitated, watching her face intently, as if considering the best method of handling her. There was a fractional beat of time during which she could sense he was trying to decide whether or not to pursue his earlier discussion. He shook his head in quick exasperation, but his voice was dangerously calm.

"None of that has anything to do with what we have been discussing. Do you prefer a frank, if unpleasant, answer or a tactful evasion?"

Sophy frowned, thinking that was a strange way to phrase it. The knowledge confused her. She put out a slim hand and touched his arm lightly. "While I have not seen men killed, I know sufficient of what bloodshed means to prefer an honest reply."

"I have my doubts, but I value your opinion."

"Trust me. We haven't let each other down yet, have we?"

Seth took her hands in his and drew her slightly toward him. He bent his head and kissed the pulse of her throat where the silver chain lay, the touch as light as a butterfly's wings, before he set her away from him.

"And we're not going to. You have my word on it." His voice was thick and husky as if he had something lodged in his throat. What was it that he was *not* saying?

"Are you suggesting a *compromise,* or a complete renegotiation of our wedding bargain?" Her body moved toward him in breathless anticipation. Something fervent glinted in the misty eyes.

Doubt gnawed away at Seth. Was it possible she was right and, together, they could overcome the obstacles facing Weston's Textiles? Or was Sophy laying siege to his heart and soul? He knew she would settle for nothing less than the real thing. Once Sophy knew what she wanted in life, she went after it. He thought of her words.

Something inside him squirmed at the prospect of being involved in such a campaign. That kind of battle was risky because it involved the emotional and passionate side of his nature. Something he had crushed for three years.

His instincts were to retreat, he realized wryly. But, deep down, he knew that withdrawal today wasn't going to do any more good than trying to resist Sophy last night had done.

His head swung down and he saw that she was staring up at him. A kind of shock traveled through his body until he was certain his very flesh vibrated. Her face was very close to his, her eyes wide. They seemed to be searching for something in his face. Then the contact was broken.

Seth shook his head. What was he fighting, anyway? And what made it so important? *Opportunity rides a dangerous wind.* He shrugged, dismissing the thought. There was an obligation to be met, a duty. To abandon duty was to destroy the essence of life. It was the only thing that had kept him going these past three years.

Having made his decision, Seth felt the corners of his mouth lift. They would do it her way. "Smart people learn to bend with the wind. A truce on business matters against full-scale attack on the personal front. Winner takes all. Is that sufficient compromise?" The gleam in his eyes dared her to refuse.

Like a warm tide following an icy current, relief flooded Sophy. Thank heavens! Matters seemed to be advancing far beyond her highest expectations. Whatever his reasoning at the moment, she had the relief of knowing he was going to play the dangerous game of love, for which she was setting the rules.

"If you're sure that's what *you* want," she retorted agreeably, beginning to enjoy herself.

"I was never more certain of anything," he murmured in tones of utmost satisfaction. For some reason, Sophy had the distinct impression that Seth had been about to say something else entirely. His fingers tightened around hers, before he released them abruptly.

"You can start by coming to visit the factory at Paterson with me tomorrow." He moved toward the door. "In the meantime, I have promised to have a look at some newfangled machine for typewriting Bernard has discovered. He swears it is a new secret weapon that will prevent forgery."

The impact of his decision made Sophy catch her breath. Glancing at his confident expression, she did not doubt that he would find a way to achieve his objective. It seemed as if she were going to be hoist with her own petard. She lifted her gaze to meet his blue eyes and smiled brightly.

"I wish you the best of luck. You're going to need all the secret weapons you have in your armory! Last night I was just checking out the possibilities!"

To her surprise, a red flush appeared across the high planes of his cheekbones. They faced each other across the short expanse of the study, and Sophy knew that he understood her motives perfectly.

Seth found himself quite unable to put into words the things she had done, and was obliged to fall back upon known ground. "A word of warning, Sophy. Don't underestimate the enemy. If you used your heavy artillery last night, you discharged a blank!"

Picking up his hat and cane, he flashed her a cocky smile. It was a question and a demand. He was flirting with her! Sophy's eyes began to dance, and she felt her cheeks dimple, but it was not until he had his hand on the doorknob that she fired her parting shot.

"You're limping, aren't you?"

Chapter Eleven

The smile was still mirrored in her eyes and curved her lips two hours later as she peeled off a kid glove to test the ripeness of a piece of fruit. She wrinkled her nose, treated the barrow man to a sideways glance, and began to haggle for the best price.

Brandied fruit would make a delicious dessert for Thanksgiving. Already in her mind's eye, Sophy was cleaning and pitting the fruit, carefully measuring the sugar, packing a combination of fruit and specially blended spices into prepared jars, and topping the container with the finest French cognac.

The colors, odors and sounds of the Orchard Street markets swept over her like an invigorating tide. It was all frenetic activity. The outdoor stalls were jammed with wares and milling customers.

Everywhere there were people. Fruit vendors briskly pushed their laden carts through the traffic. Shawled women hawked yesterday's violets at passersby. Nursemaids hurried their infant charges home in basketlike prams.

There was a biting nip in the late-autumn air. The cries of vendors filled the air like the calls of strange forest birds, carrying their strident staccato messages.

Along the side streets she could see the endless lines of roofs, pitch-black against the zinc-colored sky. From the river to the east came the hooted calls of ferryboats. Horse trams were jammed with all types of persons. The traffic had slowed to a sluggish crawl.

Sophy was watching the barrow man adjust the brass measure up another notch on his hand-held balancing scales when Agnes Weston rebuked, "Those cherries are over-ripe, Sophy. They'd give a horse colic."

"They're not for a horse, Mrs. Weston," Bernard broke in cheerfully. "Cousin Sophy's promised me a bottle of cherry conserve. The fruit has to be ripe, y'know, to have enough sugar to set the jam. Ain't that right, Sophy?"

Sophy glanced at him sharply but for once in her life saw no signs that her cousin was being deliberately annoying. "Yes, Bernard, but you don't have to be so loud about it."

Bernard had the grace to hang his head. A smile warmed her face, and she handed him the package. "Please take all our purchases back to the carriage, and then you can accompany Mrs. Weston home. The wind is getting cold, and I have to go to Rivington Street."

"You're a considerate girl, Sophy." Agnes Weston's caustic voice softened marginally. "The truth is I am rather tired. However, since Bernard has been such a pleasant escort and carried our parcels for us—as though he were indeed a horse—I shall instruct the driver to go via Ludlow Street so he can see the police parade in front of the jail."

"Gee, thanks, Mrs. Weston! You're a ripper!"

Sophy put up a slim hand, touched Agnes Weston's arm. Her voice was so soft it might have been the night wind taking away the shadows. "Don't let him eat the cherries on the way home!"

Rivington Street. Richard Carlton. So far, so good. Now the crucial question. What would the agent's reaction be on discovering the purpose of her visit? Suddenly Sophy felt all taut and alert, as if someone from within herself had leaped out and taken command.

Down the street, a cart was approaching, making its slow and creaking way. The cart trundled past her, moving as slowly as if it carried within its wooden framework all the world's worries. Sophy's brain was ticking over at full speed, assessing the situation.

Had she made a colossal mistake in believing that she was clever enough to help Seth? That a fresh method, a new approach, would make a difference to his own investigation? In believing that Seth would put the horrors and hatred of war behind him and find he still had the capacity to love? To give himself completely?

There was always the possibility she was deluding herself. Most of their conversations revolved around mundane domestic matters, but she was working to change that. On a more intimate level, he had never once told her he even cared.

She was making progress, but the truth was Seth was still very much a mystery to her in some ways. While he seemed to welcome her affectionate warmth and cheerfulness, he was still the unreadable, unknown man she had married six weeks ago.

On the whole things had worked out better than she had thought they would. She could only hope that, in the fullness of time, he would realize the depth of his feelings for her and admit them. In the meantime, she would have to be satisfied with half a loaf.

And what a half loaf it was!

The future, now that she had time to think about it, appeared bright and beckoning. A transient dimple showed at the corner of her mouth. There was a certain undeniable satisfaction to be derived from the level of passion that two people railroaded into a marriage of convenience could reach.

It was something most remarkable.

Sophy turned the corner into Rivington Street. She passed the orphanage, where small, pale faces pressed against the iron railings. The children were watching two well-dressed boys skipping around their nursemaid, clapping their hands in excitement.

At several points along the length of the busy road were small groups of people standing talking. Sophy was delighted to see a familiar figure come into her line of vision.

Richard Carlton was standing there on the curb, checking his pocket watch. The agent was impeccable as usual, white wing collar, red spotted necktie, his tailoring faultless over his solid girth. He swung round, saw her and bowed, smiling graciously.

"Mrs. Weston. What a pleasure." His soft brown eyes were half-concealed behind lazily lowered lashes. "Are you alone?" He seemed surprised.

Sophy placed her hand on his tweed-covered forearm. "Seth had some business he couldn't put off. He's expecting a big consignment of cotton to arrive in the next day or so. He seems to think I can manage this errand on my own."

Carlton shuddered. It could have been the cool of the wind. It blew constantly in this space between autumn and winter, and the wind was sharp against their faces.

"If you'd care to step into my office, Mrs. Weston, I'll do what I can to help."

His office was furnished with enough style to impress, but without the ostentation that might make a client wonder where his fees were going. A large oak desk, flanked by several high-backed carved chairs, dominated the room. On it there was a brown leather-bound journal, a pipe stand, a heavy crystal paperweight, a brass paper knife and two paper-filled metal trays.

Richard waited until she was seated before he indicated the letter Seth had dictated. "I've been expecting you." He reached for his pipe. "You've been authorized to look at invoices, payments and receipts in matters pertaining to Weston's Textiles. Is that correct?"

Richard's voice was pleasant and urbane, but Sophy felt a jolt race through her as if she had been doused with ice water. She was studying his face. Unmistakably, it creased into an expression of contempt.

Men in Richard Carlton's position were supposed to give a comprehensive service to their clients for a commission, not expect the client's wife to want specific detail. He was probably horrified that Seth would condone this odd display of feminine curiosity.

A shy smile edged the corner of her mouth. "Being newly married, I wish to devise a system of keeping accounts that is simple, but that will circumvent any attempts at dishonest practice."

Richard fumbled lighting his pipe.

Sophy looked down once before meeting the intense brown eyes. Her even white teeth became visible, and she turned to him with a small, confidential gesture. "Seth suggested I could learn something from your system."

The pipe was defying ignition.

"To tell you the truth, I don't know much about household management. Seth says your method of keeping records is superior to my own." Sophy spoke in a voice as matter-of-fact as if she were in a bakery.

Richard relaxed a little, and propped the pipe on its stand in front of him. "Only too glad to be of some assistance, Mrs. Weston. While you're browsing, would you care to partake of a cup of tea?"

"Thank you, that would be most refreshing."

Sophy's heart hammered in her throat and she felt a knot in her stomach. The papers she was studying were the lists of manufacturing supplies that had been imported in the past six months. There were sixteen lists in all.

Of the sixteen, five had been tampered with.

She studied the last entry in the journal very closely. The figure had been altered cleverly, from $101,000 to $109,000.

Her heart raced. There might be others.

She had spent the past two hours checking payments against invoices, and found some other small mistakes, but all of those could be put down to error. There was no question of error with the last one.

There was also the evidence of the invoices themselves. Several appeared to be duplicate for the same goods. Sophy had found these after scrutinizing every entry that seemed even slightly suspect.

Charles Lethbridge had endorsed all of them.

A swirl of anxiety pulled at Sophy. Involving the designer had validated her worst fears. Something wasn't quite right, but she couldn't put her finger on it. There was no reason.

It simply felt all wrong.

The alarms in her head sounded louder now. Sophy frowned. Motive. Opportunity. It was a simple explanation, yet it ripped at her mind with a whip of fire. There was no way around the issue.

The timing was wrong.

The haze of preoccupation in her eyes cleared. "I don't know that I'm much of a judge, but it seems one learns a lot about a person when they look at their record-keeping system."

Richard was busy lighting his pipe from a spill ignited at the grate. He glanced up, surprised. "Really?" He looked genuinely intrigued. "What have you learned?"

"That you are very precise, meticulous in detail, don't take a lot of senseless risks or do wild undisciplined things, that's all."

"You have a nice line in flattery, Mrs. Weston."

She looked into Richard Carlton's brown eyes. For a moment they stared at each other. His gaze was fixed on her with something that was either contempt or almost unbearable anguish.

"Tell me, Richard, do you deal only with importers and exporters in America, or is your client base more extensive?"

Dense clouds of gray smoke belched from the pipe. "Cast your net wide is my motto. I have clients on both sides of the Atlantic."

Her head bobbed. "Good thinking. Business must be booming since the war?" It was a question rather than a statement.

Carlton's heavy gold watch chain, almost as thick as a small cable, draped across his solid girth, rose and fell. "Real estate is set to spiral since the war, as are contracts with the government."

She changed the subject abruptly. "How long have you known Seth?"

"For about ten years."

"As long as that?" It startled Sophy. "You didn't first meet him through Weston's Textiles, then?"

"No. I was a friend of his father. When Seth joined the army, he wanted someone he could trust to handle his affairs."

His answer seemed quite frank. Sophy let it go at that for the time being.

"I like your little stamp."

Richard leaned forward in his chair. "Would you like it? I have several." His voice was deep, amiable. He picked up the stamp and extended it to her.

Sophy looked at the offering lying across his palm and experienced an unexpected wave of uneasiness. The hand that held the small wooden block was a strong, square one, capable of far more than pencil pushing. The blunt fingers curved like talons, ready to snatch a prey.

Why did she feel so reluctant to accept it from him? Her mind was a tumult. It flew from one possibility to another. She wished her imagination weren't quite so vivid. Stop it! Don't start imagining terrors that don't exist. She reached out quickly and took the small gift.

"You found the system helpful, then?" His voice was soft, almost expressionless.

A sick, sinking, heavy feeling grew in her stomach. Her face went rigid, and she turned to watch a lazy spiral of pipe smoke. The air hummed with purpose and power, or maybe just the twanging of her nerves. There was a moment's pause, before Sophy answered.

"The information I discovered was most useful." She prayed he wouldn't ask her what she was going to do with it. She didn't have an answer. Not yet.

A clock struck the hour. The chimes were light and clear, a friendly sound. Sophy stood up and began assembling the papers.

"I must be going. I have another appointment."

"If I may say so, it's deuced dangerous wandering around the city on your own, Mrs. Weston. I'll hail a carriage."

A smile curled her mouth. "That's very kind, thank you." She offered her hand. "If it's convenient for you, I'll visit again next week."

"Yes, of course. I look forward to the occasion." To her surprise, he lifted her hand and brushed his lips over her knuckles.

Sophy's next call was to the bank. Matt Tyson greeted her warmly. "What brings you here, Sophy?"

Sophy was aware of a curious tightness in her chest, but when she spoke, her voice was very controlled, business-like.

"A desire for information. I'd like to check the securities and records of large debits in the bank accounts. The first essential thing is to have a look at checks drawn in favor of the same firms and to get access to the bank statements. Can you arrange that?"

Matt's smile of greeting died. There was a small pause. He cleared his throat. "You intend to challenge my figures, perhaps?"

Sophy shook her head. She flashed him a quick smile. "Oh, no," she reassured him. "I'm sure your accounts are all quite accurate."

Tyson clicked his tongue against the roof of his mouth. "What's the problem, then?"

Sophy lifted her chin, and her eyes, full, unwavering, met his. "There's no problem, Matt. I'm merely seeking confirmation."

"Are you, then? Confirmation of what?" There was an edge to his voice.

"Have I your assurance that you'll listen to what I have to say?"

Not sure how to answer that, Matt became poker-faced. "Obviously you want something from me, but I have no idea what it is."

"That's all right for now. Can I assume that I can...talk to the clerk who tallies the accounts?" She put her hands together.

"Depends about what."

This was it. She kept her eyes on his face. "I don't want Charles Lethbridge to know I have been seeking your assistance, Matt. It's best if you don't know too much more."

"He will never know," Matt said bracingly. He took hold of Sophy's hand and pressed it to his mouth. His eyes were twinkling as he handed it back. "*My* lips are sealed, Sophy. No need for deception, either. I'm sure Seth will agree that this is a case of *least said, soonest mended.*"

Sophy released her breath with the air of a rider to hounds who has cleared a formidable fence. "Thank you, Matt," she murmured in a low voice.

Seth knocked lightly. Charles looked up from his papers. His desk was littered with folders and flimsy sheets. He raised a hand in greeting. "Hi."

Seth closed the door behind him. "Am I disturbing you?"

"Not at all. I am used to being harassed." Charles raised a hand in token surrender.

Seth tossed his hat and gloves onto a chair. "Out with it, Charles."

"You'd never believe me. I—" Charles stopped in midsentence. "Forget it. I think I'm going to be in enough trouble as it is."

"With whom?" The ebony cane twirled through the air, neatly hooked its target, the silver tip clattering against the wall.

The designer stretched out one hand. "You see all this? It's my monthly accounts. I *hate* getting monthly accounts. I'm already two months behind, heading for three, and the tradespeople are on my back."

Seth hoisted himself onto one littered corner of the desk. He stretched his leg up, then down. Sophy insisted the exercise strengthened the damaged tissue.

He paused mentally to hover on some invisible brink. It was an odd sensation. His fingers rubbed his thigh, as he sat intently staring at his leg, and tried to analyze the feeling.

The fingers dug into muscle, and his stomach tightened abruptly. He could never yield to what was burning up his heart! Indeed, he could not. For if he did, he would be naked, exposed, then he would shatter, be open to all hurt, pain, loving....

And yet...

Seth drew a long, long breath. Errant thoughts arrested, he raised the leg again, and contemplated the polished toe of his boot. "Are you saying I don't pay you enough, Charles?"

Charles flushed a dark puce red. "Hell, no. It's just that Abigail has no idea how to live within her means." He rubbed his hand across the back of his neck and heaved a sigh.

In spite of himself, a grin welled to the surface as Seth thought of his wife. He throttled it. Bright, reckless, impudent female! Life with Sophy was never dull!

"Women can be the very devil at times."

Seth thought about that for a minute. The ghost of an idea danced around the periphery of his consciousness. He was thinking of Sophy, of what she had said to him, the pact they had made.

"I'll tell you what. I'll take these papers home tonight and get Sophy to give them the once-over."

The designer rubbed his chin, and looked out the window. "It's still blowing a gale."

"Changing the subject, Charles?" Seth scoffed.

He glanced around at piles of small boxes and cartons. All were filled to overflowing with fabric samples and pattern designs. There were stationery compartments, holding letter headings, envelopes and oddments, some in black print, some in red, and there were several different designs of printing.

"Sophy's a very clever lady." His voice was even. "Suspects someone wants to damage our export trade in their own small way. Any ideas?"

"Bloody hell."

There was a long pause. Seth picked up a small wooden block marked "O.K. to Pay." It served as a check between the Paterson plant, which placed the orders; the warehouse, where goods were delivered; and the agent, who paid the bills. Accounts were stamped and initialed in both the buying office and receiving warehouse.

"I'm off to Paterson tomorrow. I want to check some orders with George. The suppliers are querying his last requisition."

"Bloody hell," Charles repeated again. "When will the paperwork be processed?"

"It must be before the deadline. It can be at no other time. We must be ready." He rolled the block between thumb and forefinger.

"But how?"

Seth swung his leg to the floor, and limped over to collect his cane. He stood tense, poised, motionless. When he spoke, his voice was heavy.

"That I don't know, but I'm taking Sophy to Paterson tomorrow."

Sophy's final call was to the factory on Forty-First Street. Seth was attending a meeting about the Water Street tenements, so she knew the designer would be alone.

Charles was sitting at his writing table, facing the door, with books and papers scattered in front of him. His elbows were on the table, his hands clasped under his chin.

She reached the desk, casting a shadow. Charles glanced up and started with surprise, even appeared to know a moment of discomfiture. He stood up slowly, and closed the ledger.

"I didn't hear you come in, Sophy." The moment of discomfiture past, Charles became the gracious host seeking to put his employer's wife at ease. "Seth has left. Did you want something?"

A fine tingling feathered along her spine. Sophy stood there, reminding herself that it was important for her to follow her instincts.

"Seth mentioned that you were preparing a proposal about producing paper dressmaking patterns in conjunction with Ebenezer Butterick. Is it in order for me to have a look at it?"

Charles did not smile in response. For some minutes, he showed no reaction at all. In fact, Sophy couldn't read anything in his narrowed eyes.

"No," he said finally.

For an instant Sophy hesitated, aware of the repressive quality of his expression. Unconsciously her chin angled a fraction higher. "I'd have thought, if you put your mind to it, you could turn a blind eye."

"It's out of the question. Matter of ethics."

Sophy swallowed. Looked away. At least the man was consistent. He knew she was on to something, no doubt about it, but what was his game? *Was* Charles Lethbridge the enemy?

The questions flung themselves at Sophy. Her tongue went dry and tasted suddenly of lemons. She bit her lip. To be able to differentiate an enemy from a friend was not easy.

White-lipped, every fiber in the whole, lean length of the designer was taut. It seemed interesting that this man should be under so much stress. What was he frightened of? An inquiry into questionable practices?

"I strike you as a selfish brute, hmm?"

"Not selfish. Single-minded. Gifted people generally are."

"I appreciate the compliment, Sophy," Charles said, apparently oblivious of her sarcasm. "Flattery is the one thing designed to put a man in a good humor."

"Perhaps if I were permitted to read that report, I'd get to know you better and you'd receive an entire catalog of humor."

"It'd be an exercise in logic and deduction, no doubt."

"Perhaps. It's a matter of trust, isn't it?"

When she glanced back quickly, it was to find Charles casually handing her the report. But there was an amused smile at the corners of his mouth. As if he knew she was wasting her time!

Wishing the butterflies in her stomach would find someplace to settle, Sophy flipped open the album. She read the proposal. It was interesting. In fact, the idea was almost brilliant. Charles had an easy prose style, and he didn't waste words. The description was factual and thorough.

Charles had signed it, heavily, in ink.

Her mind leaped to the truth.

It was as if red-black gunpowder exploded in Sophy's head. Her mind was whirling. It was more than just this moment. It was all the moments of Seth having to wait, of not knowing.

Charles had the devil of a lot to answer for.

Some of the tension seemed to ebb from Sophy. She felt a peacefulness wash over her. It was like a complicated jigsaw puzzle, incomprehensible until one missing piece—the key—was produced, linking all the pieces together.

Sophy felt the truth of it at the core of her being.

Seth tilted his head slightly, looking over the linen and crystal at his wife. Sophy sparkled. The gaslight streamed

down on her dark head, making the crimson silk of her dress
shine as if it were jeweled. Her flawless skin, magnolia tinted
with honey, held in either cheek a flush that owed nothing
to artifice.

She turned her head, and her black hair gleamed in the
low light. The hollow of her throat was filled with darkness. Seth felt as if he could drink the darkness from that
hollow.

Catching his eye, Sophy pressed a tooth down on her underlip. Incalculable creature. Watching her wide uplifted
look and those parted lips, so invitingly red, Seth lost himself in the urge to rush to the other end of the table and kiss
his wife.

Sophy had swept him as it were with a fan of flame. She
had made him live. There was no doubt about it, Sophy was
perfectly to his taste. Hers was a face to stir the blood.

His eyes still holding hers, Seth offered her a silent toast,
the grip on the stem of his glass rather fierce. In return, he
received a smile so radiant that he was momentarily dazzled. *Tonight,* she promised, the smile like a caress.

There was a knot in his stomach at the thought. This, too,
was pain, but sweet, swelling into pleasure. There was no
defense against that smile. Soft, gentle, relentless. A rare
and precious thing, to be savored slowly, in silence.

Seth shuddered deep and painfully as he remembered to
breathe again. A diamond glittered briefly among starched
ruffles descending his shirtfront as he inhaled.

His burning blue gaze pierced Sophy, making her shiver.
It was as though he had touched her. Her whole being stirred
in response. She flushed, aware that the hot color started as
low as her breasts and rose upward. It was a heady sensation, a sweet drenching madness that sent the blood in a wild
unreasoning race to her heart. Struggling to control her
runaway pulse, Sophy threw him a smile.

"I don't think that dreadful man should be allowed to get
away with it."

One eyebrow arched. "What dreadful man?"

"Why, Charles Lethbridge, of course. He let me have a look at the Butterick proposal, but wouldn't let me near the books. Not proper, he says. I think he could have been more helpful. Matt Tyson and Richard Carlton were most cooperative."

Seth's attention was focused on Sophy, on the mobile curve of her lips, the fine, soft line of her throat. "So you discovered nothing?"

"Not really. I'm no nearer the proof that we so badly need."

"Am I to take it that you have found something, then?" He shifted restlessly and took another sip of his wine.

"Naturally I've formed my own opinion, but you may not agree with that."

"It is always dangerous, Sophy, to have a preconceived idea."

Sophy was aware of an uneasy feeling in the pit of her stomach. He raised his eyes to meet hers again, and Sophy found it took an effort of will not to lower her own against that hard gleam.

"It seems to have some basis, though. Charles is an expert designer, and could forge anyone's initials or falsify any documents. He has the motive."

"I am quite sure that Charles is trying neither to embezzle from the firm, nor to murder me."

A quick throb of anger shot through Sophy, and exploded inside her like a burst dam. She could have stamped her foot in pure vexation.

"What does 'quite sure' mean? A hunch? Blind faith? Or have you evidence? Have you forgotten he's been around at each of the so-called *accidents?*"

A lengthy pause. She watched Seth get to his feet and come away from the table to her side, conscious of the slight uncoordination of his stride. The cane remained where it was, leaning against his chair. For short distances he no longer used it.

He captured her chin, cupping it so that she looked directly into his eyes. Their blue fire was sending out a tangible heat that she could feel throughout her senses.

From some far-off vacancy, she heard his voice, soft and compelling. It seemed to have substance, both burning and cool.

"Of course he's not trying to murder me," he said, smiling, and kissing the tip of her nose. "It may not be prudent, but I trust Charles in the same way I trust you."

Words failed Sophy. Her throat constricted. Every sinew and bone seemed numb. There was a singing in her ears and a misting of her sight that seemed suddenly, somehow blinded.

Sophy had dismissed her maid and begun to brush her hair when she heard a sound behind her. Seth stood like a dark shadow in her bedroom doorway, his tall figure an agreeable, but distracting image in the mirror. From the indulgent smile on his face, he seemed quite pleased with himself.

Seth came forward with his uneven step and stood behind her. Her hair was down, a gleaming blue-black cascade stretching straight down her back. He watched her in musing silence for a long moment, as if considering how to begin.

Heart beating fast, Sophy continued brushing her hair, glancing at him from time to time in the mirror. The ivory-backed brush was rising and falling like a tide through the river of her dark hair.

Looking thoughtful, Seth picked up a strand, ran it gently through his long fingers. He bent to her with a laugh in his eyes.

"You certainly know how to put the cat among the pigeons, my dear. I've had notes from Matt, Richard and Charles suggesting I find alternative methods to amuse my wife. Any suggestions?"

Sophy's heart gave a throb. Men and their damnably complicated codes and conventions! Unable to think of a suitable way to neutralize the masculine ambush, she shook her head. Her long hair swung, swaying with her motion.

She rose gracefully and made a small movement of one hand toward him. Quite suddenly she found it grasped in his. He leaned forward slowly, deliberately, pushing against her hand, forcing it back, finally trapping it between his hard body and her soft cotton-covered breasts.

"Did you think to escape retribution, my little brown elf?" He laughed again with a hint of mockery, letting her feel the promise of him.

Sophy let out a long sigh. "I could if I wanted to!"

"And do you want to?" His voice was very deep.

She shook her head, her long dark hair straying across his cheek and shoulder. Seth grinned with satisfaction and bent his head once more to hers.

Much later, at the edge of sleep, Sophy came awake. It was important for both their sakes that any doubts about Charles Lethbridge be dissolved. Seth trusted Charles in the same way he trusted her. Charles was his friend. Did that mean he trusted her with his life?

She curled herself against Seth, her eyes soft and glowing. Proving the designer's innocence would be the most important job she had ever tackled. Seth's trust must not be found wanting.

Her own happiness was at stake.

Chapter Twelve

A raw wind howling across the Hudson from the mountains of New Jersey brought the first stab of winter. A vaporous fog was rolling in, billowing across the streets just high enough to reach a man's calf as Seth and Sophy negotiated the slanting passage to the ferry at Twenty-Third Street.

The sky was a sullen mass, low and roiling, spitting clouds like steam from a kettle. Half-seen in the gloomy sky, great gray gulls wheeled, crying plaintively.

From the gangplank, Sophy could make out two or three high yellow sails of the fishing boats maneuvering carefully away from the quay. Like ghostly galleons they floated eerily in ethereal splendor, their undersides hidden by the mist.

She could hear the creak of the pilings, the wash of the water. Suddenly it seemed she was standing on the brink of a very wide, very deep chasm. A boat hooted upstream, the rhythmic rumble of its steam engine reaching her as a vibration up her legs until it passed, its tall smokestack lost in the haze.

Her body bent against the wind, Sophy stepped up beside Seth, and put one arm through his, her grip tight and secure. The other clung to the rail, as if she feared falling overboard. She flicked him an appraising glance from beneath her lashes.

"It seems to me that the weather is being perfectly unreasonable. It sets my sensibilities whirling."

A strong gust of the wind, sharp and bitter, whipped the words from her mouth and tossed them skyward like a kite. For a moment, Seth was not sure whether he had heard her right, but the slender arm threaded through his was quivering as delicately as a cicada's wing.

He flicked an assessing gaze over her, noting how the heavy woolen cloak outlined the curve of her breasts as she inhaled deeply to catch her breath. He thought he could see her entire body beat with the rhythm of her pulse. Her lips trembled.

Seth turned up the high collar of his coat. He pursed his lips, blew a warm breath. Condensing in the frigid air, its mist hung in front of his face, making his voice soft. "We get this kind of weather when the wind's the wrong way."

Sophy moved closer, as if needing his warmth, but unable to quell the vague amorphous fears that invaded her mind. She looked up at the sky, full of incipient rain. Nothing. She looked down at the water, dark and light. Nothing. Only a feeling, a kind of kinetic vertigo, as if she had just stepped off a merry-go-round.

The smell of salt and coal enveloped her. Her mind was whirled by the same currents and tides as the river below, full of something dark and ugly. Not normally given to visions or fantasies, she could sense death's dark dominion in the river today. A sick feeling slashed through her.

"It's a different perspective, quite alarming really, like riding high above patchy clouds," she murmured doubtfully.

Taking another step up the narrow ramp, Seth gingerly shifted his weight onto his cane, and felt the hand on his arm tremble convulsively.

"What are you thinking?" He halted, swinging toward her, waiting patiently.

Sophy's head came up, a frown etching the corners of her mouth and knitting the finely arched brows. She looked at his face without really seeing it.

In her mind she still spun in the grip of some nebulous undertow. The terror tightened in her throat, crept up to her eyes.

"I don't think you'd believe me if I told you."

"I'd believe anything you told me." He shivered a little, and drew her closer.

"What a foolish thing to say. Especially here and now."

He shrugged. "However, it's perfectly true." He drew her closer to him as if needing her warmth. "Tell me what is on your mind."

Sophy shook her head. Tears welled from beneath her lowered lids, turning to minute rainbows, despite the lack of any direct light. The effect was startling.

Seth felt compelled to break through the genuine fear he saw in her face. He had seen it often enough to recognize the real thing. Strange how it was nearly always invisible dangers that were the most terrifying.

"I thought you promised me *no tears*. Breaking your bargain, already, Sophy?" he baited softly, hoping for a reaction.

He got one.

The biting remark startled her, as he had intended it should. Sophy winced inwardly as she saw the undeniable glint of challenge in his eyes. Her eyes squeezed shut and she shook her head with sudden vehemence, irritation flaring within her.

"Of course not!" Her eyes snapped open, all traces of incipient tears vanished. "If you think that a bit of fog and a vivid imagination truly frighten me, Seth Weston, you can think again!" Her voice was like an ice floe. "If anything, this is a lesson on how foolish it is to travel without the beneficial effects of an early breakfast!"

Seth nodded, as if he fully understood. A strange tingle of relief spread through him, as Sophy responded to his challenge. Better to have her angry than fearful, he decided as they reached the top of the gangway.

Sophy deliberately withdrew her hand from Seth's arm. Her gloved hands were still shaking, but she told herself it was from the cold. Without a backward glance she made herself walk, not run, to the safety of the cabin.

Seth grinned with satisfaction, his eyes bright and alive, as he slowly followed her. The air seemed brighter, the haze fainter. It was an illusion. Above, a distant rumble of thunder punctuated the surly sky. Below, the fog settled like spilled cream on the dark, surging water.

The day went surprisingly smoothly after that. Sophy was unnaturally quiet until they cast off. But once they were moving, her apprehension seemed to slip away.

It was as if the episode on the near shore had never occurred. Seated not too uncomfortably on one of the wooden benches in the tiny first-class cabin, she soon dismissed her foolish fancies and began to enjoy the commotion.

Oddly the sounds heartened her. Somehow, the screaming calliope, the hoarse commands of shirtsleeved deck officers and the mournful, reechoed whistling of other riverboats complemented the feral wind.

The vessel began to swing as the ferry gathered momentum and drew away from her mooring. They were now moving out at a tangent, away from the shore. A deep humming filled the air, permeating it until it seemed to flutter before her eyes.

To get a better glimpse, Sophy twisted her head over her shoulder and peered, eyes straining, through the condensation clouding the glass windshield. This put her profile into prominence, so that Seth could see the arch of her wide forehead, the straight little nose, the angle of the high cheekbones and stubborn jaw, the long delicate sweep of her curving throat.

He knew without having to see them now the cheerful sparks of her soft gray eyes, the sweet, feminine line of her mouth. Her eyes always reminded him of a dawn sky, clear and serene. Genuine eyes. Generous lips. He could tell any nuance of changing mood just by a glance at those lips.

Seth sat down beside her, propping his cane against the bench and stretching out his legs, feet slightly apart. A boy handed him two cups of coffee, grateful for the modest tip.

"I've ordered some refreshments from the stall near the pilothouse. Not terribly appetizing, but I guess the coffee's hot and the food's edible. I'm afraid I'd forgotten an army marches on its stomach." He didn't realize how gentle his voice had become.

The sharply delineated profile dissolved into sweeping shadow as she turned her head to look in his direction. At the heat in his glance, Sophy felt as though her throat had constricted so much that not even air could pass through. There was a beat of silence before Seth grinned, and leaned forward holding out one of the cups as a peace offering.

Eyes wide, lips slightly apart, Sophy gratefully accepted, feeling unexpectedly lighthearted. She liked seeing him smile. Color rushed to her face, and she hurriedly took a sip of coffee. It was hot and sweet, but it could have been brackish water for all she tasted it.

"I am hungry enough to eat anything," she replied lightly, taking her tone from his.

Deep down in the core of her being, she felt an inexplicable movement. It was as if her loins had turned to water. Her gloved hand tightened around the cup, and she turned to watch the shore retreat steadily, as powerfully thrusting machinery imparted to the vessel a gentle, jouncing motion.

Seth felt her presence close and warm beside him and he wondered if it had been prudent to bring her. He thought not. He drank deeply from his cup.

Well, he thought in mild irritation, whatever I may feel now about the matter, the die is cast, and she is here beside me, wriggling like a friendly puppy. The sensuous rustle of silk against firm flesh seemed louder to his ears than the muted conversations around them.

Out of habit, one hand strayed to his leg. He rubbed his palm up and down his thigh as if it ached. Somehow, Sophy's hand crept beneath his. It felt warm. He flicked her a speculative glance.

There was nothing furtive in her movements, nothing carnal. Her fingers flexed. The side of one breast pressed against him. He kept his body very still.

Sophy felt a constriction fluttering around her heart, and for a moment, thought that it would burst through her chest. Her belly knotted and unknotted. Every iota of rational thought told her to remove her hand from his leg. But the reality was that she couldn't bear to think of him in pain.

He didn't move, but she could feel the tautness in him. It fairly sizzled across the space between them, enveloping her and feeding her own tension.

She took a deep breath, let it out as a shudder and marshaled her attention to their conversation. Her voice was very soft.

"I concede your superior knowledge of strategy. Dawn raids are often the most successful kind. If we're to take advantage of the element of surprise, I agree it's best that we arrive at the factory early and unannounced."

Unconsciously Sophy rubbed her cheek against the fabric of his jacket. Along the ridge of injured flesh she tenderly stroked the tight muscles. It was an astoundingly intimate gesture, coming as it did in the midst of a crowded ferry, even if this was modern, liberal-minded New York.

Seth felt his blood pounding. Her fingers seemed weightless as she rubbed them steadily back and forth over the thick broadcloth. Warmth spread upward into his groin. He willed his body not to respond, but it ignored him. He felt a tightening in the region of his hard, flat belly. The stroking became rhythmic, the pressure more insistent.

I must stop this. The thought fuzzily entered his mind. *I must!* Yet he could not seem to muster the willpower he needed to demand that she cease her ministrations. He scarcely dared to breathe lest some precipitate move of his embarrass them both. He curled his hand over, staring at the back, fingers clenched, knuckles white.

The ferry's horn sounded at regular intervals, hoarse and mournful. Voices of other passengers, muffled and odd sounding, echoed within the confines of the small cabin.

The boy returned with their meal. For a moment, he stood frozen and staring down at the immodest tableau. His thin hands fluttered like birds as he set down the tray of food, his face all smiles at the tip he received for so little effort. Deceit was a currency he understood.

Sophy gasped and withdrew her hand, a swift convulsive movement, as if she suddenly realized what she had been doing. At that moment, Seth experienced an acute and inexplicable sense of loss.

There was an awkward pause, but the food seemed to restore Sophy's equilibrium like magic. As soon as they began to eat, she started to question Seth about the factory at Paterson.

The food had also restored her common sense. There were certain items to be investigated, and a few specific details she would like to follow up when she visited the warehouse at Forty-First Street.

She continued talking, staring up into his eyes. Under her intense gaze Seth felt himself suffused with a peculiar feeling. Her lips opened and she said something. It might have been as mundane as "Do you want this?" He couldn't tell. He was so acutely aware of her, it was almost painful. He felt as if he were a stringed instrument and something he could not see had plucked a thawed cord.

He stared down at his coffee as if he might find answers there. He wondered what it was about her that drew him so powerfully. And could not even decide why it seemed so important for him to know. He took a deep breath, let it out slowly, settled back more comfortably in his seat, and answered her questions.

A deep humming filled the air. The general din of conversation slackened as passengers prepared to disembark.

Sophy and Seth remained seated, talking of inconsequential matters, until at long last the calliope emitted a final, wheezing gasp and, dribbling condensed steam, fell into a blissful silence.

At the top of the narrow aisle, Seth carelessly threw one arm around Sophy's shoulders and tucked her close to his side. A strange smile played briefly around his firm mouth.

"If you don't mind, I'll take advantage of your meager height and lean on you. I find the cane awkward on this sloping ramp." It was a sheer fabrication and Seth wondered whether she knew it.

Sophy did not. The public admission of human frailty in him had an instant tenderizing effect on her. Her throat convulsed. She supposed even experienced assault commanders must yield to weakness occasionally.

His nearness, the warmth that radiated from his body so close to hers, made her pulse quicken. She wanted to throw her arms around him and press her body to his.

Instead, she wrapped her arm around his waist and helped him down the narrow passage. In the process, she completely forgot her own fears. Seth's hard mouth quirked.

Ashore it was cold and damp, the fog still swirling with curling tendrils underfoot, the sun diffused and ragged within the clouds. Sophy shuddered as the wind nipped savagely at her face and ankles, and icy blasts crept up under her skirt.

To Sophy, the omnibus ride seemed interminable, even though it took a fraction of the time the ferry journey had. Perhaps the inclement weather had something to do with it, but she now felt filled with energy and a desperate longing to be busy. To do something, anything, to keep her mind occupied with thoughts other than Seth.

New Jersey was a rapidly growing industrial center, with numerous smokestacks stretching like long fingers toward the sky. Through the mist, which now appeared to be lifting, Sophy could distinguish the dark mass of the mountains to the west.

In no time at all, they arrived at Weston's Textiles, an enormous one-story structure in the heart of Paterson.

Sophy was fascinated by the great, high-roofed building where textile production took place, and not a little impressed by Seth's knowledge. She had never been in a factory before, and the sight was dizzying.

Long aisles of machinery spread before her, whirring and clanking as workers toiled to produce the cloth. Her eyes traced the endless movement of the long wooden pins, frantically hurling strands of thread against the rollers several feet away.

"Are you ready?" Seth asked, watching her mouth.

Sophy raised her head and her eyes met his. There seemed to be a smile buried in them, trapping her gaze. Time froze. The look in his eyes squeezed the very breath from her body. Her head went light and fluttery, though her heart was racing. Taking a deep breath, she smiled, the radiant smile of a rainbow across a clouded sky.

Seth stood quite still, watching her. She was smiling at him in that open way of hers, her eyes bright. He suddenly realized how much he cherished that smile. If he had been a less controlled man, he might have succumbed to the urge to touch her face, even allowed his fingers to brush her mouth.

As it was, he remained exactly where he was, his hands hanging loosely at his sides, fingers inert. But the blazing intensity in his gaze belied the outward calm of his voice. "Let's go and find George Dunwoody."

They reached the main processing section before they found him. Footfalls approached, echoing on the wooden floor, sharp above the dull hum of the machines, heralding the arrival of George Dunwoody. The manager was a ruddy-complexioned man in his forties, shortish and a bit stocky.

"Good morning, sir, ma'am." His voice bland, he turned to Sophy with a stiff little bow. Heavy brows and a flowing mustache hid any expression in his eyes or mouth. "Mr. Lethbridge mentioned that you would be visiting today."

The smile that still played around Seth's eyes was replaced by a face-crinkling frown. "Charles is here?" he echoed in disbelief, dark brows climbing.

"Certainly, sir." George Dunwoody's striped waistcoat drew tight over his solid girth, and his mustache twitched. "Mr. Lethbridge is in the Engraving Room. Courtauld's have put in a big order for the new 'Summer Palace' design, and he wants to check the print run."

"Fair enough." Seth cut him off with a flick of his hand. "I'll see him later. In the meantime, we'll just wander around for a while." His voice was even, but Sophy could feel the tension that vibrated through the tall frame.

Grasping her elbow firmly, Seth steered her over to where great lengths of fabric were rolling off the calenders. Light came from an unidentifiable source lost somewhere above them. The air was filled with the whirring of the cylindrical rollers. Seth showed her a new design that was running through. It looked sensuous and rich, and the varying textures gave it a heavy sheen.

"Mr. Weston, sir!" a voice called over the droning of the machines.

Seth excused himself, went to the foreman and exchanged a few words with him. Sophy studied her husband's broad back. She was consumed by her aching need for the full and thorough loving of this man. He looked so good to her, appealed in such a fundamental way to her senses, she wanted to surrender unconditionally.

No! Every scrap of her intuition was fairly screaming that advice. What sort of marriage would it be to a man who didn't understand about love? The sting without the honey!

Realizing that she was staring, hungrily, she felt the warmth rise in her cheeks and looked away from him back to the blur of colors in front of her. Dancing like dust motes on a beam of sunshine, or on the wild singing in her bloodstream, they were trying to tell her something.

Love is like that fabric, she thought musingly, a shifting plenum of color lending it a dazzling and illusory solidity.

When Seth came back to her, he was frowning. "We need copper rollers for this process. It is an innovative time. If we want to progress, we have to keep up with it." He lowered his voice. "Expansion is expensive, and both George Dunwoody and Matt Tyson argue that it is the bread-and-butter lines, the run-of-the-mill products that keep us going."

There was a tiny silence while Sophy thought rapidly. "I don't know about Mr. Dunwoody. He's probably content with what he has to manage at present. Is that not so? I do know Matt Tyson only talks money, especially what *not* to do with it."

Two thin vertical lines appeared in the center of Seth's brow. He continued to stand, unmoving, his scrutiny intense.

"Is that not so?" she repeated, putting one small gloved hand, fingers outspread, on his arm. Her grasp contained an urgency she could not have explained, even to herself.

At the touch, Seth sucked in his breath. "Yes. But I fail to see what..." He shrugged, his eyes narrowed to thin blue slits.

With feminine intuition guiding her, Sophy went straight to the point, her voice quiet and earnest. "Take my advice. Don't let anyone tell you dreams are only illusions, castles in the air. Follow your dreams. I'll wager they can become reality." She blinked rapidly, her love for him making her appeal fervent and personal. "If you want something, go after it, boots and all! Forget the cost!"

A slow grin suddenly revealed very white teeth, but his eyes were still gleaming with an unreadable emotion. He cocked his head to one side. "Are you encouraging me to go into debt, Sophy?" He met her eyes, daring her to deny it.

She stared at him for a minute, a blank, curiously opaque look. Then she blinked as if she were trying to remember a stray thought that had just crossed her mind. Around them, the din of the machines continued unabated, crashing off the walls and ceiling, echoing back upon the ear.

Sophy inhaled slowly, trying to find the words. She knew by the tone of Seth's voice he was trying to provoke her, but could not think why. She wondered what he wanted. Wondered what sort of answer would be best to give. In the end, she told the truth.

"I'm saying don't be a pattern card. When a door opens, go through it. If you want something badly enough, then you must do it." The smoky eyes she raised to his were full of warmth. "Those who sit and wish for things accomplish nothing."

"You're talking money. Weston's is on an even keel just now. Wouldn't it be a pity to—" he gave a short, dry laugh "—rock the boat?"

For a moment, they studied each other. Sophy stopped breathing for a few seconds. Then she sucked in a breath of air and stood very still to conceal the fact that she was trembling. She felt him go unnaturally still beside her. She paused to lick suddenly dry lips.

"Sometimes it's necessary to go against sound logic. I'm certain you don't need me to tell you that. Anyway, who wants profits from mediocrity?"

The cool question hung in the air like a beaded curtain.

He looked a little taken aback, as if he hadn't expected such a direct charge. "Damn it, Sophy, do you have to twist everything I say?" He exhaled deeply. "That's no answer, and it's too early for dramatics! I know there's another market to be tapped, material for the discriminating, but it would cost money to expand. Money I haven't got!"

"Money is like muck. It's useful only when it's spread around. If you're too proud, or too paranoid, to use my inheritance, let it rot in Matt Tyson's bank vault. Who cares?" She swallowed convulsively. Reminding him that he had married her for her dowry was no way to win his heart! "You'll have sufficient funds from your own resources when I finish my assignment and plug any financial leaks!"

"Ah." He said it as if it were a word with meaning. "Your assignment. I had forgotten," he murmured dryly.

Sophy felt a moment of irrational chill, and shivered involuntarily. His mouth twisted into a smile, and he took a step backward, deliberately changing the subject. His voice was as tight as a coiled spring.

"You had better begin your investigations while I talk to Charles."

Sophy thought furiously. "Charles seems to have a finger in every pie. Set him up as our spy. He could help us locate the traitor."

"You have nothing in your head except your tongue, which is as loose and heavy as the clapper of a church bell, and just as meaningless," Seth rasped furiously.

"Now who needs a strong dose of reality?" Her furious voice was as determined as his own.

Sophy knew it was the wrong thing to say as soon as it was out of her mouth. She mentally felt him pull away and experienced a shaft of pure self-disgust. Echoes of Tessa's lectures rang in her head. Around her the hum of machinery was like a constant admonition. *You'll catch more flies with honey than with vinegar!*

Seth was still as a statue, thinking, abruptly suffused with a curious kind of ache. He wondered how he could explain his doubts and fears to Sophy. How could he, when he was not even sure he could explain them to himself? He only knew it was as Shakespeare so cleverly put into Ophelia's mouth, "We know what we are, but know not what we may be."

He caught the eye of the manager, hurrying from the sanctuary of his office deep in the back of the building. When Mr. Dunwoody joined them, Sophy accepted his offer to escort her through the remainder of the complex. She was intensely aware of Seth, knowing his eyes, like chips of blue quartz, were following her as she passed through the door into the next section.

It was a new world to her, this world of technology. The swatches of fabrics, wovens and prints, as well as passementerie, were exciting. Because she'd always been interested in color, the dyeing operation had special appeal. Especially the molten metal process, which completed in several seconds, George Dunwoody told her, stroking his mustache lovingly with one forefinger, what had previously taken an hour or more.

Standing on the threshold of the cramped clerical area, Sophy noted the stacks of papers and binders on every available surface. Bookshelves climbed the walls on either side of a narrow fireplace. A shaded lamp burned, suspended on a chain from the high ceiling, swaying slightly so that shadows moved and perspective was shattered.

Empty shadows and dusty silence. Dust motes danced in the flickering heat of the lamp. Gray air hung in sheets in the dim corners and on high-backed leather chairs. The machines could scarcely be heard here, only as a faraway sound, a kind of persistent thrumming.

Sophy wandered casually between two desks, working her way around behind one of them, considering carefully how to begin her financial audit. She stood and moved her fingers over a leather-bound journal. Her gloved hands were like white flowers against the dark binding.

Momentarily startled, George Dunwoody watched beneath heavy lids, his colorless eyes barely discernible, as she idly opened a ledger. He made an exasperated noise, as if clearing his throat. When she began leafing through the pages, he bent forward slowly and gently put his hand on hers.

"There is not much of interest here for a woman, Mrs. Weston. I am sure you would prefer to enjoy a cup of tea or coffee with your husband and Mr. Lethbridge," he told her a little shortly.

Sophy thought she heard anger mixed with the sarcasm in his tone. She primly removed her hand. His contemptuous calm was amusing. It took a violent effort of will to stifle the laughter that threatened to bubble over inside her. As it was, the humor was clear in her eyes although she managed to keep her expression suitably haughty.

"Not at all, Mr. Dunwoody. I am not an empty vessel without an opinion of my own. I am interested in all of my husband's affairs... not just color and design. It's all fascinating... the politics, economics, the lot."

George Dunwoody evidently did not think such a foolish objection worth answering because he disregarded it totally. His eyes narrowed to slits. He watched her in musing silence for a long minute, as if considering carefully how to continue.

"Refreshments will be served shortly, ma'am," he said in his deliberate way, with a glance at the clock on the mantelpiece.

Pompous, self-opinionated man! The rage that exploded in her middle, that went whistling like shrapnel along her veins, was at that moment precisely what Sophy needed. No more vacillation! She had so much to do and so little time to accomplish it all. She felt impatient to begin. George Dunwoody's arrogance hardened her resolve as nothing else could have done. Which was good.

He thought he was dealing with an ingenue! Fleecing the innocent seemed a pastime for many people since the war. Seth needed her business acumen. She bent forward to peer at the papers on the table, suddenly very intrigued.

"Oh, but Mr. Dunwoody, you know what they say about new brooms!" she claimed with relish, looking up again abruptly.

Her eyes met his. For a moment they stood assessing each other, each sizing up the opposition. He appeared to turn the situation over several times in his mind, and then he nodded.

"I think that new brooms sweep very clean." His smile was thin and frosty. He picked up the ledger and held it in his hand.

Staring at the cover, he shook his head once, slowly, as if still reluctant to allow her access to such confidential information. But if he had learned anything, George Dunwoody thought, it was that he would do well not to underestimate the woman opposite him. It was clear to him that this particular female suffered from a curious perversity, and he would be a fool to ignore the hints of its scope.

After a moment he spoke and his voice was quiet and earnest. "I would be lying if I told you that you were welcome here, Mrs. Weston. It isn't my style to trust a woman with figures. I have been manager of the Paterson factory since before the war. You'll find none better."

Sophy heard him in attentive silence, and all the time watched him. Her gaze didn't falter. When he finished speaking, she did not say anything for a moment, but looked thoughtfully at him. He squirmed uncomfortably.

After a pause, she said, "It might be a nice learning experience for both of us to find something I do better than you."

Two spots of color burned on his cheeks. He had no illusions why she was here. He had been privy to too much detail, and too many contracts had gone wrong. His solid girth trembled. He gave a mental shrug and watched her mouth quirk up.

Sophy had read his thoughts accurately from the expressions flitting across his face. Drawing a deep, steadying breath, she looked him directly in the eye.

"Or it could be a question of us both being better at different things. Figures don't lie. I am a potential threat only if we are on opposite sides. The ledger, please, Mr. Dunwoody!" She reached for the sheaf of papers and account book he slowly extended.

"Thank you." Her expression changed. She smiled sweetly across the space that separated them, her eyes clear and bright. "You knew my husband before the war, Mr. Dunwoody. Tell me, what was he like then?"

George Dunwoody surrendered to the inevitable.

Chapter Thirteen

The boisterous wind and the ceaseless hiss of rain drowned out all other noises. Although the sky had faded to a luminous melon green, and the landscape was blurry with mist when it was time to leave New Jersey, they were safely across the Hudson before the storm struck.

On arriving back at the house on Fifth Avenue, they had gone their separate ways to dress for dinner. Immediately after the meal, Seth had shut himself in his study, saying he wanted to check a portfolio of new designs. Still not feeling one hundred percent, Sophy had retired for the night.

Outside, the wind drove the rain down in heavy sheets that in their turn were dashed away by more gusts of wind—and out of it, the hail, a deafening pounding, bouncing like golf balls from the ground in white streaks.

Sophy loved it. It was the perfect excuse to go back to basics. To spend some time making final arrangements for the Thanksgiving menu. To be alone. To think. It was growing more and more difficult to think clearly around Seth. One could think in the kitchen, come to some conclusions. The trouble was, her mind was a blank.

She still had no idea what . . .

The new cook was slicing fresh vegetables for tomorrow's bouillabaisse when she came into the kitchen. He waved a knife distractedly in answer to her query.

"I'm sorry, Mrs. Weston, but I can't seem to find them jars of preserved cherries you was lookin' for. You know, the ones you brung from Yonkers that you wanted special for Thanksgiving. They're not in the pantry." His face held a pained expression.

Sophy had already gone across the room to pick up a kerosene lantern, which stood on the bench. She selected a large latchkey from a hook on the wall, and picked up a box of locofoco matches, dropping both items into her apron pocket.

"Don't worry, Alphonse. I'll check out the cellar. They were probably taken down there in error. The jars were packed in similar containers to my father's wine collection."

She frowned, furiously trying to concentrate her mind. When Seth had questioned her about the results of her audit, she had been deliberately evasive. Her suspicions were aroused, but she mustn't give him any specific information until she had absolute proof.

Heart thundering in her rib cage, she had been sure he knew she was concealing something. For a moment he had seemed engulfed in thought, then had deliberately changed the subject.

Absently staring at the toe of his polished boot, his voice quiet, his words deliberate, as if he chose them with care, he had spoken to her about Ulysses Grant's terrible trepidation before an action against a particular rebel camp.

The general had arrived to find the troops gone, giving a whole new perspective on the question. *The enemy had as much reason to fear my forces as I had his. The lesson was valuable.*

The anecdote about Grant did reveal the empathy that attends true understanding of human limitations. Was Seth trying to give her a view of the investigation she had not considered? That he knew the situation, but was facing a terrible problem, seeking vainly for a solution? Or that he feared the evidence she might uncover could lead to disillusionment and danger?

In either circumstance, how could she tell him of her deductions? Dry documentary evidence was not the solution, and she saw the impossibility of conveying in words how a man had drifted into a vortex from which there seemed to be no return. She had to choose a strategy to deal discreetly with her conclusions.

The trail of evidence led directly to Charles Lethbridge. Cast-iron circumstantial evidence. All very plausible. But Charles remained an enigma. He had evaded her usual quick diagnosis, and remained in many respects a closed book.

Undoubtedly he was a brilliant designer. Seth trusted him. Didn't that mean something? She paused, adjusting her thoughts. Or was it sharp thinking on the part of the real villain?

Putting the worst possible construction on events, suppose someone else was the culprit? Wasn't it a smart precaution to have a suspect in reserve? It was useless to speculate. Speculation led, more often than not, to false conclusions.

Sophy lit the lantern wick, carefully adjusting the brass screw until the flame flickered, tall and even. No, she was almost sure of the truth. But it was like making her way through five layers of cotton candy. The feeling gave her just enough hesitation not to confide in Seth. She would wait until she had positive proof.

A large wooden door barred the entrance to the cellar. She fumbled for the key in her apron pocket. The lock opened smoothly.

The narrow staircase, made all shiny in the lamplight, reeled into the darkness like a filament of some mammoth spider's web. There was no handrail on the inner side, and it seemed a terribly long way down.

Sophy did not want to venture into that dank, dark cellar. It made her dizzy just thinking about it. She hesitated a moment. She should go down there. It was why she had come, after all.

Fear rooted her to the spot. The terror of her own private nightmare reared up at her. She seemed frozen in her tracks as if split apart, one half not obeying the other. *I don't like the dark.* How stupid could she be! That was no answer!

Perhaps it was only from looking down into the solid blackness? She took a deep breath, and shook her head as if to clear her mind of her thoughts. Some of the tension ebbed out of her. There was no choice, really, and it would only take a minute.

Sophy took a step forward. Another. Every step forward took the effort of two in reverse. She thought of Alice down the rabbit's hole and wondered if Mr. Carroll could have had this in mind when he wrote *Alice's Adventures in Wonderland.*

Inside it was cool and echoey. The silence seemed appalling and absolute after the long siege of the hail. Dust lay thickly along the stairs, clung to the wall.

She tried to ignore the hammering of her heart, which felt as though it had lodged in her windpipe. The creak of the steps, the soft slap of her shoes against the stairs, the whisper of her gown as it brushed the wall, all seemed to be swallowed whole in that vast bowl of quietude.

Shadows flitted, larger than life, skittering along the brickwork like a magic lantern show as she held the lamp high and slowly descended the stairs. An odd, tingling sensation manifested itself between her shoulder blades. She felt a movement, the quiet humming as of an inquisitive bee.

Suddenly, the door swung shut, clanging home with funereal finality. The silence seemed absolute. It was as if the outside world did not exist. Sophy felt very vulnerable indeed.

A hand went to her throat and the silver disk that hung there. She felt the first painful flutterings of panic take wing inside her, and wished she could touch Seth. Wished she were sitting quietly on a couch in the study watching his beloved dark head. Instead, preoccupied with his designs, he probably hadn't even noticed her absence.

This was a new fright, and she gave a little start. Her heart was thumping uncomfortably, as loudly as a blacksmith strikes his anvil. She squared her shoulders as if she faced something hostile. The feeling of being sealed as in a tomb had unnerved her a little, that was all.

Time had no meaning down here. A dankness hung in the air like a steel curtain. It was a vertiginous sense of space, echoing minutely. Silence almost. Only the sound of her own breathing.

Fear touched her heart anew. She staggered, blindly put an outstretched hand against the wall beside her to steady herself. Her foot kicked out from beneath the hem of her gown, tangled in her skirts and caught for a moment in the steel hoop. Then she was free, tumbling, rolling.

The breath whooshed out of her, and, in falling, she dropped the lantern. There was a clatter of metal as it banged against the brick wall and bounced off again. The light went out. She was in impenetrable blackness, a dense and appalling silence.

Sophy felt giddy, lighter than air. She was utterly powerless. It was if she had unexpectedly stepped off a shelf of rock in the shallows and plunged to the bottom of the sea. She turned around the way she had come but she could see nothing, no walls, no shelves.

"Seth!" Nothing. Her mind felt like jelly. She couldn't move. She couldn't breathe. The world had collapsed, and she was adrift in the dark, directionless, alone and dazzled. What was happening to her? The years were falling away like crimson leaves whirled in an autumn storm. She was spinning out of control.

"Seth!" she called again, her voice echoing off the brickwork hollowly, seeming to mock her.

Like a key jarring open a lock in her mind, a memory had surfaced. Years melted away before her open eyes like veils parting before a freshening wind. She was a child of four again, frightened, alone in the darkened nursery, alone with her nightmares.

"Seth!" Her voice seemed thin and strangled now, one she could barely recognize. She felt as if reality were slipping through her fingers, dreamlike, lost within her imagination.

Then, with an immense indrawn breath that midway through turned into a gasping shudder, she clasped both arms about her body and began to rock back and forth as she had when she was a child, terrified by phantoms springing out from the pitch-blackness of the night.

Seth's head jerked as if he had been abruptly reminded of something. He glanced across to the empty spot on the couch where Sophy normally sat.

For a moment, he had an odd sensation, as if she had called to him. The presence of her stole over him like a mantle of reflected light from the lurid streaks rending the night sky.

A strong gust took some hail pebbles and shot them against the window, strewing them along the sill where they lay like pristine pearls along a pretty girl's throat. For a long moment, he stared at them while all manner of thoughts flung themselves like rain in his mind. A smile edged his lips, as it did sometimes, in anticipation of a funny story.

He shrugged, long lean muscles rippling with the movement. First things first. His head lowered again, and he went methodically on with what he was doing, but not for long. The sensation came again, too strong now to be ignored. So acute was the feeling, he was aware of the thunder of his heart pumping, his accelerated pulse.

Seth's head turned again from the brief he had been reading, as if of its own volition. His peculiar sixth sense was warning him...of what? Sophy! Yes, he thought now, there was no doubt.

Sophy. His senses were full of her. Something fierce tugged at his insides. It was imperative he go to her. What was wrong? He began to move even before fully coherent conclusions had been reached.

Walking stiff legged from sitting so long, Seth went through the darkened hall and into the kitchen, wondering that none of the lights had been lit. He stopped, still as a statue, just over the threshold, listening and watching the shadows.

The kitchen was deserted. No one answered his call. She was not there. Nothing moved. He paused for a moment, confused.

Hadn't Sophy said she was going to the kitchen? She had given him one of her bright smiles, and promised to return shortly with a pot of hot chocolate. That had been two hours ago.

Seth cursed softly and, returning to the doorway, leaned against it, trying to make sense of it all, feeling a moment of irrational chill. There was a sighing in the room as if the winter wind outside had somehow crept through a crack in the window sash and now swirled around him.

Perhaps she had simply gone to bed? His heart contracted, as if a heavy weight had been placed on his chest. It made no sense. He shrugged inwardly. In matters like this, he reflected, one never knew. For a long moment he simply stood there, collecting his thoughts.

From deep within him came a secret fear that, somehow, Sophy had managed to uncover some undisclosed error in the accounts, and was deceiving him. This afternoon when he had tried to glean how the audit was progressing, she had stared down at her laced fingers.

Her face, calm and composed, revealed nothing of her inner feelings. He could scarcely discern the rise and fall of her breasts as she breathed, but he had the distinct impression she was struggling with herself. Which was absurd. Was she keeping something from him?

He could not say, and he did not know why it should worry him. When she swallowed he had seen the play of light along the side of her throat, the small shadow lying in the hollow like a teardrop. In that split instant, a brief shudder contracted the muscles ridged along his straight back as he was struck by a new and horrible suspicion.

He had been about to challenge her, when she had lifted her head and smiled, her teeth white and even. Her candid, open smile, untainted by sarcasm or cynicism, was like coming home after a weary journey. Locked, their eyes had stared within and through.

At the time it had been enough to allay his doubts. He had even sought a further closeness by deliberately telling an anecdote from a war he would rather forget.

Now, he shrugged away a prickle of dismay, and made his limping way into the drafty and desolate hallway. His eye caught something pale on the tiled corridor. He bent his broad back, retrieving a white linen handkerchief in long, trembling fingers.

He straightened, holding it to his nostrils, inhaling the faint scent of lavender. For a heart-stopping moment, his head buzzed with swirling emotions, and he felt a sudden tightening of his stomach, as if all the air had suddenly gone out of his lungs.

Nothing had ever felt so heavy. Trying to squelch the wild panic inside him, he gripped the scrap of fabric until his knuckles shone white as the linen.

Images enwrapped him. Sophy's violet-gray eyes, large and direct. They were always the first things he saw when he looked at her. A shining warmth that stayed with him wherever he went. He let out a light, unconscious sigh.

Lightning flickered, and the thunder followed almost at once. Seth's head snapped up, and he took a quick look around. That was it! The only doorway nearby was to the cellar. He tried the knob but the door was locked.

He assumed the worst.

Logic dictated he go search for the key, but Seth, for the first time in his life perhaps, did not heed logic. He stepped back and, using one booted foot, smashed at the lock. It gave somewhat but still held.

Crushing down the pain that shot through his leg like a steel spike hammered home, he kicked again, putting all his strength into it. The lock shattered with a crack like a rifle shot, and the door flew inward.

Recoiling, stumbling backward, Seth looked down the narrow flight of timber stairs leading to the cellar. There was no light. He stood perfectly still for some moments, though his heart was racing.

Wood creaked somewhere downstairs, a settling rather than a footstep. The cloying smell of aged yeast and fermentation was in the air. Fine dust particles, floating, caused a soft dry tickle at the base of his throat.

While lightning flashed and thunder rumbled farther off, here there was total silence, stretching itself, filling the dank void with an odd chill. But a kind of deafening noise pounded against his eardrums and Seth realized he was listening to the sound of his own pulse.

Struggling to control his breathing, the intense pounding of his blood in his veins, he scanned the darkened mass before him. His thoughts were chaotic.

"Sophy?" His voice was strange and thick, even to his own ears.

Within Seth now swirled many emotions. He recognized the fear for Sophy that dominated that other, more insidious sentiment, which was welling up inside him, threatening to overcome his hard-won control. He was not ready for that yet.

He felt torn, at odds with himself. Marriage with Sophy had changed his life. To feel. Not to feel. With Sophy, he wanted to do both. He was drawn to her like a moth to a flame, without reason or logic.

Seth shivered, remembering how one of Sophy's hands had gripped his arm on the ferry. Under the cotton of his shirtsleeve, he could almost feel an afterglow from the contact.

Emotion welled up in him. So many memories. So many sensations. There were qualities about Sophy that had begun to affect him, to creep through him like a fever.

For one thing, she was fiercely loyal. She would try to bring the sun down from the sky for one of her family who was genuinely in need. For another, her blossoming friendship with his difficult mother was touching. Her abiding understanding of Abigail Lethbridge's weakness was laudable. Even her outrageous attempt to provoke him was honest.

Suddenly Seth heard the soft rustle of silk, like reeds in the wind. Then he saw her, a figure blacker than the stygian night, her pale face rising like a waxen flower in the heart of the darkness.

His breath caught in his throat and his belly contracted painfully. He struggled to control his runaway pulse.

"Sophy?" The word stuck in his throat like a needle.

Sophy's heart leaped as the door burst open. Disoriented, she sat, transfixed. Her vision was going in and out of focus and she couldn't identify the tall silhouette framed in the square patch of dim light. A menacing figure, a demon or a rescuer?

Which was the illusion, which the reality?

"Sophy?"

There was an edge to the voice now, as if its owner had just woken up. The figure moved, all angles and black shadows, descending now into the labyrinth.

Small, chilled, miserable, Sophy huddled against the wall. She had an active imagination. Now, it had shut down entirely. Obviously, this was another illusion. She stirred slightly like a sapling in a sudden gust of wind, giving way minutely.

"Sophy?"

The huge featureless shadow had a deep voice. Seth's voice, yet not Seth's voice. Stealthy, yet full of passionate delight, as though he had found his love. The sensations touched her, beating like rain.

Sophy's eyes, weeping silent tears down her high-boned cheeks, blinked, trying to calibrate the thick, black shape, all wavering and hazy. Thighs like water, unable to support her, she scrambled to her knees. Her heart contracted as the figure took another halting step closer to her.

It was him! This time there was no doubt. Sophy's mind was jolted into recognition, and her body mobilized simultaneously. It was as if some obscure weight that had been crushing her had been lifted from her. The elation of relief seemed to fizz the blood in her veins. She came up from her knees and, heart exploding with joy, threw herself forward in one wild rush. Hurled herself into his arms with the force of fireworks.

Seth's arms automatically encircled her, to embrace her or to stop them both from falling, he did not know. It was as if he had been dropped into the center of a whirlpool, in the grip of forces he could no longer hold in check. Her head immediately tucked into the hollow of his shoulder as her upper body melted against his. He held her quietly for a moment, marshaling his thoughts.

"Sophy, are you all right?"

He felt as if his vocal cords were in spasm. The whites of his eyes took on a slight sheen as they tried to decipher her indistinct features.

She sniffed heavily. "C-certainly I am."

"You're shivering. No wonder. It's bloody freezing down here."

"I'm not c-cold."

Sophy couldn't go on. She felt him around her, his arms coiling, a great masculine figure, hard and strong. Though she was safe now within the sanctuary of his beloved embrace, still a dark part of her mind hammered to be heard.

Her chest contracted, her heart full of an unnamable anguish, she could do nothing but nestle into his robust vitality. Suddenly, she was crying against his shoulder, great gulping sobs, as she clung to him, shoulders shaking.

Seth touched her face gently with his fingertips. He could not help himself. Her eyes were half-shut, her lips partly open. He could feel her warm breath on him, and trace the moisture on her cool flesh as twin rivers gushed from beneath her quivering lids.

"Sophy..."

Her name was torn from his heart like a tattered battle pennant. His mind was working furiously, considering the improbabilities. He did not know how she came to be locked in the cellar, but he promised himself he would soon find out.

And when he did...

He felt her smaller body trembling uncontrollably against him, and his arms secured her to him like steel manacles.

"It's all right, Sophy. It's all right." It sounded like another's voice but he knew it was his.

Sophy just held him, needing to feel his warmth, the stir of his breath against her neck, the substantial masculine strength of him reassuring her that he was real rather than an illusion born out of her fear, a fear that had been part of her for so long that she had taken its existence for granted.

Slow, careful, patient as a man winning the trust of a wild creature, Seth eased one arm away and raised a hand. His long fingers caressed the nape of her neck and the base of her skull.

Sophy stirred against him, her chest heaving. A lump in her throat made it difficult to get the words out. She sniffed heavily.

"Ever since I was a child the dark has terrified me. It is an uncontrollable fear." Her voice had the quality of chalk rasping along a slate board.

"It's all right, Sophy. It's all right," Seth said again, his tone soothing. His chest moved up and down slowly with his breath as his body absorbed the deep racking shudders of hers, his soft incoherent murmurs calming her anguished sobs.

Sophy hung there against his chest, absorbing his strength as she tried to regain her own. She could no more disentangle herself from him than she could still her pulse. All sense of reality had slipped from her mind. All coherent thought was an effort.

"In the dark, I feel so alone, adrift, absolutely cut off from everything and everyone," she said, the words sounding foolish to her own ears.

Seth thought about that for a moment. His head bent until his lips brushed her ear. "Even a soldier must feel fear." His deep, rumbling voice filled Sophy's ear. It sounded odd and muffled. "A soldier must have his nemesis just as he must do battle."

He felt her soft and yielding against him, and his arms closed more tightly about her, as protectively as a mother's around a small child. Using the wall behind him as a bolster, he began to ease himself back up the stairs.

In the confined space, Seth's now-damp jacket gave off a clean, earthy smell. The solid arm around her shoulders felt heavy, warm and protective. Sophy hugged this core of comfort to the center of her being. It had the ability to make her feel safe enough to divulge her fears.

"In darkness there is betrayal and death." She gave a little hiccup.

Seth felt a spasm grip him. Not for him. Not for Sophy. She needed his protection. She was his in the most fundamental way. She had given herself to him. He would keep her safe.

There were words he longed to say, words that would free him, perhaps, from his own inner torment, but that would also certainly make him vulnerable to her. And words sometimes had no meaning at all.

"The enemy may come in many forms, in many guises, but always unseen and, therefore, the more terrifying. Fear has many eyes and can see things underground," he said softly, his face in her hair.

There was a minute trembling in his arms, and Sophy detected the slight vibration in his frame. Her head lifted. She peered at him through the shadows. Couldn't keep herself from asking in a voice that throbbed with emotion and uncertainty, "You have felt it?"

Seth thought about Gettysburg then. Something had changed. Abruptly, he realized that the sense of bitter guilt that always stung him whenever the war entered his thoughts was missing. Recognized that the unmitigated disaster of carnage and death was no longer so cruelly fresh in his heart, in his mind. Rejoiced that that particular chapter of his life was closed, forever.

It was as if a great weight had been taken off his chest. He became vividly aware of Sophy nestling deep in his arms, clinging to him. He breathed into her hair. He dragged her lightly back into his warmth and swung her up another step.

"Honor rules me. It is my weapon and my weakness." His voice was deliberately light, bantering and more full of truth than he thought it was. He had not meant to make any such admission, and immediately felt as if he had lost a battle.

Sophy could feel the nearness of his body, the tension that pulled at every muscle and sinew. A wave of love welled up within her, banishing her fear.

"Honor is but another name for love," she whispered in a voice that vibrated with the intensity of her emotions. Her words stirred the hair at the base of his neck.

Seth felt her lips open against the exposed cords at the side of his neck as she spoke. Then an extraordinary, wonderful sensation, the licking of her tongue, inquisitive and naive as a child's, licking the salty skin. All the more erotic for its simplicity.

"Sophy?"

He said it as if tasting a new flavor, testing out its sound on his tongue. His mind was numb with disbelief at her action, even as he felt the heavy pulse of his blood through his veins . . . a delicious dissolving of defenses. He lowered his head, his mouth unerringly locating hers in that well of darkness.

Sophy was quivering with the strength of the sensations running rampant through her. She couldn't give him an answer, not in words. His lips held hers while his arms walled her in, pressing her body to his. Her mouth opened under his like a flower to the sun.

Their breaths mingled. She felt his hand on her hair, stroking down it to her shoulders, his fingertips delicately exploring her neck, her jaw, her ear.

Sweetly paralyzed, her body went limp with pleasure. She melted inside at the gentle drift of his fingers against her skin and the warmth of his mouth tracing moist kisses along her jaw. He kissed her ears, her nose, the corners of her eyes where moisture still lingered soft as early-morning dew on a petal.

Wherever he touched a little fire darted through her, melting her further. When she arched lovingly against him, he buried his lips in the hollow of her throat.

Sophy felt his hands kneading the curves of her body through her gown. His fingers slid over the silky material of her bodice, followed the pearl buttons to her waist, caressed her hip, and trailed down the little angle between her belly and her hip.

There was a tiny moan, and Sophy knew in a dim way that she had uttered it. The tremble was back within her, a frenzied desire for more intimate contact. She wrapped her arms around him, pressing her face against his shoulder, almost afraid of the depth of her need for him.

Sophy felt an unknown force seeping into her body as if it came from Seth himself. Too, she became aware of an incipient urgency, a throbbing sensation deep in her stomach.

The liquid female fire within her leaped and surged, longing to engulf this other male flame, longing to fuse and become one with it. Awash with sensation, she could hear nothing but the roaring of her heart, compelling, demanding, surrendering.

She crushed herself against him, murmuring endearments. The taste of him was an intoxicating wine taken in through the senses. She trembled in his embrace as her thighs turned to liquid.

It was Seth who drew back, reluctantly, breathing fast, the timbre of his voice deep and husky. "I'm not having this."

"Wh-what?"

"This is not the right time to renegotiate our contract. It is a matter of honor."

He chuckled hoarsely and, though she could not see it, Sophy could sense the ghost of a smile on his lips. She could also sense the restraint he was exercising. She felt her heart contract, and struggled with her disappointment.

"Blast that stupid bargain! You know, sometimes I think..."

How could he not realize that the only thing she wanted was to stay here in the circle of his arms, to be drawn into the waiting pool of passion and excitement, his hard mouth on hers, his hard body her governor and shield against the world? All he could think of was to make her agree to the formal settlement of their contract!

She stood for a moment irresolute. It had all sounded so grand and heroic, this modern independence thing, but now it seemed really silly when she felt so soft and yielding. But a foolish, obstinate pride kept her from saying so.

"We can thrash it out later. Kiss me again here, just once more."

Seth drew a deep breath, aware of the sexual voltage coursing between them, of himself on the verge of a powerful, all-consuming love. "Wherever and however you give yourself to me, Sophy, I should always consider it the most priceless gift in the world. I agree with you, we can thrash it out later, but not here."

He leaned down to brush her mouth with his own. "That'll do to be going on with." He straightened up, smiling. "While we're down here, do you still want to check out the contents of the cellar?"

Sophy screwed up her face. She locked both arms around his neck, hugged him fiercely. "You can wait for your cherry cake!"

They both laughed at that, and they did not stop until they were at the top of the stairs. It was good to be on familiar territory. To have Seth take command. To witness the easy, masculine authority of him as he summoned servants to his bidding. He was a man who inspired one with a comfortable feeling of security.

Good, too, to have Tessa sweep her away to a hot bath, marvel over her misadventure, wonder at Seth's ingenuity and, generally, fuss over her. She was a little unnerved by all that had happened that day, so the pampering was savored.

An odd thought flew through her head like a bird, circling in the sky of her mind. *The fault is not in our stars, but in ourselves.* She felt all her old buoyancy surge over her.

There *was* a way!

It was like a salmon struggling upstream, fiercely fighting the current. The key was within. Seth must find the hurdle within himself and make the leap. She was quite certain of that now. Seth was a man who could be taught how to love. He just needed a little practice.

The gaslight shone brightly on the walls and ceiling, only the bed was in shadow. Light and shadow, love and laughter, a crazy quilt of images, *the most priceless gift in the world.*

Think of it! All that loving saved up for her, only for her.

Sophy's heart sighed, contented.

Chapter Fourteen

It was while he was bathing that Seth's reasoning processes finally began to function again. He stretched his long legs outward into the hot sudsy water, sighing deeply. It had been a long hard day, full of concern for Charles and fear for Sophy's well-being.

Thunder still boomed, made dull and echoey by distance, but the rain had ceased. Racing clouds ran before the wind, but they were no longer heavy and threatening. At intervals, they slid apart and the cool opalescent light of the full moon illuminated the sky.

A nagging self-blame had invaded his mind since he'd discovered Sophy trapped in the cellar. But now the hot water was working its magic on his tensed body, loosening his knotted muscles, the cords in his neck and shoulders relaxing, the day's accumulated tension leaching away from him.

Not that his anxiety about the entire incident had disappeared completely, but somehow the perilous urgency of that thought was fading. As he had interrogated the servants, the edge of his anger had dulled. Never suspecting anybody would be down there at night, a very repentant butler confessed to locking the cellar door.

Sophy came to Seth's room, a feeling of vast happiness expanding inside her. Love was warm and comforting and tender. Love was... "Seth, I..." Her words trailed away in confusion.

She swallowed, her hands tightening on the brass knob. Golden shadows from the fireplace flickered on the sinewy sleekness of Seth's chest and shoulders as he lay in a hip bath. His shuttered gaze reflected that peculiar hot light that often crept into his eyes when he stared at her.

"Well, come on in," Seth rasped with feigned impatience. "Don't just stand there letting in the cold air."

Sophy hesitated again. "I'm not sure..."

"You want your pound of flesh, don't you?" he taunted in a rough growl, deliberately closing his eyes.

What a strange phrase for him to use, Sophy thought vaguely, edging into the room. She went on watching him, tracing each contour of his head and face as if she were touching him physically. There was power in that face, the lines the burden of command had etched into it, giving it character and substance.

Slowly, his heart beating faster than he would have wished, Seth opened his eyes. She stared down at him for an instant and something flickered in her gaze. Satisfaction? Pride? It was as if he were her secret treasure.

He sucked in his breath. Nothing in his life had prepared him for Sophy. Everything in his life seemed a little brighter for her presence.

His chest rose and fell as he drew in a deep breath. Despite all his military training, his careful discipline, his sharp intellect, he felt lost beside her, as if she were a doorway to some world for which he had been totally unprepared.

Tiny, feathered lines radiated from Seth's eyes, but there was no mistaking that she had kindled something fierce and hot in those glistening blue eyes. It was like being wrapped and caught in an embrace. A new delight that made her thighs tremble, her throat constrict.

Sophy pressed a small hand to herself in the region of her waist. Suddenly she started to lose her nerve and turned to leave.

With surprising agility, given the nature of his handicap, Seth surged from the tub and moved around behind her, cutting off her retreat. He was standing naked, legs braced slightly apart.

"Welcome to my parlor, little fly."

The sight of Seth's powerful torso and long muscular legs sent a spasm of excitement through Sophy. She wanted to rush forward, to embrace him, to love him. She wanted to step back, away, to break the magic spell that bound her, to flee . . . to flee . . . but she was powerless.

"Not retreating, Sophy? Not when your ambush worked so well!" Self-deprecating humor lacing his low-pitched voice, Seth glanced down at himself. The overwhelming physical testimony of that simple truth was quite apparent in his rampant manhood.

Moisture filmed his body. Little runnels of water streamed through the shadowy hair on his chest, flowing down to bead the dark forest at the base of his trunk like pearls on a seabed. Glory! There was even a drop quivering on the tip of . . .

Face blazing, Sophy shifted her eyes from the bold and blatant evidence of his masculinity to his face. That was a mistake. Staring into those all-knowing eyes, it was difficult to think.

The air between them seemed to tremble.

Sophy made a sharp movement, a movement that was almost fierce. Her head came up. A wave of color heated her face, and her eyes darkened to a stormy violet.

At this moment, clad only in his masculine boldness, Seth felt strangely vulnerable. If she would just take one step toward him, he would gladly surrender, tell her what he knew she wanted to hear.

"I've found out something you ought to know." The words trembled on Sophy's lips. She heard them in her mind, but they were never uttered. Her lips murmured something soft and indistinguishable.

She lifted a hand, wiped back a stray strand of hair behind one ear. The long-sleeved cotton nightgown billowed around her bare ankles and her hair was an ebony ribbon of silk, but she was totally unaware of the soft, inviting picture she made.

Seth drew a breath as if about to plunge into a cold stream, and his black brows met above his brooding eyes. Something fierce showed in his blue eyes.

Sophy watched his eyes follow her hand, and wondered whether she ought to tell him about her meeting with Charles. It might be the wrong time. She didn't want to destroy that expression of hungry longing on his face. Why? Why? She asked the question, but she did not seek the answer. She already knew.

"Have you decided?" Seth asked her suddenly, and his voice sounded hoarse and unlike himself. He seemed rooted to the spot, transfixed. Despite himself, Seth felt the quickness of his pulse, the heat of his own breath firing in his throat. He wanted this woman with all his being, wherever she would lead him, at whatever cost.

Sophy gazed at him in growing uncertainty. Licking a drop that had landed on his lip, he met her eyes with perfect composure. He was not touching her, yet was all around her, enveloping, encircling, enclosing, filling her insides with warmth and softness.

It was becoming impossible to think.

At the sight of him, naked, all wet and dripping, something inside her, high up at the top of her brain, seemed to rise, beginning to float away. She had to get a grip on her emotions. In the morning, she told herself, she would sort it all out.

Right now, she could only surrender to the pull of this unbearable attraction. Standing before her without the faintest hint of shame, with that careless animal magnetism of his that made him in some fashion superb, he drew her toward him. She could not help herself.

It was as if he'd deliberately entered her mind. As if he had used some magic of his own to conjure up the desire that only he could quench, all she wanted was for him to lead her to that tingling secret world where carnality was all.

Ignoring her common sense, her inner self leaped over the bounds of her being and demanded to be joined, made double, made whole. Somehow the distance between them was closing. There seemed to be no conscious volition on either of their parts.

Sophy stepped closer, her fragrance enveloping him. A warm wind blew through his soul and he closed his eyes as he felt her arms steal about him, her lips trace the contours of his cheek. She paused as if uncertain whether to go on, then, standing on tiptoe, she gave him his answer with a feathery kiss.

"Yes." The syllable came out in a gasp, but it sounded so right, so perfect, it might have been intended since time began.

Sophy shuddered as Seth suddenly surged against her, his maleness asserting itself, the impact of him a shock to her senses. She gave a small cry deep in her throat and he swallowed the sound hungrily.

They strained to each other, mouths mingling and exploring. Seth's hands caressed her back, moving down to draw her even closer to him. In a haze, Sophy was aware of the gentle drift of his fingers against her skin and the warmth of his mouth tracing lazy kisses along her jaw.

"This is how it should be." He kissed the tip of her nose.

In a haze, her hands moved up the back of his neck and entwined in his hair, pulling his head down to hers with a sigh of yielding abandon. Her palms were damp, Sophy realized vaguely. His mouth returned to possess hers with a tenderness that stirred her heart.

Her fingers traced his earlobe, his neck, the rough hair at the nape, liking the way it felt. She nuzzled her face into the curve between his shoulder and his neck. Her tongue licked the hollow at the side of his neck before, lost in pleasure, she gave him a little nip.

Rubbing her cheek against his big warm chest, Sophy found the dark shadowed places, the damp texture of hair. She found it fascinating, and burrowed her face and fingers through it. Her hands caressed the springy texture, enjoying the way it curled around her fingers, sprang back into tight curls. She turned her head to sample one masculine nipple with the tip of her tongue, and Seth tensed, groaning.

The fingers that had been tugging at the ribbon fastenings of her night rail finally worked them free, and curved to cup the smooth, pale flesh of the breast they had exposed. Her breasts were high and round, the dark nipples gathered now into thrusting peaks clamoring for his touch.

"Please," she begged, not knowing if she meant him to stop or continue. "Please."

Seth touched the tip of one nipple as if it were a valuable gem, delighted when Sophy nestled closer. Endlessly gentle, he nuzzled the soft skin beneath her breast, his tongue making ever decreasing circles around the globe until he reached his goal.

Sophy was unaware of holding her breath until she released it with a shudder as his lips closed warmly over her nipple. She was only aware of an inordinate pleasure pooling in her loins. There was a sound, a moan, from her own throat, she realized, thick with a growing urgency.

His fingers seared her skin everywhere he touched as he divested her of her cotton night rail. As his hands molded her breasts and slid over the curves and hollows of her body, Sophy felt the sweet tingling surge of desire deep within her.

The feel of his lips on her mouth, murmuring her name over and over, was the sweetest sound she had ever heard.

Slowly, gently, Seth lifted her onto the bed and cradled her against his body. There was no passionate demand in his embrace, even though his hard lean body surged continually against her in minute ripples. His eyes glowing with some inner fire, he shifted slowly onto his back, inviting her touch.

Seth could feel her trembling response as she flowed, all soft and pliant woman, against him. There was a tightening in his stomach. His heart was racing, knocking against his ribs.

Her hair floated over him, drawing forth a deep, guttural groan that told Sophy of his rising need. She wanted to touch, to hold, with a wantonness that took her by surprise. His body was firm and corded, the wide muscular chest, where the strong heart raced beneath her palms, all damp and silky.

The hard ridge of his backbone was strength to her, the soft indentation at the base of his spine was gentleness. Her hands traced circles across his chest, belly, nipples, while her lips hovered at the edge of all of this new territory she wanted to make her own.

Trembling with the force of her excitement and growing need, she passed a hand across that flesh at the core of his being. His breath sharpened involuntarily. She teased gently, every movement incredibly slow, infinitely tantalizing, touching him with questing fingertips, drawing out his own ribboning desire.

Suddenly he had moved, and his fingers caressed her contours as if he were a blind man needing to imprint their image on his mind forever. He was making her feel as though she was floating on a cloud of pleasure. Her fingers caressed his ears as his tongue streaked hotly across her nipples.

Strong hands moved over her from ankle to throat, learning and possessing every place in between. Then, his hand was at that other secret place, where all sensation lodged. A sudden shyness caught Sophy unexpectedly, and she clenched her thighs together tightly.

"Open yourself, my love. Let it go. Any way you want, any way you ever imagined. Come on, I'll show you."

Gentle caressing voice, even though she could hear his fierce breathing. Gentle caressing hand, even though he held her anchored, as though he already possessed her. The momentary stiffening in her spine and legs slowly relaxed as his fingers lightly, delicately, danced over her feminine center.

Something indeed was opening within her, like a flower new to the sun. Opening and releasing a stream of sweetness, which carried her along on its hot, demanding flood. Felt the shaking begin, deep inside her.

He raised his head, and took her mouth. One of his hands smoothed her thigh, her hip, her waist, until she made a small impatient noise. He threaded his hands through her long, silken hair, and spread it out like a fan over her breasts, laughing as its lustrous, dark strands separated, her nipples peeping through the veil like inquisitive mice.

With infinite slowness, he parted the stems of her legs and gazed lovingly down at the moist petals of the flower thus revealed. When Sophy felt the heated stab of his tongue in her core, she arched up with her hips, crying out in inarticulate delight. Her thighs trembled uncontrollably as Seth worshiped her body with his mouth.

Then the urgency of his own desire compelled him to complete the union. Gently at first until she was accustomed to the feel of him, then, with infinite tenderness, he propelled her into the rhythm of his need. Her body answered with a surge of excitement.

She loved him so much it made her mind spin, as if she were drunk with too much wine. This was what she had wanted, what she had craved.

When the vibrations began, for a brief time Sophy believed that an earthquake had begun, then she realized that the sensation was entirely internal. It seemed perfectly natural and not at all shameless when she pressed more directly against him in order to pass on the sensation.

Seth's body, too, was making its claims. Sophy heard his breath come in great jagged gasps, like steam escaping, as he buried his face in her tossing hair. Felt the powerful play of muscles in his body as they bunched in excitement, ready for the ultimate discharge.

The trembling came to Sophy again, this time in great racking pulses, so that she moaned with the exquisite perfection of the moment. Like the burst of a cannon's fusillade he went rigid against her, the tension draining out of him as he shot his seemingly limitless seed.

They lay together as one person, all passion spent, bathed in the fire's glow and the aftermath of loving. Drifting back to reality, Sophy smiled up at Seth as he placed a gentle kiss on her nose. His eyes were as still and deep as a mountain pool.

Without a word, he pulled the covers over them and laid his head on the pillow next to hers. It was as if he were reluctant to move away from her. Tenderly, he put out his arm and drew her next to his side. She cuddled near him and they both slept.

Drowsily, Sophy opened her eyes. There was a heavy weight across one leg, and a soft warmth was blowing, quietly and evenly, at regular intervals against her face.

Seth lay sprawled beside her, his black hair stuck up endearingly in little points, his dark eyelashes tangled at the edges. He was still asleep, his face turned to the side, toward her.

He was on his stomach, stretched like some great cat, one leg straight out, the other bent at the knee. It was this leg that secured Sophy to the bed as effectively as a butterfly on a pin. It was as if, even in sleep, he wanted her by his side.

Turning carefully, she slid her numb limb from beneath him, wriggling her toes experimentally. They still moved. She braced herself on one elbow and studied his sleeping face.

He looked totally at ease as, in the manner of some great conquering hero, he took command of more than his share of the bed. The covers lay in a tangled heap on the floor. Only part of a sheet remained on the bed, and this, already sliding to join the others, trailed across one of his ankles.

Even in sleep, the powerful contours of his body reflected the intrinsic strength of the man. The driving energy and strict discipline that had enabled him to overcome an injury that would have totally crippled a lesser man were evident in the relaxed sweep of muscle and sinew.

Quietly Sophy slid off the bed and tiptoed to the cherry-wood dresser for her wrapper. She needed desperately to think before she faced him. She knew she had made the right decision, but that did not make her resigned to the inevitable results of that decision.

Seth grunted and turned his head. The sheet slipped to the floor with a mere whisper of sound as he moved his leg. She shot him a covert look, but he was still again, breathing steadily. He was still sleeping when she let herself out the door.

Seth lay quietly, blinking himself into awareness. Sophy! He turned to greet her eagerly, but there was only the dent in the pillow where her head had lain.

Yet the tenuous connection was still there, last night's events somehow linking them like a length of twined silk. There was a dull ache behind his eyes when he thought of Sophy's fear in the dark cellar, the generous gift of herself, his inability to say aloud what was burning inside him.

His thoughts and feelings shifted, rearranged themselves, as he made a determined attempt to understand and to find some steady ground. The same desperate search for steady ground had been his focus after Gettysburg, and his life felt as shattered as his leg.

He had regained his iron control, and was just preparing to shave when Sophy returned, fully dressed. Today she had on a deep crimson velvet gown with some sort of trim at the hem. Around the low neckline was a little frill, and the silver choker she favored was at her throat. Her hair swirled in a delicious loop over the curve of her cheeks, then twisted in a spiral to coil in a little knot on her crown.

There was a huge bow at the back that perched provocatively on top of the draped-up skirt. It swayed when she moved. Knowing the real contours and the sweet flare of the hips beneath all that padding sent a fresh surge of excitement clear down to his toes.

It took an extreme effort of will to simply stand there and pretend he wasn't burning up inside. Two patches of dull red stained the ridge of his cheeks but his voice was calm and steady.

"Good morning, Sophy. Going somewhere?"

Sophy blinked rapidly. "I promised your mother we would purchase some of that wonderful new flexible webbing that is now being imported from France.

"For garters," she explained patiently in response to his blank look. She lifted the front of her skirt to show him her own white silk stockings with the elastic ruching just below the knee.

"Oh." The tremor grew in him to hard stiffness.

"Are . . . are you cross with me?"

Seth was pouring hot water into his shaving mug, his brow furrowed in thought, as if he had no idea what she was talking about. Determinedly, Sophy continued, "For being such a watering pot?"

"Christ, Sophy! It's too early in the morning to needle me like this. At least let me shave first! The water's getting cold." He smiled to take the sting out of the words. Something in his eyes suddenly melted. "If you shut up, you can even stay and watch me!'' He waved a hand as if in dismissal, fully expecting her to go.

Cheeks crimson with pleasure, Sophy needed no further invitation. She sat down promptly, her heart hammering, feeling suddenly like a child who had discovered her love of sweets. Once in the shop she was reluctant to depart. She smiled at him, a shy and pleased expression.

He was giving her the opening she needed, but was there a catch? Every time she thought she knew him, another aspect of his personality would pop up like a rabbit out of a magician's hat. She was reviewing the situation with commendable detachment when he rinsed his face and began his morning routine.

It was perfectly fascinating to see Seth perform such a masculine task. Stripped to the waist, towel draped around his neck, he ran his razor down the strop. The action was like some barbaric ceremonial ritual.

Wide-eyed, she sat ever so still and watched the expertise and dexterity that were needed for such a seemingly simple procedure. Desire was in her eyes. She knew it, but couldn't disguise the emotion.

Seth looked at her reflection in the vanity mirror, and smiled in indulgent humor, the satisfaction in him plainly visible. ''Why don't you think out loud?'' He mixed shaving soap and began to lather his face.

If possible, Sophy turned a brighter shade of crimson, a sudden shyness catching her unexpectedly. She propped her elbow on her knee, and lodged her chin in her hand. A thick coil of hair slid across one side of her face like a midnight waterfall.

''I was thinking of our wedding bargain,'' she told him with soft candor.

Seth dipped his shaving brush in the mug so violently, the hot water ran over the edge, pooling on the marble bench top. He irritably topped up the mug from the steaming copper jug that had been sent up on the dumbwaiter.

"Do we have to talk about that now? Can't you leave that out of our conversation just this once?" Seth growled as he leaned over the bench top and lifted his chin, trying to see himself in the mirror.

"I suppose so."

Sophy stifled a sigh in her throat. She had given of her love freely to him and he had accepted it, giving only the physical side of himself in return. Don't think. Don't think about that, she chided herself.

"I think," she said slowly, at length, "that I see my duty more clearly now."

Seth's hands stilled. "Duty? Duty!" he repeated blankly. "You would never call what we did together last night *duty!*" he demanded, a baffled expression on his half-lathered face.

Sophy looked up wonderingly, staring at him in disbelief. No, it had been the wildest, most intense emotion she had ever known, but the physical intimacy had been only the totally consummate expression of her deepest feelings. Last night she had placed her trust in the palm of his hand.

Her tongue came out to dampen her lips. "Are you saying that you felt the same outpouring of love that I did?"

Seth swung around, his blue eyes narrowed. *Yes,* came the sound in his mind, and he started in spite of himself. Should he tell her that he wanted her, all of her: her energy, her contrariness, her spunk, even her downright bossiness?

He glanced at Sophy, and blinked a little, as if trying to assess her mood. She was very still, her huge luminous eyes fixed on his, waiting for his answer. He hesitated to answer.

What did he have to say to her? That she was an incredibly loving woman? That he wanted to sink into her flesh? Or that he was a man of honor?

Somehow, without his consent or knowledge, Sophy had wedged herself into his heart. As soon as he had his financial situation sorted out and they were on an equal footing, he would tell her. In the meantime...

"You want me to be honest?" His voice was dark in timbre, ebony velvet.

Sophy flinched at the blunt question, and her heart gave a sudden quick throb of dismay, but she nodded bravely. She realized with a swiftness that took her breath away just how fragile the illusion of love was.

"Love is not on my agenda, as I told you when we sealed our bargain," he said, making his voice as gentle as he could.

Sophy shivered as she faced him, the pain in her clearly reflected in the taut line of her mouth and in the depths of her eyes. It wasn't right, but he meant it. She knew he meant it. His absolute assurance struck her dumb.

Seth stared at her for a long moment, and then he seemed to draw a deep breath. His face softened and he lifted his hand to flick gentle fingers along the line of her cheek.

"I care for you, Sophy. I care a great deal. You have given me more than I ever dreamed or imagined. I don't want to jeopardize our relationship with introspection. Is it wrong to wish to count my blessings and leave it at that?" he added, surprised by the softness in his voice.

Out of the small silence that built itself, Sophy said softly, "I would not call it wrong. Merely shortsighted, for in avoiding suffering and risk and danger, one loses out on much of what makes life exciting and pleasurable."

Her voice was low, but not lacking in strength. Every word came with the steady force of unwavering conviction. She took a step toward him, reached out her hand to touch his face, forefinger lightly brushing his mouth.

"The heart is a house with a room for every person it loves. It is a very special gift. You have the capacity to love, do not deny it!"

Sophy couldn't keep the passionate appeal out of her voice, and the emotion cut through the space between them. Her eyes glittered as she looked up at him, diamond bright with the hint of tears she was holding back with a supreme effort of will.

"Maybe."

He said no more, knowing that anything he said would be superfluous. His throat closed, and there was a peculiar pucker around his mouth as he turned back to the mirror.

Sophy swallowed her chagrin, her dark hair swaying with her motion. Had the man last night only been an illusion? A creation of her own mind brought about by a desire to justify her surrender to the compelling fascination Seth had for her?

Then she suddenly remembered Madame Bertine's counsel. For every person, there is always another who has followed in the same shoes to the same fate. She would not take Madame Bertine's path. But she would take, whatever the cost of shameless or indelicate conduct, that provocative and intemperate advice.

A smile hovered on her wide, tender mouth. He would be shocked. But perhaps the shock would jolt his stupid notions on love just as Bernard's experiments with electricity jolted bits of wire.

Sophy put her arms around Seth from behind and kissed him between the shoulder blades, enjoying the pleasant taste and scent of his smooth skin. She had to rub her cheek against him, to press the smile from her lips.

"You didn't expect me to give up just because of last night? That was a draw!" She deliberately injected a measure of lightness into her voice. Standing on the tips of her toes, she blew at the lather under his chin, gently laughing at the shudder that went through him.

"Our war of love has just begun. I realize now there may be a number of small skirmishes before the decisive battle!" she said, smiling at his reflection.

He looked taken aback. As well he might, she thought, suppressing a chuckle at his expression. Not knowing the emotion, he did not know that love, perfect love, never gives up, and its faith, hope and patience never fail.

Glory! What would St. Paul think of Madame Bertine's advice? Sophy put her cheek against his broad back and began to giggle.

A slow sense of satisfaction grew in Seth. He made a small sound that might have been a laugh. There was an honesty about Sophy, a genuineness that had touched him, transcending circumstance.

She had approached him without guile, making no bones about what she needed. *Can you give this to me?* she had asked him in the wedding bargain. *And this? And this? And I, in return, shall give you—* More than he could ever have anticipated.

Life with Sophy was never dull.

He began to shave his face. Her palm came up to stroke his neck, and he shuddered at the fiery lick the caress engendered in him. The fingers trailed along his wide shoulder, down under the armpit, and here they stopped to explore the wiry softness of hair.

Seth made a little hissing noise, his breath sharply drawn in through his teeth. The fingers continued their examination, dancing now along his rib cage as though it were a musical instrument. His shoulders quivered, as if they had a will of their own.

He grimaced as the razor scraped his cheek, and he compelled his mind to turn to other thoughts, else he would end up cutting his own throat.

"Call it what you will," Sophy murmured beneath her breath, pressing her breasts against his back. "Whatever you may say, you are mine, and in your heart you know it. Sooner or later, sooner or later, I will make you own it."

She couldn't see over his shoulder to watch his reaction in the mirror, but seconds later, as her hand slid down from his chest and across his flat belly, she felt it.

Her fingers curled around him, tentative at first, but rapidly becoming more confident. His reaction when she touched him was gratifyingly vigorous. Feeling him spring to life against her palm, she was filled with a warm and secret delight. It had suddenly all become so simple.

Maneuver according to circumstance. Seth dabbed his face with a towel, and unlocked his thoughts, allowing the keen sense of anticipation to enfold him like a cloak on a winter's eve.

And as he did so, he smiled like a man well pleased.

Chapter Fifteen

Sophy was just about to cross into Rivington Street when, somewhere in the vicinity, a deep-toned church bell began to ring, and soon more bells of varying degrees of pitch and resonance began to clang.

Along with most of the hurrying crowd, she halted, trying to determine what was amiss and where. An icy dart shot the length of her back when she saw a palpitating orange glare light the sky and heard someone bellow, "Hey! It's a fire!"

Windows banged open and heads emerged, yelling for information. Residents ran out of doors, pulling on scarves and coats. A flood of shrieking, ravening humanity quickly surged in the direction of an increasingly dense pillar of gray-blue smoke, rising only a block or so away.

Cries of "Fire! Fire!" split the air.

A shout went up. "Where is it?"

A shout came back. "Somewhere in Rivington Street!"

More bells joined in, raising the tumult; billows of acrid, eye-stinging smoke thickened as the deafening cacophony increased.

"Clear the way for Hose Company Nineteen!"

Down the avenue it raced, the red-and-gold fire engine, billowing smoke and vapor from its steamer, three galloping horses abreast, nostrils wide, manes flying, the helmeted driver laying on an unfelt whip. Clinging to the stubby water tank as if to salvation itself, six helmeted fire fighters shouted futilely to clear the way.

So rapidly did the crowd thicken from all directions that Sophy was hard put to maintain her footing. She felt herself spun about, her ears numbed by the din.

Trapped by the mob, she pressed flat against a brownstone wall, watching the fire fighters dash past. Their little engines and wooden pump handles appeared absurdly inadequate.

Pandemonium increased. Terrified carriage and dray horses snorted, reared and plunged, dragging wrecked vehicles. Some of the animals broke loose, trampling and charging aimlessly about the crowd.

Amid howls, yells and the pounding of feet, it became apparent to Sophy that this was a fire of major proportions.

"It's spreading!"

Three other big buildings had started to ooze smoke before flames burst through the upper windows. The clouds of smoke thickened, as increasing numbers of blazing brands and sparks billowed along the street.

A small space opened in front of Sophy, and she darted into the fray. The shrill screams and screeching of humans aware that flaming death was about to close in upon them now began to sound over the infernal crackling roar.

Suddenly she was free of the worst of the crowd and started to run toward Rivington Street. Her small figure was soon swallowed up amid the billowing, choking smoke.

As Seth turned stiffly into Delancy Street, each step carefully measured, his heart was filled with a double joy. He was meeting Sophy at the agent's office in Rivington Street in fifteen minutes, and he had discovered today he could manage without the aid of his walking stick.

Every night, Sophy diligently massaged his wasted muscle, and every day he exercised assiduously. Somehow, the unorthodox treatment had restored his sense of balance and poise. He was still too slow, too awkward, but given time...

He grinned into the wind that nipped at his ears. For the first time in too many years to count, he felt free. Happy and free.

Bells clanged, coming nearer and nearer. A horde of people came yelling, tearing down the street past him. All around him arose a frightening series of yells, whoops and drunken cries.

"Fire! Where's the fire!"

Now, unbidden, Seth felt fear flutter his heart. Gray, woolly clouds of smoke came belching up Allen Street. Giant flames leaped and spewed into the darkness of the smoke like the corona of the sun seen close up in a primitive dance. People were running in every direction, screaming.

Seth felt the skin on his forearms beginning to chill and tingle when he realized where the fire was situated. His heart clenched. Abruptly, the force of his feelings for Sophy broke the surface of his mind, like a geyser rupturing the glass surface of a still pond.

The comprehension came, not from his mind, not from reason, not even from knowledge, but from somewhere in a region of his heart that he had held so long at bay.

His heart gave a wild leap and stood still as a ball of flame lit the sky. Red and orange lights led toward the East River, bulking blackly against the skyline, the bloated billowing flames twisting like fiery gymnasts.

There was a confused babble, the scurrying of many feet. The next moment he had pushed through the surge of onlookers. Rivington Street was red and ablaze.

Seth ran.

Sophy halted halfway up the stairs and leaned against the rail to catch her breath. Then she went on. She gained the office door, took a step or two inside.

Chairs lay on their sides. Drawers had been wrenched open. Papers lay scattered, giving the place the rather disconsolate air of a deserted carnival.

"Seth?" Where was he? A red eye glowed ahead of her, the opalescent glow of fire reflected in the window. She could hear the sound of harsh breathing. Her own?

The door banged shut, dislodging a piece of plaster. A distinct shiver of fear began at the base of her spine and worked upward.

"Richard?"

Every nerve in her body shrieked when, like a red lance flung into the sky, a tongue of flame caught the curtain, leaping red and gold in the window. Higher soared the flames, until the wallpaper curled. Now it was a fierce, throbbing glare that singed the feathers in Sophy's bonnet.

She wrenched open the office door. Flames raced along the baseboards of the wall and began to lick at the steps. Her knees wobbled. She closed her eyes and held her breath but she could smell it anyway. The acrid thick odor of burning timber and paint, slick and heavy as oil, filled her nostrils and stung her skin.

No way to get out.

She couldn't breathe right. Her lungs were on fire. The smoke was inky thick. She opened her mouth. "Seth! I love you!"

Seth crashed into the solid bulk of Richard Carlton. "Where's Sophy? Have you seen her?"

"No. The place has been evacuated."

"Seth!" And now he heard her, her voice clear above the din. Shouting her name, he ran into the building. Fire raced behind him, straining at his heels.

Sophy was perched on the rail at the top of the steps, limned in firelight and fear. She was balanced there, ready to jump.

He stretched out his arms to her. She hesitated, then launched herself, striking him with such force that they both went down, rolled.

He helped her up, his face white. Neither of them spoke. Words were unnecessary and impossible. The very air around them had been sucked into the backdraft. There was nowhere to go.

Seth's brain seethed in its struggle with this new problem. His eyes fastened on a narrow stairway. He pointed at the opening, grabbed Sophy's hand, and together they raced down into the smoke-filled kitchen.

He shot back a brace of stout brass bolts. Throwing open the door, he pulled her out into the rear courtyard. Coolness hit her face. The noise in her ears changed. The smoke was gone, not completely, but thin enough so they could breathe without choking.

Gasping, drawing great mouthfuls of air, Seth suddenly realized the courtyard exit was locked. They were trapped. An unnatural silence descended, broken only by a savage, spine-tingling roar of flames beating at the walls behind them.

"What is it?" Sophy managed with a steadiness that surprised her.

Seth rubbed his palms across his face and stood ramrod straight, concentrating on controlling his breathing. "It's a Yale pin tumbler lock, impossible to break."

"Is there no way it can be picked?"

He shook his head once, slowly. "Not without a flat metal tool."

Sophy fumbled under her voluminous dress. Her cagelike extension skirt dropped to the ground and she thanked heaven for Charles Worth, the French fashion king. With difficulty, her small hands began to work one of the springy metal bands free from its tape casing.

There was another explosion and the whole building seemed to shudder. An uneasy silence fell. Like scarlet serpents, flames began writhing out along the doorway until the whole area was flooded by a hellish, throbbing light.

Seth's strong capable hands took over the task, wiggling the strip of metal back and forth until the dainty braid holding the two edges together gave way. Now, thanks to the French modistes and the modish Madame Bertine, they had a lock-picking tool!

In no time at all, he had inserted the improvised key, jiggling and twisting until the internal mechanism clicked. Then they were racing to safety. As they stood there gasping, Sophy noticed with wonder that large snowflakes were beginning to fall.

Shadows danced madly around them, the central pillar of the flames still burning. In beautiful contrast with the lurid masses of flame and smoke, an arch of rainbow, brightening and fading as the northwest wind fell, formed on the spray of the engines.

Sophy sagged against the shock wave of relief, her body leaning into Seth's strength for support. His weight was like a shield, a ward against panic. She put her hand against his chest so that she could feel the breath going in and out of him.

It was real, this road, this air, this sky. They were safe and, miracle of miracles, the orphanage children were all safe and accounted for, although four citizens and three horses were later found to have been killed.

Seth's arms closed about her, and he drew her tight against him. *Sophy.* Her name sang in his bones. *Sophy Weston.* The thread of emotion had grown till it was as wide as a road, as blindingly brilliant as the fire around them. He drew a slow breath, hesitated, searching for the right way to express his feelings, his newly discovered knowledge.

Sophy let him hold her close for a few minutes, sensing his need for the quiet communion. There was a silence. All about them the air was throbbing as if with winged heartbeats. Then, with a quick, nervous laugh she released herself, her words prosaic.

"It's snowing! Let's go home."

Seth knew that he should be tired, but he wasn't. He had never felt better. He felt that somehow tonight he had opened a door, and had entered an entirely new world, though he could not for certain say what that world was. It was like the trumpeting echo of dreams.

He smiled as he bathed, and whistled as he poured himself a glass of Madeira. Then, humming, he donned a silk dressing gown. How long, he wondered, taking a generous swallow of the wine, since he had hummed a tune?

Seth shrugged mentally. It was as if a great weight had been lifted from his shoulders. He laughed, a soft sound. Excitement soared inside him. He was a fiercely painted kite riding the feral winds. His whole body seemed to be on fire with desire. This new and undreamed-of desire for Sophy, his own, his beloved, whom he had not until today realized *was* his beloved.

The truth racked him with its force. His pulse beat hard in his temples and he felt a sudden rush of blood to his head. He had never wanted any woman as he wanted her. She was made for him. She was perfection.

His hands knotted, unknotted. She must know. He shook his head slowly, struggling to do what he must do and say what he must say. It was all framed and ready when he entered her rooms.

Sophy grimaced at the reflection in the vanity mirror. Grimy tendrils of hair that had come loose from its coil hung around a face that was sweaty, dusty and smudged with ash. Her expensive couturier dress was ruined, all torn and filthy.

"The bathwater'll be cold and so will yon chocolate, if ye don't stop admirin' y'self, lass." Tessa stomped out of the room.

A bath. Bliss unalloyed. Clean hair, clean body. A smile on her lips, a sense of peace in her heart, Sophy was leaning back in the tub placidly contemplating the bright brass fittings when the bathroom door opened.

Seth stood before her, his hand on the door handle. The fat wedge of lemon light from the bedroom gilded the bridge of his nose, glinted off his eyes, turning their deep blue opaque. He stopped short. His gaze was riveted to hers, tension in every muscular inch of him from the tips of his bare toes to the jut of his newly shaved chin. It was obvious he was naked underneath a carelessly fastened black silk robe.

Sophy's head swung around to look at him, the gaslight soft on the sharply defined curve of her cheekbone, her lips. Seth's gaze slipped, and all coherent thought fled.

It was like moving through a dream. All senses were assailed relentlessly until he felt as if he had stumbled upon the atelier of one of the great artists. There was the same sensation of being in the presence of a great legacy, an immortal statement that transcended human experience.

Stillness shielded his features for a moment, then he smiled almost shyly. For just an instant Sophy thought she had caught a glimpse of him as a little boy. She found herself smiling back at him.

Seth's abrupt unease melted. He knelt and put his arms around her. "You taste of chocolate," he whispered, tilting her chin upward and sampling her lips. "Share it with me. It makes the medicine go down." His voice was thick.

"Are you making fun of me?" Sophy muttered suspiciously.

Both hands moving to frame her face, he held her a little away from him and stared at the wet hair cascading down like a stream at midnight.

"What do you think?" Teasing laughter lit up his eyes.

"I'm not sure. I'll have to think about it," Sophy countered, rubbing herself with furious energy and using the activity as an excuse not to meet those piercing blue eyes. She was all a-prickle of gooseflesh, but her face was afire.

Arm resting on one bent knee as he crouched beside the tub, he reached for an oval bar of ivory-colored soap. "Perhaps I can help make up your mind," he informed her with smiling intent.

Touching the pulse at the base of her throat lightly with his lips, he began to lather her back. Sophy felt acute excitement course down her spine and she twisted into the warm fingers. Her body had begun to sing its deep irresistible song.

"Don't be so impatient, little one," he breathed, with a small smile of satisfaction. His teeth sank lightly into her earlobe in an exciting caress that made Sophy shiver in anticipation.

He was very thorough. His fingers danced around her nipples, drew warm, damp patterns down to the curve of her stomach. Picking up each foot in turn, he soaped between her toes. His movements were deft and sure. Her tiny ankle, the flesh of the calf, the extended knee, the slender sweep of her thigh.

When he came to the tops of her thighs, Sophy pressed them together, trying to resist his questing fingers. Before she allowed this feverish excitement to overwhelm her, she must tell him about her deception.

She would tell him. Now. Today.

Loving Seth had made her realize the truth. Their marriage must not be based on illusion, all tangled up with pride and resentment and deceit. Everything had to come together, all the divergent strands, for true love to occur.

His hands went behind her, cupping her rounded buttocks. The softness of her slender body was irresistible. "A woman would only use a bath with fancy plumbing if she wanted to entice a man to share it," he teased, eyes glinting.

Ignoring the damage to his silk dressing gown, Seth placed one hair-rough leg between hers, splitting them apart. Water splashed over the floor. His knee nudged between her thighs, while his soapy hand stroked her gently.

Her protest died beneath the sharply indrawn breath that she found herself gulping as his thumb found her feminine core. Soon his experienced touch was sending little rivers of pleasure down the insides of her legs.

"Seth," she began softly, a little uncertain how to say it. Don't be foolish, she upbraided herself. It's nothing so terrible. Tell it and have done!

Seth surged to his feet, sending water flying in all directions. He leaned over, planted his strong hands on her waist and effortlessly plucked Sophy out of the tub.

"I have something to tell you." Her fingers tangled themselves in his hair. The muscles of her thighs jumped and all strength seemed to seep from her legs.

His eyes glittering darkly, Seth laughed gently, caressing her back and her tumbled hair. His tongue circled the delicate area of her ear. Instinctively, the primal dance of male and female began, their hips pressing slowly, rhythmically, against each other.

It might help to tell her, he suspected, but the throbbing hardness of him overcame all notions of wanting a conversation. He would do it later, when his throat was not so clogged and tight.

"And I have something to tell you," he managed to get out, sliding down her body as if his flesh had turned to rainwater. "But not now. Not now."

Tomorrow would be soon enough, Sophy told herself. And abruptly all her thoughts were as insubstantial as the wind.

The benches were well spaced out. Charles was at one, transferring designs for the Engraving Department. There a hand loom would be used to work out different combinations of textures, tensile strengths and general suitability.

Seth stood beside the artist, absently staring at a particular design, a rich red color without a motif. It reminded him of Sophy. All fire and passion. He smiled almost invisibly.

"That one's for the connoisseurs. Sumptuous but discreet. It would suit Sophy," he said with such complete satisfaction that he gave himself away.

Charles arched a speculative eyebrow, not fooled by the almost whimsical tone of his friend's voice. He shrugged.

"It'll be difficult to get the proper tone—red, but as if lit up from behind with a fire. And the weaving will have to show the complicated pattern by texture."

"Have you heard anything from George?" Seth asked quietly.

Charles pushed aside the patterns and put his fingertips together, elbows on the bench. "No. But a new shipment is due in any day. George is to send a message, 'Walls of Jericho,' when he is certain."

"I think we've got the Judas this time." Seth levered himself onto a stool. He stretched his leg and sighed. "The assault code is 'Alas Babylon.'"

Charles pursed his lips contemplatively. "What about Sophy? I think she is on to something."

"I'm keeping Sophy so busy she hasn't time for the prescribed audit at the shipping office." Seth tried to stifle a grin and failed.

Charles inserted some patterns into a folder, meeting Seth's satisfied look with understanding. "Marriage is a desperate thing. We have to be careful of the illusions we weave lest they become reality."

"On whose great authority do you make that pronouncement?"

"My own!" White teeth flashed in a very engaging smile. "Sophy sure is something. She discovered Abigail has no head for figures, which, as you know, is a constant source of domestic tension in our household.''

Charles tented his fingers under his chin. "Sophy has designed an accounting system for Abigail that includes a weekly budget. Thank God, it seems to be working!''

"George tells me she discovered his age, hobbies, club memberships and income in one short session!'' Seth said, obviously proud of his wife's acumen.

Charles shot up a sandy eyebrow. With the shadow of a frown behind his eyes, he issued words of caution. "We'll have to watch her.''

Seth gave a pensive smile but said nothing, contenting himself with shuffling the piles of paper littering the bench.

Charles gave him a sideways grin. "Relax. No needle is sharp at both ends, but just in case Sophy does solve the riddle, I've laid a few false trails.''

"I don't want Sophy involved in this.'' There was clear command in Seth's voice, and his blue eyes had a hint of steel in their depths as they met the perceptive hazel gaze.

Charles let that hang in the air, before making a clear effort to change the subject. "Let's hear what you think of the lithographs.''

They studied them with craftsmen's eyes, discussed designed and cost. No further mention was made of their initial exchange.

Sophy's path had diverged, and she was in the large bleaching rooms. She wanted to see the cloth they were processing. Seth had said, "You've got to feel the material. You get a seventh sense in your fingers. I can tell blindfolded where it came from, what quality it is, how much it cost.''

Should she tell him now of her deduction? Everything she had heard from the gossip mill and had seen for herself suggested her husband was a levelheaded businessman, accustomed to giving orders, convinced that profit was the only value, and not one to be taken in by parasitic friends.

Intuition warned her this was more than dissecting profit and loss columns. She decided she would say nothing to Seth. She would wait, and watch.

There was a small frown on her face when she turned away from the door and started back to the office. Once there, she flipped open a folder and began scanning the thin report inside.

She was still there when Seth and Charles walked in. Her sweet smile, filled with warm delight as she looked up from the papers, was purely unconscious, but Seth felt it like an open fire.

Unable to resist the unspoken invitation, he came over to where she was sitting. Feeling quite reckless, he leaned forward and kissed her. The feel of her, the sight of her, the scent of her, all combined to transfix him, so that he experienced again that upsurge of unexplained, oddly exciting sentiment.

Sophy pushed a folded paper toward him. He took it, his glance going to the knotted coil of hair, which had been clipped to the back of her head. Succumbing to the impulse, he tweaked a wispy tendril that trailed down the back of her neck above the low, round collar of her gown.

At the casual sign of affection, Sophy felt the red wash her cheeks. Unconsciously, the tip of her tongue touched the edge of her lip as she tried to resist the sudden surge of feminine pleasure, and concentrate on Seth's next statement.

"Good news, Charles." Seth turned to meet the designer's laughing eyes. "George Henkels, the Philadelphia furniture maker, is interested in a line of our fabrics. Weston's can produce the lines he wants, to rival those done in Europe, but less expensive."

"People are becoming more conscious of the decor of their homes." Sophy was relieved that her voice sounded light and neutral. "They follow fashion there as well as in their clothes."

"Any success in the audit?" Charles changed the subject, one sandy brow lifting curiously before shifting his glance toward Seth, who was lowering himself carefully into a high-backed leather chair.

Sophy guessed Charles was trying to decide whether or not she had discovered anything. It would be a logical move. It also seemed that a small smile curled the corners of Seth's mouth.

She glanced down thoughtfully at something she had written in the report, and quite suddenly everything came sharply into focus with stark clarity. It was simple, really. Seth must be protected at all costs.

"Nothing that can't be remedied." She shrugged lightly.

"I'm relieved." A smile dragged the corners of Charles's mouth. "There is nothing more encouraging or of greater use to a man about to face his challenge in life than a woman's kindly criticism."

He leaned forward, reaching for a file.

Something in his tone nettled Sophy past bearing. With an exclamation of profound annoyance, she gathered up several sheets that were covered with figures, stacked them together and put them in a pile just slightly out of his reach.

"The level of criticism might depend upon how much pressure is brought to bear on certain people to answer certain questions. That could be inconvenient."

Charles was staring at her intently. "What on earth do you mean?" He said it with a grin, but his tone had a cutting edge, which made outrage at the duplicity she had uncovered flash through her.

Sophy didn't think, or reason. Her response was automatic. "Who supplied designs in several forms, including drawings, engraved plates and fabrics to Globe Printworks in Massachusetts to be released under the label name *Fallon?*"

She hesitated for a moment, waiting to see if Charles had anything to say. Sophy knew suddenly she wanted him to deny her accusation. She glanced at Seth. The expression on his face was a rather alarming combination of anger and hard ruthlessness as he watched his friend's freckled hand idly tap a pencil on the wide desk.

Charles had the grace to flush. "Good heavens!" he exclaimed. "How many more trade secrets did you pick up while you were in the office?"

"Quite a few," she replied in a very low, very intense voice.

Her mind was extraordinarily calm. She could think only of Seth, and of the injustice done to him. "And I promise never to divulge them to a rival. But who is currently trading on his connection with Weston's Textiles to negotiate with Ebenezer Butterick to manufacture packaged paper patterns?"

Silence, a heavy breathing silence. The dropping of the proverbial pin would have made quite a clatter.

Sophy stood, her body shaking with shock and fear for the consequences of her flare-up of temper, unmeaning and unmeant. She smote her hands together in a passion of frustration. What had she said, done, or what would *he* do? She felt the blood run to her cheeks.

Suddenly her throat was dust dry. She swallowed. "I'm sorry, Charles. I didn't mean...my wicked tongue...forgive me..." Her words trailed off to confusion.

Seth surged to his feet, the metal edge of the pattern book clattering loudly on the table as he set it down abruptly. He stood aggressively across the desk from her, his feet slightly apart and braced in a challenging stance. His eyes were shards of ice.

Charles pushed back his chair and stood up. His slender shoulders lifted and fell. He had to stop Sophy somehow. There was too much at stake. His voice was sharp.

"You are an absolute menace, Sophy Weston! You can pin a lot of stuff on me if you want, but forget this. I don't cheat on my friends. Why don't you check out your own laundry first?''

''What!'' Seth echoed with a hint of incredulity. His eyes focused on Sophy in a swift, surprised look.

Perversely, this only seemed to infuriate her further. She gave a negligent shrug, not denying anything, but not at all certain she'd taken the right course.

Charles was at the window looking out. His hazel eyes were narrowed. Alert. Calculating. Temper seethed about the edges of his words. ''Twister of truth! Who is the cheat? Substituting one of Richard's stamps for mine! Trying to catch me out, Sophy?''

''I was right, wasn't I? Forged any checks lately, Charles?''

Termagant!

Seth stepped toward her. Sophy held her ground. His eyes locked with hers, and he set his hands on her shoulders. Did she tremble?

''Enough!''

The word came out sharply, surprising Sophy with its whiplash of command. Seth had never used that tone of authority with her before, and she acknowledged shakily it was effective. Even Charles responded to that raw, aggressive power.

''Damn!'' Charles swore in an undertone, his indignation collapsing beneath the weight of his conscience. ''I didn't mean that! It was a low shot, Sophy, and I'm sorry.''

Sophy sucked in her breath, her breasts heaving tumultuously, and lifted her chin. ''I had reason to suspect you. I needed to know the truth.''

Aware that Seth was blazingly angry, she felt a kind of vertigo, a strange frightening pressure in her chest as if the air were liquid. Wide-eyed she waited, gray gaze fixed on his thunderous face.

''In your heart you know I have discovered the truth! I know who the embezzler is and so do you!''

There was a long silence while he stared at her, his expression hard and remote. He drew a little away from her, moving stiffly, each step carefully measured. Then he spoke very softly, biting out each word between set teeth.

"If you have an ounce of common sense, Sophy, you will not say another word." Each word was a chip of ice. It sounded as though he were exercising every measure of self-control he possessed.

Charles gave Sophy a slight bow, and turned to Seth, his voice a little thick. "I'm sorry, Seth, but I have to go to Paterson today and I'm already late. I've assembled a portfolio of new designs. Perhaps the lithographs could be discussed in my absence." He laid the folder on the desk and tactfully left the room.

Desperately, Sophy tried to regain some control. Her small white teeth closed briefly around her lower lip.

"Seth. I can explain." She said it a little quickly, a little breathlessly.

"There is nothing to explain." Lean and darkly powerful, Seth stood firm and unrelenting, his logic, his reasoning suppressed and overwhelmed by a wave of majestic anger. She had blown their cover.

Damn and damn and damn her.

Chapter Sixteen

It began to snow as Seth and Sophy began their journey homeward, the sky turning white like spirit sails. The two occupants of the carriage cleaved to their respective corners, each giving a stiff mental lecture on the perils of playing with fire.

Away in the park, a crowd of people were making merry on the frozen lake. The ice was in splendid condition. It sparkled in the half-light like a sheet of frosted glass, and over it the skaters glided with much fun and laughter. It was an invigorating scene.

Sophy leaned against the carriage window and watched them. Seth heard the movement as her thighs brushed against the fabric of her gown, caught the faint lavender scent of her as she turned to speak to him.

"Oh, look at the children skating! Aren't they adorable?" She threw Seth a little smile in a small attempt to lighten the atmosphere between them. "Wouldn't you just love to be out there skating?"

As usual, when Sophy smiled, her face changed like the sky on a windy day, from clouds to sunlight. It seduced. For once, Seth didn't return her smile, but he swallowed the angry retort that rose to his lips.

"My legs are no longer a pair, so I can't even begin," he

said in an unnaturally even tone, his hands spread, palms up.

Sophy looked quickly at the skaters and then back at him. He was gazing down at her, a half smile playing at the corners of his mouth. Her fingers curled around the rim of the window.

"I'm sorry. I didn't mean to..." She flushed and bit her lip, her voice trailing off as she tried to control her emotions.

Seth forgot himself utterly, and leaned forward to clasp her hand. "It will not be long before you have a child of your own. You can take him skating." He looked directly into her eyes, all the ice in his own turned to running water and rainbows.

A jolt of shock ran through Sophy. Startled, her hand instinctively moved to her middle. Not until he loved her!

"No!" The single negative almost exploded from her. Her head shook from side to side, her normally sensual lips pressed tightly together.

Now his face was very close, and his eyes stared straight into hers. She could smell his scent, clean and strong and masculine. She felt a shiver race down her spine, as if he had reached out and touched her.

Sophy wrapped her arms around herself, clinging tightly. "Seth! I didn't mean it! It was only... I didn't expect... didn't know what I was saying. It's just that the thought of a child distracts me. It is too soon." She felt like a clockwork doll, jerking out mechanical words.

Words, empty rattling words. Sophy's throat closed. She bit her lip, distressed and wishing she could recall her words. But as is usually the case with rash words, they had already done their damage.

Seth reached down inside himself for something he did not even know existed. He dragged it up with all his strength. He clenched his fist and Sophy could see the cords of his neck standing out with the strain.

He spoke through set and aching teeth, the words bitten off sharply. "There is already the possibility that you might be with child."

Seth saw Sophy's lips move as if to protest, and put up his fingers to prevent her speaking. "It may be that nothing has happened. We need not address the problem until it arises."

His voice was low now, and he swallowed with difficulty. "In the meantime, we must just wait and ensure the chance does not occur again."

Dinner that night was quite lively, with Sophy's young cousins arriving just before the meal, and lingering on the off chance that they would be invited to stay and share a fillet of beef. And maybe *just one* of the little cranberry-pear tarts they had spied cooling on a kitchen bench.

As he graciously invited the young men to share the repast, Seth suspected he was turning out to be unexpectedly vulnerable to this particular form of attack. He was pleased they were there. One could forget, for a little while, that nothing was going right.

Sophy was also pleased to see her cousins. She listened to the men discuss the political situation, and watched Seth's mind turn over alternatives. It was a very pleasant mind to watch, quick and clear, honest yet subtle, able to analyze and evaluate in a logical and orderly fashion. She felt her dark mood lifting.

Bernard's merry quips and Pieter's jovial rejoinders concealed the cool politeness between Seth and Sophy. The strain, however, was noted by Agnes Weston.

Her eyes, bright as a bird's, went first to her son, searching his face. Seth appeared totally relaxed, but there was a hard gleam in his eyes. He was furious, Agnes realized in sudden intuition. Her speculative glance flicked to Sophy, taking in the tense look on that small pointed face in one comprehensive glance.

Agnes smiled to herself. It seemed that all was not well in the dovecote! She waited until after the meal when the men were drinking their port and they were alone in the drawing room before she turned her level gaze on her daughter-in-law.

"What have you done to make Seth so angry with you that he is heavy eyed and simply oozing displeasure?"

Sophy instantly experienced a flush of guilt. She sighed and sank into a chair near the fireplace, plucking an imaginary piece of fluff off the Chantilly lace flouncing of her skirt. There was no way she could discuss the true cause of Seth's vexation!

"I'm afraid I behaved outrageously, accusing Charles Lethbridge of unspeakable things."

How much Agnes Weston guessed about the quality of her marriage to Seth she was never of course sure, but her mother-in-law probably had a fair idea. The older woman said nothing, however, as she calmly selected a strand of colored thread from her sewing basket.

Sophy sighed again, and closed her eyes for a moment, picturing the scene all over again. Normally she would have accepted Seth's criticism of her insolence, even have laughed it off. Tonight, she felt dejected and completely enervated. Life had lost its buoyancy.

She had always believed in the triumph of good over evil, so had never doubted the inevitability of her success. However, her philosophy had never mentioned at what cost such triumph was to be achieved.

"My wretched tongue! I should not have said all those things. It is my tiresome temper . . . when I lose it there is no knowing what I will say."

Somehow she had trouble seeing. It was as if she were peering through a windowpane streaked with running water. She rubbed her eyes furiously on one deep crimson velvet puff sleeve.

"Do you know what happens to children who play with matches?" Agnes Weston remarked, but her bright eyes twinkled as, with delicate precision, she drew a thread through the eye of a needle.

"Yes." Sophy blinked at the change of topic, and her smile flashed briefly. She picked up several strands of colored silk. "They eventually see the light...even if they do get burned!"

"Poor Seth!" Agnes shook her head mournfully, placing a small stitch with great care.

"Why do you say that?"

"My son thought he was marrying a nice meek and mild little woman who would make no difference in his life." Agnes Weston's needle flashed surely, delicately, back and forth through the embroidery she was working on a tambour frame. "He wanted to be free to come and go as he pleased. He did not bargain on a firebrand like you!"

"I simply didn't think through the consequences of my actions. My impulse was stronger than my will, which compelled me," Sophy protested, her voice a husky whisper.

They had been the actions of a woman caught up between the crush of her own desire and common sense, she thought defensively. It seemed a fiery spirit like love could not be kept at one level. She should have known this, of course.

"Marriage shouldn't be a contest. Not between two sensible people." In her mind Sophy added, "who love each other," but she could not say it.

"You're human enough for that and you've got a temper. But if you can face your conscience, you can hold your head high."

While it was not the most extravagant praise in the world, Sophy colored under the pleasure of it. When she looked up at her mother-in-law, her eyes were unnaturally bright. "In all the world one can't be singled out to have one's heart's desire."

"Perhaps." Agnes seemed to be sewing extra carefully. "It would be a pity if you tried too hard, Sophy. My son might not react well to captivity."

Sophy felt herself redden even more, and concentrated on matching the threads. "He's no captive!" she protested vehemently, but with eyes firmly fixed upon the tangled skeins in her hand. "He's a very free agent...even if he has signed a contract!"

"Maybe." Agnes bit off a piece of thread. Sophy had the feeling there was more to that statement than she understood.

"But you're doing quite well at laying siege to my son's reason and logic, my dear. It would be a pity to desist now." Which was as far as Agnes Weston ever went with praise... or encouragement?

"I'm going to miss all this when I'm at Yale next year." With a cheery wave, Bernard followed his brother to the waiting carriage.

"I promise to bake a fruit-filled stack cake every week!" Sophy called to him before she closed the door and walked beside Seth down the long hallway.

When they reached the foot of the stairs, Sophy felt a warm palm on her shoulder, holding her back. She swung her head round to look at her husband, the lamplight soft on the sharply defined curve of his cheekbone, his lips. Her heart beat very fast, and a peculiar weakness came into her knees.

Seth let go of her shoulder and ran an impatient hand through the carefully combed thickness of his dark hair. "Are you going to sulk forever?"

One hand on the newel post, Sophy resisted the impulse to flee. The wildness of her pulse seemed to have invaded her head and she felt dizzy.

She had to start twice, and then could only manage to get out, "I do not sulk," wishing her voice did not sound so thin.

He stared down, the grooves at the edge of his mouth tightening, as though he could see in her flushed face the immense effort it took to utter those words.

Seth sighed. "I have given the matter serious consideration. You know, you're wrong about Charles." He lowered his voice, as if he felt himself on a precipice and in voicing this hidden knowledge he had begun to fear his own words.

"We've been friends for a long time. He had nothing but a spendthrift wife when he came to me. I gave him a job. Set him up. Let him go. He's proved himself." He gave her a half smile. "If I'd ever harbored doubts about Charles—and I don't say I had—your bombshell today dissolved them."

"As I said all along..."

"Permit me to finish. If an expert forger decides to place himself on the wrong side of the law and cook the books, to use your expression, do you really suppose he hides the main evidence under his own pillow, so to speak?"

Sophy shook her head, silently applauding his business acumen. His insight and perspective were sharp and well honed.

"Today you cut to the heart of the matter. I don't want you to be used as a weapon, either on a business or personal front. I'd prefer you not to continue your audit at the shipping office."

That stopped her. She hadn't counted on that possibility. Would he never cease doing the unexpected? It made her nervous. Sophy came closer to him and put her fingers along his arm.

"One never discards even a potential weapon unless one has to," she said, softly, fiercely. Her eyes never left his face while she waited tensely to see if he understood. His smile died and she was sorry to see it go.

"Weapons can be used by either side of a battle. I don't want you on the wrong end of this one," Seth bit back in an equally intense tone. "There's been too many *incidents* lately. The Rivington Street fire was the last straw." He struggled to master his emotions, to speak reasonably, but his eyes burned with an intense inner fire as he spoke to her.

For some reason Sophy seized on that. She decided to go on the attack. Her mind racing, she said the first thing that came into her head. "You can get that look out of your eye, Seth Weston."

She could not stop herself, wanting as she did to push him further, to needle him, to provoke in him a response strong enough to prove to her once and for all that he truly cared for her. Why couldn't he see what was so obviously hanging right in front of his face?

"Are you issuing a fresh challenge, Sophy? If so, I accept." His voice came as a soft caress and sent an eddy of sensations spiraling down through the core of her being.

"You're arrogant and domineering, and..." Sophy said, already halfway up the stairs.

"—and you're stubborn and willful, and unbelievably provoking!"

Seth slowly ascended the stairs, one hand sliding along the polished banister. His anger was oddly exciting. Now that she knew he hadn't changed his mind about sharing her bed, she felt driven to exacerbate it, to see how far she could go before his temper exploded.

They stood quite still, not touching. Her pulse beating one-two, one-two, tiny tremors in the hollow of her throat, on the insides of her wrist. Sophy tried the only weapon in her arsenal.

"What about the money?"

As soon as she said the words, she wished them unsaid. She waited tensely to see what effect they would have. He was so close to her, she could feel his heat, the passion, leaping through him. He seemed immense and invulnerable.

"If you used your head for a minute, you'd realize that no man in his right mind would put up with what I'm tolerating for the sake of a dollar or two!"

Sophy chose to take that head-on. "Force of will is an infinitely better weapon than money because it works all the time!"

Seth's eyes tracked upward to her pale face. Their eyes locked for an interminable time. There was a peculiar, tense silence.

Seth studied the rigid stance of the slender figure and the storms swirling in the wide gray eyes for an eternity before saying softly, "You're not going to win this skirmish, Sophy. So don't try my patience any more this evening. For both our sakes!" His voice, if not exactly filled with menace, had taken on a steely edge.

Sophy said nothing. There was no sense providing him with more weapons at this point. Instead, with an effort that made her gasp, she turned and ran upstairs to the security of her bedchamber.

Once there, she gave in to stubborn indignation, whirling to lock the doors behind her.

When Seth came down to breakfast the next morning he looked as though he had not slept at all. The lines upon his face seemed to have been cut more deeply, as though graven there, and his blue eyes seemed to have a touch of gray in them. His lips were tight and grim, making Sophy wonder if he had spent the night beset by pain.

"Do you have anything especially important to do today?" she began cheerily, trying to gauge his temper.

"I have to go to Brooklyn," he announced dryly, glancing up briefly from his newspaper. "The baseball league I played for before the war, the Knickerbockers' Club, has organized a meeting to discuss next season's games. I should be back by six."

Sophy poured his coffee, and handed it to him with a bright smile. Dressed in a violet-colored wool velour gown, and with her hair drawn into a snood decorated with ribbon of the same shade, she was a cool and determined little figure, sitting in the pale sunlight streaming through the shell-shaped morning room window.

"Mr. Dunwoody says you've changed since the war," Sophy heard herself say involuntarily, willing him to answer her. Watching him with wide eyes, she thought she saw him wince.

"Sure." Seth put down his paper. It seemed a very deliberate gesture. He accepted the fine china cup, blinking a little, as if trying to assess her mood.

Sophy searched his face. She knew instinctively that he was on the verge of telling her something that she very much wanted to know. Then he closed his eyes slowly, almost reluctantly, as if he were giving up a precious object.

The light, thin and diffused, slanted through the window as white and fragile as porcelain. Again Seth saw the gleam of her shining hair through the snood, a network of sea jewels, a flotsam of tiny shells. Captured light. Netted light.

Sophy's eyes seemed to be pleading with him, as if to say, *Tell me. Share yourself with me.* He took a deep sip of his coffee, then lifted one shoulder as if shaking off an unwanted memory. After a time, his voice came soft and slow, each word measured with equal, leaden force.

"How could you survive the essential hell of a civil war without being changed? The only way not to be changed by the war was to die."

What could she say? War must be an incredibly traumatic experience. Head down, her liquid eyes on her cup, the only outward sign of her agitation was the constant stirring of her coffee.

"You mustn't think of that. It's not good to store up such sad thoughts. *We* continue. *We* live. You know what you want. All you have to do is reach out and grasp it. That is all that matters."

Seth stood up. "Why does changing me matter so much?" he challenged bluntly.

Sophy blinked warily. Something in his tone nagged at the corner of her mind. She let it go and took another sip of coffee, locked in that frustrated state where reason fails utterly to convince.

"I'm not trying to change you," she retorted, feeling the pull of her stomach as it tightened. She sucked in her breath, her emotions in a state of confusion such as she had never known. They were affecting her stomach, which was definitely feeling a trifle queasy.

He watched her expressionlessly for a moment. When he spoke his voice was a sea of seething emotion, as if the words, like individual bricks, falling from his lips, anticipated the crumbling of some strong wall.

"I never in my life envisaged marrying a woman for her money, or having a wife who is richer than I am myself."

Her insides felt like a beehive. Sophy felt too weak to do more than mutter, "Does it matter?"

He was staring at her in a very peculiar way, his eyes hard and dark and filled with a quicksilver anger. "I was just going to tell you that one of the lessons you have taught me is that money is of no importance at all beside love."

Sophy was too busy fighting down a paroxysm of nausea to hear him. She scowled in uneasiness. Even her lips felt numb.

Seth narrowed his eyes and grasped the silver knob of his walking stick. He smiled compassionately at her wary expression, and laughed, a short strange sound.

"Do you know what love is, Sophy? In the words of St. Paul, *Love should not be just words and talk. True love must show itself in action.* There is imagined love, which is illusion, and real love. The two should not be confused. Love is, above all, the gift of oneself.''

He swung around when he reached the doorway and leveled his finger at her. ''To be loved as you are loved in this house is above all bargains. You know what you have to do. When you're prepared to give all of yourself to me, I'll give all myself to you!''

He spun on one booted heel and strode out of the room. The door closed shut behind him with a resounding slam.

Stomach churning, Sophy fled to her room for a chamber pot.

Sophy heard Seth's words repeating themselves over and over inside her head as she went through the morning's routine. What did he mean? She was assailed by questions that led to riddles that, in turn, brought her to enigmas.

She tried turning the situation around in her mind and looking at it from his point of view. He wanted her, had said she would have all of him if she was willing to give all of herself to him in exchange. All of him. What an overwhelming notion.

The idea of a baby hung in her mind as if slung in a shining web. It was all too confusing, she thought miserably. One of these days she was going to understand him, she vowed, as she stared blindly at a miniature of Nicholas van Houten, which stood on her *secrétaire*.

The writing desk had been a gift from her father on her sixteenth birthday. Sitting there trying to check off the stock market reports, she could still sense the vitality of the man. Feel his big, square, builder's hands grip her waist and lift her for his kiss. ''I'm home, *lief dochter*. Want to check some figures for me?''

Sophy closed her eyes, and soaked in the strong, comforting presence of her father. She could smell his warm scent, a little tangy with lumber dust, a bit musky with tobacco. How she had loved it when, laughing with delight, he let her fill his pipe for him!

He, too, had used Seth's words when she had rejected suitor after suitor. *You know what you have to do.* Her mind slowly probed the problem until the idea crystallized and took shape. The idea that Madame Bertine might know what he had meant.

Madame Bertine did not. Nor did she think it important. "It is best to face reality. You can't fight it. Life isn't 'earts and flowers, Sophy, even if the vagaries of the 'uman 'eart are what makes life unforgettable." Madame's lilting voice crooned gently.

Sophy said nothing and, by some unspoken mutual consent, they left the subject, and shared tea and biscuits. As she was leaving, she handed over the title deeds to the house in Greene Street.

"You should have had these years ago."

"Do not delude yourself with romantic or fanciful notions." Madame's voice was thick, her accent heavy, as if her throat had closed over. She deliberately looked away for a moment and her shoulders shook.

"Love has different definitions . . . different limits . . . depending on the person." Madame's head was slightly bowed, throwing her face into shadow.

Sophy looked at her levelly. "This has nothing at all to do with your relationship with my father or any other man. It is business." Her voice was like a wisp of smoke, gently drifting. "I think you could operate an Academy for Good Manners and Etiquette quite successfully."

"I am a professional 'ostess specializing in providing polite but exciting entertainment only for select gentlemen of financial quality." It was a gentle reminder.

"It does not always have to be so. I have seen what you are capable of when you want to share your knowledge and experience," Sophy corrected carefully, thoughtfully. "Such an academy would be security in old age, and an honorable occupation. It would be a shame not to share your knowledge of etiquette and your fashion expertise with others.''

They stood facing each other. Two people from opposite sides of society. Two individuals drawn to each other precisely because of that gulf. Two people who, but for the whims of fate, would have been on the other side of that great divide.

The humor caught fire in Madame's eyes. "It would be a good thing to give tone to this neighborhood,'' she agreed, slowly smiling. "Open this when you get 'ome. Everything you need is inside.''

Madame Bertine picked up a parcel and delivered it into Sophy's hands. "The first lesson a young lady must know. It is a precept attributed to the daughter-in-law of Pythagoras....'' She put her hand over Sophy's.

"In going to bed with a man, a woman should put off 'er modesty with 'er skirt and put it on again with 'er petticoat. Now, *ma fillette,* this is what you've got to do....''

There was a fire burning in the study, but Seth was not in his usual spot. Sophy crossed the expanse of carpet to where his huge desk stood, prim and proper and glossy, in one corner, surrounded by a series of biblical prints telling the story of the Prodigal Son.

Hands trembling, Sophy stared at the note addressed simply to *S. Weston*. In Charles Lethbridge's handwriting! She opened the missive, read slowly.

Somehow it all seemed unreal. It was like finding herself inside a circuitous maze and, breaching a hidden doorway, suddenly discovering a cryptic puzzle that stretched away from her like ripples in a pond.

Shock waves had begun to radiate outward from the spidery writing, revealing real worlds and false, hitherto unknown. Sophy knew the deviousness of Charles Lethbridge all too well. She had sufficient evidence against the man to finish him forever.

The only thing that had stopped her was that it was all too neat, too foolproof, not to be the figment of a convoluted mind. That, and Seth's solid belief in the constancy of his friend.

Walls of Jericho! Sophy suddenly went cold. Her fingers tightened. Was this another of Charles's ruses? A chill ran down her spine. How could she be certain?

Alas Babylon! The second annotation was in George Dunwoody's handwriting. This time she felt a jolt, as if she'd been hit.

Splinters of memory surfaced like the returning jetsam of some enormous wreck. Coalesced. A solid weight thrusting her into the path of a tram. Blunt fingers, half-seen, on a silver urn.

A vision of the agent's ransacked office danced in front of her eyes. The sudden flare of the curtains. A moving shadow. Hurried footsteps. Her mind raced. The conversation overheard. The near accident at the shipping yards.

Doubt struck her. Had she made the wrong choice? Perhaps she should have shared her anxiety over the agent's mental stability with Seth as her first impulses had urged.

Did Seth know the reasons behind these coded messages? If he did, he should be notified immediately. *I should be back by six.* She glanced at the ormolu clock on the mantelpiece. It was still early enough to catch him at the ferry.

A light snow was thickening into whirling flurries that nearly obscured both shores of the murky East River. Strident whistles penetrated the gloom as vessels of varying size and description abruptly loomed into sight.

A lane of fast-running dirty, gray water opened among jagged, grimy ice cakes interspersed with patches of semi-frozen slush. The crowded and uncomfortable ferryboat crunched its way between ice-coated pilings into the slip and came to a halt.

Immediately, dense white columns of steam roared up from her exhaust pipes. When the ferry began to discharge its throngs of passengers, Seth was not among them.

In a burst of decision, Sophy hailed one of the horse-drawn public carriages that traveled as far as City Hall. She was not the type of woman who could sit meekly awaiting her man's return. He needed her. She would go to him. Her heart slowed its pounding.

Dismounting at the City Hall terminus, she pulled her cloak tightly around her to keep out the damp chill air. Fires, built to warm laborers, flared and burned fitfully. The jagged roofs and spires of Manhattan rose gray and ghostly through the squall, while the falling snow turned the city's lights into ethereal bursts of color.

Bursts of conversation drifted to Sophy, overlaid with echoes created in the wintry atmosphere. Ragged, pinch-faced newsboys shrilled their wares, adding to the cacophony of sound.

It was a different scene down by the river. Here, a gentle hush engulfed the wharves. Lights shimmered wanly over the broad slope of the cobblestone roadway, the rows of shipping vessels tied up along its base punctuated by their feeble glow.

Lances of light shot from the moving crests of the water. Both light and sound were distorted. It was very quiet now. She couldn't hear the river at all except for a faint swish, the soft sound of the water running up the wood piers and falling back again. Tall sailing vessels were reduced to two-dimensional shadows, their insectlike antennae sending mysterious signals to the sky.

Going to find Seth, Sophy appeared as gossamer in the swirling snow. It was hard to see clearly. Snowflakes caught on her lashes, making vision difficult.

There was no sign of Seth. She peered up and down the quay. It was quite dark now. She turned her head, thinking she heard a sound. Eerie echoes of another world. The fittings on the ships creaked rhythmically in a kind of soothing litany.

Crossing her arms against her breasts, Sophy shivered and thought of turning back but persuaded herself against it. No more vacillation. With all her strength she mastered herself and walked quickly toward the pier where they had berthed the *Orion*.

Two shadows, dark and sinister, grotesquely elongated, swept across the dock. She saw the dark shapes and ducked into the shelter of a huge bowsprit jutting over the dock.

Neither man noticed Sophy, who crouched, motionless, against the packet ship. She shrank farther into the shrouded shadows as she recognized one of them as Charles Lethbridge.

Sophy felt terribly chilled, numbed into immobility. Her vision spun, staggered, sharpened with bitter clarity. It was impossible! Unthinkable! Yet it was happening! Charles *was* the villain! And she had been so sure he had only cast a few red herrings into the accounts to mislead her!

She shivered again, involuntarily, as she thought of Seth. He couldn't know, of course, she knew that. Would he guess? She thought there was a chance. He would take care of things. Seth. He was all that mattered.

Heart pounding so hard she could feel each double pulse like a shock running through her, Sophy settled down to wait. It was so quiet, and dark, inky black now. She could barely see anything anymore. It was like being at the bottom of a well. But the dark no longer troubled her.

Seth was coming. Her thoughts kept running back to him, like a river back to the sea. Love is eternal, she thought, a soft smile on her lips. *There is no fear in love. Perfect love drives out all fear.* The thought stayed with her. She drew her image of him around her like a quilt, feeling his strength enter her flesh, her bones.

All she had to do was make sure Charles did not discover her. Seth would have to come eventually. In spite of herself, Sophy shuddered.

In the hideously compressed time while she waited, the minutes ticked by with excruciating slowness. It seemed like hours, but it was probably less than five minutes. The snow was falling more thickly now, its whiteness stifling.

The cold was the worst part, she decided as she stood shivering helplessly. She wrapped her arms tightly about herself. With an effort, she looked back, and felt her heart speed up and her knees go weak.

The two men were still waiting in the shadows at the end of the dock. She didn't move. Neither did the men in the shadows. Whoever they were, they weren't coming down the pier, or passing by. They were just waiting.

Waiting for Seth.

Chapter Seventeen

"Sophy?" There was no answer. The only sound was the subdued hiss of the gas feeding the flame. Seth shrugged off his coat, threw it over the back of a chair and walked stiff legged to his desk.

He leaned against it, and picked up the crumpled slip of paper lying there. Held it, looking at it. Nothing changed in his face or his bearing, yet his fingers curved like the talons of some predator as he turned it over in his hands.

Slowly, ever so slowly, he unfolded the missive. It contained three words written in Charles Lethbridge's odd, backward-slanting hand and, below it, two words written in George Dunwoody's easily identifiable, cramped writing.

He lifted his head like an animal questing, his face a savage and alien terrain. Sophy! Lacking the strength to push his fears away anymore, he felt the first hard pangs of panic welling up in his chest. He had no thoughts now about money and embezzlement. His overriding concern was for Sophy.

Unable to quell the feeling of mounting dread that filled him, he called for a carriage. She needed him and he couldn't get to her fast enough. She was most assuredly in danger, and he felt totally impotent being so far away from her.

Time seemed to leap forward. There was a disturbance in

the street ahead and the carriage was slowing. Snow was rushing toward the vehicle, a waterfall of white liquid metal, thick and blinding.

Seth continued to peer ahead, but the low light was making vision difficult. The encroaching darkness spread rapidly like a vast funereal shroud drawn across the heavens by an unseen hand. What people remained on the streets in the face of the rapidly building snowstorm hurried along, eager to reach the warmth of their destination.

Sounds drifted in the snow-filled air. The cries of the street vendors, drunken laughter, the heavy creak of wooden-wheeled carts laden with tomorrow's produce and dry goods, the snort of horses, hooves clip-clopping on the cobbles.

There were few people about the wharves now, one or two drunks staggering along walls of buildings, a hunched figure asleep, huddled in a sheltering doorway, a pair of fragile old men rolling dice. A bit of newspaper fluttered across the gutter, lifted, then fell, like a mammoth moth searching for a flame.

Here it was very still. The darkness was like velvet, thick, soft and impenetrable. A voice, instantly muffled.

Transfixed, Sophy held her breath, listening.

The soft down along her arms lifted. Fear crawled inside her, making her breath come hot and fast. But other than the fact that the voice was male, sounded a bit urgent and uneasy, she could tell nothing.

Consumed by the intimation of some acute danger, she shrugged the snow off her cloak. She was abruptly aware of the length of her own shadow. Angled against that of the bowsprit, it was like a finger pointing directly at her.

The shadow began to move. To swirl, to shift, to coalesce.

Sophy moved closer to the water's edge, and heard the rale of her own breathing. She was aware of how ragged it sounded. Not knowing what to do, she stood quite still.

A crunch of footsteps. The shadow moved. Faded. Grew. The darkness possessed shape now. It pulsed with life, and it was drawing closer to her. It was only a handsbreath away from her.

Sophy could see the shadowy form, hear a soft laugh as an instant later a large figure loomed beside her. His hair and long, red merino muffler were flecked with snow-flakes.

She stiffened and backed away. Her heart hammered. Her palms were cold, her head light. She was backed against the end of the wharf, her hands gripping each other with such force that her fingers were numb. Then relief surged through her. It was Richard Carlton!

Large and bulky, the man yet moved stealthily in the shadows. He blended into the darkness so well that he had been upon her before she became aware of his presence.

"My humble apologies, Mrs. Weston." Breath hissed, frosting in a miniature cloud in front of him. "I was not expecting you at this late hour."

Sophy's hands flew to her cheeks. If Charles was the villain, then the agent must be the innocent pawn!

"Be careful, Richard. There are dangerous men lurking here!" Her words were swift, urgent, her voice low and thick with suppressed emotion.

For a heartbeat the silence of stupefaction, then the agent whirled. Anger, outrage, frustration limned his features. Sophy edged backward as far as she dared. There was the sound of rushing feet over wooden boards, a yell, more footsteps.

An instant later, the man swung back, half crouched, searching, nurturing his fury. His lips curled in an odd smile. He seemed beyond reason. The hiss of his breath was like a dragon's sigh.

Raw protest transmuted into insanity. He shook his head, not knowing what he denied. Wrath rose in a bloodred tide. He lifted one shoulder, and flung his solid girth against Sophy. The breath whooshed out of him like a collapsed balloon.

"So be it! We're all dead, one way or another!"

Then a strange, hunched shadow, looming over them, springing. Dimly, distantly, Sophy knew the shock of a great weight like a cord of wood falling upon her. She staggered and fell, saw in a vision from her mind, or the real world, the lithe and slender figure of Charles Lethbridge pitch forward against her.

The world rushed by her, all fuzzy. Curiously, she felt no fear. In her mind the only thought was to warn Seth, and she cried out, one short, shrill shout of alarm.

Then she was in someone's arms. Pressure against her throat, and her breath was instantly whipped away. There was a humming in her ear, as of cicadas. But this was wintertime. There were no insects.

Sophy choked and twisted, found the edge of that quelling hand and bit hard. The terrible weight on her throat lifted and she sucked in air. Steel clamps bit into her arms.

Struggling, she struck out a blind blow. She seemed to be in midair, rocked as she had been when she was a child. The memory pierced the veil of time with pristine clarity.

She butted her forehead into that distorted face swinging in front of her like a lantern at Halloween. For a long moment they poised, stretched at arm's length like partners in a spinning dance.

A tearing sound. As the steel clamps shifted to keep hold, Sophy jerked her body downward, and she was free. She opened her mouth to scream again, filling her lungs with air.

Then weight and world were gone, swept away. She had the sensation of falling and shooting forward at the same time, spinning like a leaf in the wind, toppling from the safety of...?

The scream never escaped her throat. It was cut off by the sudden invasion of water into her mouth and nostrils. With blinding clarity, Sophy realized what was happening just as she fell into the icy water. Her mouth clamped shut.

The water was cold. Ice-cold. It bit into her face like tiny needles, the weight of her cloak dragging her down, the balloon of her skirt slowing the process.

The shock of sudden immersion cleared Sophy's reeling senses sufficiently to allow her to realize that, although totally submerged, she was rising. She hung on to that, rising.

For a long, black, nightmare time, she thought she would never reach the surface again. The water was icy and her skirts were dragging at her legs, but the air trapped under her cagelike extension skirt was providing a measure of buoyancy!

When her head struck some object and checked her progress toward the air, a hideous panic gripped her. The touch of a hand on her ankle sent her over the edge of reason into terror. She'd never make the surface. She must!

Desperate panic lent strength to Sophy's thrashing attempts to free herself. Something pushed down on her head and she twisted in panic, clawing upward. Pain was shooting through her chest.

Tiny flaming meteors danced and streaked before her eyes. There was a roaring in her ears. She fought her way up a steep path that wound through a swirling, eddying, red mist, and kicked frantically.

Her consciousness seemed to have condensed to a tiny pinprick of life. She struggled blindly, until, magically, the obstruction overhead moved aside. Her lungs were almost depleted of air when she surged to the surface, and fresh air suddenly gushed into her aching lungs.

Then she heard a splashing beside her and struggled, trying to break the death grip that anchored her body against some solid object. She opened her eyes and her mouth, at the same time taking a gulp, half air, half river water.

"Just hold on. Stop struggling. Sophy! You're all right! I've got you," the voice gasped, as if its owner's lungs labored, crying that there was no air.

Seth's voice! Sophy let wonder rise about the fear, riding on it, arming herself with it. It was as if her dream were merging with reality. Her outstretched arms folded inward. The grip shifted, tightened.

She took another gulp of precious air. For a while none of her senses, saving that of touch, seemed able to function. Coughing and half-strangled, she clung to her beloved anchor, drifting in a timeless void, only dully aware of being lifted from the water.

Sophy opened her eyes. Above her was the snow-filled sky, beneath her was the hard dock. She was gasping as she clawed at the wet ropes of hair in her eyes, sucking air so deeply that she hurt in every part of her body.

Coughing. Ragged gasps.

"I've got you. You're safe. Just breathe." Seth's voice. Low, hard, uneven, but sounding magnificently in command.

The hands upon her eased but did not let her go. Relieved and encouraged, Sophy did as she was bid. The pain in her chest was still present, but the meteors, the roaring in her ears, were gone. In her mind, an echo: *I've got you. You're safe.*

The earth was solid beneath her, cold and wet. Lying flat on the dock, gulping precious air, she turned her head. Soaked and struggling for his own irregular breath was Seth, looking just as exhausted as she was.

His beloved face was slightly out of focus, but shifting, steadying as she concentrated her vision. Around them the river rocked in tiny splashes like a child playing contentedly.

Sophy tried to form his name with her lips, but her lungs were on fire and she could only pant hungrily for air without uttering a sound. She could only muster a tiny smile as she touched his cheek with a fingertip, and laid her head weakly against his chest. Exhausted, Seth turned his head far enough to drop a tiny, tingling kiss on her wet hair.

She was drifting, dreaming, drifting. She was in a pink shimmering world of delight. The light came back slowly. Infinitely slowly. Its focus was dim, more suggestion than shape, carved bedhead, vaulted window, clustered shadow outlined in the light of the flame.

A brass lamp, squatting on a table like a giant insect, was making the shadows leap and dance on the wall. They moved up and down, up and down, the motion of a fairyland boat from tales her father used to tell her as she was falling asleep years ago.

The weight across her thighs was considerable, and inescapable. Languidly, Sophy attempted to move her foot, found it trapped beneath a heavy male leg. Emerging completely from the realms of sleep, she lifted her hands, sought the ridge of muscle, the security of warmth.

The imagined warmth and delight of Seth's strong arms about her were real. His breathing was deep and even, and his eyes were closed. She touched him, a feather-brush of her hand across his cheek. Instinctively, her fingers entangled themselves in his dark hair, caressing.

Sophy raised her head, and gave a sigh of satisfaction. Her smiled deepened, and she put her arms around Seth's wide shoulders, reveling in the hardness of his muscles. Beneath she could feel the pulse of him, the steady tide of his breathing.

She lifted her hands to cradle his face. Her fingers traced the patterns time and living had carved round his eyes. She stroked the tips of her fingers against his cheek, softly kissed him there, where one black curl fell just over his forehead.

Her lips gently caressed him there, where hair mingling with soft sideburns curled against the arch of his ear. He stirred, and shifted his weight until she lay totally pinned beneath him, his warm, even breath moving tendrils in the thick black forest of her hair.

Slowly, tenderly, Sophy held his beloved head close, wishing she could kiss the fine modeling of his mouth, just where he would be warmest, except for...

Her mouth curved upward in ancient witchcraft, and she let a light hand dance down his body, across his flesh, invitingly. Seth grunted, burrowed his head deeper into the crook of her shoulder.

Drunk with fire and sweetness, Sophy let her fingers rove over the webwork of scars that were his battle honors. A whisper, a caress, a warmth as soft as dawn.

The gentle drift of her fingers against his skin and the warmth of her mouth tracing lazy kisses along his ear awakened Seth. Her arms encompassed him, her lips touching his ear. They were moist, and she made a tiny sound.

Her slender hands roamed his body, exploring still. Seth lay passive, trying to prolong the pleasure of Sophy intent on seduction, but his muscles betrayed him. They had a will of their own, bunching and quivering at her delicate touch.

Her fingers felt good against his skin. His every nerve and sinew sang as Sophy's fingers kindled the shiver of pleasure that dwelt along his spine. Her fingers did something exquisite. For one long ecstatic moment he did not move.

Then he moved slowly, gently against her. Sophy's slender body, incredibly soft, trembled against his. They stirred together like two leaves on a branch.

Seth groaned aloud, and raised his head off her arm. Her eyes, still heavy lidded with sleep, were shimmering, dove soft. Their pupils, dilated so completely there seemed no iris at all, were full of love... for him.

As always, her mouth opened in a smile, and, as always, he blinked, dazzled, and smiled back. Her gray eyes were like whirlpools spinning him down.

Seth felt himself melting, all his energy, all his reserves of strength flowing down the ribboning muscles of his thighs to his loins, pooling like quicksilver in his masculine core.

Putting out a hand to play with the tendrils of hair falling around her cheek, Seth let the other arm slide around her back, caressing the cascade of dark hair, the indentation of her spine, the rounded buttocks. His lips quivered at her musky scent.

With a sigh of yielding abandon, Sophy reached her palm up, bringing his head down until his lips opened against hers in a kiss of sweet promise. Her spread fingers pressed hard against the back of his head. She felt as if she never wanted to let him go.

Shaken like a leaf in the tempest, Seth allowed the full force of her marvelous power to blast through him. He pulled her tightly against him, his mouth descending to devour hers with a fierceness that was startling. His fingers buried themselves in her hair.

As their lips touched, all reality fled. Her grip tightened to steel, her warmth turned to fire. She clutched him with fierce strength, yet no stronger or fiercer than he.

His mouth broke away for something more important. To say it.

"I love you."

Sophy reached out and touched the flat of his cheek with her hand. "I love you, too." It was an airless whisper.

"I am no longer empty, hollow. You have shown me that my strength is in my heart."

The fine trembling of his hand as he gently tucked a stray tendril of hair behind her ear elicited a feeling of deep tenderness in Sophy. She lightly touched his wrist in a small, intimate gesture.

"You have shown me what real love is. I am different now, content to play the role of obedient wife."

Seth did nothing to destroy that reckless illusion. For the moment it was enough, more than enough. It was perfect, exciting because of the awareness, exhilarating because of the anticipation of what was to come.

Sophy's legs were twining around him as if she sought to climb onto him, or into him. Seth moved slowly into a position of interwoven subservience and mastery, his fingers exploring every supple line of her.

His lips traced the swoop of cheek and neck and shoulder, lingered on the sweet curve of her breasts, savored their musk and silk. Slowly, tenderly he left them, seeking out the arch of her ribs, the subtle curve of her hips, the gentle hills and hollows of her belly, coming to rest at last in the meeting of her thighs.

Sophy felt the explosion of his breath against her breast, and gasped with pleasure as his mouth closed over her nipple.

His hands spanned her waist and she straddled his thighs. Strands of her unbound hair brushed lightly against him in concert with her hands. Moving. Swaying.

Suspended in time and space, all Sophy could see was Seth. All she could feel was Seth, pulsing at the very core of her. Something inside her, that same inner strength, lifted him up with her so that they moved together, united in a kind of spirit dance.

Their desire, now one living thing, could no longer be held in abeyance. The ultimate vibrations began inside Sophy. Seth felt her pulsing all around him. Tried to merge himself with her.

And almost succeeded.

By ten o'clock the grand ballroom of the Astoria was thronged with an incredible company, the room filled with the usual sounds of chatter and laughter betokening a good party. For a while, Sophy lost sight of Seth, who was monopolized by small crowds of men eager to converse with him, to congratulate him on Weston's new lines.

A delightful air of pleasure seemed to seep through the ballroom. Steeple headdresses and flowing veils of the sixteenth century vied with gold turbans from the mysterious East. A centurion danced with a gentle Juliet. Cleopatra arrived, escorted by a full-bodied Henry the Eighth, who was, surely, the editor of the New York *National?*

Sophy identified an equally stout pirate as a famous socialite lawyer, and a banking baron dressed as Julius Caesar. Brigands rubbed elbows with Puritan gentlemen in wide white collars and Vandyke beards, while ladies of the harem entertained all comers.

Imps of mischief danced in her eyes as she caught sight of a tall female Viking bearing down upon her. The enormous helmet boasted two very large, upcurving horns, which presented a distinct hazard to those in her vicinity.

"You look very presentable, my dear. You're sure to set the cat among the pigeons in that outfit. A good choice."

Sophy flushed with pleasure. Familiar with her mother-in-law's penchant for understatement, she knew the outfit was approved. She directed a gay little smile at Agnes, and pointed to a gypsy fortune-teller.

"Do you think Aunt Ella knows that posset is sherry laced?"

The older woman looked startled. "I think perhaps I had best remind her that sherry upsets the stomach if one eats immediately after imbibing. And you know Ella's penchant for hors d'oeuvres!"

Sophy smiled gently, wondering if the two women would continue their gentle feuding about their planned excursion to the Caribbean. The smile lingered in her eyes and on her lips as she drifted on to converse with Uncle Heinrich and Aunt Ilsa in the guise of Don Quixote and a Dutch farm wife.

They were full of praise, not only for the new concept of matching furniture fabrics with drapes, and for the new and lighter designs, but also for the way in which Sophy had arranged for the display to be an integral part of the night's entertainment.

Sophy looked around her. The first tension had left her. Everything was going well. The service was perfect; so, she knew, were the hors d'oeuvres and, of course, the punch.

To the strains of a waltz, the dancing couples commenced to weave brilliant rhythmic patterns beneath the gaslights. People stood in small groups talking. It seemed to Seth as if half of New York was gathered in the room.

A dashing buccaneer, twirling a milkmaid on his arm, nodded his scarfed head to Seth. Pieter? He looked around for Charles, but there was no sign of him. He wandered through the rooms with a glass of burgundy, hearing bits of conversation. Great peals of laughter.

"—The best buy on the market is American...."

"Did you hear the one about..."

"St. Nicholas Hotel has earmarked that silk brocaded with gold."

"Charles." Seth ran his fingers through his dark hair. "I never got round to saying 'thank you' for your help the other night."

Charles shrugged. "It was a close thing. Sorry the bastard drowned. Without the pressure George and I put on him, the affair might not have blown up as it did. We didn't mean Sophy to be involved."

"Sophy had already discovered Carlton had found a way to funnel profits out of Weston's by assigning stock transfers to the Paterson factory. She started her own investigations with George, hoping to protect me from harm, and to catch the villain in the act. She suspected everything was too neat, with you channeling funds into a nonexistent corporation."

"But you knew all that already, didn't you?"

Seth shook his head. "I didn't."

"You mean you never did any...investigating on your own? You were so sure...." Blood came to Charles's face, making his freckles fade. His eyes were wide. "How could you have known I was not deceiving you?"

"Because—" Seth returned his friend's bruising hand-clasp "—I knew." Charles heard the heavy emphasis in Seth's words and felt the truth of them at the core of his being.

Unmindful of the web of drifting conversations, Seth's eyes searched the room for Sophy again. He liked to know where she was. Bright, vibrant, enthusiastic, she was dancing with George Dunwoody, in the guise of a portly lord justice. In her dark Puritan outfit with its square white collar, she was as distinctive as an egret among a flock of crows.

Seth folded his arms and leaned one shoulder against the wall, amusement and something far more intense gleaming in his blue eyes. A child. Dreaming in her dark womb, not yet making his presence felt. He would be something, this child of his and Sophy's. Something wonderful.

Noticing his piercing regard, Sophy stared back, half fascinated, half defiant. She felt the corners of her mouth lift. There was something about him that made her want to smile, and yet there was a part of him, a dark, sensual side that touched her deep inside.

Then she grinned in open challenge as she was spun wildly, her little foot kicking out from beneath her demure skirts. Swirl of movement, swirl of laughter as her partner whirled her round and round.

The ancient silver talisman that she never took off was around her throat, winked as it caught the light. Seth watched her do one or two twirls, enjoying the way her red petticoats glittered beneath the black skirt of her gown.

Glitter? Red petticoats? Seth straightened, looking at Sophy through dangerously narrowed eyes. He felt his blood pounding. His gaze moved from the toe of her dainty shoe to the frill of French lace on her red pantaloons. He stiffened, incredulous.

The imp had *mirrors* on her shoes! Sophy really was the limit! His temper came to the surface. Thrusting aside a gentleman of the cloth who was dancing cheek to cheek with Joan of Arc, he aimed straight toward Sophy.

With his uneven gait, he looked like a big, savage animal that had somehow wandered into the ballroom. It was, Agnes Weston thought, like watching a prowling panther in its cage at the zoo, fascinated by the motion, too late realizing that it has abruptly padded out the open door in the side, leaving beast and watcher alone together with no barrier at all.

Almost knocking over a Chinese mandarin who was clasping Queen Elizabeth to his bosom, Agnes Weston hurried to catch up with her son. She might as well try to turn the tide. It would be easier.

"Seth!" Her fingers closed on his arm.

"Not now, Mother," Seth muttered irritably, cutting her off with a gesture. "I'll kill her. No, I'll strangle her for this!" He growled under his breath, softly, dangerously.

Agnes Weston's fingers tightened their grip. "Be careful, Seth. She is not aware of it, but Sophy carries my grandchild."

She saw the tremor at the side of his mouth. He hardly seemed to be breathing. Seth bared his teeth in a smile.

"It's all right, Mother. Sophy doesn't need your help." He prized her hand off his arm.

"You've got yourself a good woman, son, and I'm right glad of it." Agnes looked squarely into her son's vivid blue eyes. "It has something to do with the daughter-in-law of Pythagoras, I believe," she said, watching his face intently.

It sounded as though some of her customary biting wit was lacking clarity. For a moment, he looked as if he were having trouble following the conversation, then he began to laugh.

A statuesque beauty clad in a flowing cream silk gown that left one dimpled shoulder bare, and was tied crisscross about the breasts with ribbons of green satin, passed by. Delilah. Seth grabbed the surprised woman's hand almost roughly in his own and dragged her toward the dance floor.

Attuned to the fine element of danger that seemed to reverberate across the room, Sophy slid out of George Dunwoody's arms seconds before Seth, with a great ruffle and flourish, thrust the hapless Delilah at the poor man.

Seth planted his considerable bulk directly in front of Sophy, a threatening glint in his eye. He seemed to her like a wild animal on the loose, dangerous and deadly and totally unstoppable. For an instant, she felt a slight shiver of fear crawling down her spine. Then it was gone.

He arched his eyebrows, inclined his head and held out a steady hand to her. Sophy felt hypnotized by that unwavering glance. She had no choice but to place her hand within his.

Seth raised it. Kissed it. Her skin was honey and fire. Her eyes wide and wickedly bright. A dull fire smoldered beneath his cheekbones. He was shocked to hear himself say involuntarily, "I'm as useless as a chocolate soldier, and this could be termed gallantry under fire, but would you care to dance with me?"

Aware of the heat in her cheeks, but totally unaware of the warmth in her eyes, she moved into his arms. How could she resist this closeness, this enchantment, when she had been seeking it all her life?

Seth held her close, moving her sedately around the room. His lips were in her hair. She felt his open mouth brush the shell of her ear as he said quite calmly, "Don't tell me it's my community duty to dance with the wallflowers. I am here dancing attendance on you only to discourage any of the others."

Sophy pulled her head back in order to see his face. "I think I like your idea of gallantry under fire! To have one's husband's undivided attention will set a new fashion!"

He laughed and hugged her tighter to him. She felt the reverberations throughout his body. "Hell, Sophy! Do you want to take odds on how long it will be before all the women in New York are wearing mirrors on their slippers and red underwear?"

"When Madame Bertine opens her Academy of Good Manners and Etiquette. Now that she has secure title over the house in Greene Street, she is giving up her present occupation."

Seth stilled abruptly, utterly. Though he showed no sign of anger, Sophy saw his lips move as if to protest. She put up her fingers to prevent him speaking.

"Scandalous, is it not? But education is women's great weapon. Should we not have a voice in our wielding? Why bind us? Why deny us the full freedom that men grant to themselves?"

Seth's head tilted. His eyes glinted. Did he have a choice? She was the most obstinate, the most unreasonable, the most maddening woman in the world.

And he loved her.

"Now I know why so many men try so hard to keep their women locked in cages. They're strangers to reason. Freedom is not worth the price women set on it. It is an illusion."

Sophy's breath escaped in a rush. "And what price does a woman have to pay? If, after all we have shared, you are going to be unreasonable, I shall bore you to death with conformity!"

Seth grinned, watching the loving expression in her wide violet-gray eyes. No reasonable man would love a woman so much. But love has no logic in it. He accepted the truth of it. Whatever came of this venture, he would not perish of boredom.

"I never said I would bind you. I was just going to say that there are some finer points in our marriage contract I would like to go over again." He glanced round at the assembled gathering. The way was simple. He met her eyes.

"If we are to keep up with the orders your brand of advertising is likely to generate, there is a little question of additional machinery to meet the demand. I thought you might be interested in increasing your loan, if we can negotiate suitable terms of repayment."

The laughter of relief began to build inside her until it threatened to erupt. "You'll be sorry! As a woman of considerable experience and a sharp usurer, I shall expect one hundred percent for my money... in kisses!"

Firm hands seized her about the waist, lifted her, spun her, set her down again with gentle force.

"I would pay no less! And what of my kisses, Sophy?"

Sophy laughed. It was light, free. "Your kisses are mine, just as mine are yours. We share everything we possess, so that it is impossible to know where your half starts and mine begins."

Seth smiled, tasting the sweetness of his victory. "It is too early yet for certainty, but could you not consider this one of your *worthy causes?*" He touched her flat belly.

Sophy's cheeks went hot pink as the blood rushed into them. She spun, turned to him, curtsied, laughing delightedly up at the man who seemed to know more about her than she knew about herself.

"This and the dozen others I will gladly bear you!"

His eyes tore her soul. "A dozen others! Sophy, how scandalous! New York society will think we spend our time in bed!"

A small secret smile broke out over her wide lips, the

gaslight turning her teeth to dazzle. Her merriment rippled in his ear.

"Let society enjoy its illusions. Only we will know the real truth."

She stepped into his open arms, which closed tightly around her.

*   *   *   *   *

![BRIDE'S BAY RESORT]

UNLOCK THE DOOR TO GREAT ROMANCE AT BRIDE'S BAY RESORT

Join Harlequin's new across-the-lines series, set in an exclusive hotel on an island off the coast of South Carolina.

Seven of your favorite authors will bring you exciting stories about fascinating heroes and heroines discovering love at Bride's Bay Resort.

Look for these fabulous stories coming to a store near you beginning in January 1996.

Harlequin American Romance #613 in January
Matchmaking Baby by Cathy Gillen Thacker

Harlequin Presents #1794 in February
Indiscretions by Robyn Donald

Harlequin Intrigue #362 in March
Love and Lies by Dawn Stewardson

Harlequin Romance #3404 in April
Make Believe Engagement by Day Leclaire

Harlequin Temptation #588 in May
Stranger in the Night by Roseanne Williams

Harlequin Superromance #695 in June
Married to a Stranger by Connie Bennett

Harlequin Historicals #324 in July
Dulcie's Gift by Ruth Langan

Visit Bride's Bay Resort each month wherever Harlequin books are sold.

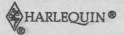

BBAYG

Bestselling author

MARGOT DALTON

Catches you in a web of

Tangled Lives

Meg Howell has no idea how she ended up in a hospital
in Salt Lake City, or why everybody is calling her Lisa
and insisting she's the wife of wealthy businessman
Victor Cantalini. Even though Victor has the pictures
to prove it, Meg knows she's not Lisa. As she searches
desperately through Lisa's life, she is propelled
dangerously close to a shattering secret. Can she prove
that she's being forced to live another woman's life—
before she's forced to die that woman's death?

Available this February at your favorite retail outlet.

MIRA The brightest star in women's fiction

MMDTL

◈ *Harlequin®* *Historical*

**Why is March the best time
to try Harlequin Historicals?
We've got four great reasons.**

FOOL'S PARADISE by Tori Phillips—A witty court
jester woos the goddaughter of a queen

THE PEARL STALLION by Rae Muir—A daring
socialite captures a wild sea captain

WARRIOR'S DECEPTION by Diana Hall—A bachelor
knight jousts with a quick-witted noblewoman

WESTERN ROSE by Lynna Banning—A gentleman
rancher corrals a hot-tempered schoolteacher

Don't miss our **March Madness** celebration—**four
new books from four terrific new authors!**

Look for them wherever
Harlequin Historicals are sold.

MM96

Harlequin® Historical

This is what critics and award-winning authors
had to say about Nina Beaumont's
first time-travel novel—

ACROSS TIME

"...a tale to treasure!" —*Romantic Times*

"Truly spellbinding..."—Anita Mills

"...a reading trip worth taking." —*Affaire de Coeur*

"Exhilarating reading adventure!" —*Rendezvous*

"A marvelous read!" —Anita Gordon

"A breathtaking achievement." —Shirl Henke

And Harlequin Historicals is proud to be able
to bring you her second time-travel novel
coming this February—

TWICE UPON TIME

This is an exciting reading opportunity
that you won't want to miss!

BIGB96-1

What do women really want to know?

Only the world's largest publisher of romance fiction could possibly attempt an answer.

HARLEQUIN ULTIMATE GUIDES™

How to Talk to a Naked Man,

Make the Most of Your Love Life, and Live Happily Ever After

The editors of Harlequin and Silhouette are definitely experts on love, men and relationships. And now they're ready to share that expertise with women everywhere.

Jam-packed with vital, indispensable, lighthearted tips to improve every area of your romantic life—even how to get one! So don't just sit around and wonder why, how or where—run to your nearest bookstore for your copy now!

Available this February, at your favorite retail outlet.

HARLEQUIN®

NAKED

Yo amo novelas con corazón!

Starting this March, Harlequin opens up to a whole new world of readers with two new romance lines in SPANISH!

Harlequin Deseo
- passionate, sensual and exciting stories

Harlequin Bianca
- romances that are fun, fresh and very contemporary

With four titles a month, each line will offer the same wonderfully romantic stories that you've come to love—now available in Spanish.

Look for them at selected retail outlets.

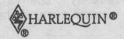

SPANT

INTRODUCING…

A collection of award-winning books by award-winning authors! From Harlequin and Silhouette.

Heaven In Texas
by Curtiss Ann Matlock

National Reader's Choice Award Winner— Long Contemporary Romance

Let Curtiss Ann Matlock take you to a place called *Heaven In Texas*, where sexy cowboys in well-worn jeans are the answer to every woman's prayer!

"Curtiss Ann Matlock blends reality with romance to perfection!"
—*Romantic Times*

Available this March wherever Silhouette books are sold.

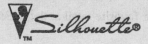

WC-3

Witness what happens when a devil falls
in love with an angel

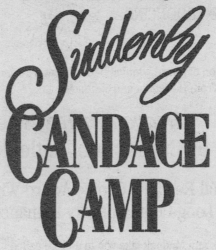

Suddenly
CANDACE
CAMP

Simon "Devil" Dure needs a wife, and Charity Emerson is
sure she can meet his expectations…and then some.

Charity is right, and the Devil is finally seduced by her
crazy schemes, her warm laughter, her loving heart. There
is no warning, however, of the dangerous trap that lies
ahead, or of the vicious act of murder that will put their
courage—and their love—to the ultimate test.

Available at your favorite retail outlet in February.

MIRA The brightest star in women's fiction

MCCS